# HUNGER

# HUNGER

## JILL WILLIAMSON

The author is represented by MacGregor Literary Inc. of Hillsboro, OR.

Cover Designer: Emilie Hendryx
Editor: Stephanie Morrill, Brad Williamson

Library of Congress Cataloging-in-Publication Data
An application to register this book for cataloging has been filed with the
Library of Congress.

International Standard Book Number: 978-0-9985230-8-8

Printed in the United States of America

*To Stephanie Morrill*

*Thank you for your kindness, wisdom, and friendship.*

# Books by Jill Williamson

**Thirst Duology**
Thirst
Hunger

**The Safe Lands series**
Captives
Outcasts
Rebels

**The Kinsman Chronicles**
King's Folly
King's Blood
King's War

**The Blood of Kings trilogy**
By Darkness Hid
To Darkness Fled
From Darkness Won

**The Mission League series**
The New Recruit
Chokepoint
Project Gemini
Ambushed
Broken Trust
The Profile Match

**RoboTales**
Tinker
Mardok and the Seven Exiles

**Stand-Alone Titles**
Replication: The Jason Experiment

**Nonfiction**
Go Teen Writers: Write Your Novel
Go Teen Writers: Edit Your Novel
Storyworld First: Creating a Unique Fantasy World for Your Novel
Punctuation 101: A Fiction Writer's Guide to Getting it Right

# PROLOGUE

Eleven days ago, the earth passed through the tail of a comet that poisoned nearly all freshwater sources on the planet and caused a great pandemic that killed billions of people. We had not only survived, we had picked up several new friends along the way. Rumors of a safe water source in the mountains where all survivors were welcome drew us farther north. Unbeknownst to us, two rock stars were building a community that wasn't nearly as safe as it sounded.

As we headed north to see if the rumors were true, little did we know that the community had already started building a wall.

You could go in, but you couldn't come back out.

# 1

## HANNAH
## AUGUST 1

I woke hungry.

I got up and entered the bathroom, trembling. Morning light filtered through the slats on a small window over the shower, giving me enough light to see by. I reached for the sink, but found the faucet covered in a black trash bag and duct tape.

Right, right. No water.

There was an outhouse in the back yard, but I wasn't going out into the wilds of Colorado alone.

I studied my reflection in the mirror. The creases under my eyes. My stringy hair, oily skin. Even my teeth felt gross. I splayed my hands over my face, rubbing my cold fingers everywhere I could, trying to cool and calm myself. My heart was still beating hard, my hands shaking. My French-manicured fingernails were caked with black grime.

Every night dreams tormented me. If it wasn't Brandon, it was the kidnappers or the dead I'd seen the past few days. Last night, it had been my home—the UCSF campus, Potrero Hill, even Lowell High School—everything looted, everyone dead, and no food anywhere.

Even in this house, a faint, fishy odor lingered, proof that people had been sick with HydroFlu here—had died here.

Had I chosen right, staying with Eli? I could have found a car. Driven home. Maybe my mom or dad were still alive. Maybe one of my friends had survived the pandemic.

A wave of despair swelled within me. Choking back a sob, I lowered the toilet seat lid and sat on the carpeted cover, tucked my head between my knees, and breathed deeply.

I grasped for shreds of logic. At the very least, Brandon could never hurt me again. I had to be safer with these people than on my own. I wanted what Eli had: deep friendships, a caring family. I hoped I hadn't ruined my chances here. Stabbing Eli had been . . . impulsive. I'd replayed the moment over and over in my mind, wondering why I hadn't aimed for Brandon's hand? Why Eli's?

Because it had been his strength holding Brandon up, trying to save him.

My stomach growled. It was then I noticed the smell. Someone was cooking. I left the bathroom and crept along the second-floor hallway of Andy Reinhold's home in nowhere, Colorado, stopping at the rail at the top of the stairs. Laughter below. Male and female.

"No, you can't." Jaylee. Eli's crush. Her voice sent a shiver of revulsion through me. I rarely hated anyone, but I did not understand what Eli saw in that vapid, selfish fool.

"Yes, I can." Eli. Of course he would be with her. "I won't, but I totally can."

"A whole package of eggs yourself? That's disgusting."

"They're good, is what they are. Scrambled with salsa."

"Gross. I hate eggs."

My mouth quirked into a grin. I liked Eli. A lot. Not only did my stomach tingle every time he looked at me, but he oozed potential. He was kind and strong—not physically. He had an inner strength that was so compelling. I'd never met anyone who could see problems before they happened and strategize so thoroughly. He was the kind of person who would survive this pandemic and live until he was old and gray, and yet . . . he was young. That blushing baby face and the way he ogled Jaylee. That girl was ten kinds of wrong for him, yet from the sounds of the friendly banter below, whatever had happened last night had been in Eli's favor. I hoped he didn't crash too hard when Jaylee moved on.

Eli was not her type.

A door at the end of the hall swung open. I jumped, embarrassed to be caught standing alone at the top of the stairs, eavesdropping.

Seth McShane emerged wearing khaki shorts and a gray T-shirt that said "Essential Oils" but pictured three types of motor oil. Though Eli had told me his dad was white, it had still surprised me when I met Seth yesterday. The man had a bit of a Hugh Jackman look, though he wasn't much taller than my five feet six inches. He seemed to have the same inner strength and kindness that Eli had.

He saw me and smiled, yet grief lines creased his mouth and eyes. "Morning, Miss Hannah," he said, walking past. He paused at the top of the stairs and glanced at me, concern etched on his brow. "You okay?"

"Someone's down there," I said, wincing at how ridiculous that sounded.

Seth started down the stairs. "Let's go see who."

I followed, fighting to ignore the sound of the creaking steps. I didn't like that sound.

"Eli, Miss Jaylee, good morning," Seth said when we reached the bottom.

Eli stood behind the counter, spatula in hand. Jaylee sat on a bar stool on the other side, leaning forward on both arms, her purple tank top showing more cleavage than a Victoria's Secret model.

When Eli spotted us, his face turned three shades of bashful, which did nothing to hide the bruises on his face and neck. The boy was black and blue because of Brandon—because of me. My only consolation was that Brandon would never hurt anyone ever again.

"Morning, Mr. McShane!" Jaylee leaped off the stool and greeted Eli's dad with a flirty embrace that he deftly maneuvered into a side hug.

I skirted them and sat on one of three stools, farthest from the one Jaylee had vacated. "Good morning, Eli," I said.

The flush in his cheeks darkened, and he turned toward the stove, avoiding my gaze. "Want some eggs?"

He seemed to be asking the cast iron skillet as he stirred with his spatula, left-handed, I couldn't help notice. This brought my gaze to the splinted fingers on his right hand, which hung limp at his side. I ached to have a look at the wound but knew he wouldn't let me near it.

Why hadn't I stayed in bed?

I forced myself to answer. "I'd love some. Thank you."

Eli retrieved a paper plate from a stack beside the stove and dished up a steaming pile. He set the plate in front of me. "You want salt? Pepper? Salsa?" Still ducking eye contact. I missed the easy way we'd talked before the incident on the bridge.

I really couldn't believe I'd stabbed him.

"I'll take some salsa," I said.

Our eyes met briefly, but he quickly turned away to fetch the jar of salsa from where it sat on the counter by the stove.

I'd never had salsa on eggs before. I rarely ate eggs, or breakfast at all beyond a yogurt, but I'd do what I could to make peace with this kind-hearted boy I'd so traumatized. If times had been different, would he have called the police after Brandon had fallen? I imagined myself sitting in a jail cell, awaiting my arraignment for voluntary manslaughter.

"And . . . salsa," Eli said, sliding the glass jar toward me, directly followed by the clattering of a long-handled spoon.

"Thank you. This smells great." I scooped some salsa onto my eggs and took a bite. Wow. So much going on at once. The eggs were hot, the salsa cold but spicy. Good, though. I liked it. While I ate, I watched Jaylee follow Seth into the kitchen. The girl started snooping in cupboards while Seth approached Eli at the stove.

"Got enough in there for me?" he asked, peeking into the skillet.

"Yep," Eli said, filling a plate for his father.

Seth carried his eggs to the center stool, the one on my right. He helped himself to the salsa. "So, Miss Hannah, what's your story? Give me the works."

I caught Eli looking at us and pretended not to notice. "The short version is: I'm from San Francisco. I finished my first year of med school. First and last, it seems. I'm one of those annoying overachievers who graduated early."

He grinned. "Reminds me of Leti. She took a program in high school that gave her a head start toward a nursing program. She worked in labor and delivery and . . . uh . . ." His grin faded, and he stared at his eggs as if they were a mirror to the past.

Leti must have been his wife. When we'd arrived yesterday, Eli and Lizzie had given their dad the news that their mom hadn't survived the pandemic. I'd never seen a man cry before, but Seth McShane had wept when his kids had delivered that bad news.

The front door opened, making me jump, but it was only Andy Reinhold, the owner of this house. With his bushy black hair and beard, and that red plaid shirt, he looked like Paul Bunyan stepping out of a children's book. He stomped his feet on the mat by the door, then traipsed into the kitchen.

"Jaylee, what you looking for?" Andy asked, his voice a deep growl.

She had a jar of applesauce in one hand and was reaching into a cupboard with the other. "Can I open this?" She lifted the applesauce higher.

"Nope," Andy said. "We've got to eat what's going to go bad first. Save the canned stuff for when the perishables are gone. Come have some eggs."

"But I don't like eggs."

"I'm afraid it's time to get used to eating what you don't

like," Seth said. "Choice is going to become a thing of the past."

"True enough," Andy said. "Eat an apple or a banana." He gestured to a bowl on the counter. By the look of the spots on the bananas, they'd been there a while.

"The apples are mushy," Jaylee said.

"Suit yourself." Andy came to stand on Seth's right. He leaned both hands onto the counter. "You tell these knuckleheads the plan?"

Seth shook his head, his mouth full of eggs.

Andy delivered the news himself. "We're going to drive on up to the ski resort and see about that rumor of safe water."

Jaylee squealed and ran toward the stairs. "I have to tell Antônia!"

"Once we know for sure, we can decide what to do," Seth told her fleeting form.

"Lots of good land up around Crested Butte," Andy said. "If there's a fresh water source, we could build our own place."

"Is there a hospital there?" I asked.

"Not sure," Reinhold said. "Why do you ask?"

"It would be wise to stock up on some medical supplies," I said.

"Love that idea," Seth said.

"Zach and Lizzie found plenty from the pharmacy at Target," Eli said. "All kinds of stuff." He was actually looking at me now, for an extended period of time, but there was no warmth in his gaze.

"That's great," I said. "But there are some things only hospitals will have."

"The hospitals are *really* bad," Eli said. "Remember Cree's mom? Imagine that times . . ." He glanced over my head. "How many dead in the hospital in Phoenix, Liz?"

I glanced back as Lizzie McShane bounded off the last few steps. I'd first thought Eli and his sister were twins, but Eli was a year older. They both had brown hair, eyes, and skin, taking after their mom, who'd been Mexican.

"Too many." Lizzie stopped between Seth and me and draped an arm around her dad's shoulders. "Hundreds in every hallway."

Seth rubbed his daughter's back. "I'm sorry, baby girl."

"Banner was awful," Jaylee said. "I felt like I was in a horror movie when we went there."

Eli, still looking at me, raised his eyebrows as if Lizzie and Jaylee's experiences had ended some sort of argument.

They hadn't. "We're still going to need medical supplies at some point," I said. "Why not face the unpleasant now to avoid the unpleasant happening to one of us later? I'd rather be prepared for a medical emergency than have to rush out for supplies when someone is sick or injured and not make it back in time."

"That sounds smart," Lizzie said.

"We'll swing by the hospitals in Gunnison and Montrose on our way back," Andy said. "See what we can find. Today is just a day trip, people. For now, this house is still home base."

I caught Eli staring but couldn't read his expression. "Eat up, Liz," he told his sister. "There are eggs on the stove."

"I need to use the outhouse first," she said.

"I'll come too," I said, eager for my chance at an escort.

Lizzie and I slipped on our shoes and went outside. The sun was up, the morning chilly. Andy had built a wooden outhouse in the back yard. Lizzie went in. I hugged myself and twisted the ring I wore on my right hand, half expecting Brandon to jump out from behind the bushes in back of the house and grab me.

My turn came, and Lizzie waited for me. Afterwards, we explored the property a little, even going inside the teepee in front of the house. It looked authentic.

"Why do they have a teepee?" I asked.

"Andy's wife was a Ute native," Lizzie said. "It was important to her to that her daughters know their heritage and traditions."

"Kimama had a sister?"

"Two," Lizzie said. "She was the oldest."

The words were heavy and pulled on my heart, reminding me just how much everyone had lost. Why wasn't I more grieved that my parents were likely dead? I had no desire to travel to San

Francisco and find out for sure. What did that say about me?

We went back inside, and Lizzie joined her brother at the table, leaving me alone at the kitchen counter. I finished my eggs, all the while feeling like an outsider with this group. I wanted so desperately to belong here. Before I had stabbed Eli on that bridge, he and I had gotten along well. But now . . . ?

Voicing my extremely opinionated ideas about medical supplies certainly wasn't going to help make peace between Eli and me.

I wondered if anything ever could.

## ELI

Sensation overload. As I knelt on the floor, trying to roll up my sleeping bag one-handed—left-handed—I didn't know what to focus my thoughts on. First and best, Jaylee and I were . . . something. Not sure what, but it was something good. Just thinking about it . . . Gah. I couldn't stop smiling.

Until Hannah showed up with her "I stab people" presence and her smart talk, impressing my dad, who seemed to have no problem with the fact that she'd caused a man to plummet to his death in the Chinle Wash.

Now we were headed to Crested Butte to see if the French rock stars really had access to clean water. How was that even a logical sentence? Then on the way back we had to stop at *two* hospitals and wade through dead bodies so Hannah could stock up on vague medical supplies. She was probably hooked on Benzos or Tranqs and needed a fix.

I lost my grip on the sleeping bag, which unrolled completely. I batted it away, ticked off that my left hand was so useless. I'd gone off the deep end on this Hannah thing. Truth was, I didn't know the girl well enough to guess what kind of person she was. I'd liked her from the start, though—really liked her—which should count for something now.

Was I being too harsh about what had happened to Brandon? Probably. The guy *had* beaten me up and shot at me. Plus, he'd kidnapped Hannah, and from what I'd surmised from her bruises, he'd beaten her too. When I considered the situation as a whole, preemptive self-defense wasn't that far-fetched.

Just thinking about how I'd been ignoring her made guilt pool in my chest. After all the ways she'd supported me, too. I stroked the bandage on the back of my hand and down my two middle fingers, recalling the shock that had possessed me the moment Hannah had stabbed me so Brandon would fall— practically crippling me in the process.

Maybe I just needed a little more time to adjust.

I glanced at my stuff. What did I need for today? Not much, since we were coming back. Dad said to bring a change of clothes on the off chance there really was safe water and we could shower. I stuffed a fresh set of clothes into my pack and headed outside.

We'd emptied the supplies from Zach's van so we could drive both north. With the backs empty, we'd have plenty of room to load any medical supplies we picked up on the way back. I grabbed two of the walkie talkies and put one in each vehicle, realized I wasn't going to be driving—couldn't anyway with my hand messed up. It made me feel powerless.

The bed of my truck was open. I'd given my keys to Logan with a mission of packing lunches for the day. He was, at the moment, regaling my dad with his theories on Comet Pulon. Needing something to keep my mind occupied, I climbed up onto the bed and took over his job.

I was digging through one of the coolers when someone tugged on my pant leg. "Baby, can I talk to you a second?"

Baby? Wow. Would my face ever stop flaming when Jaylee talked to me? I crawled out of the truck and turned to face the most gorgeous girl in the world. She smelled tropical, like sunscreen and sand, and had pushed a pair of black sunglasses on top of her head. She ran her fingers up my arm and tilted her head in the most adorable way.

"You still have some of those applesauce pouches we picked up at Target?" she asked, stepping into my space until her body pressed against mine.

Yi yi yi. "Uh . . . I think so."

"Can I have one? I'm hungry."

Really? This again. I took a breath. "What about the apples Reinhold told you to eat?"

She held up a baggie filled with sliced apples. "I cut them to take on the drive, but they're already brown. It's so gross."

Hannah appeared, holding Cree on one hip, and dropped two zippered lunch boxes on the tailgate. "Andy said to give these to you," she said.

"*Na'*," Cree added, dropping a third lunch box.

I smirked at Cree, amused. He seemed too old for baby talk.

Zach was right behind them and set three more lunch sacks beside Hannah's. "Applesauce is made from mashed apples, Jaylee," he said.

"He's right," I said, stepping back from her. I needed a little personal space if I was going to stand my ground.

"So?" her bottom lip poked out. "It tastes way better than these. They're mealy."

She wasn't nearly as pretty when she was complaining. I pushed past her and reached for the lunch packs, but Jaylee slid her hands around my waist and tucked them into the back pockets of my jeans.

"Whoa," I laughed. "Jaylee, I've gotta make lunches for—"

She raised onto her tiptoes and kissed me. Just like that. As if we weren't surrounded by a dozen onlookers, including my sister and my dad. Her lips were magic, though, and I suddenly found myself joining in, wondering if I was doing it right, urgently hoping I wasn't bad at this.

She pulled back, leaving me dazed. "Please?" she said faintly. "Just one? I'm *so* hungry."

I stared into those chocolatey eyes rimmed in thick black lashes. "I'll see what I can do," I whispered, though I didn't want to. Why couldn't she understand how serious things were? And if I let her play me on day two of our—maybe it was a relationship?—was I setting myself up for a future of being bossed around?

Probably.

I decided to give her a task, even things up a bit. "Go see if Reinhold has a Sharpie so I can write names on water bottles."

"Okay!" She gave me one last peck on the lips and jogged off, leaving her baggie of apple slices on the tailgate.

I could see the blurred forms of people staring at me, so I turned back to the load, pulled out one cooler, then another.

My dad stepped up beside me. "How long has this thing with Jaylee been going on?"

I peeked into the first cooler, found snacks. "Uh . . . since last night?"

Dad chuckled a little too long. "Okay. You be careful with her. She's a wild one."

I studied my splinted fingers and sighed. "I know."

"Not sure you want a wild one?"

I met Dad's serious gaze. "She wants me to give her applesauce from our stash since Reinhold told her she couldn't have any of his."

Dad nodded. "I saw that."

Perfect. The idea of my dad watching me get played made me feel twice as stupid. "I told her I'd see what I could do." The confession felt good, at least.

"Guess you'd better see, then."

Really? "But I agree with Reinhold. We need to be smart about the food."

Dad grabbed my shoulder at the base of my neck and squeezed. "You're a smart man. You need to trust your instincts. If your instincts say one thing, and your girl talks you into another thing with absolutely no logic on her side, you know what you are?"

I winced. "Whipped?"

"Exactly." He released me. "You must like her, so give it a try," Dad said, "just don't let her change who you are."

"So you're okay with this?" I'd never had a girlfriend before.

"It's a new world, Eli. You've got to make your own choices. Now, let's talk weapons."

With so many kids, Dad and I agreed we needed to lock up any weapons that weren't in hand. Reinhold had some portable gun safes, so we locked Dad's rifle and one of the handguns I picked up at Ace in the back of the Honda Odyssey and my new Winchester rifle and another handgun in the back of the Sienna. The only other supplies we brought were sack lunches and stacks of towels Reinhold had gathered in hopes of us showering. Reinhold would keep his rifle with him in Dad's van.

By the time we had that figured out, I headed toward Zach's Toyota Sienna, curious how our group had divided themselves. Zach and Lizzie were in the front. I peeked in the open sliding door and saw Antônia, Krista, and Shyla in the middle seat. Hannah, Kimama, Cree, and the boys must be in Dad's van.

Predictable. Just like it had been for the past few days. The only difference was that Dad and Reinhold had taken my place. I wasn't in charge anymore. I wasn't needed.

I wasn't even capable now.

"Sit here, Eli!" Jaylee said from the back.

"She saved you the whole row, man," Zach said, grinning.

Wow. Okay. I climbed into the van, and we headed north.

Jaylee sat in the middle of the back row to be closer to me, she said. It made me feel awesome, until about five miles down the road when she turned to me, eyes hidden behind her sunglasses, and asked, "You have my applesauce?"

Moment of truth, Eli. What was it going to be? Man or boy? "Sorry, Jay," I said, my pulse racing "I brought you these, though." I dug into my pack and pulled out the baggie of apple slices she'd left on the tailgate.

She tipped down her chin to look at me over the top of her shades, eyebrows raised in two sculpted arcs. "You're kidding."

"We've all got to play by the same rules if we're going to survive."

"One tiny dish of applesauce won't starve anyone."

"That's not the point," I said. "If we let everyone do what they want, it'll be trouble."

"Your dad caught you, didn't he?" she said, her tone nasty. "He told you no, and all this is what he said to you."

"No, it's how I feel." Dad had just backed me up.

"Sure, Eli. Whatever."

She pulled out her iPhone, and in a few swipes of her glittery fingernails, "Vivre La Vie Dixième" by Loca and Liberté Champion blared from her iTunes.

Krista turned in her seat. "Ask Zach to play it over the speakers."

Jaylee was all for this, and soon everyone in the van was blessed with the indecipherable French lyrics and electronic dance music beat. Forty minutes from Reinhold's place, we hit the San Juan National Forest, and the EDM was still playing. The Sienna had a nice sound system, but after three times through Jaylee's playlist, I sort of wished it had no sound system at all.

Jaylee fell asleep, leaning against me like a pillow, which was nice. I had wanted to kill Zach last night when he'd revealed my crush on Jaylee, but it had worked out. I was still a little dazed that Jaylee wanted to give us a try.

At some point, Antônia and Krista fell asleep. Lizzie took over as DJ and started a game of "Name That Disney Tune" with Zach. The intro to *Aladdin*'s "Friend Like Me" woke everyone.

Jaylee straightened and yawned. "Where are we?"

"About halfway there," I said.

For a few miles, Jaylee and I just listened as Krista and Antônia joined in on "Name That Tune." Jaylee found her bag of apples on the seat beside her and started eating them. She lifted the second apple slice to my mouth.

"Have some," she said.

How very . . . awkward. I bit off the end and chewed it some. "Thank you." It wasn't bad, certainly not mealy.

When Jaylee finished the apples, she reached up and started

playing with my ear. "How long have you liked me, Eli?"

Her touch sent a tingle up my arms. "Since Mrs. Muir's class."

"Fifth grade? Are you serious?"

"You wore your hair in braids with different colored rubber bands that matched your outfits. I thought it was cute. And you smiled. A lot. You always seemed so happy."

"I can't believe you've liked me that long." She fisted the front of my T-shirt and pulled me into a kiss. Lips cold and sweet from the apples parted against mine, and her tongue was suddenly in my mouth. She kissed kind of angry and wild, and I had no idea if this was normal or just Jaylee.

A giggle broke through my euphoria. My eyes flashed open and met Shyla's. The five-year-old was out of her seatbelt, backwards, elbows hooked over the top of the bench seat.

"Shyla, turn around and buckle up," I said. "That's not safe."

"Kiss, kiss, kiss," she said, puckering her lips.

Krista grabbed Shyla's waist and yanked her down. "Stop messing around," she said.

"Don't be mean!" Shyla said, her voice whiny and defensive.

I'd picked up Krista, Shyla, and Davis in Phoenix. Krista had been babysitting the kids, and she regularly bossed them around.

"Check it out," Zach said. "Now entering Montrose, city of debris."

I looked out my window. Whoever had looted in Montrose had just dragged everything outside and left it—the clothing, anyway. Parking lots and sidewalks were covered with stuff.

"Oh, my gosh, there's a dead person!" Krista said.

"Where?" Antônia leaned over Shyla to look out Krista's window. "Eww!"

Shyla began to cry.

"Guys!" I said. "How about you ixnay the eadday eoplepay alktay, huh?"

Both girls stared at me over the back seat, their expressions clueless while Shyla continued to weep.

"What did you say?" This from Antônia, the female sponsor from our outdoor survival camping trip. She was a Mexican

17

citizen here on a student visa to study programming at PVCC.

"Unbuckle Shyla and send her back here," I said.

The girls complied, and Jaylee had to move over a seat so Shyla could sit between us. I hugged the little girl while we drove through Montrose. Told her everything was going to be fine. I had no way of knowing whether or not I was telling the truth, but what else was I supposed to do? Let her stare out the window at dead bodies as we carelessly drove past?

Lizzie started up the Disney songs again, which calmed Shyla. I noted it was 12:35. "You hungry, Shy?" I asked.

She nodded, and I dug out the lunch bags I'd packed for our vehicle. Peanut butter and jelly sandwiches, more apple slices, mozzarella sticks, and Capri Suns. It almost felt normal.

We ate and talked. Shyla eventually drifted off to sleep. Jaylee moved between Krista and Antônia. This left me in the back corner of the van, a not-so-squishy pillow for a five-year-old. After several days of feeling like it had been my job to get everyone safely north, it was kind of nice to have one simple task.

Until my thoughts started drifting.

I saw Mom's face in my mind, the last time she had grilled steaks. She'd been laughing at Sammy, our golden retriever, who'd been sitting with his head on Dad's lap, tipped to the side while he stared beseechingly at the meat sizzling on the grill, eyes lazy, hypnotized by the aroma.

Mom had laughed so hard, tears had run down her cheeks. In retrospect, it hadn't been all that funny. Mom's laughter had been contagious, though, and we'd all cracked up, more at her reaction than at Sammy. I'd laughed until my side hurt.

Tears filled my eyes, blurring my vision. Mom's death had warped this memory––made it sad. Everything was sad now. I wanted a different ending for Mom. I wanted it for everyone.

My chest tightened. I blinked, flushing tears from my eyes. The way Shyla was lying, I didn't dare move to wipe them off my face. Instead I gazed out the window to the sky, pale behind the treetops as we sped past.

"Why?" I whispered.

I knew God had heard me. I just didn't know if he'd answer.

# 3

## ELI

I woke to the exclamations of my friends. Shyla was no longer sleeping, but staring out the side window at yet another ravaged city, her orange pigtails askew.

"Where are we?" I asked, my voice raspy from sleep.

"Gunnison," Antônia said from the middle row.

Only a half hour left.

Gunnison was a bigger town with a Walmart, several hotels, and, of course, the hospital we'd be stopping at on the way back, thanks to Hannah. I didn't see a single store that had slipped through unscathed. Broken windows . . . doors swinging on their hinges . . . graffiti everywhere. The people of Gunnison had done a better job of keeping their loot off the ground, but every few blocks there was a body, just lying there for the elements to have their way. How had people died on the street like that? Had they gone out, thinking they weren't really that sick, then keeled over? Or had they been shot by looters?

Sitting in the back like this, I couldn't see much of the road. "You still seeing abandoned cars and road kill?" I asked Zach.

"Plenty," he said.

"See anyone driving the other way?"

"A few trucks, actually," Zach said. "Industrial ones. Wondered what you'd think of it, but you were asleep."

I wasn't sure. "Single driver?"

"Yep."

Strange. That sounded almost occupational.

Static fizzed from the walkie talkie on the dashboard, then my dad's voice said, "You guys see this?"

I peered out the windshield and saw that Dad's Silver Bullet had slowed behind an industrial flatbed truck that was hauling a load of bright blue portable bathrooms.

Chatter erupted—and so did my heart—at the first sign of life I'd seen all day.

"We see it, Dad," Lizzie said into the walkie talkie.

"Why would someone want a bunch of porta-potties?" Jaylee asked.

"With all the survivors coming up here, they must need them," Antônia said.

We came to a straight stretch of road, and Dad passed the truck. Zach did too, and I counted twelve bathrooms on the back. Someone up here was hard at work.

Ten minutes later, Jaylee and the girls cheered when we passed a freshly painted sign that said "LLC Safe Water Mountain Refuge: Clean Water for All" and had an arrow pointing ahead. Five miles south of the ski resort, we entered the town of Crested Butte. Sage green streetlamps along the sides of the road and no traffic lights gave the place a quaint feel. We passed a school with a football field out front that was filled with army tents, semi-truck trailers, a ton of solar panels, and more portable bathrooms than I'd seen in my life. In the parking lot, a helicopter sat on a freshly painted X. Someone certainly had some resources at their disposal.

After that we passed a car dealership. Electric cars filled a car carrier trailer in the lot. I spotted three Teslas, a Hyundai Kona, and a Chevy Bolt. As we drove deeper into town, I could tell this place had been looted as well, but there were people here—work crews sweeping up glass and nailing boards over broken windows. Several trucks had magnetic signs on the side doors that said, "Safe Water Recovery Team." I didn't see one dead body.

"Recovery for what?" Zach said.

"Don't you see?" Jaylee leaned up between the two front seats. "Everyone is working together to help Loca and Liberté make this a safe place to live."

Jaylee could be on to something. I didn't have any better ideas, and these people certainly did appear to be working together.

Just as suddenly as we'd entered the town, we left it behind, driving over stretches of flat ranchland as we approached the mountain. There weren't many trees here, and the vegetation was brown and yellow. They must be having a bit of a drought, which was unsurprising for western Colorado in August. Up ahead, the sun glared off the shiny black surface of what looked like windows. As we got closer, I realized it was a solar farm. I counted eleven rows of solar panels, each reflecting the white glow of the sun above.

At the base of the mountain, we reached the ski resort. How weird to name this place Mt. Crested Butte when it was five miles from another town named Crested Butte. A little weak on originality.

Our vans slowed behind a refrigerated truck where some construction workers had set up a roadblock. On both sides of the roads, signs proclaimed "LLC Safe Water Mountain Refuge: Clean Water for All." I dared hope it could be true.

The refrigerated truck moved on, and Dad pulled forward. A chill crept up my neck as I peered across the length of the minivan and out the windshield, watching my dad interact with the workers out the driver's window of his van. The memory of

Beardo hitting me with his rifle had me on edge. These men seemed harmless, though. No one looked to be packing. Dad's van passed through, and the worker waved Zach to stop next. He rolled down his window.

"Looking for the compound?" the man asked.

"Yeah," Zach said. "We're with the Odyssey." He motioned to the Silver Bullet up ahead.

"So he said. Y'all from Arizona, then?"

"Phoenix," Zach said.

"We've had a few from there. Heard it got pretty bad."

Zach didn't bother with small talk. "So how does this work? There really clean water here?"

"A stream, actually. Comes out of the mountain onto the Champions' land."

"Why isn't the stream contaminated like everything else?" I asked.

The man leaned down close to Zach's window and peered inside. "What do I look like? A geographer? Follow the signs on up to the compound. Park along the road. We've got a no looting policy, and enforcers working to keep it so. Behave and you won't find any trouble."

"Enforcers?" Zach asked.

"The Champions' bodyguard staff."

Sounded a little extreme. I couldn't help but notice the construction happening on both sides of the road. "Ask him what they're building."

Zach repeated my question.

"A fence. We've had trouble with some local warlords coming in and looting the place. We want to keep them out and keep our people safe."

"No one died here?" Lizzie asked. "Of the HydroFlu?"

"Plenty of people died, but now that we know what water is safe, we can protect everyone. The Champions and their team have worked hard to repair the town so everyone can move on with the rest of our lives."

Sounded too good to be true. Zach thanked the man and drove on. Dad had pulled over up ahead but started moving once

Zach got close.

With the exception of rows of porta-potties in every parking lot we passed by, the town of Mt. Crested Butte looked almost normal. I saw two shops with boarded-up windows and a third with construction workers out front, replacing a glass door. I didn't see any rigs packed with survival gear or people toting guns. It seemed wrong somehow. After everything we'd been through, why would people just suddenly act normal?

The downtown area of Mt. Crested Butte had maybe three dozen buildings total, not counting residential houses. The mountain looked bare, the surrounding forest thin. We convoyed through the ski resort area, following the signs to a road that turned south along the base of the mountain. I caught sight of a few more solar panels—this time on the roofs of buildings. We entered a forested, residential area, and the road turned to gravel.

"Cows!" Shyla yelled.

Sure enough, I counted eight brown and white cows in a grassy field on the north side of the road. The sight of them filled me with hope.

"The question is, did a bull survive?" I said.

"If not, those cows are an endangered species," Lizzie said.

The farther we drove, the more trees filled the stretches between each residence. The houses got fancier too. We came upon a length of road with vehicles parked along both sides.

"It's like I'm trying to find parking for a party in Desert Hills," Zach said.

"Can't wait!" Jaylee said.

Eventually, both Dad and Zach found places to park, and we all piled out. My legs were so stiff, it felt great to stand again.

"I can't believe we're here!" Jaylee grabbed my hand— my right, splinted one—and I quickly rotated to give her my left.

"Sorry," she said, threading her fingers with mine as we followed the signs—and the crowd—along the gravel road. "LLC was supposed to tour this fall. They were coming through Phoenix in late September. I wasn't sure if I was going to be able to go since they're so expensive." She prattled on about her former plans to babysit and raise the money for tickets.

Reinhold fell in step on my other side. "They sure are busy workers here," he said.

"How do you think they got all those solar panels so quickly?" I asked.

"At the school? Who knows?" Reinhold said. "But that solar farm wasn't new. Western Colorado is big on green energy. They've got a bunch of sustainable projects out here. Solar panels, windmills, charging stations. The cops even ride electric motorbikes. I think 25 percent of power in this area was green before HydroFlu."

"Not bad for a tiny place like this," Dad said.

"If the stream is clean, the headwaters above the stream are clean," Reinhold said. "Might be worth our time to test the waters on the other side of the mountain to see what they're like."

The road ended at a black iron gate. A crowd was one-by-one showing lanyards around their neck to a guard at a gate door in order to get inside. Beyond, a gray stone mansion sat on a grassy lawn like its own version of the White House. Directly to the right of the house stood an elevated, covered outdoor stage with its back to the mansion. A huge grassy lawn stretched out from the stage. It had to be at least ten acres. Clusters of people covered the space, sitting in groups, many on top of a blanket like they were waiting for some kind of music festival to begin.

My attention shifted to the driveway. It circled a rose garden and working fountain, passed by the front door, then ran back to the gate. A gaggle of kids were playing in the fountain.

Playing *in* the water.

"It really is safe," I said.

My dad's eyes narrowed. "Seems to be."

While we stood watching the children play, and Jaylee and Antônia gushed over the Champions' mansion, a man approached from the guardhouse, carrying a small pad of paper.

"You folks new here?" he asked.

"Yes, sir," Dad said.

"How many you got?"

"Fourteen," Dad said.

"Don't know that they can put you all together. I'm assuming you want to stay together."

"We'd like to, yes," Dad said. "Mostly, we're just curious how it all works."

The guard used a Sharpie to scratch a number 14 onto a sheet of paper. This he ripped off and handed to my dad. "Go on in. Ask for Mr. Tracy."

"We can live *here*?" Jaylee asked.

"The Champions' house is full," the guard said. "Mr. Tracy will assign you to a hotel or condo for now. There's a task force working to clear the houses in the city. At some point, we'll start assigning those."

Clear the houses. I shuddered.

The guard went back to his station, and a moment later the iron gate slid open on wheels, rattling as it went.

We followed the driveway around the fountain. I couldn't help staring at the kids running and splashing and shrieking and laughing. My gut said to get those kids out of there, that the water might hurt them.

"Can we play in the fountain?" Shyla asked.

"Not right now, sweetie," Lizzie said. She had a firm grip on Shyla and Davis's hands.

I glanced behind me and saw Hannah carrying Cree piggyback. It relieved me that the kids couldn't dash off into that water. It likely was safe, but I wasn't ready to give up caution just yet.

We approached the front doors, which were oversized and made of black iron that matched the gate. We let ourselves into a spacious foyer with dark hardwood floors and a ceiling that stretched three levels above our heads. A staircase wrapped along the left side of a hallway. Gaudy red and gold carpets ran up the middle of the steps and stretched down the center of the hall. Fancy light fixtures on the walls caught my gaze. A chandelier overhead too.

All were lit.

"Electricity is on," I said.

"Wonder how they pulled that off," Dad said. "I didn't hear

a generator."

"Maybe they're putting that solar farm to work," Logan said.

"They'd need a lot more than one farm to power this whole town," Reinhold said.

Archways stood on either side of the foyer. The one on the left led to a formal sitting room with fancy furniture that had carved wooden legs. I didn't get a good look through the right archway before a woman stepped out to greet us. Tall with wavy auburn hair, a pink business suit, and black high-heeled shoes, she paused before my dad and totally checked him out.

"I'm Jennie," she said. "You here to see Mr. Tracy?"

"Yes, we are," Dad said, handing her his number fourteen.

"Such a large group, that's wonderful. Right this way."

We followed her clicking heels into an office filled with a variety of leather furniture. A man came into view, sitting behind a glossy desk. He stood as Jennie handed him Dad's slip of paper, and we crowded inside. He wore a three-piece black suit and was Jack Skellington skinny—even had a small head with cropped hair that didn't help his awkward proportions.

"Welcome, come on in. I'm Morgan Tracy." His voice was nasally, his eyes wild and more open than was normal. "Why don't y'all take a seat. Make yourselves comfortable."

Sure. Fourteen of us were going to sit on the three chairs and sofa that were available. Jaylee abandoned me to squeeze onto the sofa with Antônia, Krista, and Lizzie. Davis, Logan, and Shyla claimed the three leather chairs. The rest of us remained standing.

Mr. Tracy sat against the front of his desk, ankles crossed, arms folded. "What a great looking group of young people. We're so glad you found us. I hear it's brutal out there."

"We're not looking to stay," Reinhold said. "We're just curious."

Tracy's fish eyes latched onto Reinhold, who was standing with Kimama just behind me and Zach. "Oh, I didn't see you back there, sir. These your kids?"

"Do we look like his kids?" Hannah was standing on Dad's other side, still holding Cree.

Her voice twisted my stomach, and I tapped my splinted fingers against my leg, suddenly uncomfortable.

"My mistake," Tracy said, holding up his hands. "Well, if you do decide to stay here, and if you follow instructions, I promise we'll keep you safe, m'kay?"

"How can you promise that?" Reinhold asked from the back.

"Okay, well, let me tell you about what we're doing here," Tracy said. "About two weeks ago, we realized the river water was safe. It's the only water you can drink. It's the only water you can touch. No one else has access to this water."

"You stole a river?" I said.

"No, no, no," Tracy said. "The river is on the Champions' property. Once they realized their water was safe, they wanted to share it. We set to work immediately making a plan to build a community here."

"How do you have power?" I asked.

"Gunnison County Electric used to get its power from the Blue Mesa Dam," Tracy said. "It's only about 60 miles from here. We formed a task team and sent them down there. They got it running again. It's not ideal to have anyone living so far away from the community, but that's what it's going to take until we can come up with a new power source."

"Impressive that you found people who knew how to run the dam," Dad said.

"One." Tracy held up his finger. "We found one, and he trained a team. Anything we need—as long as we can find one skilled leader—we form a task team, and we train."

That was smart.

"We'll want to know your skills and interests too," Jennie said.

"Yes," Tracy said. "This is a community. It takes a lot of different skills to run this place, so we all have to work together."

"The guy at the gate said something about housing?" Zach asked.

"That's right," Tracy said. "We'll set you up with food vouchers and housing, free of charge—eventually *houses*. The water has been turned off all over town. You can't shower anywhere but here. You can't drink any water but ours. If you turn on the old water and you die, that's not our fault, m'kay? If you want to stay, you'll need to sign a waiver, agreeing to our rules and releasing us from liability should you choose noncompliance."

Liability? Was this guy for real? "You a lawyer?" I asked.

"Consider me the Attorney General of the Safe Water Mountain Refuge," Tracy said, grinning. "It's my job to make this place run smoothly and to keep everyone alive and healthy. The sooner everyone signs the waiver, the sooner Jennie can get you processed."

"I'm in!" Jaylee said.

"Me too," Antônia and Krista added.

"Hold on just a minute, girls," Dad said.

But Tracy snapped his fingers, and Jennie came trotting over on her high heels. She handed each of us a single sheet of paper. It was a bunch of legal mumbo jumbo. Like Tracy said, we each got fifty dollars in vouchers a day for food and access to the showers on the Champions' property. We would also be given a one-gallon water jug that we could refill. We had to adhere to the "Laws of the United States," and we had to attend a mandatory "Morning Party" every Monday at 10 a.m. on the Champions' lawn.

Basically, we had to agree to their rules or get out. I watched Dad for cues, then joined him and Reinhold as they talked it out.

"Feels weird," Dad said.

"I hear you loud and clear," Reinhold said.

"I would like a shower, though." Dad looked at me. "What do you think, Eli?"

"I think they went through a lot of trouble to keep from getting sued," I said, "but I respect their attempt at organization. It can't be easy, taking care of so many people."

"Yes, they do have a lot of good things going for them," Dad said.

"Done!" Jaylee said, waving her paper above her head.

The world stopped. If Jaylee stayed and Dad didn't, what

would I do?

"I'd like a shower, too," I said, my voice a little thick. "Maybe stay the day and see what kind of food they have."

Zach stepped into our circle. "You think they have cheeseburgers?"

"Okay, how about this?" Dad said. "We give it the night. Try the place out. Get showers. Tomorrow morning we decide who's staying and who's going back. Andy?"

Reinhold grimaced but said, "Yeah, okay."

I glanced at Jaylee again. She and Antônia were on their feet, talking and smiling like there'd never been a pandemic and both of their families weren't missing.

There was nothing on the paper that worried me. I didn't have a problem agreeing to any of it. I managed to pinch the pen with my right hand and draw my name at the bottom. I handed it to Jennie, whose fingernails were so long she almost scratched me.

"Excellent," Tracy said when Jennie set our stack of signed contracts on his desk. "Welcome to the Safe Water Mountain Refuge, folks. We're glad to have you. Jennie will get you registered and set up with housing and vouchers. Y'all have a good time out there, m'kay?"

"Mmm'kay," Zach said, grinning at me.

Jennie clicked her way out of the office and across to the fancy sitting room. We took turns on five computers that were set up along the far wall. We filled out a questionnaire that asked us about our education, training, skills, hobbies, and interests. This was for future job placement, Jennie said, if and when the right opportunity became available. She also took our pictures for our digital IDs, which ticked off Reinhold, big time.

"Dunno what you need pictures for," he said.

Jennie handled his mood with endless cheer. "Our tech team is working on a digital system to replace our voucher system. It won't be ready for a few more weeks, but I'm getting a head start on it now to save time later."

After the pictures, she said, "I put you all in the Snowcrest Condominiums," then gave us instructions on how to get there, like we might get lost in this ten-road town. She read from her cell phone, "People say the Snowcrest has the best view of any hotel in Mt. Crested Butte due to its slightly elevated and central location. It has easy access to the pedestrian footbridge, charming shops, and gourmet restaurants."

Zach lit up. "Restaurants are open?"

"Oh, yes. Everything is open, except the hot tub and pool in your condominium, of course, since there is no water to fill it."

"Does your cell phone work?" Jaylee asked.

"For Wi-Fi, yes, though lots of internet sites are down. Depends who they were hosted by and what kind of back-up power those companies had. In time it will likely all go down, but our tech team has built a website on our own servers. It's pretty basic right now, but they're adding to it every day. We'll get phones back, eventually, but that's a little trickier than internet."

"Why?" Antônia asked.

"Well, first our phone team had to figure out which cell towers were still working. Now they're out scavenging to see if they can find the right kind of phones. If they can find some that work with the local towers, we can get people set up again."

"That would be amazing," Jaylee said.

"I've given you units 33 and 34 at the Snowcrest," Jennie said. "Both are two bedroom condos that sleep eight." She handed my dad two sets of keys on plastic rings. "There is no housekeeping. There are no plumbers to fix toilets or bathtubs or sinks if you decide to do things that might break them. Avoid using the toilets in the units, since there is no means to flush them, and instead use the portable toilets in the parking lots."

"I guess we know where those porta-potties were headed," Lizzie said.

"You'll each get a lanyard with your ID number that will get you on this property for showering, filling your water jugs, morning parties, and concerts. You will also get vouchers to purchase fifty dollars of product a day—that's food, coffee, milkshakes, beer, groceries, merchandise, whatever you want."

"Cheeseburgers?" Zach asked.

"Absolutely," Jennie said.

"I can't eat burgers because of my braces," Logan said.

"How do you have cheeseburgers?" Reinhold asked. "Where you getting this food?"

"Our scavenge teams have been hard at work. They've traveled to Gunnison, Montrose, Grand Junction, and as far as Pueblo, Colorado Springs, and Denver. They targeted distribution centers. Many still had electricity, so the teams were able to transport fresh and frozen foods back here in refrigerated trucks. The teams already brought in enough to feed Safe Water for a year, but they still go out weekly to continue to stockpile resources."

"What about expiration dates?" I asked.

"We know the food won't last forever, which is why we have other task teams making plans to manufacture new foods. What our scavenge teams have found should last until we start producing new foods. Now, vouchers come in ten-dollar values, and there is no change. Sorry, but we can't deal with that. Besides, this is just to tide us over until the wristbands are set up. We do offer a budgeting workshop to help you make the best use of your daily allowance. That is listed online as well."

"Online where?" I asked.

"Oh, I'm sorry," Jennie said. "Whenever you log onto the LLC Wi-Fi, it will automatically take you to a Safe Water Mountain Refuge homepage. That's where you'll find all the information I've told you about. If you don't have a cell phone or access to a computer, there are computers in your condo lobby. When you get a chance, poke around the site and get a good feel for it. You'll be visiting there a lot."

"I brought my laptop," Logan said. "You guys can all use mine."

"What about laundry?" Lizzie asked.

"Excellent question," Jennie said, pushing her long hair over one shoulder. "Right now our laundry is dry clean only. You can make a reservation online. The pricing is listed there. I think it's thirty dollars for a 13-gallon trash bag. Pickup and delivery are free."

"That's the only way to wash our clothes?" I asked.

"For now, yes, but we have a team experimenting with using the contaminated water from the East River for industrial purposes. They believe it could be used safely for laundry, but they're still testing that process."

"Anything online about other survivors?" I asked, curious what might be going on in the rest of the world.

"Not that I know of," she said. "We hope you'll be very happy here."

"That's it?" Reinhold asked. "No charge?"

"None. It's the Champions' honor to take care of everyone. We hope you'll eventually join a task team where your skills best fit. Here are your lanyards." She handed Dad a fistful of black shoelaces with white plastic tags on the end. Then she gave him a manila envelope. "And here are your vouchers for today and tomorrow. New vouchers can be picked up in the lobby of your residence every Monday—excuse me! Don't touch that, please." She pushed past us and tottered over to where Jaylee and Krista were admiring some award statues on a shelf.

"What do you think?" Dad asked me and Reinhold.

"A little too good to be true," I said. "They can't feed all of us forever."

"At some point," Reinhold said, "they're going to start asking us to earn our keep. And I didn't see anything about that on their contract."

"That's what the questionnaire was for," I said. "She did say she hoped we'd volunteer to help with a task team."

Reinhold grinned and lowered his voice. "Good thing I said my skills were ballet and dog training."

I chuckled, glad Reinhold was giving this a try. I had to admit, what they'd accomplished already was impressive— especially the organization. I guess if you wanted people to listen to you, it helped to be famous and to have the only known safe water source in the world.

"I don't mind taking advantage of their hospitality for a bit," Dad said. "Maybe we'll find answers to some of our questions."

"I only want to get a closer look at that river," Reinhold said.

"All righty then," I said. "Let's check out this condo."

# 4

## HANNAH

As Seth drove the minivan back into town, we all took the same seats we'd had on the ride up. I sat directly behind Andy, who had claimed the passenger's seat. Kimama sat behind Seth. Between us was little Cree, the only person who could possibly feel as foreign in this van as me. We had picked him up in Kayenta after discovering he'd been living in a Holiday Inn with his mother's corpse—yet another haunting memory to add to my growing collection.

In the back row, Logan and Davis were again feeding their video game addictions on Logan's Nintendo Switch. Logan was Lizzie's age and a long-time friend of Eli and Zach. Davis was nine, brother to five-year-old Shyla who was in the other van— both beautiful white children with ginger hair and faces full of orange freckles. Eli had picked them up with their babysitter, Krista, in Phoenix.

Seth easily found the Snowcrest Condominiums. The property was made up of several sections of row housing units with dated beige siding, dark brown trim, and long, steeply pitched brown shed roofs. Most had balconies. Taller units had their own garage. Each section also had its own parking area with a cluster of turquoise portable bathrooms.

Seth drove through the place until he found unit 33. As soon as he parked, I grabbed my new camper backpack—the one Eli had helped me pick out from Ace Hardware—and got out. We all gathered on a plank walkway in front of the dark brown door with the number 33 on it.

"The next one should be 34," Seth said, holding out a key. "Boys in 33, girls in 34. Let's meet back here in ten, then we'll head to the showers."

Jaylee snatched the key from Seth and ran down the walkway, Krista on her heels. The rest of us girls followed behind. First time in my life I wished I was a boy.

The door to 34 was open when I arrived. I entered a bright space. Directly ahead, a tile floor filled an open, U-shaped kitchen. Beyond, three steps led to a raised living room. The outer wall was solid windows with a set of sliding doors on one end that led to an enclosed balcony.

The place was furnished and reminded me of a rustic mountain cabin. Almost everything was shaved logs, golden and glossy. There was a TV and DVD player—a flyer on the console listed movie titles we could check out from our lobby. A cast-iron woodstove with scalloped feet sat in the inside corner of the living room. Its black stove pipe stretched all the way up until it disappeared into a hole in the vaulted ceiling. Strangely out of place were several second-story windows overlooking the living room. Shyla waved down from the one near the stove pipe.

I followed the sound of the girls' voices up carpeted stairs and inspected the two bedrooms and bathroom from a squared landing. The rooms were small with windows on both walls, one set looking out to the parking lot, the other looking down on the living room. The master bedroom had two queen beds, a desk and chair, and a private bathroom. The other room had two twin beds. All had hotel bedding in red and blue geometric prints.

"Where are you guys going?" Krista yelled from somewhere. The age gap between Krista, Jaylee, and Antônia at thirteen, seventeen, and twenty-two intrigued me. Younger and older both gravitated toward Jaylee, and I just didn't see the draw. Krista was destined to be disappointed, though, as her eagerness to be included too often came off as desperation.

I twisted my ring. Strange places made me nervous. I peeked into the master bedroom, looking for Lizzie or Kimama. Antônia and Jaylee were already inside.

"See? This one is *way* better," Jaylee said.

"But with the other one, it can just be us," Antônia whispered. "It would be nice to have some privacy."

"The bathroom, though," Jaylee said, dragging Antônia through the open master bathroom doorway. "It's, like, a must to have our own space to get ready in—even if we can't use the shower and sink. Don't you think?"

"We'll have to share beds in this room," Antônia said.

"Four people in here," Jaylee said. "Good point."

Krista nearly ran me down at the doorway. "You guys? Where are you?"

"A *very* good point," Jaylee said, followed by the sound of the two girls giggling.

Krista ran into the master bath, and I slipped across the hall into the smaller bedroom, relieved when I saw Kimama and Lizzie standing at the interior window, looking down to the living room. Shyla had climbed into one of the beds and was under the covers.

"I'm going to sleep here!" she said, grinning.

"Looks cozy," I said, but I didn't want to be in either of these rooms. I also wanted to make that choice myself before the girls made it for me when I became the odd one out.

I went downstairs and set my backpack on the sofa, thinking I could sleep there and be perfectly happy—I glanced up—except for those windows looking down from above and the window wall exposing my sleeping area. I checked the lock on the sliding door, pleased that it had a bolt and a stick in the runner. I checked the lock on the front door next, but it had only a door knob lock. No deadbolt, no chain.

Muffled voices from upstairs caught my attention, then a shrieking reply from Krista.

"Why do *you* get to decide? You're not the boss of me!"

Disinterested in the war brewing above and weary from the butterflies crowding my stomach, I left the apartment, shutting the door behind me. Someone was leaning against the wall just outside our unit. I cried out, my heart leaping into my throat.

"Sorry," Eli said. "Didn't mean to scare you."

Everything scared me. It was nothing new. I rubbed the scar on my forearm that often ached when I became frightened. My skin still tingled as I thought of all the times I'd found Brandon waiting in a similar way. This was *not* Brandon, I reminded myself. Eli was safe.

"Kind of loud in there," he said.

"They're fighting over who gets to sleep where," I said, trying to sound normal. "Krista wants to be with Jaylee. Antônia wants to be with Jaylee. But Antônia wants the smaller room, so she and Jaylee can have privacy. Shyla is already under the covers in the smaller room, though, and Jaylee wants the master bedroom because it has more space to get ready. But she doesn't want to share a bed." I sighed. "It's been a long time since I've been around so much drama."

"I'd rather not be around it myself. But I'll tell you right now, Jaylee will win."

"Jaylee always wins?"

He grinned. "Always."

I raised my eyebrows. "Not with the applesauce, though?"

Surprise flashed across his face. "Oh. Uh . . . I guess not."

For a moment, we stared at each other without speaking. He had a good face. Boyish. Honest. He wasn't stunningly handsome like his father, nor did he have the laugh lines that graced Seth's face. I wondered why.

He was still looking at me. I fumbled to say something

neutral—something that would keep our conversation going. "Glad your dad told us to bring a change of clothing. I'm looking forward to that shower."

"No kidding." Eli ran his fingers through his greasy hair. "It's been way too long."

I smiled at him, then quickly looked away, not wanting to jinx whatever was happening here. A truce, perhaps?

The door to my condo opened, and Krista stormed out. "It's not fair!" Her gaze fell on Eli. "Who decides who sleeps where?" she snapped.

"You have to work it out," he said.

Krista rolled her eyes. "You never take my side."

"Mr. McShane and Reinhold decided for us," Zach said, approaching from the guy's apartment, Logan at his side.

"Maybe they can choose for us too since Eli won't," Krista said. She glared at him, then at Jaylee and Antônia as the rest of the girls exited our condo.

"What did they decide?" I asked Zach.

"Davis and Cree get the twin beds," Zach said. "Mr. McShane said they needed a bedtime. He and Reinhold are sharing the couch bed downstairs. They gave us three the master."

The dads had put the kids first. No surprise.

Jaylee tucked herself under Eli's arm and grinned. "Which of you are sharing a bed?"

Zach, Eli, and Logan frowned at each other.

"I didn't even go upstairs," Logan said. "I was trying to build a fire in the stove. Did you see there's firewood on the balcony, Hannah? I can come build you a fire later, if you want."

"Thanks," I said, not sure I wanted Logan in my bedroom.

"Come on!" Jaylee tugged Eli toward the vans. "Let's go shower."

Antônia and Krista followed the new couple. Logan passed by them as he ran to catch up with Eli. The rest of van two waited for Seth at door 33. Eventually the men came out. The moment Cree saw me, he came running and put his tiny hand in mine.

"You missed me?" I asked.

The sweet little guy smiled. My best friend in this group was five, maybe six years old, and I was okay with that.

"You're good with him," Seth said as we headed toward the van.

"Really? I thought about going into pediatrics, but since I've never been around kids, I figured I'd be bad with them."

Seth's gaze shifted to the boy at my side. "I think Cree would disagree."

We walked a few steps in silence, and I felt compelled to say something to this kind man. "I'm sorry you got saddled with . . ." I stopped myself, not wanting Cree to think he was a burden on anyone. "That you feel responsible to take care of everyone. I'm happy to help with Cree anytime. If you need a break."

"Not a problem, Miss Hannah," he said, his expression suddenly weary. "It's nice to have something to keep me busy."

Which was exactly why I liked having Cree around, but I kept that thought to myself.

• • •

Back at the compound, we showed our lanyards to enter through the gate and followed the crowd around the stage— quickly lost Jaylee, Eli, Antônia, and Krista, who ran off to explore an arc of fence barricades set up around the stage front.

People and tents covered the huge grassy expanse. Many were seated on blankets. On the backside of the mansion, the shower building came into sight—a single story beige structure with ten doors. The line outside was worse than the one to ride Space Mountain. Half the people were sitting on the grass. We copped a squat at the end of the line and settled in to wait.

Lizzie, Zach, Shyla, Davis, and Logan were at the front of our group. Eli and the girls caught up and claimed the next place in line. Jaylee's arms were wrapped around Eli's waist like tentacles. Then Kimama, Reinhold, Seth, then me and Cree. The day was nice. Partly cloudy. Mid-seventies, I guessed. Dry. How often did it rain here? Would rain be dangerous?

We took turns going to fill our water jugs. I took Cree with me, and we returned to the line with a bounty that felt like pure gold. My lips were chapped from being dehydrated for so long, and even though the water tasted amazing, I was careful not to overdo it. Cree, obsessed with his water jug, could barely lift it to his mouth, so he never got much of a drink without help.

"Think people can really live here like this?" Zach asked. "It feels like camp."

"How long can it last before they run out of food?" Andy asked.

A man with a goatee walked up the line, passing out flyers. "Concert tonight," he said. "Right here at the compound."

Jaylee snatched one, read it, and gasped. "LLC are playing tonight!"

"How much is it?" Antônia asked.

Jaylee held up the flyer for Antônia to see. "Free."

The girls squealed.

"I'm not going to get out of this, am I?" Eli said to his dad.

Seth chucked. "Yeah, good luck with all that."

About ten yards up the line, a group had started a drum circle, which inspired Cree to dance. Shyla quickly joined him, and the two laughed as they wiggled to the hollow rhythms. More people worked the line, some distributing flyers for the concert, others with their own agendas. One guy was selling bottles of soda for ten credits each. A woman walked past with a tray of homemade hemp jewelry. Another guy was selling marijuana.

Zach called out to a guy with wet hair. "Hey, man. How long you wait in line?"

The guy shrugged. "Got here around noon. What time is it now?"

Zach checked his watch. "Close to three," he said.

The guy swore. "Yeah, there's only ten showers, so it's pretty slow going."

Three hours to wait for a shower?

Eventually, Zach started an alphabet game that ran up and down our line, each of us naming a restaurant with whatever letter landed on us. I got N and said Nute's, which was a Thai place near my parent's house. After that the game changed to movies, then song titles. By the time round three ended, the group had lost interest. Smaller conversations developed, and with me at the end of the line, I was again left out.

I didn't mean to continually separate myself from the teenagers. I was far closer to their ages than Seth's and Andy's, but I preferred maturity to hyperactivity. I'd always been this way, even in middle school, high school, and college. The few times I'd tried to fit in, invariably I'd always chosen the wrong people. Lesedi. Shen. Henrique. Brandon.

I shuddered, recalling Brandon's control. His anger. His madness.

Part of the reason I'd stuck with Eli was that he'd seemed more mature, like me. I'd liked the leader in him. The strategist. I'd also liked how he'd risked everything to help me and later had gone above and beyond for Cree.

After the incident on the bridge, though, he'd crumpled in on himself. I'd broken him. And the moment we'd reached his father, he'd sunk back and let Seth and Andy take over. I couldn't fault him, really. What we were living through . . . this was a horror film come to life. We all wanted to curl up with a blanket and have someone stronger and wiser tuck us in. I certainly did. And this group wasn't exactly easy to corral.

I glanced at Eli, Jaylee's nose nearly touching his as she talked so only he could hear. His eyes were fixed on hers. Caught in her web. I didn't have time for such games. The world had imploded, and somehow I was still here. But for how long? I wanted to believe I could take care of myself. I had many virtues, but physical strength wasn't one of them.

I studied Seth, who sat just ahead of me, throwing a ball of clean socks to Cree. The boy never once caught the socks but seemed to like playing fetch. Seth was strong. He was also really nice and easy to talk to. Handsome, for an older guy.

Wow. Wow. Wow. Had I really just checked out Eli's dad? What was the matter with me? Eli and Jaylee were kissing now. Eww. Past them, Zach and Lizzie lay side by side on the grass, pointing at clouds with their hands interlocked. They were so cute it turned my stomach. Logan was playing a video game with Davis. Andy and Kimama had wandered to explore, Shyla on their heels. An overwhelming feeling of loneliness drenched me in sorrow so heavy, tears welled in my eyes. I blinked them away as I studied the people around us in the line, the men, the women, the children. Many were paired in obvious family groups.

I didn't care about romance or attraction. Didn't believe in love anymore. The idea of dating someone in a pandemic—after all Brandon had put me through—it held no interest for me. But I hated being alone. I needed friends. A safe place to belong and call home. A family.

Cree ran up to me and held out the socks. "Na'," he said. "Na'!"

I took the socks from him. "Thank you."

He reached out. "*Hǫh.*"

I returned the socks. This went on for a while, then he threw them and pointed to where they landed in the grass. "Hǫh. Get it."

"You get it," I said.

He grinned and hop, hop, hopped over to the socks and swept them into his hands with more drama than a ballerina. Again he held them out to me. "Na'!"

Well, this was fun. Honestly, I was grateful to have the little guy paying attention to me. Eli had guessed Cree was five or six, but I thought he might be even younger. When I asked him, he help up his hand and concentrated, like he might be trying to hold up three fingers, but then he said, "Five. I'm five years old." We'd probably never know for sure.

Andy and Kimama returned from their walk, and Cree threw the socks at Kimama.

She tossed them back to me. "Catch!"

I did, and Cree came running over. Kimama joined our game, the three of us sitting close enough to toss the socks in a circle. Cree eventually got tired and sank onto my lap.

"*Shimá bił ílyeed,*" he said. "*Aoo', t'áá ákot'é.* Yes."

It was the most I'd heard him say, and it wasn't English. Or Spanish.

41

"Dad, I think Cree speaks Diné," Kimama said.

I turned to where the men sat behind us. "What's Diné?"

"The language of the Navajo people," Kimama said.

"*Diné bizaad?*" Andy asked Cree. "*Yá'át'ééh?*"

Cree smiled, buried half his face behind my sleeve, and said, "*Yá'át'ééh, Azhé'é,*" back to Andy.

"That's all I ever learned," Andy said. "Poor kid belongs with his people."

"There was no one alive at the hotel in Kayenta," I said, panicked and defensive. "We didn't want to just leave him."

"I know," Andy said. "I know."

What if there had been people living nearby? People who could have cared for Cree? My eyes misted with tears at the very idea that what I'd seen as a rescue could have been an abduction. "He speaks English too," I said, setting my hand on his head. "You are Cree."

The boy reached up and touched my ear. "You are Nana."

I grinned. "Close. Hannah. Hhh. Hannah."

"Hhhannah. Eli *shą'?*" When I didn't answer, he said, "Where Eli go?"

"Over there," I said, pointing to the front of our group.

Cree craned his neck to the side but must have decided Eli was too far away to play toss-the-socks, because he stayed put.

Seth was on his feet now and walked past me. Our eyes met, locked briefly, then his gaze drifted down the line. "I think we should have that talk while we're waiting," he said.

My arms prickled. Was he speaking to me? Before I could manage an answer, Andy's voice came from behind. "Let's do it."

So . . . not talking to me, then.

"Everyone—Phoenix crew," Seth said. "Let's make a plan for heading back to Andy's place tomorrow."

"What!" Jaylee's volume turned the heads of people in line around us. "I'm not going back there."

"Me either," Krista said.

Seth held up a hand. "I'm not forcing anyone to leave. But I do want to hear from everyone. Zach? How about you?"

Zach glanced at Lizzie. "I wouldn't mind staying a little

longer. But I'm fine to leave too. We've got plenty of supplies."

"No way to bathe, though," Lizzie added. "Maybe we could drive up once a week for showers?"

"That might work for a few months," Andy said, "but gasoline won't last forever. Until we get a good rain, we won't know if it will be safe to harvest water."

"What about the mountain?" Eli said. "I thought you wanted to explore it. See if we could find access to the river ourselves."

"I do," Andy said. "Thought we'd leave bright and early tomorrow and drive as far east as we can, then hike up the slope."

"Why do you want to leave?" Jaylee asked. "This place has everything."

"Your definition of everything is a whole lot different than mine," Andy said. "I shouldn't have to wear a necklace to access fresh water. It ain't right, anyone claiming to own a whole river."

"There are two vans," Eli said, frowning. "Maybe some could stay, and some could explore?" He avoided Jaylee's gaze. "I mean, I definitely want to explore the mountain, but I wouldn't mind staying a little longer too. It might take a couple days to get a feel for what it would be like to live here. Right now, it's too early to tell."

"We should stay at least a week," Logan said. "That will give us enough time to make an educated decision."

"How about you, Miss Hannah?" Seth asked.

I liked how normal the town seemed. "I wouldn't mind sticking around a little longer," I said. "I like the possibility of being part of a society."

Seth nodded. "You raise a good point. We could survive on our own for quite a while—maybe for the rest of our lives—but what kind of a future would we be building for the kids if we raised them in isolation?" He rustled Cree's hair.

"A far better one than living in a place run by a bunch of nut jobs," Andy said.

"That's not fair," Jaylee said. "Just because you don't like their music doesn't make them crazy."

"Anyone who makes me sign a contract just to take a

shower is hiding something," Andy said.

"How about a compromise?" Seth said. "Whoever wants to explore the mountain can go with Andy in the morning. Everybody else will remain here. When Andy gets back, we'll revisit this conversation. Sound fair?"

No one dissented, so Seth let the matter drop.

When I finally made it to the shower, the water inside was lukewarm with low pressure, reminding me of the showers in Guatemala. They had soap and shampoo dispensers inside, for which I was grateful, since I didn't bring any. This was the first bath I'd taken since I'd been abducted, and I scrubbed myself until my skin turned pink.

I wondered, not for the first time, how much my dad had agreed to pay the "kidnappers" for my return. That Brandon had hired them still shocked me. I'd known he was a monster, but orchestrating my kidnapping and extorting money from my dad had been a new low. Had he honestly believed I'd never find out? And even if I hadn't, why would he think "rescuing" me would make up for all he'd done?

After my shower, I joined the group on the lawn and pretended not to notice Zach wrapping Eli's fingers in a fresh splint. I regretted hurting him—wished I could go back and make another choice. A knot ached in my chest, but I told myself this was good. At least Eli was letting someone take care of the wound.

I spotted Kimama lying on the ground and sat with her. Andy paced a groove into the grass in front of Eli and Zach, going on about his plan to explore the mountain tomorrow. I wondered if anyone would invite me along. Did I even want to go?

One by one our group grew until all had returned clean, hair dripping. When I saw how everyone had divided themselves, just like before, it became clear that I needed to plan for my own future. I couldn't just wait around to see where this group decided to put me. I needed to be proactive—to act—before I ended up all alone.

# 5

## ELI

Once everyone had showered and filled water jugs, we dropped our stuff at the condos, then went looking for dinner on foot. We followed the signs to a pedestrian sky bridge that led to the downtown shopping area. We explored a handful of sporting goods stores that specialized in ski gear, several tourist shops that sold Mt. Crested Butte T-shirts and hoodies, and a place called Butte Boutique and Mercantile that ended up being a one-stop shopping location. The girls bought shampoo and soap. I bought a pair of kiddie binoculars that fascinated Cree.

We ended up at a place called The Secret Pizzeria, which was serving what seemed like the frozen pizzas Mom got from the grocery store back home. I ordered a whole one for myself and inhaled it.

My nerves were still on high alert. It was strange to see so many people and not feel like I needed to point a gun at them. I felt vulnerable and had to keep reminding myself it was different here. That felt naïve, though. All of this seemed too good to be true. I kept that thought to myself. I'd voiced it to Jaylee earlier today and had gotten verbally scratched.

I liked Jaylee. A lot. Loved the feel of her hand in mine and the way her hair brushed my arm when we walked side by side. I didn't like how awkward being "with" her felt sometimes. Two-way conversation pretty much didn't happen. She wasn't interested in anything I had to say, unless I was complimenting her or agreeing with her.

I'd wanted this for so long—to be with Jaylee—but it was different than I thought it would be. I wasn't sure what, if anything, to do about that yet. I remember my mom saying she and Dad picked their battles with each other, that some things just weren't worth fighting about—or even bringing up. From now on, I would try that with Jaylee and keep my gut instincts about this mountain "refuge" to myself.

We eventually split up. Dad, Reinhold, Hannah, and the kids—all except Krista—went back to the condos. Zach drove the rest of us back to the mansion for the concert. I could feel the boom-cha pulse of the electronic dance music before we even parked the van. Once we were out and walking toward the black iron gates, the deeper the bass reverberated in my chest. It was chilly out now that it was dark, and I was glad I'd worn my Phoenix Suns sweatshirt over my T-shirt.

Our lanyards got us inside. The stage was lit up brightly, instruments all in place, but no one was up there yet. Traffic barrier fences that hadn't been there earlier today funneled us around the crowd and released us deep into the grassy lawn. We made our way to an empty pocket as close to the stage as we could get. People instantly started filling in behind us.

"At least we all smell better!" Lizzie yelled, arms around Zach's waist in a side hug.

Zach inhaled my sister's hair. "Like an ocean."

"I don't know," I shouted. "I think I needed a round two."

Jaylee tugged on the hem of my hoodie. "Can I wear this? I'm cold."

I stripped it off and handed it to her. The cool night air made me shiver, but seeing Jaylee in my shirt was totally worth it. She grabbed my hand and waved me to lean down. I was hoping for a kiss, but she spoke into my ear. "I want to get closer. Let's make our way to the front."

I considered the crowd. No thanks, was what I wanted to say. I glanced at Zach and Lizzie and yelled, "You guys want to try and get closer?"

Lizzie shot me the bug eyes and shook her head. I didn't want to go, either. For my own sanity, this seemed a battle worth fighting.

"I'm going to watch from here," I told her.

Jaylee rolled her eyes and mouthed the word, "Fine." She latched onto Antônia's arm and pushed up against two guys standing in front of us. "Excuse me!" This she yelled in a voice that somehow sounded sweet while still being extremely loud.

The guys looked back, parted, and Jaylee stepped through, pulling Antônia with her. Krista lunged forward and caught Antônia's hand.

"Wait for me!" Logan latched onto Krista's sleeve and was slowly dragged into the crowd, grinning like a fool.

I watched their progress, keeping my eyes on Logan and Krista's frizzy blond heads, but I eventually lost them in the mob. I had to admit, it felt nice to be alone for a minute. Not that I was really alone. I counted heads and tried to estimate how many people were here. Had to be close to a thousand. Had they all signed Tracy's contract to live in the Safe Water Mountain Refuge? How many more might come? Were there other clean-water streams in the world? If there was one, it stood to reason that there were others too.

Blue lights lit the stage. A new beat kicked up. Colored spotlights streaked over the small crowd, drawing an eruption of screaming cheers. I don't know why the level of enthusiasm surprised me. Most of these people *had* come to hear a concert.

"*Bonsoir, mes amis!*"

The heavily accented male voice amplified over the sound system and enticed a second round of cheers, louder than the first. A spotlight illuminated a white guy standing on the left side of the stage. He was wearing a short-sleeved shirt printed in an oversized green and white argyle print and what looked like black leather pants.

"For those of you who do not know me, I am Loca Champion. *Tous si beaux*. You are so beautiful. Your smiling faces. Your joy." He smiled like the Cheshire cat, all teeth and wild eyes. "*Je suis très heureux*. I am so happy. So happy to see so many alive!"

More cheering.

"*Oui! Oui!* We did it!" he yelled. "You did. You survived. *Ma sœur aussi*. My sister."

"*Bonjour, amis sûrs*." A woman's voice. Low. Almost humming.

A spotlight shone on a woman on the right side of the stage, and the crowd went wild. Liberté, I gathered. She wore a long-sleeved, purple and black striped swimsuit with some kind of stiff, white collar that belonged on a vampire cape.

"We survived the end of the world!" She lifted both hands above her head in victory, drawing more cheers. She brought a dagger-like fingernail to her lips. "Shhh," she said, and the crowd fell silent. "We will continue to survive as long as we stick together."

Before the next round of applause could get too loud, Loca spoke. "But we're not going to sit around and be afraid," he said. "We are going to party. Every. Day."

The little crowd lost their minds screaming. I glanced at Zach and Lizzie, and we all chuckled. LLC sure knew how to work the audience.

"We've got a lot to party about," Liberté said, walking toward her brother like one of those supermodels on a runway. She stopped before him, and they stood there, staring at each other, eye to eye.

"Because we . . ." Loca yelled.

"Are . . ." Liberté said.

"Survivors!" they yelled in unison, and the music kicked in.

The crowd went nuts, jumping and cheering as the siblings began to sing. It took me a minute with the overly loud music, but I eventually recognized the "We Are Survivors" song from Jaylee's indoctrination on the ride up. A breeze made me shiver, and I crossed my arms, missing my sweatshirt. My gaze caught on a shirtless man moving through the crowd. He was ripped and wore blinking bicycle safety lights strapped across his chest. The crowd danced around him, but every-so-often someone stopped and bought something from him. There were a few others like him. I counted four. Four people here colder than me.

"What do you think they're selling?" I asked Zach.

He shrugged. "Buttons? Stickers? Some kind of paraphernalia?"

Weird. From the reaction of the crowd, it appeared that Loca and Liberté Champion were putting on a good show. I recognized every song they played: "Fast Lane," "Rage Right," "Bon Bon Breakfast," "Everywhere Love," and "Brown Sugar Night."

When the concert ended, Zach, Lizzie, and I waited while the crowd milled away. Once the area around us had emptied out, Lizzie sat on the grass, and Zach joined her.

Logan found us first. "What did you guys think?" he asked.

I shrugged. "Just like the ride up, only much, much louder. You liked it?"

"Yeah. Good energy," Logan said. "I lost the girls. Made it all the way to the fence, and Liberté looked right at me. She's much prettier in person. Not as pretty as Hannah, though."

We waited another half hour before the girls returned. By then we were all sitting in the grass.

"There you are!" Krista said. "We've been looking for you for, like, forever."

"We're right where you left us," Lizzie said, a fake smile on her face.

Jaylee dropped onto my lap, grabbed my face, and kissed me. "That was . . ." Another kiss. "Amazing."

"Can we go now?" Lizzie asked. "It's past my bedtime."

"Yes, I'm so tired," Antônia said.

"Let's do it." Zach jumped to his feet and helped Lizzie stand.

Jaylee leapt off me and scrambled after my sister. "Lizzie! I have to tell you about this security guy up by the fence. He was so nice! The crowd kept pushing me against the fence. I couldn't breathe, and I was too small to protect myself. Then this hot security guy grabbed me and moved me to the other side with him!"

I got up and followed. Logan fell in beside me. "They had twelve security guards up front," he said. "Do you think they were here when the pandemic broke out? Or do you think this is a new crew?"

"Don't know," I said. "Maybe Tracy just recruited the biggest people who signed his contract?"

We left the compound and walked along the roadside, past the long line of parallel-parked vehicles, heading for Zach's van. Jaylee, Antônia, and Krista finished each other's sentences as they filled in Lizzie on all that went on in the mob, which were their favorite songs played, and their opinions of Loca and Liberté's outfits. Logan was doing his version of the same to me and Zach, though he was talking about the sound system and the scaffolding of the stage.

"Oh. My. Gosh!" Jaylee broke away from the girls and ran ahead. "You guys!"

A few steps later, I caught on. Jaylee was jumping up and down next to a red Land Rover Evoque. When I reached her, she threw both hands around my neck. "Riggs is here!"

I hugged her, enjoying the warmth of my sweatshirt. "We don't know for sure that's his rig," I said. "Someone might have the same car."

Jaylee abandoned me and tapped on the windshield where a pewter skull hung from the rearview mirror inside.

"Arizona plates too," Antônia said.

Well, nuts. Three days ago, Rigley Orcutt had driven us back to Phoenix after a pitiful job of being our chaperone on the survival trip that had saved us from the HydroFlu. I didn't want him to die or anything, but he was not my favorite person. Plus, Jaylee had always had a huge crush on him. Our day-old relationship wasn't ready for that kind of competition.

Jaylee squealed. "Riggs is alive! And here!"

"Unless someone stole his car," I said.

"*Eli!*" Jaylee wacked me. "Why would you say such a horrible thing?"

Because I was a horrible person, apparently. I just looked at her, unable to form any words to dig myself out of the pit I'd just created.

"Yay for Riggs," Zach said, waving two invisible flags. "I'm going to bed." He and Lizzie kept walking, so I did too.

"You guys are just going to leave?" Jaylee called after us. "We have to wait for him!"

"It's late," Lizzie said. "The concert ended forty minutes ago."

I turned around but kept walking backwards. "If he's here, we'll run into him eventually." Look at me. I'd picked two battles in the same evening. Wish I could ask Mom if I was pushing my luck.

Jaylee climbed up onto the hood of the Evoque. "We're going to wait," she said, extending a hand down to Antônia. "We'll catch up with you guys at the condo."

Her words made my chest tight. I glanced at Lizzie, trying to look like I didn't care. "We shouldn't just leave them, should we? It's almost midnight, and they don't have a vehicle."

"Stay with them if you're worried," my sister said, "but we can't really outvote them anymore."

"The Montgomery Shuttle is departing," Zach said. "Board now or hoof it."

It was hard for me to walk away like I didn't care, because I really didn't want Jaylee to see Riggs tonight, but I wasn't going to sit on Riggs's car and wait for him, either. So, I waved at my girlfriend and left.

As Zach drove us back, I thought about this place and wasn't sure I wanted to stay. "It felt weird to watch people dance around and cheer tonight like everything is resolved," I said.

"I thought it was kind of nice," Lizzie said. "People needed something positive."

"I get that people have been devastated and could use cheering up," I said, "but something about that concert just felt off."

"What?" Zach asked.

I couldn't put my finger on it. "I don't know." Maybe it was all in my head.

When we reached the condos, I hopped up and sat on a half wall of stone that bordered the sidewalk leading to the front office.

"You going to wait out here?" Zach asked.

"How will they get back without a vehicle?"

"They made their choice, man. They'll be fine."

"I don't know."

Zach offered me the keys. "Drive back up there, if you want."

I took the keys but followed Zach inside. "It's probably fine," I whispered, not wanting to wake my dad and Reinhold.

"Do what you got to do, E." Zach climbed the stairs to the bedrooms.

I didn't go up. I sat in the dark for a while on one of the kitchen barstools, then decided to drive back over and look for the girls. When I reached the Evoque, it was still there, but the girls weren't, which only made me worry more. I looked for them walking as I drove back, took the long route through town, trying to travel every street. A few places were open, but I didn't bother getting out and going inside to check them all. I wasn't *that* much of a mom.

Yet when I got back to our condo, I went out onto the balcony, parked myself on one of the deck chairs, and settled in to wait.

●   ●   ●

I was dreaming about my dog, Sammy, when Jaylee's giggle

pulled me back to consciousness. I slid to the edge of my seat and scanned the darkness until I saw the girls cutting across the parking lot from the sky bridge that led to the restaurants.

I checked my watch. It was 3:25. Anger and relief warred in my chest. I wanted to go hug her. I wanted to yell. I should have gone to bed, content that they were, in fact, still living. Instead, I climbed over the half wall and iron pipe rail of the balcony and lowered myself, instantly regretting it. Pain shot through my right hand, so I held on mostly with my left. While I was hanging there—my splintered fingers sticking up like a pair of rabbit ears—the memory of Brandon on the Chinle Wash Bridge came back. The look of horror on his face as he fell, arms pinwheeling for purchase.

This wasn't that far. I let go and fell, scraping against the rough wood siding. The distance to the asphalt had been a bit farther than it looked. My feet landed hard, and a sharpness near my belly button signaled that I might have gotten a sliver. I recovered quickly and started toward the girls, the bottoms of my feet still stinging.

Krista saw me first and elbowed Jaylee.

"Eli!" Jaylee jogged over and gave me a quick hug. "What are you doing up?"

"Waiting for you. I drove back up the hill to see if you needed a ride. The Evoque was still there. No sign of you guys. So I came back here."

I was suddenly well aware of how pathetic I sounded. How needy and controlling and desperately uncool.

"Oh, Eli . . ." Jaylee's bottom lip poked out, and she literally batted her eyes. "You didn't have to do that."

"I was . . ." Didn't really want to admit it, but at this point it kind of felt like I had no choice. "Worried."

"We were fine," she said. "Riggs never showed, so we walked back. We met some people and hung out with them at the Brown Jug Pub." She bobbed up and kissed me. Her breath smelled weird. Sour and smoky.

I didn't know Jaylee smoked.

"Don't they card at pubs?" I asked.

"Not here," Krista said, smiling. "I ordered a beer, and they gave it to me!"

"That's a good thing?" I asked. "You're thirteen."

"Safe Water has no legal age for drinking," Antônia added.

"What?" I said. "They made us sign a contract that said we'd adhere to the laws of America. They can't just go changing the laws."

"Teens who want to drink always find a way," Jaylee said. "The new law will keep them from drinking in secret and making more trouble."

"The legal drinking age of twenty-one has to do with maturity," I said, eyeing Krista. "Letting teens drink in public doesn't change the—"

"Yo! Lime-a-Rita!" someone yelled.

Jaylee spun around and waved to a pack of guys who looked to be in their early twenties. "Hey!" she yelled, then softer to Antônia, "That guy with the gauges, what did he drink?"

"Bourbon," Antônia said.

Jaylee waved again. "Hey, Bourbon!" She blew him a kiss and laughed.

I'd reached my limit. "Goodnight," I said. "Glad you're alive and everything." I walked toward the path that led to my condo.

"You're such an old man, Eli." Krista's voice.

I paused, turned back. "Yeah, well, I doubt Mr. Bourbon would have saved you from those creeps in Phoenix."

"Let's go talk to them," Antônia said. "Just to say goodnight and tell them where we live."

"Wait one minute?" Jaylee asked me, wincing. "We'll come right back."

I didn't wait. I walked the path that led to our front door, which was locked. Nuts. I thought about the balcony but knew I couldn't climb it. Maybe if I drove the van around, I could stand on its roof. Nope. I'd left Zach's keys inside on the counter.

Footsteps approached along the path. Jaylee. She grabbed my arm with both hands, hugged it. "Why didn't you wait?"

"I've been waiting for hours."

"You're mad."

"I thought something had happened to you. But you were just off drinking with some random guys."

Her eyes lit up. "You're jealous!"

I pulled away, but I had nowhere to go. Literally.

Jaylee stepped in front of me. Hands on my chest, she pressed me against the wall of the condo, whispered, "Don't be jealous," then kissed me.

It was a good kiss too. She was putting in a lot of effort, and while I tried to enjoy the moment, all I could think of was how she tasted like ash.

The kiss ended, and she leaned back, her eyes reflecting two glistening sparks from the distant street lights. "I want to hang out with those people. I want to make new friends. Come with me?"

Anger rose inside me, casting whorls of frustration along every vein. I appreciated that she was throwing me a rope here—trying to include me—but I didn't see any reason to make myself miserable just to be with her. If we were going to work, I was going to have to accept that we were different people. She clearly wasn't going to change herself for me, but I didn't want to change for her, either.

"No thanks," I said as nicely as possible. "But could I ask you a favor?"

She kissed me again. "You want more of this?" she asked, keeping her lips on mine as she spoke.

I chuckled. "Um, always, but . . . could you let me into your place? I'm locked out."

•  •  •

I would have slept on the couch, but someone was already there. Jaylee took me up to her room and woke my sister to tell her I was coming in.

"You can sleep in Antônia's and my bed until we get back," Jaylee said, "then we'll figure out something."

And she left me to share the room with my sister.

"What are you doing here?" Lizzie asked from the darkness.

"I got locked out of the guys' apartment. The girls wanted to go hang with some new friends, and I didn't."

"So you're just going to share the bed with Jaylee and Antônia?"

"No. I don't know."

My sister groaned. "This is weird, Eli. You and her."

"Why?"

"You really have to ask?"

"Well, you and Zach are weird for me," I said. "How long has that been going on?"

"Valentine's Day."

I rose up onto one elbow. "Six months? Are you kidding me right now?"

"We wanted to make sure it was going to work before we told anyone."

"Why?"

"Because we knew you'd all freak out and worry. No sense making everyone freak out and worry if there was nothing there."

"But there is. Something there?" I asked.

"Yeah." I could hear the smile in her voice. "I've liked Zach ever since he slept over when I was in seventh grade, and you guys let me watch the *Lord of the Rings* marathon with you."

I gagged. "I knew that was a mistake."

She laughed and the sound slowly faded into a whisper. "Are you really not okay about us?"

"I'll be fine," I said. "As long as you keep the PDA to a minimum. Nobody needs to see that."

"Oh, like you can talk. Jaylee is the queen of PDA."

"Yeah," I said, "it kind of embarrasses me."

My sister giggled. "That's obvious because you turn five shades of pink every time she kisses you."

"Do I really?"

"Yep."

Well, that was embarrassing. "Why is my misery fun for you? Haven't I been a good brother?"

"Because if I don't laugh about it, I'll cry."

"Oh, come on."

"It's creepy. She's playing with you."

"I disagree," I said. "You think seventh grade is a long time to like someone? I've liked Jaylee since fifth grade."

Lizzie sighed. "I know. Just . . . be careful, okay?"

"I will." Though the very thought of sleeping next to Jaylee in her bed kept my mind spinning for nearly another hour. I eventually fell asleep.

The next time I woke, I was still alone and desperately uncomfortable in my jeans. I had to pee but not badly enough to go out into the cold where I might not get back inside. I pressed the light on my watch to check the time—5:16 and they still weren't back.

A sign of things to come, no doubt. I liked to think Jaylee would get all this out of her system at some point. That the novelty of the freedom offered here would wear off, especially if what Jennie had said was true about everyone getting jobs.

I knew I was being naïve, though. Jaylee was Jaylee. Time and responsibility wouldn't change that the girl did what she wanted to do without apologizing. In a way, I was jealous of that. Why couldn't I do what I wanted to do? Or had I? I was currently lying in Jaylee's bed—something that would have gotten me grounded back home in the old world—so it seemed like maybe I could.

A girl's voice drifted from downstairs. Hope and shame rose in me. Had I misjudged Jaylee too soon? Maybe they had come back and were downstairs pulling an all-nighter and talking about girly things.

I slipped out of bed and approached the window overlooking the living room below. Too dark to see. The sun hadn't risen yet, and the lights inside the condo were off. Outside the living room windows, the parking lot sat illuminated in a golden glow from the streetlamps.

I heard the voice again. Kind of a yell. I shoved my feet into my shoes and crept downstairs.

"Hurry!" the voice said.

Prickles ran up my arms to my neck. I used the light of the microwave oven clock to see as I made my way through the kitchen as quickly as I could.

"Hello?" I said.

"Leave me alone."

I slowed, confused.

"Don't! Get away from me."

Okay . . . Left hand on the wall, I walked slowly until my feet found the stairs to the raised living room. I took them one by one. Once I'd reached the living room, the light from outside was enough to illuminate an open sofa bed, occupied. Someone thrashing in sleep.

"Please put it down?"

Hannah. I recognized her voice that time. She'd said something similar to Brandon on the bridge. She must be having a bad dream. About him. The thought broke something inside me. I'd been so shocked and angry about what she'd done that it made it easy to forget what she'd been through. Yeah, stabbing me had been way out of line, but a person probably wasn't at her best with a psychopath like that chasing her down.

The girl clearly needed help, and I was done putting myself first.

# 6

## HANNAH
## AUGUST 2

"*Hannah.*"

*Familiar footsteps creaked on the stairs. My pulse accelerated. Brandon was coming. If I didn't get away, he would hurt me. Again and again I sliced my thumbnail against the ropes binding my wrists. I'd been working on them for days now and had finally severed some of the fibers. Not enough, though. Never enough. Still, I had to try.*

*The footsteps stopped. The door swung open, and Brandon stepped into the basement.*

"*Hannah,*" *he taunted.*

"*Leave me alone!*"

*Brandon raised his arm, gun in hand.*

"*Don't!*" *I yelled.* "*Get away from me.*"

*Brandon aimed the gun at me.* "*If I can't have you, we'll die together.*"

"*Please put it down?*"

*"Hannah? It's Eli."*

*Eli?*

I was no longer bound, no longer sitting. I lay on a bed, looking up into Eli's face as he leaned over me. Beyond, a high ceiling, a stove pipe. My heart raced. "Lock the door!"

Eli nudged my shoulder. "Hannah, wake up."

"What?" Time seemed to shift.

"You were dreaming," he said.

A few blinks and I understood. I breathed deeply, willing my heart rate to slow.

"You okay?" he asked, sitting on the edge of the sofa bed.

I would be soon enough. "How did you get in? The door was locked, wasn't it?"

"Uh . . . yeah." He turned away, as if this admission embarrassed him.

I processed this. "I didn't hear you come in," I said, "but I'm kind of a heavy sleeper." Like he hadn't just witnessed that. "What time is it?"

He gazed out the window into the dark, the street lamps making him look pale. "Oh, about 5:20."

"In the morning?" Had he been here all night?

My insinuating tone made him blush all the way to his ears. I fought the urge to roll my eyes. Half the time Eli seemed twenty-eight years old, efficiently managing a regiment of soldiers. The rest of the time, he was thirteen, caught in the juxtaposition of raging hormones and timidity.

"Listen, Hannah . . ." he said. "I'm sorry."

*He* was sorry? I hadn't been expecting that. "For what?"

"How I've treated you the past couple days. It wasn't right."

Was this really happening? Or was I still dreaming? He was staring at me, though, brown eyes glinting from the light of the street lamps outside. What to say? "I'm really not a horrible person," I said. "Usually."

Eli smirked and lifted his gaze above my head, out the windows. "I know." His smile faded, but his gaze remained elsewhere. "He was though, wasn't he? A horrible person?"

He was still bothered by Brandon's death—probably always

would be. It said something about who he was—how different he was from Brandon. By the time I managed to speak, I could barely see Eli through the tears that had filled my eyes. "He enjoyed hurting other people," I said. "Trapping them. Controlling them." As the words left my lips, memories flashed in my mind, different moments when I'd been the one hurt, trapped, and controlled. "I wasn't the only person he hurt. There were others. He couldn't control his anger."

Eli looked at me then, and I was surprised to see his eyes had clouded too. He swallowed, his Adam's apple looking sharp in the low light and from the strange angle of him sitting above me. "Forgive me?" he said finally.

"If you forgive me." I reached for his splinted fingers, gingerly took his right hand in mine. My stomach flipped at my bold action, but I ignored it, not afraid to touch Eli. Besides, I needed the moment to work. I wanted peace between us.

He squeezed my hand with his thumb and pinky. "Deal."

He was so cute, looking at me like that, a little crooked smirk on his face, which drew a smile from me in return. Then he ran his other hand over his head, which reminded me of Seth, who often did the same thing.

"Thanks," I said, releasing his hand. "How are your fingers?"

He studied them. "Uh . . . kind of the same. They still bend funny."

"It might take ten to twelve weeks to heal completely," I said.

"Oh. Wow."

"Could be as short as eight if you wear your splint."

"I'll wear it every day. Well . . ." He stood. "Guess I'd better take off."

"Okay, thanks for pulling me from my nightmares."

"Yeah. Sure." He walked away, descended the steps to the kitchen, then turned back at the door and raised his splinted hand. "Bye."

"Bye, Eli."

Then he was gone.

I yanked the pillow out from under my head and dropped it on my face. *Thanks for pulling me from my nightmares?* Gosh. Such witty banter.

But yay! Eli had forgiven me. I threw the pillow aside and grinned into the darkness, awed at how something so small could feel so big inside me. The relief alone had taken off five pounds of stress.

I lay there for a while, thinking about Eli and this place. I had the urge to go take a shower to start my day, but that wasn't a possibility at present. Even the porta-potties in the parking lot seemed a hundred miles away. The memory of waking up tied to the chair in that basement brought a flash of panic over me. That was over. I was as safe as I could be now. For a post-pandemic world, this place seemed almost normal.

I got dressed and folded up my bed. The sound of the creaking steps made my hands sweaty. Someone was coming down. It wasn't Brandon. It couldn't be him ever again.

Kimama emerged from the landing, shoes on, backpack over her shoulder.

"Are you going out?" I whispered.

"Dad wants to explore the mountain," she said.

Right. I'd take the chance while I had it. Who knew when the others might get up. "I need to use the bathroom," I said. "I'll walk out with you."

Kimama decided to visit the porta-potty too, for which I was grateful. I'd only met the girl two days ago, but at eleven, she was already more mature than Krista.

Dawn had broken, but it was still creepy in the parking lot. Kimama let me go first, then I waited for her. On our way back to the guys' condo, I spotted a dog, brown with floppy ears. He trotted across the parking lot, stopping to sniff here and there.

"Look," I said, pointing.

"Wow," Kimama said.

His presence kind of stunned me. We just stood there, unable to look away until he had moved out of my line of sight.

"The average dog is nicer than the average person," Kimama said.

I didn't doubt that was true. "Wonder how he survived?"

"His owner gave him safe water?"

That made sense. "Sometimes it seems like this Safe Water Mountain Refuge is somehow separate from the rest of the world, the way people joke that Disneyland is protected by the happiness bubble. This place is protected too."

"I've never been to Disneyland," Kimama said.

"I'm sorry," I said. "It was a fun place."

The door to the boys' apartment was open. Cree poked his head out. His gaze landed on me, and he slipped outside.

"Hannah! *Áltsé!*" The boy ran toward me, his bare feet slapping the asphalt, his long hair fluttering behind him. When Eli had first found him playing in the back of his truck with Shyla, he'd assumed Cree was a girl. He'd assumed wrong.

I crouched down to Cree's eye level. "Good morning," I said.

"Look." He bared his teeth and used his fingers to wiggle his left incisor.

I gasped. "You have a loose tooth?"

He pointed to the door. "They're fighting," he said.

I stood, lifting Cree in my arms and settling him on one hip. "Who?"

"Eli and *Azhé'é*," Cree said, continuing to wiggle his tooth. "*Azhé'é* is mad."

Curious, I pushed inside the boys' condo with Kimama.

"I don't want to bother with that," Andy said. "It'll be faster this way."

"Well, I just don't want to spend the whole day gone," Eli said.

"Why?"

Kimama and I stepped into the kitchen and spotted Andy and Eli at the far end of the counter, facing one another. The tension between them reached all the way to where we stood.

"Because," Eli said. "I want some time to see what it's like here."

"Why?"

"Stop asking me that!"

"Hey, hey, hey." Seth appeared, descending the last few steps from the second floor. He positioned himself between Eli and Andy, easily the shortest of the three. "What's the problem?"

"Eli doesn't want to come with," Andy said.

"Seth, Seth." Cree wiggled in my arms, suddenly intent on getting down. His little voice drew the attention of the others, who all looked at us.

"Morning, Miss Hannah, Miss Kimama," Seth said, flashing us a wide smile.

I lowered Cree to the floor. The boy ran to Seth and collided against his legs.

Seth mussed Cree's hair, but his eyes were on Andy. "And?"

"And I could use his help," Andy said. "He's got a way of looking at things."

"I was going to go for a run," Eli told his dad.

"You? Run?" Seth said, looking amused by the idea.

"I want to get some exercise," Eli said.

"We're going to hike up a mountain," Andy said.

"But you might be gone for days," Eli said.

"Fine." Andy pushed between Eli and his dad. "Enjoy your vacation while Kimama and I figure out how we can actually survive this mess." Andy stormed past Kimama and out the front door. "Let's go, girl," he called back.

"Sorry," Kimama said. "He's been strange lately. I think he's just missing my mom."

"Of course he is," Seth said. "We're all missing someone. Here, take one of the walkie talkies with you so you can call us if you need anything."

Kimama took the radio and left.

"Going on your run?" Seth said to Eli.

"After I give Reinhold a little time to drive away."

One side of Seth's mouth quirked up in an almost smile. "Looks like someone would like breakfast." He lifted Cree to one of the stools at the counter.

"*Tį'! Ła' nisin*," Cree said. "I'm very hungry."

"I know it, buddy. Me too." Seth entered the kitchen and opened the fridge. He removed a zippered lunch bag and opened it. "Looks like you still have some sandwich from yesterday." He offered it to Cree, who snatched it up and eagerly bit into the half-eaten peanut butter and jelly. "That ought to tide him over." Seth glanced at me. "His leftover pizza is in here too. You want some? Didn't you share with him?"

"My half is in our fridge," I said. "I'm not really hungry."

"What about you?" Seth asked Eli.

"I'll eat after my run."

"Suit yourself." Seth removed a Styrofoam container from the fridge. "Looks like I'm having leftover pastrami on rye for breakfast." He claimed the stool beside Cree and started to eat. "What this place is missing is a grocery store."

"I can stop and get something on my way back," Eli said, heading toward the door.

"Hold up," Seth said. "What was that with you and Andy?"

Eli glanced at me, like he didn't want to say in front of an audience. "Tell you later. I want to run while it's cool."

Seth waved his hand in a dismissal. Eli grabbed his empty water jug and left, giving me a half-smile as he passed by.

Seth bit into his sandwich and chewed. He and Cree looked fairly adorable sitting side by side, both intent on eating their sandwiches. My time for intruding was over. I stepped toward the door, searching for the right words to politely depart.

"So, San Francisco, huh?" Seth said.

Oh. Guess I'd stick around a bit longer. "You ever been?"

"Nope. Didn't travel much in my life."

"Native Arizonan?"

"Grew up in Montana, actually."

"That explains Eli's affinity for guns."

Seth laughed. "My dad took me hunting often, so I did the same with Eli. Lizzie never cared for it."

"How did you end up in Arizona?"

"Mom was from Tempe. My parents were older. Dad retired the summer after my eighth-grade year, and they moved."

"That must have been hard. To leave home at that age."

His eyebrows shifted, as if he were thinking it over. "You know, it was, and it wasn't. I grew up in Shelby—town of about 3000. Not much in Shelby. I had friends, sure, but sometimes in a small town, you get pigeonholed, and it sticks forever."

Story of my life. "How did the town of Shelby see Seth McShane?" I asked.

He smirked, the laughter in his eyes clear. "I was the bad boy."

This surprised me. "You?"

"Yeah, I did some dumb stuff. What thirteen-year-old boy hasn't? And I wasn't the greatest student. Dyslexic, I found out in sixth grade. So for me, leaving town for the big city was the adventure of a lifetime."

"More," Cree said, reaching for the sandwich in Seth's hands.

"What about me?" Seth said, passing the boy what was left of his sandwich. "What am I supposed to eat?"

Cree didn't pause, just lifted Seth's half-eaten sandwich to his mouth and took a bite. His eyes went wide as he chewed, and he turned to look up at Seth. "Is good."

"I know it." Seth shot me a look. "Can you believe this kid?"

Cree was adorable, but before I could think of a response, someone knocked at the door. Since I was still standing three steps away, I answered it.

Two policemen stood outside. One looked Middle Eastern, the other white. Something about the white guy's posture and bored scowl reminded me of Brandon. I closed the door a little, peering out the crack.

"Hannah Cheng?" the white guy said, as if he expected people to jump at his command.

Adrenaline shot to my head. "She lives next door," I said.

"They said to check over here," said the white guy.

I felt a hand on my back, and suddenly Seth was beside me, steering me behind the door.

"What do you fellows need?" he asked.

"Hannah. Cheng." The white cop had grown annoyed.

None of them were Brandon, I reminded myself. I was safe.

"Did she break some sort of law she wasn't aware of?" Seth asked.

"No, sir." This voice was deeper. It must have come from the other cop. "Her assistance is requested at the hospital. We have a great need for anyone with medical training."

Medical training. Relief chased away my fear, and I suddenly felt embarrassed. Why did I always assume someone wanted to hurt me?

"All right," Seth said. "I'll see if I can find her." He shut the door on the policemen, and his eyes met mine. "What do you want to do?"

His kind concern was so foreign I barely knew how to acknowledge it. "I'll go," I said. "I'm happy to help where I can."

He pressed his lips into a line. "I know they're dressed as cops, but I don't feel right sending you off with two strangers. Wait here. I'll be right back." He jogged toward the stairs and disappeared, his steps continuing to creak through the condo. I heard his voice, muffled, and then he was back, socks and shoes in hand. He sat on the bottom step and pulled them on. "I'm coming with. To make sure it's all legit."

"You don't have to do that," I said, but inside, I felt immensely grateful.

A bleary-eyed Zach appeared on the stairs behind Seth, who jumped to his feet and headed toward me.

"Find Lizzie if you need help," Seth told Zach.

"I got it," Zach said, sitting beside Cree. "We'll be fine."

I opened the door, wanting to exude some sort of independence. The officers had wandered into the parking lot, standing in front of a police SUV. The sound of the front door closing behind us pulled their attention our way.

"Hannah Cheng?" the white guy said.

"Yes," I said. "And you are?"

"Officer Harvey. This is Officer Vrahnos."

"This is Seth McShane," I said. "He's coming along."

Officer Harvey turned a bored expression on Seth, then headed to the passenger's seat. "Get in the back," he said.

As I opened the back door of the SUV on the driver's side, I noticed the logo on the driver's door. A sticker that said "Safe Water Mountain Refuge Enforcers" had been affixed over whatever words had previously adorned the side.

Seth was already seated in the back. "I see you've repurposed the Colorado State Patrol vehicles and uniforms. You two used to work for the CSP?"

"I'm former LAPD," said Officer Harvey. "Vrahnos was a

Marine. We both worked for the Champions and were up here with them for the summer when the HydroFlu hit."

Officer Vrahnos started the vehicle and steered toward the exit. He turned right out of the Snowcrest parking lot onto Marcellina Lane. I wished I'd brought something to write directions on so I could find my way back to the condo later.

"Mr. Tracy plan to conscript everyone to some kind of work?" Seth asked.

"We don't know Mr. Tracy's plans," Officer Harvey said. "Right now, the need is medical, which is why the hospital administrator asked us to bring in Miss Cheng."

"Is there a situation?" I asked.

Officer Vrahnos glanced at me in the rearview mirror. "Not that we're aware of. You'd be surprised how many people flock to the doctor's office for the littlest thing."

No, I wouldn't. I'd spent enough time in hospitals and clinics to know that much. "It makes sense considering all we've been through," I said.

"I didn't realize there was a hospital here," Seth said.

"Yep," Officer Harvey said. "Pretty good one, too."

Officer Vrahnos stopped the vehicle at a T, glanced both ways, then took a sharp right onto Gothic, which took us back toward the mountain. We passed under the pedestrian sky bridge that connected the Snowcrest Condos to the shopping area and eventually turned left onto Snowmass Road. Another quick left brought us into a combination driveway and parking lot shared between two buildings, each about the size of the Snowcrest's six-condo units.

Both buildings were beige with dark brown roof tiles and railings on the upper floor balconies. They sat end to end at the base of the mountain's ski slope. On the end wall of the eastern building hung a blue medical sign with a red cross. Officer Vrahnos parked the vehicle in front of the building, and I noted a vinyl banner tied over a thick pine overhang that said "Safe Water Mountain Refuge Hospital."

"Well, this wasn't far," Seth said. "I can see the Snowcrest roofs from here."

"The roads sort of circle all the buildings," Officer Vrahnos said. "Pretty much everything ends at the foot of the mountain. She'll have no problem walking back and forth."

"Go on in and ask for Susan Vail," Officer Harvey said. "She's expecting you."

I opened the door and got out. Seth had already exited. The driver's window rolled down, and Officer Vrahnos looked out.

"You going in, or do we need to escort you?" he asked.

I scowled at him. "I'm going in."

Seth and I walked toward the building's entrance.

"I find it strange they'd come recruit you at 6:30 in the morning," he said.

"It is quite early," I said, "though doctors and nurses work strange hours."

Seth opened the door for me, and I stepped into a small reception area of an air-conditioned building. A woman wearing a headset sat behind a walled, chest-high desk. She had silky, golden brown hair cut into a bob that curled under her chin, and wore hot pink lipstick.

"How can I help you?" she asked.

"My name is Hannah Cheng. Some officers brought me over to help out."

"Oh, bless your heart, yes. We hoped you'd come. I'm Monica. I work the switchboard. Have a seat. I'll page Susan." Somewhere behind the desk wall came the sound of fingers on a keyboard. The next time the receptionist spoke, her voice came magnified over a PA system. "Nurse Vail to reception, please. Nurse Vail to reception. We have a new recruit."

Feeling suddenly nervous, I turned to seek out the seating area and noticed Seth had already claimed a spot on a long beige sofa. I sat beside him, perched on the edge.

"You going to be okay?" he asked.

"I think so. You're all staying here tonight, right?" I asked.

"Yep, and maybe longer." He sighed. "We'll see what Andy finds out there."

"Right." The mountain hiking investigation.

"Hannah Cheng?" A black woman in pink scrubs was

striding toward me, her wild, poufy curls bobbing with each step. "I'm Susan Vail. The head nurse here at Safe Water." She extended her hand.

I shook it, instantly at ease. I knew a no-nonsense nurse when I saw one, and Susan Vail was the real deal. "Hannah. It's nice to meet you."

Susan reached for Seth. "You her partner?"

His eyes widened. "No, Miss Vail. Just a friend, checking out the place. I'm Seth McShane. We're brand new here and still a little unsure of everything."

"I hear that," Susan said. "We've all been through the wringer." She turned her attention back to me. "We're hoping you'll be willing to work a twelve-hour shift." She glanced at her watch. "That'll put you off around seven."

"That's fine," I said.

"Can she get food here?" Seth asked. "She didn't have a chance to eat breakfast before the enforcers came calling."

"Sure! We'll get her something. We have meals delivered. We'll even get her set up with some scrubs. No need to worry, Mr. McShane. She'll just be here all day, saving lives."

Seth grinned. "I don't doubt that one bit. I'll see you later, Miss Hannah."

"Thanks for coming with me," I said, suddenly shy.

"Anytime, my dear." He nodded to Susan, "Nice to meet you, Miss Vail," and left.

Susan watched him go, then looked at me. "Mmm mmm. That is one beautiful man."

I could feel the smile light up my face. "He's nice too."

"Oh, I caught that." Susan hooked her arm in mine, linking us at the elbows. "Best sink your claws into him quick before someone else does. Someone like me!" She laughed loud and free, which made me laugh too. "I'm kidding, hon. He's all yours. Let me show you the place, and we'll see what you know."

I followed her behind the reception wall and into the clinic, toward the familiar sounds of coughs, beeping monitors, and the squeaking wheels of medical carts, toward a place I just might belong.

# 7

## ELI

I jogged toward the compound, carrying my change of clothes over one shoulder and my empty water jug in one hand. It was quiet out this early and chilly. At first, I missed my sweatshirt, which Jaylee still had, but it wasn't long before I warmed up. I enjoyed the cool mountain air in my lungs. The long run gave me too much time to think, though, and my thoughts dwelled on my mom.

Figuring out how to survive in a post-pandemic world was hard enough, but how was I supposed to live in a world without my mom? All the things she'd done for me and taught me—there wasn't going to be any more of that. Her laugh, and her backrubs, and her cooking! No *chilaquiles* and refried beans, no quesadillas *fritas*, no *tres leches*.

How did I even get to this place? And almost eighteen years old? It had all gone by so fast. When I was little, I couldn't wait to grow up, but now I just wanted to go back to when Mom was Mama, and I was her *mijo*, and my only job was to spend the entire day at her side.

By the time I reached the compound, I was heaving for breath and had a cramp in my side. According to my wristwatch, the run had taken me twenty-nine minutes. I had no idea if that was a decent time or if I should be embarrassed. I wasn't in the greatest of shape, and the second half of the route had been uphill. Plus I was pretty choked up from thinking about my mom.

I trudged onto the Champions' grassy lawn to the water spouts and filled my jug. It felt good to be able to guzzle as much water as I wanted without having to worry about rationing it. I drank a quarter of the gallon right then.

Working out felt good, too. I never wanted to find myself going up against someone like Brandon again and not be strong enough to protect myself. Cardio wasn't going to be enough. I probably needed to start lifting weights. Weakness wasn't an option in this new world.

I heaved in a deep breath all the way to my navel, filling my lungs with fresh air, then released it slowly. I fell onto the grass, took a few more belly breaths, then did forty-three sit-ups and twenty-six push-ups, which was awkward with my splinted fingers. Again, no idea if those numbers were good or not.

I rolled onto my back and stared up at the sky, bright blue and filled with puffy white clouds. I lay there in the grass, pondering the madness of life. How everything had just ended and would never be the same. That Riggs had somehow survived. Riggs had lived, and Mom hadn't. I berated myself for that unkind thought—Mom wouldn't have liked it—and that made me cry. It felt safe to cry here where no one could see me, and I kind of just let myself go.

At some point, I started watching the clouds drift slowly across the sky. I wondered when it might rain, and when it finally did, if the water would be safe.

I eventually got up and joined the shower queue. It wasn't as long as yesterday. It was only 7:12 a.m. Late-night parties kept the lines short in the mornings.

I wondered where Jaylee and the girls had been all this time. It wouldn't have surprised me to learn that the restaurants and bars were open 24/7. Or maybe they'd gone to Mr. Bourbon's condo. I wanted to be cool with it. To give Jaylee the space she needed to be herself. I just wasn't sure I'd like it if this became regular thing.

I showered, re-filled my water jug, then headed back, walking slowly. My body was sluggish—I probably shouldn't have started a new exercise program coming off so little sleep. Still, I was pleased with my plans. It seemed like a decent do-it-yourself workout, and the walk back should keep my legs from cramping. I'd still need to find a way to lift weights, though.

I took my time in the downtown area, looking for breakfast options. I found a place that made breakfast burritos and ordered enough for everyone—used over half my daily allowance. I figured someone would share with me if I ran out. If not, I'd just eat breakfast burritos all day.

I ate one of the chorizo burritos on the walk back. I was halfway across the pedestrian bridge when I spotted a brown lab trotting along the road below.

The hairs danced on the back of my neck as I watched the familiar way it stopped to sniff every few yards. It couldn't be. Could it?

I was tempted to run back into town and see if I could follow it, but it had already passed under the bridge. I turned to the other side and watched it continue down the road, wondering. What were the odds that this dog was the same one that had distracted me in the Target parking lot so Beardo and his wife could steal my truck? Could they have come here too?

I really hoped not.

The dog padded along the road until he was out of sight, so I continued to the apartment. It was after eight when I got back. People were up, and someone was angry. I could hear the shouting before I even opened the door. I walked inside, surprised to see Reinhold and Kimama up in the living room with my dad, Zach, Lizzie, Logan, and Cree. I joined them and dropped my bags of burritos on the coffee table.

"I brought breakfast," I said.

"Yes!" Zach lunged for the paper sack at the same time as Logan.

"You guys decide to stick around?" I asked Reinhold.

"No," he said, arms folded across his broad chest. "No one is allowed to leave."

"What?" I said. "They can't keep us here."

"Their guns said they can," Kimama said, accepting the paper sack Logan passed her.

"Start over," I said, "from the beginning."

"We were headed out of town," Reinhold said. "Guards stopped us at a closed gate that stretched across the entire road."

"On both sides?" I asked. "They're not letting people in either?"

"The roads are one way now," Kimama said. "They changed them."

"And the road out is closed," Reinhold said. "Guards said the Champions couldn't, in good conscience, let anyone leave for fear they'd contract the HydroFlu."

"Why do they get to decide that for us?" I asked.

"Enforcer had no answer. Just kept repeating for me to turn around and head back to my residence or he'd be forced to arrest me. And get this: The fence don't just run across the road, either. They're enclosing this whole town."

My mouth was gaping like a fish out of water. "But why should they care what we do? Fewer people here means more resources for everyone else."

"Which means they care more about something else," Dad said. "Enforcers came for Hannah this morning—wanted her to work at the hospital."

"The cops took her?" I asked, even more shocked.

"Twelve-hour shift, the nurse said." Dad raised his eyebrows.

"This is just the beginning," Reinhold said. "Soon they'll find *jobs* for all of us."

"Jobs that don't pay," I said. "We'll have to do them in exchange for the housing, food, and water they're providing free now."

"Civil conscription," Logan said. "Poor Hannah. We should rescue her."

"I don't think she's asking to be rescued, Logan," Dad said.

Freedom was important to me, and I didn't like being forced into a way of life I hadn't agreed to. I should get to choose. To vote. To have a say.

I suddenly had the urge to drive the Silver Bullet over to the gate and see for myself. "What about climbing over the mountain?" I asked. "We might not be able to drive it, but if we can hike Mt. Crested Butte, we can make our way north on Highway 317 or even follow the East River south until it meets up with Highway 135, then follow it back to Gunnison."

"Sounds good to me," Reinhold said.

"It's a fine idea, Eli," Dad said. "But Cree and Shyla and Davis would struggle. We'd have to haul our own food and water for who knows how long. And don't forget the girls want to stay."

Jaylee. No way she would ever leave, especially not to hike over a mountain in hopes of escaping to live forever at Reinhold's house. She'd think we were nuts for even wanting to.

"Was Hannah upset about being forced to work?" I asked.

"No, just surprised," Dad said. "She strikes me as someone who wants to help where she can."

Yeah, she was that.

"How about this?" Reinhold said. "We hike up the mountain and see if we can get through. If this place is already fenced in, what we're talking about might not even be an option."

We agreed that was the best place to start. Lizzie volunteered to stay with the kids, which made Zach offer to help. When Kimama also offered to stay, Dad jumped on it.

"Let Kimama have a turn," Dad said. "You two come with."

Translation: Dad didn't want Lizzie and Zach here alone. I found this hysterical and failed to hide my grin.

"Laugh it up, chuckles," Zach said, throwing my own words

back at me. Didn't matter. I only laughed harder.

Everyone ate a breakfast burrito, and Lizzie checked next door to tell the girls where we were going and wake Shyla.

"They're not home," she said when she returned only with Shy. "I'm not sure they ever came home."

Of course they hadn't.

"Never came home?" Dad said. "Where would they be?"

"They stayed out late," I said. "Met some people they wanted to hang out with."

Dad's eyes met mine. "What kind of people?"

I shrugged. I wasn't about to nark on anyone, least of all my girlfriend.

We set off toward the downtown area. Reinhold and Dad led the way. Logan walked beside me, the two of us behind Zach and Lizzie, who were holding hands. This annoyed me. My best friend would rather hang out with my sister than me, and my girlfriend would rather party with strangers. Welcome to my life.

"Where were you this morning, Eli?" Logan asked.

"Went for a run," I said. "Ended up down at the showers, so I cleaned up and walked back. Got breakfast for everyone on the way."

"I didn't know you were a runner," he said.

"I'm not. Just felt like it today." I didn't share my workout plans with Logan for fear he'd join me. I rather liked having that time to myself.

We began our hike at the bottom of the main ski lift near the Grand Lodge. A short trek up the grassy slope and across the mountain bike trail led us to a dusty service road. We followed it for a while and took a shortcut up a few steep slopes, which about killed my legs that were sore from my morning run. Thankfully, Dad decided to keep to the road that ran along the south side of the mountain. Purple wildflowers covered the hills. It crossed my mind to pick some for Jaylee, but she'd probably think it was dumb.

I caught my dad eyeballing Zach and Lizzie, who had stopped so Zach could thread purple flowers in Lizzie's hair. I guessed Dad would rather have them together where he could see them than together where he couldn't. I wondered if he'd given them his talk on being adults in this new world and making their own choices.

Somehow I doubted it.

The road switched back to the north, but Dad continued on a narrow trail to the south that forced us to walk single file, putting Lizzie ahead of me—Zach before her—and Logan behind me. They'd been talking about last night's concert and continued while we walked.

"It didn't sound like music to me," Zach said. "Just noise."

"People like that," Lizzie said. "EDM is fun to dance to."

"Did you know there are different types of EDM music?" Logan asked.

"That's redundant," Lizzie said. "You wouldn't say electronic dance music music."

"Right. I know. But there's hardstyle, jumpstyle, breakbeat, rave, electrohop . . ."

"Like you know any of those dances, Logan," Zach said.

". . . electronica, trance, club, drum and bass, ambient, speedcore . . ."

"Techno is the grandfather of EDM," Lizzie said. "It originated in the 80s as any kind of music made with electronic technology."

Shockingly, that comment silenced Logan. We were high enough now to get a good look at the town below. It would be another half mile at least before we were above the Champions' compound.

We reached the creek long before then. It looked to be coming down out of the mountain on the diagonal, from north to south.

"Why don't we build our own camp up here?" Reinhold asked.

"They'd know we were here," I said.

"Let's see what the land looks like a bit farther in," Dad said, heading upstream.

We wove our way around bushes, purple flowers, and trees. The sky was clear, and the sun was making me warm. We were approaching a cliff, and I could hear the rushing of a waterfall. The trees grew taller and thicker here, so we slowed and fought our way through.

We exited in a small clearing on the shore of a plunge pool. The falls weren't overly high, but the water was coming down hard and fast. My first thoughts were how much fun it would be to dive in.

But we were not alone. Two dozen men were gathered on the upper ledge, sitting on the ground, eating. Upon closer inspection, they appeared to be construction workers. A bulldozer sat off to the right, a heap of freshly dozed soil and stacks of aluminum fencing beside it.

One of the men saw us and alerted the others. The next thing we knew, one of them had pulled a handgun, and everyone was yelling.

"We don't want any trouble!" Dad said. "We're just hiking."

"The mountain is private property." This from the guy with the gun.

"No one owns an entire mountain," Reinhold said.

"My gun says differently, old man."

"Actually, I think some people from Vermont own the Mt. Crested Butte resort," Logan said.

"Well, the Champions own it now," the gun guy said.

"Did they buy it?" Logan asked. "Because I—"

"Shut up, Logan," Zach said.

"Let's go," Dad said, turning around.

"About face, people," Reinhold said. "We're leaving."

"Spread the word to any other hikers that this mountain is off limits," someone yelled after us.

We didn't answer. Not even Logan, thankfully.

"It ain't right," Reinhold said as we picked our way back through the trees. "They got no business keeping people away from that crick."

"Who'd have thought you could steal a mountain," Logan said.

"I guess they're fencing the mountain too," I said.

"There was more than fencing there," Dad said. "Looked

like they might be going to build a dam. That would give them complete control of the river water."

Reinhold muttered some kind of Ute curse under his breath. "You're right. That's exactly what they were doing."

A chill flashed over me. That wasn't fair. "Why should they get to control the whole creek?"

"They've got the upper hand," Dad said. "And because of their wealth and fame, they came out of the pandemic with a lot more resources than the rest of us. Plus, they were here first, so they had a head start staking their claim."

"It's still not fair," I said.

"Life has never been fair, son," Dad said. "It's even less so now. We're going to have to find a way to make the best of this."

"Not me," Reinhold said. "I'm not going to let a couple of hippie rock stars dictate my life."

"What are you going to do?" I asked.

"Those falls ain't the start of the crick." Reinhold gazed up to the mountain peak. "I'd like to hike the other side of this rock and see just how much of that crick they're not using."

Zach's eye twitched. "That's a long ways on foot," he said.

"Turns out I've got a lot of free time just now," Reinhold said.

"The summit is only about 12,000 feet," Logan said. "That's only eleven miles or so."

"I want out before they get the perimeter fence done," Reinhold added.

"Maybe we should all go," Dad said. "If we wait a few days and gather enough food, the kids could make it."

"I don't want to risk the set-up here if we can't get through," Reinhold said. "Who knows what might happen if you don't claim your vouchers. No, Kimama and I will hike up there tomorrow before dawn. Make sure none of them enforcers see us. We'll take one of the walkies and radio back what we find."

That was all that was said until we reached the bottom. Even though it was early for lunch, we stopped by the Woodstone Grill, ordered a bunch of sandwiches, and took them back to the apartment. Lizzie ran to her place to see if the girls were back.

I wasn't holding my breath.

Ten minutes later, though, my sister returned with Jaylee, Antônia, and Krista in tow.

"Eli!" Jaylee threw her arms around my waist and squeezed. She smelled like dead flowers and stale smoke. She'd changed her clothes though, so I guessed she'd decided this was a new day. No sign of my sweatshirt. "You'll never guess who we ran into last night."

"Riggs?" That *was* who she'd been looking for, after all.

"Nope, but we found him too." She beamed at me. "Cristobal and Josh are here! Isn't that amazing? We're going to meet them for lunch at the Avalanche Bar and Grill. Want to come?"

I whirled around to face Zach. "Did you hear that?" Cristobal and Josh had been on the camping trip with us when the comet had passed by. We hadn't heard from them since they'd left for Phoenix.

"They're okay?" Zach asked.

"Perfectly," Jaylee said.

"Oh! Praise Jesus," Lizzie said. "That's such good news."

"Where did you find them?" Logan asked.

"Last night at the Keystone Apartments," Antônia said.

"Josh is *so* cute," Krista said.

"This is incredible," I said, then to Krista, "and Josh is way too old for you."

She scowled. "You're not the boss of me."

"What time are we meeting them?" Zach asked.

"Where are they staying?" Lizzie added.

"In the Keystone," Jaylee said. "It's at the foot of the mountain. Lunch is at noon. You coming?"

I looked to my dad. "We just got sandwiches . . ."

"Go," Dad said. "The sandwiches will keep until dinner."

"Thanks," I said, grateful for a piece of good news in a day that had started off pretty rocky.

## HANNAH

"This hospital used to be called the Gunnison Valley Health Mountain Clinic," Susan told me as she led me down a wide, but short and deserted, hallway. "It was tiny but mighty. Built to serve tourists skiing the mountain. Top three floors are condos."

"How funny," I said.

"You won't think it's funny once Dr. Bayles starts sweet-talking you into moving up there. He has this crazy idea all the medical staff should live in this building. Know what that means?" She quirked an eyebrow but didn't wait for a reply. "No days off. Ever. 'Cause if you live upstairs, and there's an emergency on your weekend . . . You gonna say no when they call?"

"Probably not."

"Mmm hmm. We're all up there right now—even Monica.

Hold out, if you can. I'm serious."

"Thanks for the warning," I said.

"Okay. While this facility is top notch, we don't have the staff to work it—yet. We've got three doctors, three nurses, and now one med student."

"That's it? For this whole town?"

"Yep, and that's okay for now. Some days we've had over thirty patients in a twelve-hour shift. Other days, no one comes in until after two in the afternoon. The work is a lot like you'd see in an urgent care facility. People just show up—very few have appointments. We see a lot of minor injuries and illnesses—a lot of HydroFlu scares still, though it's been three days since we've had a real case, so hopefully that'll taper off now that everyone understands how to keep themselves safe. We get a steady stream of respiratory infections, cold and flu, sore throats, ear infections, gastrointestinal, UTIs. We've seen a fair amount of heat stroke and personal injuries. Sprains, minor fractures, lacerations, burns, some physical abuse."

I flinched, but Susan continued, listing more ailments as if "physical abuse" was the same as a sore throat or a twisted ankle.

"There've been an overwhelming number of poison ivy cases from people hiking up in the mountains," she said. "That should end too, though, once they close off access to the trails."

That piqued my interest. "Why do that?"

"To keep out the rabble." She paused outside a set of double doors. "We've had a couple pretty horrific incidents where someone drove through and tore up the place. Two deaths last time. One man was shot and killed for refusing to unlock the door to the refrigerator at one of the local restaurants. Another was struck by one of the vehicles."

"That's awful. Why do people insist on hurting others?" The latter I said softly, to myself, but Susan didn't miss a beat.

"Selfish people do selfish things. I'm glad Admin is taking care of it, but that means everyone is going to have to stay put for a while, until our safety can be ensured." She sighed. "People don't like staying put. Know what I mean?"

"Yes, I do." A sense of gratefulness washed over me. It

meant a lot to suddenly have a purpose. Something to do. A way to contribute.

"Let's introduce you to the other two nurses." Susan pushed through the double doors and into an empty nurses' station. "The hallways run a perimeter." Susan gestured as she talked. "Exam rooms on the outer walls. Interior holds restrooms—currently off limits, of course—supplies, and our employee lounge." She headed down the right hallway. "This facility already had electronic charting, which is fabulous. I created a master list of everyone who registered a pre-existing medical condition. You'll be able to access it as well. I'll show you."

She led me into an empty exam room and approached a computer on a rolling cart. She entered a username and password, then turned the cart toward me.

"The charts list only what people disclosed. Click on a person's name, and you'll see all their info. You can also click on the condition, and it'll show you how many cases we've had." She clicked on "diabetes" and a list of names populated on the screen. "So, 106 people who registered claimed to be diabetic." She clicked back to the former screen, scrolled down, then clicked on pregnant. "Thirty-five pregnant women in town. And so it goes. When you log a patient, use their ID number. That keeps all the info in one place."

"So I'm going to work as a nurse?"

"Yes, I'll be training you as a nurse. But Dr. Bayles, he's our Chief Physician, he wants to train you as a doctor, since that was your interest. This'll be vastly different from what was previously normal training. We're going old school master-and-apprentice on this thing."

That should be sufficient. "What will my responsibilities be?"

"For starters, I'm going to get you trained—"

"Susan?" A petite, dark-haired woman entered the exam room and stopped when she saw me. "Oh, hello."

"Finally," Susan said. "I was beginning to think you'd all gone on vacation."

"What's a vacation?" the woman said, grinning.

"This is Asiya Hassan," Susan said, pronouncing the name

Ah-see-yah.

"She worked as an ER nurse. For how many years?"

"Seven," Asiya said.

"Wow," I said.

"Asiya, this is Hannah Cheng."

"The med student, hello," Asiya said. "You're very welcome here and needed too." She looked to Susan. "My hypertensive patient wants to leave, but her BP is still too high. She's demanding to see Dr. Bayles, but he said to have *you* talk to her."

Susan sighed. "Tell her I'm with someone but will be in to see her in about a half hour. And keep an eye on her. I don't want her sneaking out."

"Thank you. It was nice to meet you, Hannah." Asiya waved and left the room.

"She's nice," I said.

"She's amazing. Our entire staff is. Our other nurse is Linsey Morales. Worked in pediatrics. He's a gem."

"He?"

"Linsey's a man. A handsome man too," she added with a grin.

"What's your background?" I asked her.

"Worked sixteen years as an oncology nurse. Since I have the most experience, Dr. Bayles made me head nurse. Let's see if we can find Linsey before I leave you with Dr. Bayles."

I followed Susan out into the hallway, feeling nervous about meeting the doctor. Too often, men in positions of power intimidated me, and I really wanted to do well here. We passed by several more exam rooms, many of which were occupied.

"So, I'm going to train you on charting and tracking admits and discharges," Susan said. "While you're on duty, you'll need to know who's here, who we're expecting, who might be getting ready for discharge."

"Bed manager?"

"Exactly." She grinned at me. "You're a quick study. I like that. As a nurse, you'll check weight and height, take blood pressure, urine samples, blood draws, strep tests, that sort of thing. We do x-rays here too, so Dr. Bayles will teach you how and the basics of x-ray readings. You'll also be back-up response,

HUNGER

which means if we're shorthanded, you assist any way you can, even if it's holding open the door and fetching supplies."

We turned the corner. A male nurse was walking toward us, rolling an IV stand at his side. He wore navy blue scrubs that strained just enough to hint at a muscular physique beneath the thin cotton. He was about Seth's height and build, but his skin was two shades darker than Eli and Lizzie's. His left arm was inked in black, red, and green tattoos. I thought I recognized a rose and a skull, but I didn't want to stare.

"Yo," he said, slowing to meet us. "You the new recruit?"

"Yes, I'm Hannah," I said, apprehension creeping up my spine.

"Linsey Morales," he said, his surname heavily accented as it rolled off his tongue. "You're our savior, girl. We desperately need another set of hands around here."

His friendly manner set me at ease. "Susan said you used to work in pediatrics," I said.

"Yeah, but now we all work everything, know what I'm saying?"

"I think so."

"Angel from heaven," he said, continuing on. "I'll see you around. Got a patient waiting."

Susan and I set off again. "Isn't he great? His wife is one of our pregnant women. They've got two little girls, and Linsey is convinced Clara is carrying a boy."

"Do we have ultrasound equipment here?" I asked.

"Oh, yes, but they're waiting to find out."

"That's sweet."

"Sickeningly sweet, actually. Especially for those of us who are single. Pretty ring, by the way. That from your friend?"

"No," I said, splaying my fingers to admire my ring. "It was my grandmother's."

"It's stunning." Susan led me down the final leg of the clinic's perimeter, back toward the double doors through which we entered. "You got into med school, so you're likely used to juggling a lot of things at once. Nurses always have to be thinking one step ahead. So be a sponge. Soak up everything you see and

85

be helpful. If you don't know, ask someone who does."

"You said three doctors work here?" I asked.

"Yep. Dr. Jason Bayles is a cardiac surgeon, Dr. Vicky Carter is OB-GYN, and Dr. Albert Russell is family practice. We also have a psychologist, Dixie Wells, who specializes in marriage and family but is learning to serve a wider base. Everyone is being extremely flexible and generous with their abilities."

We left the clinic and wove our way to a section of offices—toward Dr. Bayles's office. My stomach fluttered, and I reminded myself that I was wanted here. There was no reason to be intimidated because the acting chief of medicine was male. Yet I still found myself comforted by Susan's mention of the female psych and OB-GYN.

Susan approached an office with its door open wide. She paused on the threshold and knocked on the frame. "Sorry to interrupt. I've got Hannah Cheng here to meet you," she said.

"Right. Excellent," a man said, then softer, "I'll see you later." Then loud again. "Come on in. Please."

Rather than enter, Susan stepped back and Monica the receptionist slipped out. "Excuse me," she said, a guilty smile on her face.

I moved aside so she could pass between us, then followed Susan into a spacious office. The back wall was solid windows that overlooked the mountain. A thirty-something Caucasian man in a white lab coat stood behind a cherry desk, hands on his hips. He had blond hair slicked back over his head and gray eyes. A short reddish beard shaded his chin and top lip—lips that were smeared with hot pink lipstick.

My stomach sank. Oh dear.

Besides the lipstick, Dr. Bayles was all business—shirt, tie, and slacks under his lab coat. A man in power. He circled the desk and reached out a hand, bringing with him the Old Spice smell of citrus and cloves that reminded me of the feel of Brandon's fingers on my throat. I willed myself to stay calm. I needed these people and couldn't afford to do anything embarrassing.

"Jason Bayles," he said, arm still outstretched.

We shook, and I found his hand cold and soft. Not one of Eli's callouses. I wanted my boss to like me, but I also kind of wanted to leave. I reminded myself that Dr. Bayles wasn't Brandon and managed to say, "It's nice to meet you, sir."

"Call me Jason. Everybody does. Have a seat."

I sat in the firm leather chair before his desk, knowing I could never call this man Jason. Too familiar, which in my experience always led to trouble.

"I'll see you later, Hannah," Susan said.

I turned and caught her wave. She was leaving me alone with him? "Okay. Thank you."

On the opposite side of the spacious desk, Dr. Bayles leaned back in his leather chair, crossed one shiny black shoe over his opposite knee, and tucked his hands behind his head, making himself look far too comfortable. "Tell me about yourself, Hannah."

I explained how I'd graduated early, volunteered with Doctors Without Borders, and completed my first year of med school. Telling my story calmed me some.

"What kind of doctor were you studying to be?" he asked.

"General practitioner. Wanted to work abroad. Save the world."

"Considering there are only three doctors left in the world—that we know of, anyway—you *will* get your wish. The good news? This facility was a Top 100 Critical-Access Hospital. I couldn't have built a better hospital for such a small population if I'd tried." His lips pressed into a thin line. "But I won't lie to you. You're at a disadvantage without having completed med school. I gave Mr. Tracy's medical scavenger team a list of textbooks. If the books can be found, they'll be an asset to our on-the-job doctor training program."

"That sounds amazing," I said.

He nodded, like he agreed. "You'll be learning from the three of us. Dr. Russell and Dr. Carter will teach you everything you need to know about general medicine and OB-GYN. I will teach you internal medicine and surgery—when the opportunity arises. It's important that the hospital staff be open to new areas of education—myself included. Never thought I'd be practicing general medicine on children, but when that's the need of the day, that's what I'm going to do."

"That's admirable," I said. "I've always seen myself as a lifelong learner."

"Glad to hear it. That kind of attitude will keep people alive in this new normal. We all need to be flexible. It's imperative that we get this hospital running smoothly."

It was easy to imagine the chaos that could happen in a very short time.

"Mr. Tracy tells me the vast majority of our population is blue-collar workers with few professional skills," Dr. Bayles said. "Don't get me wrong. We need all types to run a society, but when cold and flu season hits, our staff is going to be the ones to feel the pressure. What's your living situation at present? You have a partner? A spouse?"

I felt my face warm. "I'm living with friends," I said, thinking of Susan's warning, thinking of Monica.

Dr. Bayles steepled his fingers. "Fine. Should you ever find yourself seeking a move, this building has three floors of apartments above the hospital, if you can believe that. Perks of a ski resort town. Mr. Tracy gave me authority over housing placements in this building, so if you'd ever like to see any of the open units, I'll show them to you. Just ask." He paused, as if he was waiting for me to ask to see the apartments this very moment.

"Thanks," I finally said. "I'll let you know if my situation changes."

"Excellent." He lowered his foot and stood, set both palms on the desk, and leaned forward, looming over me. "You're one of us now, Hannah. This staff—we belong to each other. We're going to be close, I promise you." He smiled, flashing a very white smile that seemed simultaneously genuine and predatory. "Welcome to the family."

I smiled back, but one thing was very clear to me in that moment. I was going to have to be careful around Dr. Bayles.

# 9

ELI

According to Jaylee, the portable bathrooms at the Avalanche were disgusting, so the girls insisted on a visit to the porta-potties in our parking lot before we all went to lunch.

While we were waiting for them to return, Dad answered a knock on the door. Zach, Logan, and I were sitting in the living room with Reinhold.

"Who you looking for now?" Dad asked.

"Zachary Montgomery," a man said.

"Come on in." Dad strode toward the raised living room, hands on his hips and frowning.

Two enforcer cops trailed him. They were both male, wore slate blue shirts, tan slacks, and belts packed with gadgets and heat.

"Zach, officers Harvey and Vrahnos would like a word," Dad said.

I quickly spotted the surnames on each officer's uniform.

Zach popped to his feet, the backs of his legs still flush against the couch. "What'd I do?" he said.

"We're here to give you a ride to work," Officer Harvey said.

"That's funny," Zach said. "I don't remember applying for a job."

Officer Vrahnos grinned and looked away.

"Everyone needs to do their part," Harvey said. "You listed having emergency medical training on your application for residency. Turns out, that's our greatest need at present."

"I was a lifeguard," Zach said, forehead wrinkling. "I'm no doctor."

"You're being placed as an EMT," Vrahnos said. "They'll train you."

"That's awesome!" Logan jumped up and approached the cops. "You guys have an ambulance?"

"Of course," Harvey said.

Zach seemed to relax. "I could do that, I guess."

"Thrilled to hear it," Harvey said. "Let's go."

"Now?" Zach said.

"Yes, now," Harvey said.

"The sooner they can start your training, the better," Vrahnos said.

"What about the rest of us?" I said. "You going to come for all of us?"

"Eventually," Harvey said, shooting me a look that dared me to argue. "You'll know when you know."

Logan followed the officers toward the door. "My dad was a pharmacist," he said. "I was planning to go into the field . . ."

Zach looked at me, then to my dad. "I should just go, then?"

"Might as well," Dad said. "The hospital is three blocks away. Even if you're in another building, you won't be far. Take a sandwich or burrito for lunch."

"All right." Zach said.

While he put on his shoes, I grabbed the last two burritos and a sandwich from the fridge and set them on the counter so Zach could take his pick. Logan had cornered the officers by the door and was still telling stories about his job qualifications.

"For programming, I know Java and C++ and Unity," he said.

"I'll be in the car," Harvey said, letting himself out.

"If there is need for your skills, you'll be contacted," Vrahnos said.

"But I didn't list any of those things on the questionnaire," Logan said. "I didn't realize it would be important."

"You can update your answers on the website," Vrahnos said.

"I'll do that," Logan said, striding to where he'd plugged in his laptop to charge.

"Hey, do you guys have a dentist here?" Logan asked. "Because I'm supposed to get my braces off in two months."

"I haven't heard of a dental office opening up yet," Officer Vrahnos said, then he looked around Logan to Zach. "You ready?"

"I guess." Zach grabbed all the food I'd set out as he passed. "Say 'Hey' to the guys for me, and tell Lizzie where I went."

"Will do, man," I said. "You got this."

"Let's hope so." Zach pulled the door closed behind him, and then he was gone.

"They've got too much control," Reinhold said.

"Conscripting people is pretty intense," I said, yet I also understood the need for people to fill necessary roles if the town was going to function.

The front door banged open. "Dad!" Lizzie tore into the condo, eyes wild. "The cops have Zach!"

"We know," I said, my gaze shifting to Jaylee as she and the other girls filed inside.

Lizzie threw herself against Dad, and he caught her in a hug. "He's fine," Dad said. "They want to train him as an EMT. That's a good job. Something that'll use the skills he already has and give him more."

"Did they say when he'd be back?" Lizzie asked.

"No," Dad said, "but the nurse at the hospital told Hannah she'd work a twelve-hour shift, so I wouldn't expect him back for a while."

"Twelve hours?" Krista's mouth gaped.

"What about the rest of us?" Jaylee asked. "I can't be a nurse or an EMT. Blood makes me queasy."

"Which is why you're still here, Miss Jaylee," Dad said.

"Jaylee, you can use my computer to update your skills survey. I'm doing mine now."

"No, you're not," I said. "The guys are waiting."

"Oh, right," Logan said, slapping his laptop shut.

"Plus, Josh and Cris know more about this place than we do," Jaylee said. "They've been here longer."

"A whole day longer," Antônia said.

"A lot can happen in a day," Jaylee said.

No one had an argument for that, so we left the condo and went to meet our friends.

•　　•　　•

On the walk to lunch, I got the story of how Jaylee and the girls had gone to their new friend Marco's apartment in the Keystone last night where a party was underway. They'd found Josh and Riggs there. Turned out they were Marco's neighbors. The girls ended up watching a DVD at Josh's house and fell asleep. On the couch. That's all the information I got except that the girls were tired and planned to go to take naps after lunch.

Eight of us climbed into the booth at the Avalanche Bar and Grill. The place was dark, air-conditioned, and smelled deliciously greasy. I sat between Logan and Jaylee, across from Josh and Cristobal. Krista had somehow managed to sit on Josh's other side and was working overtime to get his attention.

Josh had always been popular with girls. His dimpled grin, "electric" blue eyes, and "great hair" were attributes I'd consistently heard girls admire over the years. He'd always had at least one girlfriend—he once dated three at the same time. Jaylee had been among his conquests, as well as Lizzie, though they had only gone to homecoming together. Lizzie wouldn't call Josh a former boyfriend. Josh, however, was counting, and Lizzie was definitely on his list.

Cristobal was practically Josh's opposite, though they both played soccer and had been friends since seventh grade when Cristobal and his family emigrated from Hermosillo. He'd never had a girlfriend, to my knowledge. He was five foot six—a fact he often lamented—quiet, and a total book nerd. He and Zach often swapped sci fi novels.

"I was placed in Admin," Cristobal said, after we'd told them about Zach's recent conscription. "*In* the Champions' house, as a translator."

"My boy's practically on the staff of this place," Josh said.

"You're so lucky," Jaylee said.

"Are there many Spanish speakers here?" Antônia asked.

"Just over twenty percent of the population," Cristobal said. "Not many of them fluently bilingual, but they put me to work right away. I basically do what Jennie does for anyone who speaks Spanish. Plus, I answer questions and translate during conscriptions too."

"He's the man," Josh said. "And I'm stuck as a flipping busboy at the flipping Avalanche. I've asked to be promoted to host, but nooo . . ."

I grinned. For as long as Josh and Cristobal had been friends, it had always been Cristobal following Josh, Cristobal struggling and Josh riding easy. I rather liked that their places had been switched.

"Can't Riggs help you?" Jaylee said, then to Lizzie, "Riggs works here as a bartender."

"Of course he does," I mumbled.

"Naw," Josh said. "Riggs and I both started three days ago. I'm just going to have to tough it out for a while. Did you know Riggs is friends with one of the Champions' dancers? She's totally hot."

"Miranda," Jaylee said. "I met her last night. She's super sweet."

I tried to process this but was too hungry to give it much effort. The waitress took our orders. I chose a buffalo bacon cheeseburger and could not *wait* to pack it away. Since that used the last of my vouchers, I asked Lizzie to order one for Zach, to go, in case he was hungry later.

"Why did you guys get jobs and not us?" Logan asked once the waitress had left.

"Because we were here first," Josh said.

"Last week had the highest registration," Cristobal said.

Josh leaned forward on his arms. "Which was why there was this huge need to put people to work so there would be places to eat and shop and whatever. Now that those jobs have been assigned, you guys lucked out."

"Except for Zach and Hannah," Lizzie said.

"Who's Hannah?" Cristobal asked.

"A girl Eli and I rescued from a psycho killer," Logan said.

"She hot?" Josh asked.

"Oh, yeah," Logan said. "I think she likes me too."

Josh flubbed his lips. "If she's hot, she doesn't like you, man."

"Hey," I said to Josh. "None of that."

"Well, Hannah and Zach are lucky," Josh said, ignoring me. "I'd love to be an EMT or work at the hospital. But I'm a flipping busboy, up to my elbows in trash and wet wipes."

"Why wet wipes?" Lizzie asked.

"No water. I have to clean everything with wipes. Until they run out. Then who knows?"

"They sent a team to scavenge for non-water-based cleaning supplies and disposable plates and forks, that kind of stuff," Cristobal said. "The task manager figures we have enough to last two years, though he thinks products like Clorox wipes might dry out before then."

"Are there salaries that accompany these jobs?" Lizzie asked.

"No pay," Josh said.

"What?" Jaylee said.

"Admin would like to get there," Cristobal said. "It'll take time, though. Right now they're just trying to get everyone housed and fed and make sure people are safe."

"A curfew might help with that," I said.

"Eli!" Jaylee nudged me with her elbow.

Josh laughed. "There's no way. These people are all about having a good time."

"Admin too?" I asked Cristobal.

"Pretty much," he said. "The majority of the Admin staff worked for the Champions before all this happened. And, while many celebrities would run this place totally differently, Loca and Liberté . . . fun is their *número uno*."

"Which is what their fans love about them," Josh said.

"Which is what *I* love about them," Jaylee said.

And what I found dangerous for people leading a community.

"This place . . ." Cristobal said. "Some came for the promise of safe water, like you. But a lot of people came because their favorite band invited them. I'm sure there are other places around the country where survivors holed up. There might even be other clean water sources. But this place was broadcasted on the news a few days before the networks went down. And people came."

"How did you hear about it?" Lizzie asked.

"The TV at my place. My parents, uh . . ." Josh bowed his head.

"We found them first," Cristobal said. "They'd been watching TV in bed. Mark's parents weren't home. Mine left a note saying they'd gone to St. Joe's. At that point, we figured Mark needed a doctor, so we went."

"That place was a nightmare," Josh said, staring at the salt and pepper shakers.

"My mom died there," Lizzie said. "I was with her."

"That's awful," Cristobal said to Lizzie, then looked to me. "I'm sorry, man."

"Did you find your parents?" Antônia asked.

Cristobal shook his head. "Walking around that place . . . No one was alive. I knew they were gone. So we took Mark home. He wanted to look harder for a note from his family, and we wanted to help him. We stayed there."

"Until he died." Josh growled. "It was all so stupid."

Krista rubbed Josh's back. It was a little creepy to watch her work, knowing she was only thirteen—knowing exactly what she was thinking. Josh didn't seem to mind. Go figure.

"After that we went to your place," Cristobal said to me. "You weren't there, so we went to Logan's. Then Zach's . . ." He shook his head. "After what we saw there, we figured you guys had been back. We ended up at Riggs' house and found him packing. Jaylee had left him a note. He invited us along."

"Riggs got my note." Jaylee beamed up at me. Gave me a little peck on the lips.

"What was that?" Josh straightened, bloodshot eyes flicking between Jaylee and me. "You and her? Seriously? Since when?"

Jaylee linked her arm with mine. "Since it's none of your business."

Josh narrowed his gaze. "That doesn't even make sense."

"Whatever," Jaylee said. "I'm going to go check my hair. Lizzie? Can I get by?"

Lizzie, who was sitting on the end, got up, and Jaylee was able to slide out of the booth. The table was silent as we all watched her cross the restaurant.

Josh broke the silence. "My tongue has been in her mouth."

"Oh, come on," I said.

"Don't be rude, Josh," Lizzie said.

Another moment of silence, and then, "Lots of guys' tongues have been in her mouth," Cristobal said.

Josh and Antônia busted up laughing.

"Cristobal!" Lizzie shot him The Look—the one she gives me when I push my luck too far.

"Change the subject," I said.

"No, no, not yet," Josh said. "It is my duty as a fellow male to warn you." He patted his chest. "That girl dragged my heart through the mud three times. Three, man. Don't be the fool that I was. She can't keep her hands off other guys. I swear to you."

I ignored him, but under the table, I squeezed my left hand into a fist to distract myself from the frustration rumbling inside me.

"What about the morning parties?" Lizzie asked. "Are they really mandatory? What happens if we don't go?"

"Why wouldn't you go?" Krista asked.

"They dock your vouchers for a week," Cristobal said.

"A whole week?" Lizzie said.

I raised my eyebrows. "Wow."

"What about emergencies?" Logan asked. "What about a pregnant woman in labor?"

"Because there are so many pregnant women here," I said.

"No, he's right," Cristobal said. "Medical staff are exempt from MPs if they're working. Same for EMTs and enforcers—unless they're stationed there for security, which some always are. Childcare, adult care." He frowned. "Anyone considered an essential worker, really. Nonessential businesses are closed until after the Monday meeting. Admin is also excused, though most of Admin is usually working behind the scenes at the meetings."

Our food came then, thick paper plates gloriously overflowing with massive burgers, French fries, and garnishes. Not everyone got their food. Jaylee's hadn't come, but she wasn't back yet. My morning workout had left me a bigger appetite than usual, so when the waitress set my burger in front of me, I picked it up and took a bite, groaning with pleasure.

"*Eli,*" Lizzie said. "How about I pray first?"

I set my burger back on the plate, shame washing over me as my sister gave thanks and asked for God's blessing over our meal.

After Lizzie's prayer, we all ate in silence for several seconds. Josh was the first to speak.

"Nobody prays here," he said.

"I do," Cristobal said, then added, "Not out loud."

"Well, they should," Lizzie said. "*You* should. Especially now. After everything that's happened. After we've been spared."

"I'm sorry," Josh said. "Maybe I have nothing to say to any god who'd allow most of earth's population to keel over and die in less than a month. Didn't God promise not to kill off the entire world after Noah?"

"He promised not to flood the earth again," Lizzie said.

"Oh, well. Guess that clears that right up," Josh snapped.

"It's the great battle of Armageddon," Logan said. "It's got to be."

This led us to yet another debate on end-times theories from the book of Revelation. It made me feel tired.

The waitress brought the rest of the food—all except Jaylee's. "We're still missing one," I told her. "For the girl who's sitting here." I tapped the empty space between Lizzie and me.

"She said she was sitting at the bar now." The waitress motioned across the restaurant. "I delivered her food there."

Every head at the table turned toward the bar, some of us craning more than others to get a good view. Sure enough, there sat Jaylee at the counter, twirling a piece of her hair while she talked to Riggs, who was leaning on his forearms on the other side of the bar, tattooed biceps on full display.

Josh busted up.

I felt, like, six emotions at once: anger, jealousy, frustration, hurt, betrayal, and above all, humiliation. While I was fighting to look like I didn't really care and ignore the looks of pity from my friends, it became very clear that all of the doubts inside me had been justified. All along my intuition had known better than my heart.

"Told you, man," Josh said, shaking his head slightly, his dimple tucked *way* in as he grinned, beyond amused at my misfortune.

# 10

ELI
AUGUST 3

Monday morning I spent my run trying to plan a way to break up with Jaylee. I came up dry. How did you break up with a girl, anyway? I had no idea.

When I got back to the apartment, I found Cree and Davis eating at the kitchen counter, various leftover containers around them. The refrigerator door was wide open.

"Hey, you guys need to close the fridge when you're done," I said. "You'll let all the cold air out."

Cree held up someone's leftover hamburger. "Breakfast."

"Sorry," Davis said, his glasses so smudged I could barely see his eyes.

"How can you see?" I asked him. "Do you know how to clean your glasses?"

Davis shrugged. "I should wash them?"

"No. Just kind of polish them to get the smudges off." I pulled them off his face and smoothed the lenses with the hem of my T-shirt. "Where is my dad?" I asked, returning his glasses.

"He's sleeping." Davis put his glasses back on. "Hey! That's better!"

I walked up the stairs to the living room. Sure enough, the hide-a-bed was still open, and Dad had somehow slept through all the noise the boys were making ten yards away. "Dad?"

A grunt told me he wasn't really sleeping.

"Reinhold leave?" I asked.

Another grunt. "He wanted you to go but said he wouldn't put you on the spot again."

Regret washed over me. I should have gone with. It would have been a much better use of my time than trying to figure out how to break it off with Jaylee.

Dad sat up and rubbed his face. "You have a nice run?"

"Yeah. I beat yesterday's time by two minutes."

"Nicely done."

"Thanks. I'd also like to find some weights. After what happened with Brandon, I just want to be strong enough to defend myself."

"I doubt you'll ever have to fight for your life like that again, but if you do, bar none, the most effective close range self-defense is eye gouging."

My whole life, eye gouging had been the extent of my dad's self-defense advice. He'd had plenty of advice about Jaylee before we left Reinhold's place. Maybe he could tell me how to break up with her. "Hey, Dad. Uh, how do you—?"

The rap of knuckles on the front door pressed pause on our conversation. I opened the door, expecting Lizzie, but it was our neighborhood cops, Harvey and Vrahnos.

"Job placements for Seth and Eli McShane."

I'd suspected it was coming, but hearing Harvey say my name still came as a shock. "Tracy mentioned volunteer task teams," I said. "He didn't say anything about conscriptions."

Harvey just held out a sheet of paper, looking bored. I

snatched it from his hand, found my name, then the words "sanitation engineer" next to the words "Mt. Crested Butte Department of Water and Sanitation."

"Are you kidding me?" I said as Dad came alongside me. "I'm a garbage man?"

Vrahnos grinned. "Hey, ten points, kid. You're the first person who knew what a sanitation engineer was."

"Hooray for me," I said, looking to Dad, who was now holding his own sheet of paper. "What did you get?"

"Mechanic," he said.

My posture slumped. "Come on! I can fix cars too." I turned to Vrahnos, because Harvey intimidated me. "Dad taught me everything he knows."

"Sorry, kid," Vrahnos said. "Change your profile on the Grid if you want a better job. Until then, sanitation engineer it is."

"Report times are listed," Harvey said. "Have a nice day." He walked toward a set of Zero FXP electric motorcycles.

Vrahnos remained. "Any questions?"

"Dad said you guys drove an SUV," I said, nodding at the bikes.

"We share the vehicles with the other officers," Vrahnos said. "Take turns depending on our shifts."

I examined my paper again. I was scheduled Tuesday through Saturday. "Five a.m.?"

Vrahnos looked me up and down. "Be sure to eat a good breakfast. You'll need it."

• • •

At ten o'clock, everyone but Zach and Hannah went to the morning party. Loca and Liberté sang a couple of songs, then Tracy came out and went over all the ways people were committing infractions, as he called them.

"First, we need y'all to only order food you're going to eat. We're working hard to make Safe Water feel like a home, but the truth is, we don't have unlimited resources. Too many of y'all are wasting food. If this continues, we'll have to make some changes to your weekly allowances."

I didn't envy Admin's job of trying to make a couple thousand people understand the severity of the situation. "Rationing will come next," I told Logan, "especially as we approach winter and traveling becomes harder."

"They won't be able to send their scavenge teams out as often then," Logan said.

"Second," Tracy said, "urinating in public is forbidden. Men, there are portable bathrooms all over this town. Please use them. We don't want to have to withhold anyone's weekly vouchers, but that's exactly what'll happen if you're caught violating this rule, m'kay?"

I didn't see that one coming, and it cracked me up.

"Finally, we can't have people crowding the town gates and hassling the workers. Find something better to do with your time, or you'll lose your weekly vouchers for loitering."

"Wonder who's crowding the gates?" Logan asked.

"Don't know, but I'm going over there later to find out," I said.

"Just keep your distance," Dad said, scowling at me. "We don't need you losing your vouchers for the week."

Next, Tracy brought up some guy named Arthur Fairchild who used to run a custom embroidery shop in Monticello, Utah. Tracy had asked him to take over an abandoned embroidery shop in Crested Butte, and the guy had designed a bunch of logos for the town. "Patches are being manufactured as we speak for our new Enforcer uniforms," Tracy said. "Mr. Fairchild, your contribution has made Safe Water a better place. We thank you."

Tracy went on to tell us how important we all were, and to be sure to register our skills on the Grid—which was what he was calling the Safe Water website—so we could all help make this town a better place.

What a waste of time.

• • •

After we got back from the morning party, I asked Jaylee if

she wanted to drive over to the gate with me and spy on the protestors. I was also hoping it would give us a chance to be alone and talk.

"Why do you want to go over there?" she said. "Mr. Tracy just said people who went there would lose their vouchers."

"I'm not going to join them," I said. "I just want to see what all the fuss is about."

"No thanks," she said. "And didn't your dad tell you no?"

Dad had gone upstairs to take another nap. "He also told me I was old enough to decide things for myself," I said. Besides, Lizzie was watching a movie with the kids, and I only planned to be gone ten minutes.

I took Logan with me instead. Like Kimama had said, the roads had been rerouted, and I couldn't get near the original entry gate. I finally parked the van in an apartment complex, and we walked over. Logan talked nonstop about Hannah the whole time.

"She could like me, don't you think?" he asked.

"Hannah? I don't know, man. I think she's still, you know, getting over Brandon."

"Right. I should give her some space for that," he said.

"Good idea," I said. What a nut.

There were a bunch of flyers on the ground with the heading: "We are Americans: This land is free." On them was a short article about how the administration had no right to keep anyone in this place. When we reached the gate, there were forty-some people dressed in variations of red, white, and blue. Many were waving U.S. flags overhead and chanting, "We are Americans! Let us go!" over and over. It was like seeing fans cheer on Team USA at the Olympics.

"Patriotic," Logan said.

It was. Enforcers had surrounded them, though, and we couldn't have joined in even if we'd wanted to. Still, it encouraged me to see that we weren't the only ones annoyed with being stuck in this place.

Logan and I went back to the Snowcrest to show everyone the flyer and share what we'd seen.

"Dad still sleeping?" I asked my sister.

"Yep," Lizzie said. "I'm worried about him."

"He's just sad," I said. We all were.

"While you were gone, Antônia and I got jobs," Lizzie said. "You, too, Logan. They left you a paper. It's on the counter."

"Awesome." Logan pushed past me to retrieve his assignment.

"Antônia has to work in the laundry," Lizzie said. "She was pretty annoyed. She wants to borrow your computer, Logan, to change her skills page. Cristobal told her she'd get moved right away if she added that she speaks Spanish, but she really wants to get assigned to something with computers, so I don't know if she'll tell them that. I got childcare!"

"That fits," I said. My sister loved kids.

"Programming, yes!" Logan said, beaming.

"Antonia was pretty annoyed about that too," Lizzie said.

"Lucky you," I said, thinking I'd better take my turn with Logan's computer and change my skills as well. Pretty much anything had to be better than sanitation engineer.

•   •   •

When Zach got off his shift and found out about my job, he razzed me the rest of the night—Zach who was riding around in an ambulance with his partner Travis. I couldn't help but notice Zach's uniform had a patch that said "Safe Water Emergency Medical Technician." Way to go, Mr. Fairchild.

Logan was quick to join in the fun. "Should have changed your profile when I did, trash man," he said.

"Yeah, don't be nervous about tomorrow, McShane," Zach said. "There isn't much training in being a garbage man. You just pick it up as you go along."

"Ha ha," I said.

"It might be harder than that," Logan said. "I really hope you aren't *canned*." He laughed so hard, he sounded like some kind of cartoon.

Zach chuckled. "Nice one!"

"Laugh it up, both of you," I said, nervous about my new job. I'd gone onto the Grid that afternoon and updated my resume section, so there wasn't a whole lot I could do at the moment but wait and see if they moved me someplace else.

•   •   •

Tuesday morning, I didn't have time for my run. Dad drove me over to the Mt. Crested Butte Department of Water and Sanitation and wished me good luck. I was set up in a team of three. A middle-aged man named Nigil had worked as a UPS deliveryman in Albuquerque, so he was assigned as our driver. He introduced me to Bong, a twenty-something British guy who looked like he belonged in a mixed martial arts ring.

"Nice to meet you, Bong," I said, making sure not to smile, but there was something in my voice. A slight mocking I'd failed to hide.

Thankfully, Bong only looked at me, bored, liked he'd heard it a million times before. "Bong means *phoenix* in Korean," he said, his accent thick.

I stared at him.

"Like the bird. Dumbledore's bird. In *Harry Potter.*"

"Oh," I said, then added, "Those are cool." Because they were.

As it turned out, Bong had worked as a *bin man*, as he called it, in a town called Redditch in the UK. He'd come to Tucson for his sister's wedding and gotten stuck here.

"Most bin men cover a thousand houses a day," Bong said. "This place is loads easier. We've four trucks to basically cover half what one truck normally runs. They're wise to start you out that way, since being a bin man is physically demanding." He eyed me up and down. "It's going to leave you a bit knackered, I'm afraid."

I scowled and said, "I can handle it."

"Sure, you say." He motioned to my splinted fingers. "How long you have to wear that?"

"Eight weeks."

Bong grunted. "Well, we're going to ease you in, yeah? Most crews have two blokes. One driving, the other fetching the bins and loading them, putting them back. Because it's such grueling work, our crew has two on back. One expert, one novice. This is so you can take it slow, learn the job. You'll only run every other bin for the first week or two. Or however quickly you catch on or your body takes to shape up."

I felt like I should be insulted, but he and I were physically in two different leagues. If he said the work was hard, I believed him.

I had no idea how right he was. Bong said the job would still be physically demanding if everyone disposed of their trash properly, but people didn't. I don't know how many times I had to squat or crouch to pick up stuff that was just lying on the street beside the trash cans. And while most cans rolled easily, too many didn't. They were heavy or had lost one or more wheels, and I had to push, pull, or drag them to the truck, all mostly one-handed, since I couldn't get the other glove on over my splint. Also, jumping off and on the truck all day worked over my back and feet.

By the end of day one, I was spent. That night Lizzie had mercy on me and used her sewing skills to remodel my right glove. She cut open the middle and fourth fingers, then sewed them together so that I could slide my hand—and the splint— into the glove. It fit perfectly.

Wednesday, I woke feeling like someone had taken a rubber mallet to my body. Having gloves on both hands made things easier, but I still limped around, muscles I'd never used screaming in protest that I hadn't prepared them properly for my new occupation.

But that was okay. The more I hurt—the more I watched the ease at how Bong moved and lifted things—I realized this job was a better workout than my morning jog and handful of sit-ups and push-ups. This job would make me strong. And if I did it well, I might even get promoted to the crews that went outside the gates to drive the trucks to the landfill. Having the freedom to get out of this place was something I wanted very badly.

•   •   •

Thursday evening, a bunch of us walked over to the new park, which was nothing more than a collection of scavenged playground equipment from people's backyards on a grassy lot edged in sidewalks. The kids loved it. Jaylee ran over to a swing set and demanded I push her. I complied, thinking this might be my moment to break things off. Unfortunately, Krista tagged along and begged me to push her as well. I was working up the courage to just say what I wanted to say right in front of Krista when Jaylee leapt off the swing.

"Marco!" she yelled, jogging toward a dark-haired guy on the sidewalk.

Krista leaped off her swing and followed.

I sighed and sat down on Jaylee's abandoned swing, feeling sorry for myself and wondering how I was going to get myself out of my newfound relationship.

Hannah and Cree approached. Hannah helped Cree onto the swing, and soon Cree was soaring beside me, no shoes, his long hair flying around his face.

"How was your first week at the hospital?" I asked.

"Good," Hannah said. "It's a lot to learn, but I like it. How about you?"

"It's really hard," I said. "I'm exhausted."

Hannah gave Cree another push. "Missing your mom probably adds to that."

"Yeah," I said. "Dad's in worse shape, though. He's been sleeping a lot. He yelled at Cree for peeing in the toilet. Then he duct-taped the lid shut. He never used to yell about anything. Of course, we were practically perfect children, so . . ." I shrugged.

"Gotta pee outside," Cree said.

"That's right," I said, watching him soar. "This one is sad too, I think. He keeps asking me about his Shimá."

"*Shoo, Shimá bił íłyeed,*" Cree said.

I had no idea what he was saying. "I know, buddy. It stinks."

"Looks like Jaylee is trying to get your attention," Hannah

said.

Sure enough, Jaylee was beckoning from where she, Krista, and Marco were standing on the sidewalk. Josh had joined their little group, which honestly didn't sweeten the prospect of me walking over there. I was still annoyed at him for prophesying the impending doom of my relationship, then mocking me when it pretty much happened in front of everyone. The last thing I needed right now was to let anyone take more shots at me.

Yet I said goodbye to Hannah and Cree, pushed myself out of the swing, and trudged across the grass, fully aware that Safe Water wasn't the only trap that had caught me.

# 11

## HANNAH
## AUGUST 7

Friday, Dr. Bayles brought special guests into the hospital. Mr. Tracy, Jennie, and a man named Eric Wilson, who Dr. Bayles introduced as the head of the medical scavenge teams. Mr. Wilson's team unloaded over two dozen boxes of medical supplies and equipment. I was the lucky person who would get to inventory everything.

"We come bearing gifts for y'all too," Mr. Tracy said.

Jennie set a small box on the counter and opened it. "We have iPhones!" she sang. "Enough for everyone. They already have service and phone numbers. You'll find all that information on the slip of paper inside each box."

Susan whooped and dug in the box. She pulled out an iPhone box. "I cannot wait to have a phone again."

Linsey, Asiya, and Dr. Carter each claimed a phone as well.

"We don't have enough phones for everyone," Mr. Tracy said, "so we decided to share our new cell service with some of our most important citizens. Y'all who work here in the hospital are invaluable to Safe Water. We want to make sure you are connected to each other."

Susan pushed the box toward me. "Pick a phone, girl. What are you waiting for?"

I peeked inside and withdrew a red iPhone 11. "Thank you," I said, a little giddy about the prospect of connecting to the internet to see what was out there still.

"Thank *you* for your service," Mr. Tracy said.

"We also have the prototypes of our wristbands," Jennie said, withdrawing a translucent silicone bracelet out of her box. "If you'll hand me your lanyard IDs, I'll get these set up for you."

"How do they work?" Linsey asked.

"Ever been to Walt Disney World?" Jennie asked.

"No, and thanks for rubbing it in," Linsey said.

"Aww, well, they used a technology called Magic Bands that linked to each customer. Once you set it up, you could enter the park with your Magic Band, pay for food and merchandise . . . It even worked as your hotel room key."

"Handy," I said.

"We thought so," Jennie said. "Loca and Liberté have been using LED wristbands at concerts for the past seven years. Our tech team found a way to combine both technologies into one. Not only will your new wristband hold your ID and your credits, it will light up whenever LLC plays a concert, making you part of the show."

"Pretty groovy," Linsey said.

Dr. Bayles led the guests out of our wing. Jennie remained until she set up all our wristbands. "You should be good to go. Every shop in Safe Water can read these with their iPad registers, so you can start using them today. If you have any trouble, call me." She handed each of us one of her business cards.

I got busy with the inventory, which was going to take me weeks to unpack. I was working intently when Susan whisked back into the nurse's station.

"Wasn't that great? Giving us phones? I'm so excited!"

"Me too," I said.

"Oh, after Mr. Tracy and his team left, Jason asked about you," Susan said. "I told him about your man. That won't stop him from trying, but it might slow him down a little."

"Excuse me?" I asked. "Dr. Bayles asked what about me?"

"If you were involved with anyone." She raised one eyebrow.

"But I thought he and Monica . . ."

"Mmm hmm. This week." She twisted her lips. "Last week he was with Asiya. And you didn't hear that from me."

For the rest of the day, I was hyper-aware of everything Dr. Bayles said and did. He had the tendency to stand a little too close when talking to me, but that was all. With Asiya, though, there was way too much touching going on, which didn't make sense if they'd broken up.

Discovering that my boss had poor professional boundaries was not only a disappointment, it unsettled me. I didn't want to feel unsafe at work. I never wanted to feel unsafe again. Thankfully, I had the Snowcrest to go home to. The more time I spent with my new friends, the more I felt like one of their number.

Since I was off on Friday, I asked Lizzie to leave the kids home with me, rather than taking them with her to the childcare facility. I didn't like being alone in that big apartment, and watching the kids kept my mind from wandering from one fearful scenario to another. We had a full day watching DVDs we checked out from the lobby, playing hide and seek, and walking over to the playground park.

That night I ordered dinner from The Divy, a restaurant that served the best food in town, as far as I was concerned. Linsey had talked me into ordering lunch from them a couple days ago, and I had fallen in love with their food. I didn't know how much to order. Zach and Logan were working late. Eli and Seth were both off at four, but they always went straight to the showers after their shifts. Seth was usually home by five, but Eli usually had his dad drop him at the Avalanche where he ate dinner with Jaylee and then did who knew what. I hadn't seen him all week. Lizzie would be home by six but had told me that morning not to make the kids wait until she got back.

I used my new iPhone to order as much as I could get using the kids' vouchers and my credits. This got me four barbecue salmon dinners and three chicken dinners.

Shyla helped me set the table with the paper plates and plastic forks Seth had bought at the mercantile. It still felt nice to set a table as if this were a home.

It wasn't a home. I slept on the foldaway couch in the condo next door. Still, I was making an effort and determined to have a nice evening.

"Your grandma's wedding ring is so pretty," Shyla said.

I'd forgotten I'd told her about it. "Thanks," I said. My father had given it to Brandon when he'd asked his permission to marry me. Since it was a family ring, I didn't give it back after we broke up.

"I hope I can have a pretty ring someday," Shyla said.

I considered the number of abandoned jewelry stores out there. "I'm sure you can."

Dinner arrived. I gave the delivery man the kids' vouchers, and he buzzed my wristband to deduct the rest. I then carried the warm bags to the dining table.

Shyla skipped alongside me. "Can I help you?"

"You certainly can," I said.

We set the salads on each plate but kept the hot food covered so it would stay warm. Cree crawled onto a chair, eyes fixed on his plate as if he hadn't eaten all day—and he had. Twice!

"Hungry, Cree?" I asked.

He brushed his hair from his eyes and nodded, his now toothless grin making his cheeks look as if he'd already packed away some food for winter.

The door opened, and Seth entered. "Smells good in here," he said, kicking off his shoes by the door.

"Go fetch Davis," I said to Shyla. "Tell him dinner is ready."

The red-headed girl streaked up the stairs like a comet, her shrill voice muffled by the walls as she called her brother's name.

Seth approached, wearing a stark white undershirt and shorts, his hair damp and flat against his scalp. His jaw and chin were covered in dark, almost-a-beard scruff, likely from lack of shaving more than trying to look like a hipster. Over his arm, he held the slate blue overalls he'd been given to wear for work. "Well, this is a fine looking table. Smells good too."

"I hope you like salmon," I said, glancing at him, briefly. He looked tired.

"It's one of my favorites."

"No Eli?" I asked.

"Dropped him at the Avalanche," Seth said.

I was disappointed but not surprised.

Seth set his hand on Cree's head and mussed his hair. "And how was your day?"

"*La' nisin.*" Cree pointed at the salad, but the sounds of footsteps pounding down the stairs made his eyes roll back to watch Davis and Shyla launch into the room.

Seth chuckled. "Always hungry, this one. Lizzie say what time she's off today?"

"Six," I said. "She said to start without her. Are we ready for the main dish now, or shall we eat our salads first?" I reached for the paper bag.

Davis said, "Main dish!" at the same time as Shyla said, "Salad!"

Cree waited patiently.

"Mind if I pray first?" Seth asked.

Right. I always forgot the praying part. "Not at all." I took the seat to Seth's left since Davis had taken the spot I had intended for myself.

Seth reached out his hands, and I set mine in his, unsurprised by the roughness of his skin. This man had raised Eli, after all. How different they were from Brandon, my dad, and even Dr. Bayles. I had to reach for Davis, who was kneeling on his chair and practically lying on his salad as he stretched his freckled arm toward me.

Seth winked at Cree, then closed his eyes. "God, we thank you for this bounty that Hannah prepared. We thank you for bringing us together in the aftermath of such tragedy. Thank you for your provision and your continued protection. In Jesus' name, amen."

"Amen!" Shyla and Cree yelled together. They had made a game of this new praying tradition the McShane family practiced.

I passed one of the bags with a salmon dinner down to Seth, then divided the chicken between the kids.

"How are you liking the hospital?" Seth asked.

"It's nice," I said. "My feet are always sore, my mind cluttered with new facts and procedures, but I like it there. I'm glad to have a place to make a difference. I want to do well. I mean . . ." I was rambling. "I've made so many mistakes. I hope they won't give up on me."

"Everyone makes mistakes," Seth said. "I'm sure you're going to pick it all up in no time. If you decide to switch career paths, let me know. I'd be happy to teach you how to clean a carburetor."

I grinned. "No thanks."

Seth turned to Cree. "You see how fast she rejected that offer?"

"I could clean a car bird ray-tar," Davis said.

Seth chuckled. "One of these days I'll show you."

The boy beamed at Seth, his eyes lost behind a sheen of light reflecting off his glasses. I was struck at how easily Seth had filled the role of father for these three.

As if reading my thoughts, Shyla said, "Are you gonna be our parents now?"

I almost choked on my salmon. All three of the kids were staring—not at me, but at Seth. He was the one they really wanted, and I honestly couldn't blame them one bit. But I was honored Shyla had lumped me in as part of a package deal.

"That's a good question, Miss Shyla," Seth said. "Krista took care of you before Eli met you and brought you here. I think we're all one big family. How does that sound?"

Shyla sighed slowly, as if this wasn't at all acceptable. Her freckled face fixed on me. "You too?"

"Me too," I said, though I wasn't quite sure I understood the question.

"Krista doesn't want us," Davis said. "She just wants to kiss on boys."

Seth frowned. "What boys?"

Davis shrugged. "All of them, I guess."

I bit my lip and glanced at Seth. He, too, was fighting to keep a straight face, but his eyes totally gave him away.

"Krista is more like a big sister than a guardian," I said.

"Right," Seth said. "She's part of our family, but we're not going to rely on her to remember to fix us dinner."

"She would never fix dinner," Davis said, shaking his head.

"Chicken is good dinner," Cree said, holding up his drumstick.

Shyla forced out an over-the-top giggle. "Krista wants to kiss all the boys. Grr-ross!"

"Don't you knock it, girl," Seth said. "Someday that's going to be you."

Shyla yelped, eyes even bigger, and wrinkled her nose. "No way, Mr. Seth. You're wrong about that. Grr-ross!" Then she pretended to spit. "Puh, puh!"

"Puh!" Cree mimicked her.

"My mistake," Seth said.

A stretch of silence passed. My heart felt light from the innocence of these children and how they made me smile.

"You can be our dad," Davis said to Seth. Then he looked at me. "And you can be our mom."

Shyla lit up. "You can get married! Hannah already has a wedding ring."

Seth stared at me, lips parted as if he'd lost his ability to speak. He quickly recovered. "I can see why you might think that's a good idea," he said. "But Hannah and I . . . we just met last week. People need to get to know each other before they get married."

"I'm going to marry Cree," Shyla said, gazing at the boy.

Clueless, Cree tore off another bite of his chicken leg.

Seth and I laughed.

Later, when the kids were draped over the living room furniture, watching *WALL-E*, Seth and I cleaned up, then sat at the table, talking.

"Hey, I'm sorry about that, with the kids and us getting married," Seth said.

"It's fine," I said. "It will take a while for their understanding of marriage to change."

He met my gaze. "Change how?"

"Just that with so few people, I think partnerships will rise out of convenience and respect more than a deep love."

"Really?"

"Modern American culture has taught us that true love is out there, and you shouldn't marry unless you've found that perfect match. That's a lie sold by novelists and Hollywood and the bridal and tourism industries to make a ton of money."

"That's kind of a cynical view," Seth said.

"Maybe, but the data matches. Divorce statistics prove that people don't care about commitment. Deeply devoted couples 'fall out of love' every day." I used air quotes to make my point.

"But some stick it out," Seth said.

No one I knew. "I just think that in Safe Water, where the population is 2,462, last I heard, people are going to have to think in a new way. I mean, for those not interested in long-term companionship, it'll quickly be worse than six degrees of separation. Before they know it, they'll have all dated each other."

"That's a disturbing thought."

"But if someone wants a commitment—or to have a family—I just think it's foolish for them to hope they'll find their perfect match in this tiny populace."

"From the angle of a community where everyone looks out for themselves," Seth said, "I suppose you might be onto something. Relationships are supposed to be a two-way street—a 50/50 balance where no one keeps score."

"People are always keeping score," I said.

"Not me. Well"—he grinned—"at least not for long."

We laughed. But then Seth sighed deeply, and though he was

still smiling, he sounded sad and tired. "If you're right, Miss Hannah, the dating scene in this place will be like a game of draw straws."

"You snooze, you lose." I suddenly realized this applied to me, as well. "Then maybe we should consider Davis's idea," I said, throwing caution to the wind.

Seth's eyebrows shot up his forehead. "That *we* get married?"

"Not now," I said, shrugging. "But we're both smart and capable people. We get along. Work well together. We have as good a chance as anyone else at a successful partnership."

His eyes met mine, studied my face. "You're serious," he said.

I shrugged, suddenly embarrassed. "It's like those deals friends make. Give it ten years. If we're not married by the time we're thirty, we'll marry each other."

"I'm forty-two."

Oh. Oh gosh.

Seth's forehead crumpled. Apologetic. "Hannah. I follow your logic. In a way, it makes perfect sense. And I'm so very flattered. Really." He got up and walked into the kitchen, hands perched on his hips as he passed behind the U-shaped counter. I got the feeling he wanted some kind of boundary between us.

My pulse throbbed in my temples. My face burned. I hoped I hadn't offended him. "Don't worry about it." I shrugged like it didn't matter. "I was just postulating. Trying to think ahead. Skip all the hard stuff. Survive this, uhm . . ." Wow. Could I even form a coherent sentence right now?

"It's not you." He looked at his hands—at his wedding band. "I met Leti the summer before ninth grade when my family moved in next door to hers. We had a connection right away." He shrugged, like he couldn't help how he'd felt. "We'd have been married twenty years this December." His voice went high. His shoulders curled in and shook. He was crying.

My face tingled. Oh my gosh. I'd forgotten his wife. "I'm sorry," I blurted. "I shouldn't have made marriage seem like it didn't matter. Forgive me. I didn't think." I got up from the table. "I'm going to . . ." I motioned toward the door.

"Hold on." He stepped out from the kitchen and into my path. "This conversation . . ." He waved his hand between us. "Just a conversation. We're good. You hear me?"

"Sure," I said, trying to sound like I wasn't about to die from humiliation.

"Also, I understand why a marriage of convenience appeals to you," Seth said. "Why you'd want to skip the hard stuff. Knowing what you've been through, it makes perfect sense. But, Hannah, please hear me. Don't give up on love. Yeah, it's hard sometimes, but getting to the other side of that hard stuff is what makes it all worthwhile."

My vision blurred. Traitorous tears filling my eyes. I shoved past him, annoyed that I'd just ruined one of the few new friendships I had in this world. Thanks to me and my big-mouthed opinions, my small world had just gotten smaller.

# 12

## ELI
## AUGUST 10

By the time next Monday rolled around, Zach happened to be off, so we were all together for once—except for Hannah, who was sleeping. She worked nights at the moment, which was unfortunate now that we were friends again. I hadn't seen her all week.

It was weird to be up so early and not have to go to work. I grabbed one of the walkie talkies and tried to call Reinhold. Still no answer. What had happened to him and Kimama? I felt sick just thinking about it.

When Zach and I went out to pick up breakfast for everyone, the ground was wet.

"It rained last night," I said, awestruck and a little freaked out.

"What do we do?" Zach asked.

"We get breakfast," I said, looking up at the sky, which was pale white. This part of Colorado had low humidity at this time of year—it wouldn't rain often—but I was eager to know if the rain would be safe.

As we walked toward the shopping area, Zach told me about a call he and Travis had taken last night.

"The call came through the Grid. A civilian said the cops were beating some guy."

"Is that how you get calls? Email?" I asked.

"Sometimes. Mostly enforcers call us on the scanner. Anyway, we show up at this dinky little apartment complex over on Emmons Road. People are everywhere, running, terrified. Officer Vrahnos is guarding the entrance, keeping people out. He doesn't want to let us in, but I said we had a call that someone's life is in danger, so he'd better move."

"Did he?"

"Yeah, and get this. Inside, Officer Harvey is interrogating this guy, trying to get him to confess to working with some people on the outside. I don't even know what he's talking about, but the guy's a mess. So I step in."

"Look at you being a hero," I said.

"Then Harvey came at me, telling me to stay out of it and everything. At that point, Vrahnos decided to stop looking the other way and backed me up. Harvey was ticked."

"This place is a disaster waiting to happen," I said. "Where's the accountability for the enforcers?"

"Doesn't look like they have any," Zach said.

• • •

Zach used his new wristband to buy egg sandwiches that made me wonder if the scavenge teams had ransacked the freezer at a McDonald's. Only Zach, Hannah, and Cristobal had wristbands. Cristobal said we'd all have them soon. They were also given iPhones since they were essential workers, but the general public would not be getting phones, which about made Krista and Jaylee blow a gasket.

When we got back, the girls were moving slowly, as usual, so we dropped their share of the breakfast at their place. It was another hour before Lizzie arrived with Shyla.

"You get the boys dressed?" Lizzie asked.

Zach and I looked at each other. Davis was lying on the couch, still wearing the adult T-shirt/dress Dad had bought him for pajamas, and watching *WALL-E*. Again. Cree was running around in his underwear, making robot sounds.

"You get Davis moving, I'll help Cree," I told Zach, then chased Cree upstairs and caught him hiding in the closet, giggling.

I held him with my right arm, biceps whining from the overuse of my muscles while I dug through the pile on the floor for something—anything—he could wear. Dad had bought him a few Mt. Crested Butte T-shirts, but as far as I knew, he still had only the one pair of cutoff jeans he'd been wearing when we found him. Andy had given him an old pair of Teva sandals that had belonged to one of his kids, but Cree was always taking them off. I didn't care if he went barefoot for now, but come winter, the kid's feet were going to fall off if he kept this up.

I finally found his jeans wadded under the edge of the bed and wrestled Cree into them and a T-shirt.

He said, "We go!" then sprinted from the room. I heard him bump down the stairs—a game he and Davis had created with an old pizza box.

I hadn't seen Dad since breakfast, so I went looking for him next. I found him out on the balcony, sitting cross-legged on the floor.

"There's two perfectly good chairs out here, you know," I said.

He jumped at the sound of my voice, sniffed. "I'm good here." His voice sounded funny, like he'd been crying. Again.

My whole life, I'd never seen my dad cry. Since Mom died, it happened daily.

"You see it rained last night?" I asked.

Dad grunted.

"It's time to leave for the morning party. You okay?"

He sighed, posture curling on his exhale. "Just missing your mom."

Mom existed now as a constant ache that I shoved away whenever I felt it rising up. Seeing my dad like this threatened to pull to the surface everything I'd been packing down. Her loss was too much for me to think about every day. I knew it must be even harder for Dad.

"I miss her too," I managed, but those four words brought a rush of emotions up my throat to my head, almost made me dizzy. I took a breath. Had to get away from here. "I'll tell them you're coming." And I went back inside.

"Well?" Lizzie was standing just inside the sliding doors, glaring, arms folded.

"What?" I said.

She rolled her eyes. "He's not the only one who lost someone. The way he's been acting lately, I feel like we lost them both."

I winced at the pain in my sister's voice. "He just needs some time."

"I just need my dad." Lizzie grabbed her bag and strode toward the door.

Jaylee was already standing there, holding the door open, water jug in hand, duffel bag crooked in one elbow, towel draped around her neck. Behind her, just outside, Zach, Krista, Hannah, and the kids were waiting, everyone ready to go. If we didn't leave now, we'd miss our chance and have to line up after the meeting. By then the lines would triple.

"Zach, why don't you go now," I said. "Dad and I will bring the kids."

"No prob," Zach said, shooing everyone toward the Sienna.

●   ●   ●

By the time the five of us walked onto the compound, there were hundreds of people in line for showers already. I figured we'd missed our chance for today. The closer we got, we found ourselves in more of an angry mob than a shower line.

"What's going on?" I asked a tan guy with spiky blond hair.

"No water in the showers, no water for the jugs, and no one is answering at the house," he said.

A flutter of panic bloomed in my gut. I reminded myself it didn't matter. Reinhold would find access to the creek from above. If the Champions had messed up, maybe they'd let everyone leave.

We walked the line looking for Zach and the others. We found them sitting on the grass about halfway up.

"No reason to wait here, I guess," Zach said.

"It's probably a broken pipe," Logan said. "So many people showering probably overwhelmed the plumbing, which likely wasn't installed correctly from the start."

"Could be," Zach said. "That's a good theory, Logan."

For once it was.

"I bet they joined mismatched pipes when they put all this in," Logan said. "Galvanized steel can't be joined with a copper pipe without a dielectric union. It corrodes and will leak. They should use brass."

I smirked at Zach. "You had to encourage him, didn't you?"

"I felt bad about his job."

Logan had been picked up to work in IT, but he'd been mysteriously fired by the end of his first day. Antônia had been moved to programming too, and she said Logan had grossly exaggerated his abilities. Two days later they moved him to janitorial at the hospital, where, according to Zach, he was constantly chatting up Hannah, rather than cleaning. Hannah had told Zach if Logan wasn't careful, he'd be fired from there too.

"He earned that job," I said, grinning. "They found out he was more of a sweeper agent than a secret agent."

"I know!" Zach said. "I'm so proud of our broommate."

"Hey, at least I get to work with Hannah," Logan said. "We have fun together."

Zach and I exchanged crippling glances. Poor Hannah.

"Let's move over to the lawn and wait for the morning party to start," Lizzie said. "Mr. Tracy will probably have something to say about the water."

Everyone got up and headed toward the stage. Jaylee fell in

line beside me, took hold of my hand. "What if there's just no water left?" she asked as we followed the others. "I need to wash my hair, Eli. It feels gross."

I slowed down, hoping we'd fall behind the others long enough to for me to tell her I wanted to break up.

"Hey, Jaylee, I've been thinking . . . I'm not sure—"

Krista appeared from nowhere, barging between us from behind and grabbing Jaylee's arm. "Josh said we could come over later," she said.

"Not interested," Jaylee said. "I'm going to the Avalanche after this. Riggs thinks he can get me hired as a waitress."

"You want to be a waitress?" I asked.

"More than a janitor or laundry worker," she said. "Antônia was miserable doing all that dry cleaning, and now that they moved her to programming, they're going to need to replace her at the laundry. I'm not touching anyone's dirty clothes, even with gloves on. I need a job, now."

The Champions' version of a wake-up call ended my chance to break up with Jaylee. Rather than the military "Reveille" that once frequented summer camps across the country, the Champions had remixed an instrumental version of "We Are Survivors" that sounded like a Mario Brothers video game.

When the song ended, Morgan Tracy strode onstage, microphone in hand. Applause burst forth, until a half dozen enforcers joined Tracy on the platform, lining up right behind him, Harvey and Vrahnos included.

"Good morning, everyone!" Tracy said. "How are y'all this fine day?"

He received scattered applause. For most of this crowd, it was still pretty early. The rest seemed guarded, expecting an announcement that would end the so-called "good life" here.

"I'm sure y'all noticed there was no water this morning," Tracy said. "I'm real sorry about that, but we needed to get everyone's attention. Thing is, we've had too many rules broken lately. I need to remind everyone that y'all signed a contract agreeing to certain terms. We've kept our end of the bargain, and we really need y'all to keep yours, m'kay? Going forward, the penalty for breach of contract will be the forfeiture of water privileges."

Angry murmurs broke out among the crowd, and all of a sudden I was very thirsty.

Tracy hurried on with his speech. "How long a person loses water privileges depends on how badly that person violated the contract, m'kay?"

"Not m'kay," I said to Zach. "Water is a human right."

I wasn't the only one objecting to this declaration. Around us, pockets of dissenters were getting louder.

"We hate doing this," Tracy said. "But if the party life here is going to work, we need y'all's cooperation. Our goal is to keep everyone safe, but we can't do that when people are breaking rules."

"What rules are people breaking?" someone yelled out.

"I don't want to get into specifics," Tracy said, "but y'all need to behave in town. No vandalism. No assault. No stealing. Be nice to each other and respect the establishments, the enforcers, our construction workers, and the boundaries. We need to keep the fences in place, and we need y'all to stay off the mountain, at least for now. This is all pretty obvious stuff.

"Also, if you've been assigned a job, we need y'all to go to work. We're doing what we can to make this place a safe home, and we need y'all to do your part, m'kay?" He paused for a full second, then dove right into a new topic. "We'll have some construction here today that will change the way y'all enter the showers and the water refill area. We'll also be distributing wristbands to replace the voucher system. Those will hold your credits for making purchases and be your tickets to showers, to fill water jugs, and to attend the morning parties."

"And so they can track everything we do," Antônia said.

I didn't like the sound of that one bit.

"A couple other things," Tracy said. "Too many people are still wasting food, so we're dropping the daily allowance to thirty credits instead of fifty, and one gallon of water per person per day."

This was met with booing. So much for guzzling water and

refilling the jug before I left the compound.

"I'm sorry, folks," Tracy said. "Once we see the waste stop, we'll consider raising the allowance again, m'kay?" Before the audience could get too loud, he changed the subject. "Also, night parties are changing to once a week. The Champions have been stellar to give us so many concerts, but they're getting tired. They need a chance to rest. And we love them, don't we?"

Scattered applause rang out.

"That's right. We want to make sure they're getting the rest they need. So, fewer night parties, but they'll be longer and wilder than ever! Mandatory morning parties will remain here every Monday. Anyone who skips without authorization will be docked their weekly credits. That's nothing new. We're only asking y'all to wake up early one day a week. Y'all can handle that, m'kay?"

But Tracy wasn't done. "The showers and water spouts will remain off today while the construction crews install the new kiosks. To those of you who've been following the rules, we're real sorry about all this. Those who have no violations, y'all will get a credit for a special meet and greet with the Champions."

The crowd went nuts, Jaylee and Krista included. How did a chance to meet two rock stars make everyone forget everything Tracy had just laid out?

"That's all for today," he said. "Short and sweet. The Champions and I, we love y'all so much. Have a good one!"

He waved, and people started to disperse. Our group clustered closer together.

"So much wrong," I said.

"The UN's resolution explicitly states that the human right to water and sanitation is included in the right to a habitable living environment," Logan said.

"Exactly." I tapped fists with Logan.

"Doesn't sound like the Champions care about anything but their own rules," Lizzie said.

"If people would follow the rules," Jaylee said, "there wouldn't be any problems."

"The contract they asked us to sign specifically referred to the laws of America," Zach said. "Our country has never withheld water as a punishment for breaking the law."

That much was true. "We should protest," I said. "Peacefully. Remind them that they asked us to comply to the laws of this country, so they should too."

Jaylee frowned at me. "Eli . . ."

"We can get materials for signs at the drugstore," Lizzie said. "I saw they had poster board there."

"I'm in," Zach said.

"Me too," Logan added.

"No, thank you," Antônia said. "I like my new job, and I don't want to lose it."

"According to the constitution, we have the right to peacefully assemble," I said. "It's the First Amendment."

Krista groaned. "Who cares?"

"You don't have to come with us," I said.

"I would never come with you," she said. "Not to protest this. It's not even a thing worth protesting."

"Yes, it is," I said. "Water is a human right."

"What does that even mean?" she asked.

Sometimes I forgot Krista was only thirteen. "Human rights are defined by the United Nations," I said. "They list the things that every person should have access to just because they're human. Safe drinking water is one of those things. Without it, a person can die. For Tracy to use drinking water as a punishment, well, he's messing with people's right to life. Not even mass murderers are denied drinking water."

"Are you going?" Krista asked Jaylee.

"I'm going to the Avalanche," Jaylee said, kissing me goodbye with a peck on the cheek. "I already told you."

"Will you come with me to Josh's place after?" Krista asked.

"Maybe," Jaylee said, already walking away. "First I want to find out how to meet Loca and Liberté. Bye, Eli!"

"I'm coming with you!" Krista said.

"See you," Antônia said, following them.

"You're going to have to get your own ride back," Zach yelled after them.

Jaylee turned and waved, like this was no concern.

"Where's Dad?" Lizzie asked.

We rounded up the kids and headed for the vans. We found Dad waiting in the driver's seat of the Honda.

"Protest? Why?" he asked when I'd told him our plan.

I stood on the driver's side of the Silver Bullet, talking to him through the rolled-down window while Lizzie helped the kids load up. "What they're doing is wrong," I said.

"You think they care about that?" Dad snapped.

His tone made me flinch. "We have to try something," I said.

Dad sighed, as if he had long ago lost patience with me. It seemed out of character for him. These days, almost everything he did seemed out of character. "Do what you got to do, I guess."

"So, you'll watch the kids?"

"Oh, I see how it is."

"We'll only be gone a couple hours," I said. "We'll bring back dinner, and you can have the night off. We'll put the kids to bed and everything," I said.

"I guess I can put that Wally movie on for them," Dad mumbled.

It cracked me up that Dad still thought the robot's name was Wally. "Okay, cool." I glanced at Lizzie and shrugged.

"Thanks, Daddy!" Lizzie sang, then blew him a kiss before jumping into Zach's van.

That at least got a partial smile from Dad, who said, "Sure thing, baby girl."

# 13

## ELI

After lunch, Lizzie, Zach, Logan, and I walked to the everything store, bought poster board and markers, then went back to our condo to create our masterpieces. Our signs were not all that varied. Mine said: "Water is a Human Right," Lizzie's said: "Water & Justice 4 All," Zach's said: "SAFE H2O 4 ALL," and Logan's said: "Clean Water for Everyone."

We carried our signs to the southeast corner of Crested Mountain Lane and Crested Butte Drive, right on the path to the restaurants, and started our protest. It was only a little after eleven, but people would be coming for lunch soon.

The first group stopped and talked to us. They were ticked about the lowered rations and the fact that Safe Water had locked us all in. They wished us luck and went on their way.

"You guys are going?" Logan asked them. "You're supposed to join in the protest!"

"Maybe later," one of the guys said, and the group continued on.

Three teen girls stopped next, staring and giggling at Zach. Lizzie stepped up and gave them the spiel, but they just laughed harder. I elbowed Zach, who invited the girls to join our protest. At this, they shrieked, clutched each other's arms, and ran off, laughing like lunatics.

"Girls are nuts," I said.

"It's not their fault," Logan said. "Zach distracted them with his face."

Lizzie slid her arms around Zach's waist and gave him a quick kiss. "Not only your face, babe." Another peck. "You're the whole package."

I grimaced and went back to waving my sign. Most people passed by in groups of three or four. We had good conversations, but some were actually annoyed by our protest.

"Dude, it's just until they get the new system rigged," one guy said. "We went without showers for two weeks at the height of the pandemic. You guys can't last a day without protesting?"

"I can understand them saying 'No showers' while they build new kiosks," Zach said. "But they had no real reason to turn off the drinking water spouts. People count on that water. Some only come once a week."

"Plus," I said, "if people don't speak up now, Admin will think they can do whatever they want. Someone has to keep them in check."

"Who? You?" the guy asked.

"Why not me?" I said.

The guy lifted his hands. "Whatever, man. Do what you got to do. Even if it's a stupid waste of time." He walked away.

Energy flashed through me. "It's never a waste of time to stand up for your rights," I yelled after him.

"Hey," Lizzie grabbed my arm. "We're here to make people think, to remind them they have brains of their own. We're not going to convince everyone."

I knew that, of course. "I just don't like it when people make it personal, you know?"

"That's *their* freedom of speech," Zach said.

"We can't make anyone agree with us," Lizzie said. "But maybe later, they'll think about what we said and see we were on to something."

"Hey!" A man in a straw cowboy hat approached us, grinning. I knew him, but couldn't pin why. "Quinn," he said. "Met you on the side of Interstate 17 on the drive north?"

"Oh, yeah." The moment came rushing back. He had pulled over to check on us after we'd found out Erin had died. I'd feared they were going to rob us. "You drive a gold GMC."

"That's right," he said. "What this?" He gestured to our signs.

We explained our protest.

"I'm with you, man," he said, "and I'd join you, if I could. But my wife would kill me. We both lost rations last week for loitering at the gate."

"You're one of the 'We are Americans!' crowd?" I asked.

Quinn lit up. "That's right. This place is a joke, but they've got Darby scared. She didn't like losing access to food. We had enough snacks to tide us over, but . . ."

"I don't blame her," Lizzie said. "That would be scary."

"We're not doing anything wrong," I assured her.

"Neither were we," Quinn said.

Despite Quinn's rejection, we did manage to recruit some more to our cause. Rick, Finn, and Warren from Los Angeles joined us, as did two girls named Mikayla and Laura, and another married couple from Colorado Springs. Bong stopped, and I introduced him around. He had no interest in what we were doing, though.

"Just want to keep my head down and survive," he said.

Which was fair. We were about to pack it up when Riggs and Josh came by.

"What are you freaks doing now?" Riggs asked.

I let Lizzie give the spiel this time. I admit it, I was jealous of how all the girls loved Riggs. I don't know if it was because he was rich, buff, had wing tattoos all over his back and arms, or wore that stupid puka shell necklace. It certainly wasn't because he was nice.

Riggs had always gotten under my skin, and I didn't trust myself to stay calm when talking to him. That became so much harder when he started laughing.

"You guys are so intense with the signs and the attitudes," he said.

"It does seem a little over the top," Josh said. "I mean, the Champions are trying to help people. They're doing the best they can."

"Helping people is one thing," I said to Josh. "Withholding water and keeping people prisoner is another. Do you know they're building a fence around this place?"

"They won't let anyone leave," Logan said.

"I'm sorry," Riggs said. "You got someplace better to be?"

"Anywhere is better than here," I said.

Riggs shook his head and urged Josh to move along. "You guys are losers," he said. "Go play some video games or something."

"It's unconstitutional that Admin would force people to purchase water or use it as a punishment," I said.

"Whoa, boy," Riggs said. "Getting almost fierce. Might want to take it down a few notches."

I clenched my jaw as Riggs grinned, amused by himself, then turned and walked away.

"You guys need to stop being idiots!" Logan yelled after them.

"*Logan*," I said.

Riggs turned back and strode toward Logan. "Say that again, punk," he said.

Logan ducked behind Zach, who had a few inches on Riggs and held out both hands. "We don't want any trouble."

"Sounds like baby face here does," Riggs said. "Better put a muzzle on him, or your little *assembly* won't be so peaceful now, will it?"

No one said anything. We all waited for Riggs to calm down.

We'd had enough experiences with his temper to know that silence usually worked. He finally gave us all one last rude hand gesture, then continued on. Josh shrugged at me as if to say, "What are you going to do?" then followed Riggs. He'd picked his side, and it wasn't ours.

Zach punched Logan's arm. "Don't be stupid! You'll get us all in trouble."

"Sorry," Logan said, rubbing his arm. "He just makes me so mad!"

"Oh, join the club," I said. "But you can't win an insult match with him. He's too mean."

After that, we had a few productive conversations. Our protest added four more to its ranks, and another group of six said they'd go get materials to make signs. I was feeling pretty good until two enforcer SUVs pulled up, which instantly scared off almost all those who'd joined us. Only Rick, Finn, and Warren remained.

The doors on both vehicles opened, and four enforcers got out. They ambled toward us, all wearing sunglasses. I recognized Vrahnos and Harvey; Harvey was in the lead. He pushed his sunglasses up onto his head as he came to a stop before us and folded his arms. The nametags on the other two cops said Miller and Wick.

"Another idealistic display, Mr. Montgomery?" Harvey said to Zach. "Why am I not surprised to find you in the middle of it?"

We all looked to Zach. "This is a peaceful demonstration," he said. "We think it's wrong to withhold water from anyone."

"Water is a basic human right," I added. "That Mr. Tracy would use it as a form of punishment violates the U.S. constitution."

"Is that so?" Officer Harvey asked, turning his glare my way.

"Yes," I said, sounding more confident than I felt. "Mr. Tracy made us sign a contract that said we'd abide by the laws of this country."

"That *you* would abide," Harvey said, tapping his gloved finger against my chest, "not that *they* would."

I frowned, thinking that over.

"That's not fair," said Rick from Los Angeles.

"What's not fair is that we've had *two* reports that you've been harassing people," said a different enforcer—Miller, according to his nametag. "That means you all get in the cars and come with us."

"You're arresting us?" I asked.

"That's right," Harvey said, pulling a set of handcuffs from his belt. "You going to come peacefully? Or are you going to make a scene?" He zeroed in on Zach. "Mr. Montgomery?"

Zach looked at me, so I dropped my sign and offered Harvey my hands, palms up. "Do what you've got to do," I said, staring him down, as politely, and defiantly, as I could.

Harvey smirked. "You got it, kid." He slapped the cuffs onto my left wrist, spun me around, and hooked my other hand behind my back.

I glanced at my sister, whose mouth was hanging open.

Well, *that* was unexpected.

•   •   •

We were searched and divided between the two vehicles. I ended up in Officer Harvey's SUV with Zach and Lizzie. Logan somehow got put in Officer Miller's rig with the guys from L.A. Sitting there with my arms cuffed behind me, I felt guilt, regret, and fear.

Until they drove us up the hill to the Champion compound.

"Why bring us here?" I asked Officer Vrahnos, who was driving.

"Mr. Tracy would like a word," he said.

I perked up, hopeful that we would get our chance to be heard.

The enforcers parked outside the front door and led us into Tracy's office. The man was sitting behind his desk, leaning back in his leather chair, hands folded over his stomach, talking softly with a very tall enforcer, who stood on the other side of the desk. If Tracy was Jack Skellington, the enforcer was Groot from

*Guardians of the Galaxy*, thick, intimidating, and silent.

"Ah, our little troublemakers have arrived," Tracy said, standing. "Come in, come in." He chuckled, as if we had been caught starting a food fight in the school cafeteria. "This is Captain Koval. He is the head of our enforcers. We have just worked out a system for bringing order to this place. Want to hear it?"

"We didn't mean to cause any trouble, sir," I said, eager to say my piece. "The First Amendment gives us the right to peacefully protest, so that's what we were doing. We think it's inhumane and unconstitutional to withhold water as punishment."

"I see. 'Water is a . . .'" Tracy gestured to Officer Miller, who was holding our signs. Miller held them up, and Tracy read from the one on the top of the stack, "'A human right.' That's very profound. But here's the thing. The United States of America died with ninety percent of the world's population, m'kay? So, while I applaud your knowledge of its constitution, that document no longer applies in this place."

Was this guy for real? "But we signed a contract," I said. "Nowhere in that contract did it say we couldn't leave or that we'd be forced to work."

"We have the right to amend our contract as necessary," Tracy said.

"Nowhere in your contract did it say you had the right to amend your contract as necessary," I said, raising my voice.

"Captain Koval and I, we make the laws around here. Water is what gets people to obey, so water is our great motivator, m'kay?"

"You can't just declare our country dead," Zach said.

"Who is going to stop me?" Tracy asked, looking genuinely puzzled. "A half dozen teenaged fundamentalists? I don't think so. In fact, I've brought you here for a reason. We're going to make an example of you."

"You're going to put us in jail?" Lizzie asked.

"Jail sounds so . . . oppressive," Tracy said. "The Champions want to keep things positive. They know y'all just got a little carried away. We all do. It's no secret that Loca Champion has been to rehab several times for his addiction to heroin. A little heroin is an adventure. Too much, and you need to get help. No shame in that."

"We're not trying to have an adventure," I said. "What you're doing is wrong."

"Now, see?" Tracy said. "You kids, you're addicted to complaining. Negativity. I see you want to make a difference—I can respect that—but you've got to learn the rules first. And since we are still writing the rules, you need to learn trust. Your offense is minor—I could let you off with a warning—but since I need people to understand how things work around here—and how serious Captain Koval and I are about enforcing order—I'm checking you all in to Rehab for twenty-four hours, so you can learn."

"So we can learn what?" I asked.

"What it means to be a resident of the Safe Water Mountain Refuge," Tracy said.

•   •   •

Rehab turned out to be in the Town Hall, a two-story brick building that was undergoing major construction on the outside and renovation inside. It currently had eight holding cells in its basement with bars across the front of each. The bars likely had been part of the original building, but I guessed the pine bunk beds, sage green wall paint, and the framed poster of Loca and Liberté were all new.

They separated us—each in our own cell. The cells ran side-by-side along one wall and shared a plaster interior wall, which made it impossible to see the adjacent cells, though we could talk to each other easily enough through the bars. Across the narrow corridor, the wall had been freshly painted and displayed more posters of LLC, each touting song lyrics.

An hour after we arrived, we were escorted to what one of the guards called group therapy. This was held upstairs in a conference room painted pale blue. A circular table surrounded by chairs was the only thing in the room with the exception of a dozen LLC posters, three on each wall. Seeing them all together, I noticed the words weren't merely song lyrics. They'd been carefully designed as propaganda.

"You are safe in the haven."
"Rage right. Rage together."
"We are survivors."
"Party. Every. Day."
"Glory to the Safe Water Mountain Refuge."
"LLC will keep you safe."
"Let there be peace, love, and EDM."
"Be gratifiable."
"Trust LLC."
"We keep the peace."
"Be beautiful and party."
"Find pleasure in life."

As we took our seats around the table, Zach whispered, "This feels like a dystopian novel."

"Right?" said Rick from L.A.

"That would be funny if this wasn't really happening," I said.

"I don't like that they're calling this Rehab," Lizzie said. "It's disrespectful to the purpose of real places of rehabilitation. People who seek help are brave, not criminals."

"Sit quietly until the counselor arrives," one of the guards said.

So we sat in silence, looking at each other. I wanted so badly to say something, but there were four guards. They'd positioned themselves behind our chairs. They were wearing guns and tasers, and I really didn't want to push my luck any further than I already had.

The door opened, and a tiny blonde woman breezed in. She was wearing a suit with a skirt and high-heeled shoes that looked out of place next to the armed guards.

"I'm Connie Lawler," she said, "Rehab counselor. I'm here to help you work past your issues."

"Being oppressed is not an issue," I said, "it's a fact."

So much for not pushing my luck.

"If you have something to say, you may raise your hand," she said, quirking a penciled eyebrow my way, "but do not speak unless spoken to and never interrupt me ag—"

"This is crap!" Logan said, standing. "We haven't done anything wrong. We don't deserve to be here. You don't have a right to keep us prisoner when we didn't even—"

Something clicked, and Logan grunted, his face contorted in shock and pain. One of the guards had tased him. When the clicking stopped, Logan fell back onto his chair, then right off the side. Those of us at the table all jumped up at once, but the other guards trained their tasers on us. We froze.

"Sit down," Connie said.

We sat.

"I will have order in this room," Connie said. "You cannot grow and heal mentally if you are being rebellious. And if you want to stay out of Rehab, I suggest you pay attention and participate. Because if I don't sign your dismissal, your sentence will be lengthened. The Safe Water Mountain Refuge is not in the practice of putting dangerous residents on the street."

So much wrong.

"The Champions seek to create a society of freedom and joy," Connie said. "To succeed, they require residents to get along with one another. No judging. No expressing hostile ideas."

I raised my hand.

Again that thin eyebrow went up. "Yes, Mr. McShane?"

"You want conformity."

She pinned me with a fake smile. "We want kindness. Over the next day, you will learn ways to react to all situations with kindness. You will learn to adjust your attitude. To be positive. Only then will I allow you to reenter society."

So this was attitude rehabilitation. Our little protest had been too much free thinking for these people. We could do exactly what they said, or we could stay here in Rehab.

Again I wished I'd gone with Reinhold.

•   •   •

I honestly couldn't say that any of us did *well* in Connie Lawler's Rehab. We pandered, telling the woman what she wanted to hear. I don't think she believed us for a second, but that didn't seem to matter. The Safe Water Mountain Refuge didn't care what you believed. It cared about conformity. As long as we obeyed, we were "free" to go about our business.

After our community service, of course, which turned out to be porta-potty duty.

We were driven out to a field of portable bathrooms, given yellow hazmat suits, and taught how to first vacuum out the toilets—I was horrified to discover—then how to wash them down with high-pressure hoses. The water in the tanks had been pumped out of the East River, hence the hazmat suits to protect us from potential HydroFlu contamination. They also protected us from the smell, which our trainer told us was a lucky coincidence.

"Before HydroFlu, this was a hold-your-nose cleanup job," he said.

It was still beyond disgusting. As I held my vacuum hose down the toilet hole, I could feel the thing shudder as it sucked up what was inside. My hose got clogged several times, and I had to reverse the flow. Some of the toilets had been abused: graffitied, cut up with knives, burned. Three of the two dozen I worked on somehow had the walls, floors, and seats covered with feces.

It was a horror I wished I'd never been forced to experience.

We were released at the end of twenty-four hours and told we were all docked our food and water rations for the week, and that we needed to get to our jobs, which Lizzie and I were already late for. I had to change into my uniform, and Lizzie needed to take the kids with her, so we walked back to the condo.

Dad lost it when he saw us, ranting about our promise of only being gone two hours and how irresponsible we were to get ourselves in trouble. I told him not to yell, and Lizzie tried to calm him down. But Dad just kept shouting. I gave up trying to reason with him and let him vent.

To be fair, he did shift gears and show concern for our

welfare for about three minutes before he lost it again. "Where are all the adults, is what I want to know?" he said, pacing in the living room. "Hannah's gone now, and here I am, a single parent of thirteen!"

"What's Hannah got to do with anything?" Lizzie asked.

"She offered to help with the kids," Dad said. "Anytime, she said. "And she didn't constantly go off gallivanting and leave me to babysit."

"That's not fair," Lizzie said, her voice cracking. "I take the kids with me almost every day."

"Hey, hey," I said, coming alongside her. "I don't think he means it."

"Don't defend him! He's supposed to take care of us. He's the dad!" Lizzie wriggled out of my grasp and fled the apartment. Zach went after her, followed by Logan.

"Where are you going?" I yelled after Logan, but the coward just ran.

Dad ranted a bit more, so I did my best to get Davis, Shyla, and Cree dressed and ready to go. I'd never seen my dad like this. All while I'd been at the jail and cleaning toilets I'd imagined him being outraged about what had happened to us. I never expected this. Maybe he'd been holding it inside for too long.

I somehow managed to get the kids out the door and over to the girls' condo, then I went back and got Dad to leave with me for work. I drove, and Dad continued to whine the entire way. I stopped the van outside the Department of Water and Sanitation, left the keys in the ignition, and said, "Bye, Dad."

I shut the door on his mumbled reply and walked toward the building. I glanced back and saw that he was still sitting in the passenger's side of the Odyssey, but now he was bawling.

I sighed, clueless about how to deal with him, and went to work.

# 14

## HANNAH
## AUGUST 11

Tuesday afternoon, I was the only one at the condo when Eli dropped by with a paper sack that smelled delicious.

"Jaylee's not here," I said.

He groaned and walked farther inside. "Of course she's not." He dropped the sack on the counter. "This is for Lizzie. Dad sent me with his wristband to get some sandwiches for dinner."

"That was thoughtful." I joined him at the counter.

"More like necessary. You heard we lost our weekly rations?"

"I heard you spent the night in jail."

"Rehab, actually. Turns out the Champions seek to create a society of freedom and joy, which requires their residents to get along with one another. No judging. No expressing hostile ideas. No independent thought."

"Did you express independent thought?"

"I said water was a human right and shouldn't be withheld as a punishment."

"They thought that was hostile?"

"They did." He went on to describe everything that had happened to them. I'd gotten parts of it from Lizzie that morning, but Eli was a much more thorough storyteller. I watched him closely as he talked, missing the deep conversations we'd had while driving across Arizona.

"Using the portable bathrooms for community service is actually pretty smart," I said.

"Yeah, *if* we'd done something wrong," Eli said. "Would you have protested with us yesterday? If you hadn't been working?"

"Sure. I don't like the use of withholding water as part of sentencing, and I can't believe what that officer said about us having to abide by the laws of the United States while they don't have to."

"It's scary, right?" Eli said.

"Very much so." I honestly didn't want to think too much about it. Life was finally starting to make some sense with my job at the hospital and talking to Dixie. I didn't need to dig up more things to worry about.

"But you want to stay here," Eli said. "Why?"

I looked at him, at those deep brown eyes that seemed to be judging me for some reason. "You ask Jaylee that same question?"

"Wow. Bringing up Jaylee with all kind of attitude. What's *that* about?"

I looked away from him. "There was no attitude," I said, hoping to cover my blunder.

"Well, I *know* why Jaylee wants to stay," Eli said. "But I was asking you."

I stared at him, wondering why he felt this conversation was necessary. "There's security here. There's purpose. Out there, living at Andy's house, toting guns everywhere . . . that's day-today survival, which is honestly terrifying. Here, we can have a society. We can serve each other and care for people."

"Like you take care of Cree?" he said.

Blood drained from my face at his accusatory tone. "Excuse me?"

"He asks for you every morning, every night. When was the last time you saw him?"

I blinked, and my bottom lip trembled. I didn't want to hurt anyone. Least of all Cree. "Friday, I guess."

"Four days is a long time for neighbors. You avoiding us?"

"No. I'm tired, okay? My job is exhausting. What's with the third degree?"

"I'm just saying, he misses you. We all do. My dad was going on and on about how you're the only other adult and you aren't around more."

"What?" My voice came out much louder than I'd intended. I *had* been avoiding Seth ever since our awkward conversation. "Look, I'm happy to take the kids when I can. It, uh . . . it just felt weird with me and your dad together so much with the rest of you gone." Which wasn't fair. Seth had always been totally nice. I was the one who went and made things weird.

Eli seemed to consider this. "I get that," he said. "Plus, Dad isn't the most pleasant person to be around these days. Sorry we ditched you."

Footsteps creaked overhead, descending the stairs slowly. My skin tingled, and my pulse increased, suddenly throbbing in my ears.

Oh no.

He was coming.

Brandon.

"Hannah?"

I could feel the soreness of fresh bruises on my body, the pressure of his fingers on my throat.

I had to get away.

Now.

So I did. I went away where I would be safe. Where Brandon couldn't find me.

"What's she doing?"

"Hannah, will you look at me?" Someone touched my hand, and I snapped it away.

"Don't touch me!" I yelled.

"Maybe I should call Zach."

"Hannah, it's Eli. Can you look at me?"

Eli.

Eli . . . ?

"Hannah?"

I focused on the sound of his voice. "Eli?"

"Yeah, that's right." A finger waved in front of my eyes, tapped the end of my nose, then waved again. I focused on it and finally saw Eli there in front of me. He grinned. "Hey."

We were sitting on the floor in the kitchen. I gasped, confused. Shame flooded my body with heat. Why was I on the floor? Behind Eli, Krista stood looking down, arms crossed, watching me warily, her poufy blonde curls tamed by a headband.

What had I done? "I'm sorry," I said.

Eli frowned, puzzled. "What for? You aren't feeling well?"

I glanced at Krista, not wanting to explain myself to her.

She rolled her eyes. "You guys are weird. I'm going to the bathroom."

Once she'd left, I felt compelled to explain. "Sometimes I hear a sound that reminds me of him, and I get afraid. Sometimes it's a smell. My boss at the hospital wears the same kind of deodorant. Old Spice. The briefest scent of it makes my skin crawl."

"Do I smell?" Eli asked.

A breathy laugh escaped me. "No, it was the stairs. Krista coming down, I guess. My old apartment was two stories, and I could tell by how his footsteps creaked on the stairs what kind of a mood he was in. Sometimes I'd hide in the closet and wait for him to leave."

Gosh. Why was I telling him all this? It was pathetic!

"Lizzie mentioned you've had a couple more nightmares," Eli said.

Great. I tried to make it sound normal, like it happened to

everyone. "Oh, I've been having bad dreams for a long time," I said. "A guy like Brandon, he gets into your head."

"That sucks," he said.

Familiar emotion bubbled up within me. Despair. Soon it would come out in tears. I didn't want to look any weaker in front of Eli than I already did, so I stood and walked out from behind the counter.

"I think I'm going to go for a walk," I said, eager to flee the awkward scene I'd created.

"Wait." Eli followed, eyebrows sinking low over his eyes. "Um . . . I need your help with something."

"What?"

He hesitated like he was having second thoughts, then: "I want to break up with Jaylee."

The words brought such a shock that I could tangibly feel the awkwardness and despair fall away.

"You do?" I said.

He winced, his nose wrinkling in the most adorable way. "For about a week now."

Don't smile. I couldn't smile. Not yet. "What happened?" I asked.

He shrugged. "I don't know. We're just too different, I guess."

And I'd been worried she'd break his heart. Turned out she'd just bored him.

"I don't know how to end it. We're never alone. Someone is always there. Antônia, Krista, *Riggs*. The few times I thought I had a moment to try, she won't shut up long enough for me to say anything. I don't know what to do."

I fought hard to hold back a grin. This made me so very happy. "I'm not exactly a pro at breaking up with people," I said. "Maybe just blurt it out the first chance you get?"

"Won't that hurt her feelings?"

"I don't know if people can break up without someone getting their feelings hurt."

"I was afraid of that. I just don't want to make her cry. But I honestly don't think she likes me enough that this will even make her sad."

"I'm sure that's not true," I said.

The door opened, and Jaylee ran in. "Eli! Krista said you were back."

She threw herself at him. He caught her around the waist and had to take a step back to keep his balance. She started kissing him like he'd just returned from the front lines of a major war. For wanting to break up with the girl, Eli wasn't putting up much of a fight at the moment.

Antônia and Krista arrived seconds later. Krista rolled her eyes at Eli and Jaylee, then dug into the bag of sandwiches Eli had left on the counter.

Eli broke the kiss to stop Krista. "That's for Lizzie," he said.

Krista rolled her eyes and shoved the bag away.

"I was so worried about you," Jaylee said, tugging at the neckline of his shirt.

Eli frowned. "You were?"

"Yes!" She whacked his arm. "You guys just vanished. I told you not to protest."

"No, you didn't," he said.

"Yes, I did. I said the Champions are nice, and it was rude to protest them."

"We weren't protesting the Champions," Eli said. "We were protesting the fact that they—"

"Yeah, we know," Krista said. "You don't have to keep telling us."

"Can we leave?" Antônia asked. "Cristobal said to come at five thirty, which it's almost gonna be."

"We're going to Josh's place," Jaylee said.

"I'm kind of tired," Eli said. "I worked all day and didn't get much sleep last—"

"It's just for a couple hours," Jaylee said. "I have to work at eight. Tonight is my first shift."

"Where?" Eli and I asked at the same time.

"The Avalanche," Jaylee beamed. "Riggs got me hired as a hostess."

"Of course he did," Eli mumbled.

"Eli has a great story about Rehab," I said to Jaylee, hoping to urge this breakup along. "He can tell you about it on the walk over. Or you could talk about something else."

"Just don't tell me about the bathrooms," Jaylee said, pulling Eli by the hand toward the door. "Lizzie already grossed me out about that."

"I didn't hear it," Antônia said, following. "Eli? What happened about the bathrooms?"

Eli made a face at me as the girls dragged him out. It didn't look like he would get his moment alone with Jaylee on the walk over, which I suddenly found hysterical.

He would figure it out eventually, though. He would break up with Jaylee, and then he and I could be close friends again. The prospect left me feeling quite pleased.

•   •   •

I was sitting at the nursing station, reading a patient's chart, when Monica's voice came over the intercom.

"Code blue to admitting. Code blue to admitting."

A code blue signified a medical emergency. I started toward the front of the hospital, unsure if I'd be needed or not. In bigger hospitals, there was a separate ambulance entrance where EMTs brought in patients. This little hospital only had one way in.

"Hannah!" Susan jogged out of an exam room up ahead. "Run grab a SAFE kit and meet Dr. Carter in Exam Room 2. EMTs are bringing in a possible IPV."

A chill ran up my arms. A SAFE kit—also known as a rape kit—was used to gather and preserve physical evidence after an alleged assault. I quickly made my way to the supply room and brought the SAFE kit to Exam Room 2 where Linsey, Dr. Vicky Carter, and Dixie Wells, the psychologist, were in place, waiting.

"Everyone's so calm," I said.

"The key to emergency medicine is to make it look easy," Dr. Carter said. She was in her forties, the tallest and widest of the three doctors, and always wore her hair in a ponytail. "Plus patients take on the energy of those around them. A calm, confident environment communicates to patients that they're in safe hands, despite their predicament."

Susan strode into the room, the paramedics on her heels, pushing a gurney. Today it was Zach and Amber. They transferred the patient to the hospital bed, and Linsey and I worked to get her stable with some IV fluids. The patient was dark-haired and pale—didn't look any older than me. Her face was swollen and patched with gauze. Swaths of her hair had been torn out.

"Moment of silence," Dr. Carter said, and the voices stopped. "Report?"

Zach met Dr. Carter's gaze. "We have a hypotensive twenty-three-year-old female with severe bruising to the head and neck and a possible fractured cheek. The patient was assaulted by her partner approximately thirty minutes ago. We stabilized her neck and tended lacerations on temple, cheek, and forearms to stop bleeding.

"She is conscious and alert, but slow to respond. Vital signs are BP 102/88, pulse 122, and irregular respirations 24. Head-to-toe finds the cheek, temple, and both forearms as well as minor abrasions. Visible signs of bruising on the neck. Old ligature marks on both wrists. Might have been rope burns? No other significant findings. Nothing on the chest, abdomen, or legs. Lungs are clear. No significant medical history that we're aware of."

Dr. Carter gazed down on the patient. "Where is the partner now?"

"Unknown," Zach said. "Her friend called us. The partner wasn't in the apartment when we arrived. The friend promised to file a report with the enforcers and give them a description."

"Let's hope the friend did," Dr. Carter said. "Thank you. We'll take it from here."

I met Zach's eyes, nodded, then got back to the patient. We did a portable chest x-ray and bedside ultrasound, but found no internal bleeding. As we were doing all this, Dr. Carter did a complete head-to-toe examination and talked with the patient, who was named Natalie. When Dr. Carter asked what happened,

Natalie defended her partner.

"He didn't mean it," she said. "I made him angry."

I shivered, repulsed that I had said those same words before and actually believed them.

"Has he done this before?" Dr. Carter asked.

"Not like this. He would never hurt me on purpose."

"He needs to be charged with assault," Dr. Carter said.

"Oh, no no no," Natalie said, tears filling her eyes. "I can't do that."

"Well, the EMTs did fine work," Dr. Carter said, agreeing with Zach's assessment.

"We should get that handsome one in here and trained as a nurse," Susan said.

I thought to smile at that remark, but I was transfixed by Natalie. Two lumps had swelled on her forehead, looking like twin golf balls trying to escape her skull. The wounds Zach had mentioned on her cheek and over her left eye had been temporarily patched with gauze. Her scalp was bleeding where hair had been torn out. The extensive bruising on her forearms were all too familiar defensive wounds.

I folded my arms and rubbed my index finger over the scar on the back of my forearm. It came from the time Brandon had tried to hit me with a pewter picture frame. I'd lifted my arm to protect my head, and the outer edge of molded roses and leaves had broken the skin through to the bone and fractured my ulna shaft. I'd had to throw out the frame after that.

"Hannah?" Dr. Carter said.

Her voice snapped me back to the present, and I found her perfectly made-up eyes fixed on me. "Yes, doctor?"

"Vitals are stable. Let's take Natalie for a CT scan."

Linsey and I pushed the bed toward the CT room. There Dr. Carter walked me through taking scans of Natalie's head, neck, chest, and abdomen, what Dr. Carter called the trauma combo. The CT scan verified Zach's theory of a fracture. When we finished, Dr. Carter asked me to take Natalie back to the exam room and stitch up the laceration over her eye. But as I wheeled her down the hall, I didn't know if I could. My hands were gripping the bed, but they were shaking. Everything about this girl was bringing back horrible memories and the feelings that came with them.

I pushed Natalie inside Exam Room 2 and got the bed situated and hooked up, then went to the cupboard to grab a suture kit.

The door swung shut. I turned to ask Dr. Carter whether I should use silk or Vicryl suture, but a man stood there. He was middle-aged and haggard, breath unsteady and hitched. Eyes veined in red met mine, and he grinned.

"I come for Nat," he said, walking toward the bed. "Time to go home, baby."

"Oh," was all Natalie managed to say. The girl looked terrified.

I stepped in his way. "She needs stitches," I said, chin trembling. "Before she can go."

He stopped, toe-to-toe with me, and glared down, his porous, pink nose almost touching mine. "She'll heal on her own."

His breath, hot and sour, filled my senses and pulled loose something deep inside me. I felt myself sway. "No, sir," I said. "We need to get those stitches in. And she needs her antibiotics so that cut won't get infected."

Large and powerful hands shoved me aside. I stumbled, struck my elbow against the computer cart. The man advanced toward the bed. I lunged after him, managed to slip past. I threw myself across Natalie's body, grabbing the handles on the opposite side of the bed. I pressed the nurse call button with my thumb. The phone was behind me, on the other side of the bed, so for now, this was the best I could do.

"Get away from her!" The man tore at my back but found no purchase. An arm encircled my waist. A hand fisted my hair. He pulled.

"Yo!" Linsey's voice. "Get off!"

I held tight as my assailant released his grip, drawn into a scuffle with Linsey.

Beneath me, Natalie whimpered.

"I'm sorry," I told her. "It's going to be okay."

I glanced back. Linsey had pinned the man's arms behind him. I grabbed the phone and dialed zero.

Monica's voice. "Safe Water Mountain—"

"Send security to Exam Room 2!" I said. "We have an intruder."

"On it!" The line went dead, then I heard Monica's voice over the intercom. "Strong man to Exam Room 2. Strong man to Exam Room 2."

Before security could arrive, Dr. Bayles walked in. He glanced at me and the patient, then to Linsey and the man, who were still struggling.

"Want to get me five mg of Midazolam, doctor?" Linsey asked, his voice pressed thin.

Instead of fetching a syringe, Dr. Bayles hauled back and punched the man. Once. Twice. Three times.

"Yo!" Linsey said, sinking to his knees to protect the man's head as he passed out. "What you do that for?"

"Because I didn't know just then where to find the Midazolam," Dr. Bayles said.

I sank to the floor and pushed back into the corner of the exam room. Hugged my knees. Hid my face. I stayed there. Just stayed. Time passed. I heard voices. Movement. Everything was muted and distant. I'd left that place of chaos behind. Wanted no part of it.

A voice spoke in my ear. Low and warm. Male.

It tried again.

"Hannah? Are you hurt?"

Linsey.

Someone touched my arm. I jolted. Someone keened. I think it was me.

"Hey, I'm not going to hurt you."

Hands on both sides of my face. "Hannah, look at me. Lift your head. Hey." Hands forced my face to rise. Linsey, looking at me. Eyes brown and warm. Kind.

"He hurt her," I said, my voice more air than sound.

"He did. But he's gone now."

"Hannah's ex-boyfriend was abusive," someone said.

Linsey turned his head. "What do you know? Just clean that up and get out of here."

"Hannah and I are friends," the someone went on. "A bunch of us came up here together. She lives next door to me."

Logan.

"Her ex was this guy named Brandon," Logan said. "A crazy dude. Chased us all through Arizona until—"

"Logan!" I said, coming back to myself, desperate to stop him before he told Linsey about what happened on the bridge. I found his frizzy blond head over Linsey's shoulder. "That's my story to tell. Not yours."

His squinty little eyes met mine, and he nodded. "Sure, Hannah. You got it. Just trying to help."

I wiped my hair out of my face and straightened. The bed was empty. "Where's my patient?"

"We moved her to a clean room," Linsey said. "You okay?"

"I'm fine."

Linsey took hold of my hands. They were still shaking. "How about we get you up on this bed, give you a little oxygen?"

"No need." I just needed to stop thinking about it. His power. His rage.

Linsey pulled a chair over and helped me sit. The next thing I knew he was holding an O2 mask over my nose and mouth.

This was crazy. What was the matter with me? I was a professional. I needed to snap out of this before they fired me, and I ended up working as a janitor with Logan.

Yet I stayed put and breathed in and out and listened to Linsey's deep voice. I closed my eyes and saw that man glaring down at me. Saw Jason strike him. Saw the bruises on Natalie's forearms. Defensive wounds. She'd tried—and failed—to protect her face. Again I fingered the scar on my forearm. It was healed. I was okay.

*Stop it, Hannah*, I told myself. *This is ridiculous.*

I don't know how long I sat there with Linsey, circling the drain of horrible memories, but eventually he took away the O2, and Dr. Carter returned with Dixie. The psychologist was a petite

Black woman with chocolate brown skin, spiky blue hair, and cat-eye glasses.

"I need you to tell Dixie what happened," Dr. Carter said. "She'll be talking with the patient, but it would help her to have your side of the story."

That seemed reasonable, so I told Dixie about the man and how I'd tried to protect my patient and called for help.

"Have you ever been hurt by someone, Hannah?" Dixie asked me.

I glanced toward the door, but Dr. Carter had gone. I might have known she'd use the situation to coerce me to talk with the psych. But I *had* lost it in front of Linsey, so lying wouldn't help my case. "A long time ago," I said, bouncing my knees.

"Can you tell me the signs that a patient is suffering from post-traumatic stress?"

I frowned. "You think I have PTSD?"

"Honey, this is the end of the world," Dixie said. "I'd be shocked if you didn't."

I nodded, my mind racing through all I knew about PTSD from books and my psych classes in college. It had never occurred to me that I might be suffering such a side effect from what I'd gone through with Brandon.

"There's no shame in telling your story," Dixie said. "There's also no charge to your credits. Many people find talking to someone quite helpful. Why don't we make an appointment, so we can talk in private? Would that be okay?"

I didn't want to. It felt like admitting weakness, but under the circumstances . . . Two incidents in as many days. First with Krista and the stairs, then here. Could I really be suffering from PTSD? Tears flooded my eyes, and I looked away. "I guess that would be fine."

We made plans to talk tomorrow, then Dixie left. Susan came in and told me to take my lunch break. I needed some fresh air, so I walked over to The Divy and ordered a salad. The lettuce seemed a little wilted, like my mood. Were they going to grow new vegetables here? I remembered the seeds Eli had filled his cart with at the Ace Hardware store, and I got choked up again.

What if Seth told his son what I'd said about marriage that day? Eli had forgiven me for stabbing him. I didn't think he'd forgive me for suggesting his dad and I get married.

I suddenly felt like a complete failure as a human being and all alone in the world. Everywhere I went I humiliated myself. I couldn't do anything right.

My lunch passed by quickly, and I returned to the hospital and checked the board.

Dr. Bayles approached the nurse's station. "Hannah. That was pretty wild, earlier, huh? How you doing?"

"Fine," I said, unable to meet his eyes. I kept seeing him strike that man. One punch I could excuse. But three? Was it a sign? Was Dr. Bayles a violent man?

Another flash of his perfectly white teeth. "Glad to hear it. I'll be in my office if you need to talk."

No, I did not need to talk with that man. I watched him walk away, my knee bouncing wildly. I hadn't been this anxious in a long time. I knew Brandon was gone, and I was safe. I wanted to calm down, but my body didn't seem to be getting the message.

• • •

I'd scheduled my appointment with Dixie before my shift Friday afternoon. Her office was near Dr. Bayles's office. I hoped he didn't see me around Dixie's domain. While psychology had been my favorite college courses, for some reason, I didn't want anyone to know I was here.

I found her office door open and peeked inside. "Hello?"

"Come on in!" Dixie called.

I entered what looked like a small living room. It had thick beige carpeting, a blue suede sofa, a brown leather wingchair, and a wooden rocking chair. The walls were covered in bookshelves and paintings of tranquil, outdoor locations.

Dixie stood from where she'd been sitting on an office chair parked beside a small rolling desk. Today she wore a blue polka dot blouse that matched the color of her hair.

She shook my hand. "It's so nice to see you, Hannah. How

are you?"

"Fine. How does this work?"

"We talk. You tell me about yourself, your family, growing up, your ex-boyfriend. Whatever you feel like sharing."

I told her about my mother, my father, his jobs, my brother—how my parents had practically refused to grieve John's death. She asked me a lot of questions.

"It seems to me that your parents made love conditional," Dixie said. "Their lack of appropriate boundaries set a poor example for you, and in turn, when you needed to be able to set boundaries with them and with your boyfriend, you didn't know how."

That seemed profound. "I really didn't."

She went on to talk about codependency, which I had always thought was only something that happened to addicts, but Dixie defined it as an imbalance in a relationship.

"Your parents had such high expectations, it left you unable to make your own choices. It also gave them an unhealthy reliance on your obedience. They should have been able to feel your love apart from your actions. Relying on your obedience for their sense of identity was codependent behavior, and it was harmful to you all. Does that feel like it fits?"

"It does," I said. "I've always been too eager to please everyone. I say yes even when I don't want to. How do I stop that?"

"By setting some boundaries. We each have our own space that we are in charge of. It's healthy to stay in our own little yard, responsible for our space. What's unhealthy is when someone continually tells us to come into their yard and do work. Or when we start looking into other people's yards and telling them what they should be doing over there. Or going so far as to trespass in other people's yards to do things for them. Your parents came into your yard and set up everything and told you how it was to be managed and expected you to do things just as they decreed. And you're used to people doing that—calling the shots in your life. That's not a healthy relationship based on mutual love, trust, and respect, is it?"

"No," I said. "It's actually pretty depressing."

"We're not here to depress you, Hannah, or to demonize or judge your parents. They did the best they knew how. I'm here to walk with you into your past and help you see it in a different way. With a new perspective and tools like setting boundaries for yourself and staying in your own yard, then we can work on finding healthier ways to respond when you get triggered by life. How does that sound?"

I liked it very much.

# 15

ELI
AUGUST 16

The days passed by in a blur of sanitation engineering. My arms and legs were still sore, but my fingers were bending a little better now. I didn't dare remove the splint for fear I'd make them worse. I was looking forward to Hannah's promise of "healed in eight weeks."

We still hadn't heard from Reinhold and Kimama. If I thought about it too much, it made me sick, so I shoved my concern down with grieving my mother's death. If I kept this up, I was going to turn myself into a robot.

On Sunday, since everyone was off work for once, Lizzie tried to put on a spur-of-the-moment church service, but Dad, who'd gone up to sleep in Cree's bed after everyone was up, refused to come down. This sent Lizzie into a rage, then into a puddle of tears.

"It's not fair," she said. "I miss her too, but he's the parent. He's supposed to be able to handle this stuff better than us."

"Grief is different for everyone," Hannah said.

"I don't think he knows how to live without Mom," I said.

Lizzie's face crumpled. "Neither do I."

Zach hugged her while she cried.

"I have an idea," Hannah said. "When I was in college, a friend of mine lost her mom, and they had a grief ceremony. I remember wishing we could have done something like that for my brother."

"What's a grief ceremony?" I asked.

"Beforehand, everyone wrote down humorous or touching stories about the mom. They also wrote down last words they wanted to say. Then they got together and read them out loud, to share with each other. My friend told me it gave her more closure than the funeral since she didn't feel like she could really share honestly there."

Lizzie sniffled. "None of our people got funerals."

"I like this idea," I said. "We could all do it. Take turns sharing about the family we lost." It would be a lot of crying, but maybe that's what everyone needed—what Dad needed.

Everyone agreed, then they sent me upstairs to tell Dad about it.

"Not interested," he said.

That ticked me off, and I flipped on the lights and yanked the blanket off him. "I'm not asking, Dad. I'm telling you. This is what's happening. We get that you're sad. We're sad too."

A long moment of silence passed. Then Dad said, "It's an ache I can't explain."

"I know. I don't want you to stop being sad, but we need to do this. Give everyone a chance to honor those they loved. To say goodbye. Everyone likes this idea, so we're doing it."

"All right," he said. "Today?"

"Yeah," I said, deciding right then. "Today."

●　　●　　●

We invited Josh, Cristobal, and Riggs to the impromptu grief ceremony. Josh and Cristobal came, but Riggs declined. Lizzie put together a list of names, then passed out slips of paper so we could write down memories about everyone we knew. It was four in the afternoon by the time we got started. Lizzie drew names from a bowl to see who would go first. We started with Josh, but he didn't have much to say about his family. I was glad so many of us knew his parents and brother and could share stories. That got him to open up, and he said a lot more. At one point, I glanced at my watch and realized we'd been talking about Josh's family for forty-five minutes. We had twelve more groups to go.

This was going to be a long night, but that was okay.

Zach's name came up next, and we spent just as long on his family. After that we did Antônia's aunt, then Logan, then Jaylee. Lizzie had added Erin and Mark's names, as well, so we took turns sharing about them too.

When Davis and Shyla's names came up, things got a lot quieter. Davis told about how his dad liked to watch football and take him bowling, and Shyla had drawn a family portrait, which she explained in detail. They were also mourning the loss of a dachshund named Bitsy. Krista shared a story about their mom, who had worked with hers at a local elementary school. The rest of us had nothing to add, and we were done in ten minutes. I felt bad about it, but the kids seemed pleased.

Lizzie drew us next, which brought tears to my eyes from anticipation alone. Lizzie talked about how Mom taught her to cook *posole*, a soup we had on special occasions. "Mama would always play music while she was cooking and dance around the kitchen. She taught me to dance too."

"And if Dad caught her, he would dance with her," I added.

"Yes!" Lizzie said, eyes shining.

"She danced when she was cleaning too," Dad said.

I laughed, remembering Mom dancing with rubber gloves on her hands. "When I was little, she had to know where I was at all times, even though I was always with Zach or Logan."

"You didn't have any other friends," Zach said.

"Ha ha," I said.

"When I was at your place," Zach said, "your mom made sure I was never hungry or thirsty. She was always giving me food."

"Tacos," Logan said. "Her tacos were the best in the world."

We all agreed. "She made me look her in the eyes when she was talking to me," I said. "She told me it was important and respectful to engage with people that way."

"She had beautiful eyes," Dad said.

"Where did you meet her?" Antônia asked.

Dad told how he'd met Mom in high school. I was proud of how well he was holding it together.

"Leti inspired me every minute of every day," he said. "I loved her strength, her passion for life. And the way she smiled at me—it made the whole world more beautiful."

The ceremony continued, next with Hannah, who was even quieter than Josh. She lauded her father's work ethic and how her mother valued a good education. I got the feeling Hannah didn't have a close relationship with her parents. Through her whole turn, she twisted her grandmother's wedding ring as if she had to wind herself up to keep going. Since she'd mentioned she wished she could have done this for her brother, I asked her about him, and she had much more to say.

By the time we finished, it was after midnight. We were all emotionally drained. Josh, Cristobal, and the girls left. We put the kids to bed, then Dad, Zach, Logan, and I stayed up even later, telling more stories and talking until the early hours of Monday morning.

•　　•　　•

We rode to the morning party in the van and made our way to the back of the grassy lawn. The new showers had been finished—twenty stalls instead of ten. We found Josh and Riggs in the back with some of their new friends. Jaylee, Antônia, and Krista joined them, and I stayed with Zach, Lizzie, my dad, and the kids. I was too tired to care that Jaylee was flirting with Riggs or to bother trying to break up with her today. The late night had been worth it, but right now it hurt.

The morning party theme music started, and Tracy's voice came over the loud speakers. "Gooood morning, my friends! How is everyone today?"

The crowd cheered. I tried to tune it all out. Morning parties were getting old fast.

Tracy reminded us all that we were not to climb the mountain until the construction of the fence was completed. "It's just too dangerous for y'all up there, m'kay?"

Too dangerous for us to find out that they were building a dam.

"This week we are leaving the voucher system behind," Tracy said. "If you haven't already, you can pick up your new wristbands in the lobby of your building. You'll need to activate them on the Grid before you can use them. You cannot eat, take showers, or claim drinking water without your wristband, so be careful not to lose it. They also glow in the dark, which will be great for concert nights, trust me."

"I got mine!" Shyla said, holding her arm in the air.

We'd picked them up this morning at Jaylee's insistence. The technology was pretty impressive, though I didn't like that they could probably track our every move.

Next came a video, shot like a docudrama, where Tracy was interviewing the Champions about their dreams for this town.

"We want this to be home for everyone," Liberté said in her thick French accent.

"Not only that," her brother added, "we want to help people who struggle."

Zach's face appeared on the jumbo screen, up close. He was in the group room at the rehabilitation center, saying something, but the words had been drowned out by the electronic score. The camera flashed between Zach's face and Connie Lawler's.

"They recorded us?" I said, dread coiling inside me.

"Apparently," Zach said.

"Zach, you're on the screen!" Jaylee said, appearing between us and grabbing his arm.

"I see my shoulder," Lizzie said. "And the back of that guy's head. Warren, was it?"

"That's not legal," Logan said. "None of us signed waivers."

"Like they care about any laws but their own." I glanced at my dad. "Can you believe this place?"

Dad stepped beside Zach and squeezed his shoulder. "It's nice to see you're getting the help you need, Zachary," he said.

Zach made a face. "Ha ha."

I thought it was even nicer to see my dad make a joke.

The video went on to show a montage of people rocking out at concerts, eating together at restaurants in town, and shopping. It flashed a close up of Zach smiling as the words "Help is only a click away" appeared at the bottom of the screen.

"They're seriously making me look like some kind of addict," Zach said.

"When did you smile in that place?" I asked him.

"Lizzie had been making faces behind Connie's back," he said.

Lizzie put her fingers in her mouth and stretched it way too wide.

Everyone laughed, except me. I didn't think this was very funny.

Now we were back to Loca and Liberté on the big screen.

"If you are struggling to adapt to life in Safe Water, the Rehabilitation Center is here to help," Liberté said.

"We want everyone to feel at home here," Loca said. "If you are having a hard time, stop by the Admin office and let us know. There is no shame . . . no judgment. Let us help you find pleasure in life."

"They want people to check themselves into that place?" I asked.

"If they build a positive reputation for Rehab," Lizzie said, "when people end up there, they won't feel so bad about it."

"They'll probably be excited," I said.

"Oh, cool! This is that place we saw on that video at the MP," Zach said in a high-pitched voice. "I'm so happy to be here."

"Something like that," I said.

"Look!" Jaylee said. "They're talking about houses."

". . . called the Lottery Draw," Tracy said. "As houses get cleared for habitation, residents will randomly be chosen to relocate. Winners will receive a tour of the available houses and be able to choose one. There is no obligation, of course. If you'd rather stay in your current housing, that option is yours. This is totally free, totally random. There's nothing you can do to increase or decrease your odds of getting chosen, m'kay? We have eight houses ready. Eight of you have been notified. Your wristbands should be lighting up green right now."

I glanced at my wristband, surprised when I saw the bright green light glowing under the jellied rubber. I held up my hand. "Check it out."

Jaylee squealed and jumped up and down beside me. "You won! You won a house!"

Seriously?

"Winners, make your way to the Champions' front door," Tracy said. "A van is waiting to take you on our very first house tour. Where are our winners this morning? Let's see those lights. Lift up your hands! I see you in the pink jacket. Congratulations. And you, sir, in the Adidas cap, come on up. Hold them high, friends!"

"Let's go, Eli," Jaylee lifted my arm in the air and dragged me out of the crowd toward the Champions' house. "Here! We have a winner here!"

Sure enough, when we reached the circle drive, three people with glowing wristbands were waiting beside a white van. Captain Koval was there with Jennie, who seemed to be gathering information from the winners onto an iPad.

Behind us, from the sudden screams on the field, I suspected that Loca and Liberté had taken the stage.

"*Bonjour, bonjour, mes amis!*" Loca yelled, his booming mic somewhat muted by our distance from the speakers.

"Just think, Eli, a house!" Jaylee said. "I would so love to live in a house. Do you know I never have? My whole life in that same apartment."

I hadn't thought about it before, but I was glad she was excited.

When my turn came, Jennie asked my name and used some kind of scanner to connect to my wristband. "Elias McShane," she read from her tablet, then smiled at me. "Grab a seat in the van. We'll be leaving soon."

Jaylee led me toward the vehicle, but Captain Koval dropped his arm between us. "Only winners inside," he said.

"But I'm with him," Jaylee said. "He's my partner."

The word "partner" shot a pang of guilt through me. I really needed to break up with this girl.

"Not my business," Koval said. "The van only seats eight. The rest of you, get lost."

Jaylee gasped. "Rude much?" She shoved her cell phone into my hands. "Take pictures for me."

"You still carry this around? It doesn't have service."

"It can go on the internet," she said. "Plus it works for pictures. Take lots, okay?"

I climbed in the van. I was the youngest by far. Most of the people looked middle-aged. We were each given a slip of paper that listed eight addresses and were told to rank our top four. Jennie told us that she'd do her best to make us all happy.

As we drove away, I couldn't help but wonder if this van might not be going to a string of mystery houses but instead to some sort of location where they made troublemakers disappear. Maybe I'd see Reinhold and Kimama there.

But no. They actually drove us to a bunch of houses. The first two were off Summit Road and across the street from each other—super close to the LLC compound. Everyone went nuts over the places, but I had no desire to be the Champions' neighbors. After that, we drove out Gothic and down a bunch of side streets where we found the next three houses. These were suburban, three-bedroom, two-and-a-half baths with tiny yards like I might have found in my neighborhood back in Phoenix. They were all nice inside. Jennie said the houses came furnished.

The experience reminded me of the few times I'd gone with

my mom to an estate sale. It always felt a bit creepy to traipse through the house of someone who had died, picking over the personal belongings they no longer needed. I wondered about the families who had lived in these houses. I knew some of these places were vacation homes or rentals, but the owners must have died if Tracy and his staff had sent their people in to clear them out. Whoever had coined the phrase "You can't take it with you" wasn't kidding.

The plumbing in all the houses had been turned off and a porta-potty had been placed in each yard, which Jennie told us was temporary.

"The Champions plan to re-route the safe water to all the houses. It's a major project, though, and will take several years to complete."

After that, we went north and stopped at a house on Cinnamon Mountain Road that was 3,986 square feet. It had four bedrooms, three and a half baths, a great room, and a wet bar. The seventh house was even better. A bit farther north on Gold Link Drive, the five-bedroom, 4,200-square-foot behemoth looked like a log cabin hotel resort. It had massive windows overlooking the mountain, quick access to National Forest hiking trails, and bathrooms and balconies in each room. Everyone went nuts over the place, so there was no way I'd get it.

I got caught up in the fun of it all and had to keep reminding myself I didn't want to live in this town with these people who kept making up new rules every day.

The last house was on the north side of the mountain way down Prospect Road. It had been built into a steep hill. The ground level was stone masonry around a two-car garage. The next two stories were sided in pine. A porch wrapped around the front of the second story, and unless you entered through the garage, you had to climb a full flight of stairs to reach the front porch and door. Everyone complained about this, as if walking a flight of stairs was too much work. My recently conditioned legs didn't have a problem with it.

Jennie said the house had been built in the '80s. It had three bedrooms and two baths. The inside was clean but outdated. It smelled old. There was a framed ski resort map on the wall that marked all the hiking trails and got me wondering which way Reinhold had gone.

Several people said the place was ugly and too far away from the LLC compound to make it to morning parties and meals.

I liked it. I especially liked that no one else did.

As we drove back toward the compound, everyone was talking about which place was their favorite. I wasn't sure if people were being honest. I mean, we were competing with each other for these houses. Why show your hand? Most everyone raved about the two that were near the compound and the mansion on Gold Link Drive. Several pointed out that moving away from the downtown area would make access to the restaurants difficult. One lady said she liked the houses next to the compound, but if she didn't get them, she was going to stay in her apartment.

While I had no plans to stick around long term, I would much rather live in a house than the condo, though I agreed it would make meals complicated. If I could get one of the houses close to the mountain, we might be able to explore. Since everyone was obsessed with Gold Link Drive, I chose Prospect Drive as my number one. It was perfect for our needs, and the fact that no one else seemed to want it made me hopeful that I'd actually get it.

When we got back to the compound, Jennie told us to wait while she took our surveys inside to tally them. It took forever for her to come back out. They were probably drawing straws between seven people having chosen Gold Link Drive as their number one.

Jennie finally returned with a shoebox of keys. Gold Link Drive went to a middle-aged guy who looked like weight-lifting was his life. He pumped his fist in the air while several others in the group shot him death glares.

When Jennie handed me the keys to Prospect Drive, I was a little giddy. She had me sign for the keys, then told me I was free to move in.

I checked the lawn just in case the others had decided to

wait for me, but we'd been gone a long time. I figured they'd returned to the condo. I was used to the walk by now, but it was frustrating to have to make it when I had news to share.

Out on the road, however, I found Zach, Lizzie, and Jaylee waiting for me in the Sienna. They saw me coming and climbed out. Jaylee ran toward me.

"Well?"

"I got a house," I said, dangling the key in front of her face. "Want to go see it?"

"Yes." She snatched the key out of my hand. "Did you take pictures? Where's my phone?"

Whoops. "I totally forgot."

She punched my arm. "Eli!"

"Sorry!"

"Why are you sorry?" Zach asked.

"He forgot to take pictures," Jaylee said.

"You evil beast," Zach said, climbing back into the driver's seat. "Where are we going?"

"North on Gothic," I said.

Zach started up the Sienna, and we headed toward the house. Lizzie and Jaylee peppered me with questions. I told them about the other houses, leaving out the fact that two had been neighbors to the Champions.

"It's really far out here," Jaylee said. "You think that's why they are giving these away?"

"Maybe," I said.

"Is it big? Tell me about it."

Jaylee would never have chosen Prospect Drive, so I tried to make it sound like it had been the best of the choices.

"Check it out," Zach said. "A dog."

I followed his gaze to the side of the road where a brown lab was trotting through the weeds. "I've seen it before," I said. "It looks just like the one that belonged to the couple who stole my truck in Flagstaff."

Jaylee gasped, her eyes wide. "Maybe they're here!"

"I sincerely hope not," I said.

We arrived at the new house, and Jaylee jumped out before

Zach had fully stopped the van. I heard her squeal, which I considered a good sign. I got out and joined her where she stood before the garage, looking up.

"I like that deck," she said. "Race you up the stairs."

She took off. I chased her but let her win.

She slapped the front door. "Ha! I beat you." She fiddled with the keys. "Which one opens the door? How many bedrooms again? Is there one we can share?"

Share? "Are you nuts?" I said. "My dad is going to live here!"

She smirked and set one hand on her hip. "So?"

I snatched the keys and held them behind my back. A glance down the steps showed me that Zach and Lizzie were inspecting the garage. It had to be now. Gosh, I was such a jerk. And suddenly nervous. This girl had always made me anxious, but what I was about to say . . . it would probably go badly. "I'm not going to share a room with you," I said.

She narrowed her eyes. "Because of your dad."

"No, because I don't think it's smart. Or right, actually. I want to . . . wait until I'm married to, you know, live with someone."

She laughed, reached up, and played with the hair at the back of my neck. "You're so cute, Eli."

I shrugged her off. Zach and Lizzie were coming up the stairs now. "I think we should stop this."

"Stop what?"

I waved my splinted fingers between us. "Whatever this is."

"You're breaking up with me?" She sounded totally shocked. "Because I wanted to share a room with you?"

"No," I said. "We don't even like the same . . . anything."

"I've been trying to do things with you," Jaylee said, glaring. "I really have. But you haven't even tried to do anything I want to do. You never come hang out at Riggs and Josh's place. You refuse to meet any of my new friends. That's not really fair."

The statement hit hard. She was right. I'd been asking her to change, but I hadn't been willing to change anything about myself. Not that I would, either. And that *did* sound unfair.

I peeked over the porch railing, noticed Zach and Lizzie had moved back down to the ground. They must have overheard us. "You're right," I said. "Which only proves my point that we're a bad match."

Jaylee exhaled a growling, eye-rolling, exasperated sigh. "You're such a bore, Eli."

"And you're mean," I said. "Look, if it makes you feel better, tell everyone you dumped me, okay? I don't really care."

I jogged down the steps and climbed into the van. I felt a little tense, but mostly I felt relief. I had done it! I'd broken up with Jaylee. And it had only taken me two weeks.

Zach sauntered over and opened the door, which slowly rolled aside, then propped one foot on the baseboard. "What's going on?"

Movement caught my eye—Lizzie, headed up the stairs to where Jaylee was standing. "Jaylee and I are done. I'm sure you're completely shocked."

"What happened?"

"I broke up with her." I held out the house keys. "You and Lizzie want to look inside?"

"We can wait."

I hit my head against the back of the seat. "Do you think I was stupid? To like her?"

"Naw, man. You like who you like. You had to give it a shot. Now you know."

That was true. "Now I know."

"They're coming."

I glanced to the stairs. Jaylee was running down. Behind her, Lizzie was taking her time. Jaylee got in the front passenger's seat and slammed the door.

"I'm dumping you," she said without moving to even look at me. "You're a jerk."

I released a slow breath and shot Zach a look. He patted my shoulder twice, then rolled the side door closed, and climbed into the driver's seat. Once Lizzie was buckled in beside me, Zach backed out of the driveway.

•   •   •

Three blocks from the condo, Zach stopped to let some people cross the street. Someone knocked on Zach's window.

I jumped, saw that it was Riggs.

Zach rolled down the window.

"Hey, losers," Riggs said. "You really get a house or what, Eli?"

"Yeah," I said.

"Dude, you should have a party, man. That would be sweet."

"Eli doesn't party, Riggs," Jaylee said. "He's too good for that."

"Well, sure he is." Riggs hunched down and winked at me. "You're such a good boy, McShane. Yes, you are a good boy." He was talking to me like I was a dog. He sounded a little drunk, and it wasn't even eleven.

Someone honked behind us. "See you later," Zach said, stepping on the gas.

Riggs held onto the window and ran alongside the van. "Wait! Whoa! You guys should come meet my friends. We're going for some pizza."

"Some other time," Zach said.

"I'll come, Riggsy." Jaylee climbed out of the van and slammed the door.

"I told you not to call me that," Riggs said to Jaylee, his voice muffled.

Zach met my gaze in the rearview mirror. I shrugged, and he drove on.

Good riddance, right?

Right.

# 16

HANNAH

"I think about death a lot more than I used to," Logan said. "And not just because I work in the hospital."

I pursed my lips to stifle a sigh. Logan was in the nurse's station, talking to me instead of cleaning. He'd made a habit of following me around at work. It was hard to get anything done with him going on and on.

"I mean, a pandemic will do that to anyone, right?" he said. "And the whole grief ceremony was hard. But also, working here. That man died last week. It really made me think it might not be that long for all of us."

I lost my place on the chart I'd been updating. What had I been trying to do? I glanced around and spotted the container of penicillin sitting right where I left it. Right! The man in 4B had broken out in hives, and Susan had asked me to mark the allergy on his chart.

"We all could be infected with the HydroFlu but just aren't showing symptoms yet," Logan said. "One of these days something will trigger it, and then the rash will break out, we'll all start to smell like fish, and that will be the end."

Good grief. Would he never stop?

"Logan," I said, just as Susan strode behind the counter.

He looked up. "Yeah?"

"I need to concentrate here for a moment," I said.

"Oh, sorry. I'll just get the trash." He pointed behind me.

The trash that he'd emptied two hours ago. I stifled a sigh, got up, and moved out of his way, waited while he removed the trash and replaced the bag.

"There you go," he said, carrying the practically empty trash bag out of the nurse's station and adding it to the big can on his cart.

"Thanks," I said.

He grinned, baring his silver braces. "Did you know that by the time you turn forty, you'll have outlived every cat and dog that was alive when you were born?"

"Logan, hit the road," Susan said.

He jumped. "Oh. Yeah, okay. Sure. Uh, see you later, Hannah."

"Bye," I said.

While he waved and pushed his cart out the double doors, I went back to my chart and added the note about the penicillin allergy.

"I'm going to see if I can schedule him at different times from you," Susan said.

I perked up at that comment, relief ballooning inside me. "Can you do that?"

Susan's lips twitched, like she didn't want to laugh. "Like that, would you?"

"Yes," I breathed. "He's a really nice person, but it just seems like he's always here."

"He likes you," Susan said. "You're going to have to let him down."

I dropped my face into my hands. "Must I?"

"The sooner you do it, the easier it will be."

I knew she was right, but I really didn't want to hurt Logan's feelings.

●　　●　　●

Around noon, Monica paged me to the reception area. When I arrived, I was surprised to see Eli waiting.

Heat flooded my cheeks at the sight of him, which only made me feel embarrassed. I had no idea why.

"Hey," he said, hands stuffed in the front pocket of the Crested Butte hoodie he'd picked up at the mercantile. "Sorry to bother you at work, but I have some news, and I didn't know how else to tell you."

"That sounds ominous," I said.

Eli smiled, which completely lit up his face. Why did boys always seem to have the best eyelashes? "It's nothing bad," he said. "Remember how Tracy has been talking about giving away houses in a lottery? Well, this morning I won a house. Pretty crazy, right?"

"Oh." My mind spun through possibilities of what this might have to do with me.

"Yeah, well, I wanted to tell you that, you know, you're welcome to live there too."

"With you?"

"No. Well, sort of. With all of us. Mostly. But anyway . . . The house is on the outskirts of town. It's old, but it's nicer than the condo and a lot bigger. Farther from the food, but we have the vans."

"Until they run out of gas," I said.

"No, they've got a gas station going now," Eli said. "You have to use your credits, but since no one drives very far, we won't have to fill the tanks very often."

"True," I said.

"So, anyway . . . We're all moving out there today. I mean,

not everyone, but . . ."

His cheeks were pink now. Why was he suddenly being shy around me?

He rubbed the back of his neck. "Lizzie was going to pack up your stuff and just move it, but I said that wasn't right. That we should ask you. See what you wanted to do. I mean, you can stay in the condo if you want. Antônia and Krista and Jaylee are staying."

Oh, interesting. This was bigger news than the house. "They're not moving into the new place?" I asked.

"They'd rather stay in town." He glanced away. "I, uh, finally broke up with Jaylee."

My whole body tingled. "You did?"

He scrubbed his hands over his cheeks, fingers still splinted. "I know! It was really hard. I don't think I handled it very well, but . . ."

"Congratulations, I guess."

"Yeah, it's a relief. So, anyway. If you want to come, I can pick you up at the end of your shift. Drive you to the condo to get your stuff. Take you out to the house. It's pretty cool." He was looking at me again, excited now. "It has a huge balcony and a great view of the mountain. The bedrooms in the house are way bigger than the ones in the condo. Lizzie said you can share a room with her and Shyla. Um, it does have some stairs."

"Actually, I've been doing better with stairs lately. Not as many nightmares, either. I think this job is helping. It gives me purpose, which keeps my mind busy, you know?" And my conversations with Dixie had helped too.

"That's good," he said. "I'm glad to hear it. So, you'll come?"

I hesitated. This was my chance to break away from them, if I wanted to—distance myself from Seth and the shame I felt every time I saw him. But there was no way I was sharing a place with only Jaylee, Antônia, and Krista. No, thank you. And I wasn't ready to say goodbye to Cree or Lizzie or Shyla or Eli.

If it didn't work out, I could always ask Dr. Bayles about the apartments here, though I didn't think this was the right place for me, either. Could be I didn't belong anywhere, but at least Eli was asking me.

His brow crinkled. "You okay?" he asked.

"Yes. Sorry. Just thinking."

"Thinking about how you're going to tell me you're sick of us? Or that you'll come?"

Eli could be very intuitive when he wasn't completely distracted by Jaylee. Which thankfully he wouldn't be anymore. I grinned. "That I'll come."

"Okay, great. Uh . . . I'll be back at four, right?"

"Yes, perfect." I was on the day shift this week, which was a nice change.

Eli just stood there, looking around the lobby like he suddenly found the place interesting. He rubbed the back of his neck again, and I chuckled.

"What?" he asked.

"Your dad does that too. Rubs his neck like that. Did you know?"

He suddenly looked self-conscious. "My mom always said so."

A moment of awkward silence stretched between us, and I knew he was thinking about his mom.

*Nice job, Hannah.*

"Well, I'll let you get back to work," Eli said, already heading out the door. "See you at four."

"Bye," I said, watching him go.

"Who was *that*?" Monica asked, arms folded across the top of her desk wall. "How do you know so many cute guys?"

"That was Eli. He's Zach's best friend—EMT Zach—and Seth's son."

Monica's eyebrows jumped. "Interesting," she said.

I shot her a smirk. "It really isn't."

But as I headed back to the nurse's station, one thing I did find extremely interesting was the news that Eli and Jaylee were no more. Now *that* made me smile.

● ● ●

I'd barely made it back to my station when a code-blue page sent me back the other way. I missed the handoff and spotted Susan and two enforcers rushing a gurney into an emergency exam room.

I started to run. By the time I had scrubbed up, the enforcers had stationed themselves outside the door and Susan was trying to stop abdominal bleeding on an unconscious bearded man.

It was Andy Reinhold.

"Hannah, place two large-bore IV lines. Two liters of Lactated Ringers," Susan said.

I grabbed my supplies and got to work, tingling all over. Susan was on Andy's left, so I went to his right, wondering where Kimama was and what had happened to them both.

I removed the IV materials from the bag and started setting it up. "Is he sedated?" I asked. He looked dead already.

"Enforcers asked paramedics to sedate him with ketamine," Susan said. "That's why I had to intubate. He was having trouble breathing."

"Why would they do that?" I asked as I tied a tourniquet above Andy's elbow.

"They've been doing it a lot lately," Susan said, "despite the calls Dr. Bayles has made to Admin, asking them to stop. Apparently this man was resisting arrest, even after being shot, so enforcers made the call."

Andy resisting arrest didn't surprise me. "But sedation is an abuse of law enforcement power," I said. "I can't believe the paramedics complied. Was it Zach?"

"Amber and Jermaine brought him in," Susan said. "Amber said she refused, until the enforcer put a gun to her head."

"What!"

"Apparently it's not the first time, either, according to Amber," Susan said. "I'm not sure Mr. Tracy has the best screening process for his enforcer recruits. They're all about making things as easy on themselves as possible, even if it risks killing people."

"That's incredibly disturbing." I turned Andy's arm and looked for a vein. My hand was shaking. I didn't know if I was shocked to be working on my friend or angry about the behavior of the enforcers and Mr. Tracy's apathy toward protecting lives. "Did he come in alone?" I asked.

"Yes, why?"

"Just wondering what happened."

"Paramedics had to hike the mountain and carry him down," Susan said. "No one mentioned what he was doing up there or why enforcers shot him."

I pulled on a pair of gloves, prepped my tubing and flushed it, then got my tape ready. A piece stuck to my glove, and I couldn't get it off. It ended up tangled around two fingers, and I had to remove the glove and pull on a new one. I cleaned the site with an alcohol swab, then readied my IV. My eyes kept flicking to Susan and all the blood.

"Is it bad?" I asked.

"He needs a laparotomy. Dr. Bayles is on his way. Linsey should be here too. Monica called him back from lunch. He went up to eat with Clara."

I inserted my needle into Andy's arm and glanced at the cannula, relieved when I saw blood filling the chamber. I'd gotten it on my first try. I slid the cannula forward and removed the needle, dropped it in the sharps box, attached my extension tubing, then ran my saline flush. I was taping it down when Dr. Bayles came in, hands scrubbed and raised above the waist.

"What do we have?" he asked.

"Single GSW to the right upper quadrant," Susan said. "Heavy bleeding and sanguineous drainage. Paramedics could find no visible exit wound. They also administered 125 mg of ketamine intramuscularly."

Dr. Bayles swore, mumbling a derogatory remark about enforcers. "Where's Linsey?"

"On his way."

"I need a scrub nurse, and I need the patient prepped for laparotomy," Dr. Bayles said.

"And I need a second pair of hands," Susan said. "Hannah,

how's that IV coming?"

"Done," I said, "I just need to get the fluids going."

"Leave it for me and help Jason," Susan said, though she did not remove her hands from Andy's wound.

I jumped up and grabbed fresh scrubs for myself and the doctor.

"Yo." Linsey strode into the room, passing the enforcers at the door. He saw me struggling to get into my gown and rushed over to help. "What's with the popo?"

"Our unconscious patient is considered dangerous," Susan told Linsey. "Hannah already put in the IV, but we still need two liters of Ringers. He also needs prophylactic antibiotics—400 mg of Ciprofloxacin, 500 mg of metronidazole. When you're done, can you do the catheter?"

"I didn't mark date and time on the IV," I said.

"I'm on it," Linsey said.

I helped Dr. Bayles into his gown and put on his gloves, holding my breath to avoid the overwhelming scent of Old Spice. Then I prepped the surgical tools on the Mayo stand.

"Who shot him?" Linsey asked. "Do we need to take photos for evidence?"

"Enforcers said no," Susan said.

Linsey looked like he might argue, yet said nothing further as he inserted the spikes into the fluid bags and zip-tied them in place.

"Do we have lab work and blood?" Dr. Bayles asked.

"I'll have it soon," Susan said.

"Then let's get started," Dr. Bayles said.

As scrub nurse, I was right beside him, handing him the surgical tools when he asked for them. He narrated his every move, always teaching.

"Avoid any presumption of wound severity based solely on what you see," he said. "The wound may appear small on the surface, but internally it can be devastating. Cavitations, fractures, hemorrhaging . . . You don't know until you're inside, so always assume the wound is severe. Hand me a sponge."

I took the scalpel Dr. Bayles was holding up, then passed

him a sponge.

"You also have to consider the possibility of spinal trauma. It might not look like it from the entry wound, but the bullet may have gone in at an angle and hit the spine. Also, bullets create dirty wounds, so there is a great potential for infection."

By the time Dr. Bales shifted into teaching about the laparotomy and removing the bullet, I went into medical mode. Andy's identity faded away, as did the corresponding emotions.

Being able to separate myself from my emotions was something that made me a prime candidate for a career in medicine. Blood and gore had never made me squeamish.

My stoicism was not without end, though. By the time I stumbled out the sliding front doors of the hospital and into the minivan that sat idling in a nearby spot, I completely fell apart. Maybe it was the isolation of the van and that only Eli was inside. Maybe I was simply exhausted. I suspected it also had a great deal to do with the nagging feeling that Eli was right, that the people in charge of this community could not be fully trusted.

"What happened?" Eli asked.

I poured it all out to him. Andy and his gunshot wound that had happened somewhere on the mountain. The enforcers ordering Amber to administer ketamine. How two officers were still stationed outside the door to Andy's hospital room.

"I can't believe this," Eli said, his face ghostly. "Is he going to make it?"

"Dr. Bayles thinks so. The enforcers wanted to take him to Rehab, but Dr. Bayles called Mr. Tracy and got permission to keep him at the hospital for now."

"What about Kimama?"

I shook my head. "No word. And I can't ask Andy because we're keeping him sedated until he recovers."

"I should have gone with him," Eli said.

"Then you might be the one shot," I said.

"He might not have been shot if he hadn't been alone. Did you tell anyone you know him?"

"No. What good could I do for him, then?" I said. "They'd probably make sure I didn't get to see him at all."

"That's what I was thinking," Eli said.

We sat in silence, the engine purring softly around us. My tears had gone, for which I was grateful. I didn't like crying in front of people.

"I'm glad you were there," Eli said.

Though it had been horrible, I said, "Me too."

# 17

ELI

At the condo, I waited in the Odyssey while Hannah went in and grabbed her things. I doubted Jaylee was in there, but if she was, I didn't want to see her. Hannah was in and out in less than five minutes, then I drove over to the house, and we told the others about Reinhold.

"Wish Travis and I would have taken that call," Zach said. "That enforcer would have had to shoot me before I would have injected ketamine. I bet it was Harvey."

"Zach!" Lizzie said.

"He shouldn't be wearing a badge," Zach said, his eye twitching. "Amber found out he was discharged from the LAPD. His sister is one of the Champions' dancers, and she got him a job on their security team."

"What was he discharged for?" I asked.

"Excessive force and falsification of evidence," Zach said. "I'm the only EMT brave enough to stand up to him. Everyone else is too afraid."

"Please don't start a war with an enforcer," Lizzie said.

"I'm not starting a war," Zach said, tucking his arm around my sister.

"We should break Andy out of the hospital," Logan said. "I've got keys."

"He's in critical condition," Hannah said.

"Yeah, he needs to stay put for now," Zach said.

"What about Kimama?" Lizzie asked. "What if she goes back to the apartment, and we're not there? Should we try looking for her?"

"Kimama is a smart kid," I said. "She'll find us."

"Unless something happened to her," Logan said.

"We can't go up that mountain," Dad said. "Not if enforcers are shooting at people."

"Reinhold could have shot first," I said.

"True," Dad said, "but there's still no reason to go up there when we know it's not safe. Let's wait until Andy can tell us what happened. Hannah, you're in the best position to get that information from him. Think you can?"

"If I happen to be working when he wakes up," she said. "Once the doctor takes him off the sedatives, the enforcers are going to move him to Rehab."

I sighed. "Then we'll need to move fast. Let us know when you think they're going to wake him. Then we'll make a plan to break him out."

"That's the best we can do for now," Dad said.

"Maybe not," I said, walking toward the framed ski map on the wall. I lifted it off its hook and carried it to the kitchen table. "We can use this to come up with some ideas of where Reinhold might have gone—where we might go to look for Kimama if we get the chance."

"I like it," Dad said. "But we're just planning. No one goes up that mountain unless we're all in agreement, deal?

"Deal," I said.

•　　•　　•

Lizzie found a cupboard with board games in the new house, so after dinner, we played Sorry, Monopoly, Boggle, and Pictionary. Much needed laughter filled our night, which made me feel better after worrying about Reinhold and Kimama. Hannah had to work at four in the morning, though, so she went to bed around nine. Lizzie quit then too. Both girls volunteered to put the kids to bed, so us guys went out and sat on the deck.

"Too bad you guys wouldn't play Trivial Pursuit," Logan said. "That's my best game."

"It's the 1984 version," I said. "None of us know any of that stuff."

"I do," Logan said. "She likes me, don't you think? Hannah? She volunteered to be on my team."

There was no way Hannah liked Logan, though he'd certainly made himself an idiot around her. "That's because she didn't know any better," I said.

"We did good together, though," Logan said. "I guessed everything she drew."

"Because she's a good artist," Zach said. "She didn't guess half the things you drew."

Logan ignored that. "Hannah said she could take off my braces when it's time. She just needs some pliers and a needle."

"Glad to hear it," I said. "No one wants braces for life."

"I've been thinking," Logan said. "Remember how Reinhold said we'd all need to pair off and procreate? Repopulate the world?"

"I love Reinhold," I said, "but he's a bit of a nut."

"Besides, he didn't mean today," Zach said. "He was talking long term."

Logan shrugged. "Still . . . You and Lizzie. Eli and Jaylee. And me and Hannah. Right?"

Guess I should tell Logan the news. "You can cross me and Jaylee off that list," I said.

"Why?" Logan asked. "What did you do?"

Heat flashed up my spine. "Why do you assume it was my fault?"

"That's true," Logan said. "She always did like Riggs."

That annoyed me even more. "She's not with Riggs," I said. "Yet."

Zach snorted. "Yeah, give her time. She'll snag him eventually. It won't last, though."

We all knew that well enough. Neither of them were the long-term relationship type.

"It was weird from the start," I said. "Jaylee and I are just too different."

"You need to fix this," Logan said. "Fast. Before Riggs or Josh find out."

"I'm not fixing it," I said. "I'm done."

"But, Eli . . ." Logan gave me a very serious look. "Don't get any ideas about Hannah."

I chuckled, surprised I hadn't seen that coming. "Oh, I see. *That's* what you're really worried about? Forget that Jaylee broke your friend's heart. You're just worried about yourself."

"I'm serious," Logan said. "I call dibs."

"You can't call dibs on a person," Zach said. "Besides, Hannah should get a say in this, don't you think? What if she's into Eli?"

"She's not into me," I said. "And don't worry, Logan. I don't like Hannah that way." Which maybe wasn't quite true. We were friends, though, and I didn't see her getting together with someone like Logan.

"She needs stability," Logan said. "Someone who knows her past like I do."

"What do you know about her past?" I said.

"About, you know . . ." He lowered his voice. "Brandon. She lost it the other day. Some perp came into the hospital, looking for a girl he beat up. He shoved Hannah, and she lost it. Linsey had to give her O2. So I told him about Brandon, and now she's seeing the counselor."

So much was wrong with everything Logan had just spilled.

"Dude, that wasn't your business to tell anyone about Brandon," I said.

"She practically went catatonic," Logan said. "No one knew what to do."

"Sounds like Linsey did," Zach said.

"My point is, she's getting help. Because of me." Logan's eyes were wild with excitement. He actually looked proud. "And I don't need you swooping in and impressing her with your survival skills and new muscles."

Wow. My friend had really lost it this time. "Oh, yes. I'm so strong after two weeks of moving trash cans around."

"Stronger than me," Logan said.

"Don't sweat it, Logan," I said. "Reinhold wants me to marry Kimama, so I'm all set."

Zach and Logan stared at me, mouths gaping, then they cracked up.

I don't know if they thought I was joking or not, but I'd had enough talk about girls. There were more important things on my mind. "We've got to get out of this place before we end up stuck here forever. That's all I care about right now."

"I'm with you, man," Zach said.

"Me too," said Logan. "Unless Hannah wants to stay here. Then . . ." He shrugged.

I fought the urge to shake my head. Logan in denial was a familiar story, but for his sake, I hoped he made his move sooner rather than later. Then Hannah could reject him, and he could get over it and move on to someone more his . . . type.

•   •   •

The following afternoon, Dad took a turn with the kids while Zach, Lizzie, and I went to pick up Hannah from the hospital. Zach and I would have assigned the job to Logan— more to razz him than to help him—but he was working until six.

We took Zach's van, in case Dad needed his, so I let Lizzie sit shotgun and jumped into the middle row. The moment Zach pulled into a spot at the hospital, Hannah came out, looking tired.

She was wearing royal blue scrubs and had her hair up in a ponytail. The hair around her face was all frizzy, and she had creases under her eyes. She was still strikingly pretty.

She climbed in beside me and sighed. "Thanks for coming to get me."

"You hungry?" I asked.

"Pizza," Hannah said. "Then a chocolate ice cream cone. Rocky Road if they have it."

"How very specific," I said.

"I know what I want," she said.

"You got it." Zach said. He steered out of the lot and turned toward The Secret Pizzeria.

"Logan wanted to come get you, but he's working until six," I said, meeting Zach's gaze in the rearview mirror.

Zach grinned and shook his head. I was being a jerk, but I couldn't help myself.

"I've seen enough of Logan for one day," Hannah said. "He follows me around."

"Aww." Lizzie turned in her seat. "Maybe he likes you," she said.

"Oh, that's clear enough," Hannah said.

Zach started laughing.

"What?" Lizzie said. "What's so bad about Logan?"

"Nothing," Zach said. "You like him so much, you date him."

Lizzie punched Zach's arm.

"It's nothing personal," Hannah said. "He's just not my type."

Poor Logan hadn't even made his move, and already he'd been rejected. Talk about a record.

"And his lack of boundaries is bothersome," Hannah added.

"He doesn't know he's being annoying," I said, suddenly wanting to defend the guy.

Lizzie again turned to look at Hannah. "What is your type?"

She shrugged. "Someone with boundaries?"

We all chuckled at that.

"How was Reinhold today?" Zach asked.

"The same," she said. "Why do you guys call him by his last name?"

"Because when I first met him, he called me Montgomery," Zach said.

"And he called me McShane," I said. Hopefully he would again, too.

Zach parked on the street in front of the pizza place, and we went in and claimed a booth by the windows. The waitress was able to divide an extra-large pizza and three sodas between our credits. Hannah ordered a water with lemon.

"Check it out," Zach said, pulling a sheet of paper from the drink menu on the table.

It was another flyer. The headline said, "Safe Water: A Gilded Cage." It ranted about the unfairness of trapping people in this place under the guise of helping them. It questioned the Champions' motives and claimed they could not continue to feed the current population if they kept up the rate of thirty credits a day.

"They make a lot of good points," I said. "I'd like to talk to whoever is writing these."

"What kinds of things do you do at the hospital?" Lizzie asked Hannah. "Besides hide from Logan?"

"I'm in charge of greeting new patients, assigning them a room and a doctor. There are only three doctors and usually only one working at a time, so that's not a very complicated task. I'm also training to be a nurse *and* a doctor, so everyone tries to include me in every call, which is great, but also exhausting."

"What kinds of problems do you see?" Zach asked. "I'm assuming it's anything and everything since that's what we see as paramedics."

"Pretty much," she said. "This week we saw colds, a second-degree burn, some seasonal allergies. There was a twisted ankle, a few cases of dehydration, a guy whose back went out. There was another guy who had just finished chemo two weeks before the HydroFlu hit. He really needed to see a specialist, which is unfortunate because we don't have one. I also saw people needing meds: bipolar meds, HIV retrovirals, and diabetics needing insulin."

"Should you be telling us this?" Lizzie asked. "Isn't that doctor-patient privileged information?"

"I didn't tell you who had what," Hannah said. "I'm just talking about my day. That's allowed."

"Were you able to help those last few patients?" Zach asked. "I'm concerned about the availability of meds. Won't we run out eventually? And when we do, what will happen to people who need them to live, like diabetics?"

"We have a great pharmacy right now," Hannah said. "The hospital was nicely stocked, and the population isn't so large that we're using it very quickly. Expiration dates will be a problem before we'll have to worry about running out. Dr. Bayles is working with Mr. Tracy on that. Admin has put together some research teams to learn ways to reproduce various things like foods and medicines."

"How can they reproduce medicines?" I asked.

"I don't know their plans," Hannah said, "but all three of our doctors and the two pharmacists are part of the medicine committee."

"I'm glad to know they're thinking about this stuff," Zach said.

"Why?" I asked. "It's not like we're going to stay here. Once Reinhold is awake, we'll find Kimama and get out of this place."

"But other people will stay," Zach said, "and it's just nice to think that they'll be taken care of."

The pizza came, and it wasn't just frozen pizzas anymore. They'd found someone to make real pizzas, and they were good. I wondered if the new chef had noted some kind of cooking ability on his survey. How weird would that be? Picked up by the cops and conscripted to make pizza? Maybe Tracy would pull him up on stage at the next morning party so we could all cheer.

When we were done, we decided to walk to the ice cream shop, since it was only a block away. The sidewalks were crowded. We'd eaten an early dinner, and now that we were ready for dessert, everyone else was looking for food.

We turned the corner and ran into Jaylee, Krista, Antônia,

and Cristobal. The latter two were holding hands.

"Well, that's new," Zach mumbled to me.

"You guys found Hannah!" Krista said, hugging a very surprised Hannah.

"Was I lost?" Hannah asked.

"We didn't know," Jaylee said. "Your stuff just disappeared."

"On the day the rest of us all moved," I said, my sarcasm obvious.

Lizzie elbowed me. "We just had pizza," she said. "What are you guys doing?"

"Going for pizza," Krista said. "Jaylee won't eat anything else."

"I like pizza," she said, looking just about everywhere but at me.

She was so cute it made me ache. It shouldn't be fair that some girls looked like Jaylee, especially when they were mean inside. Okay, so maybe I was overreacting a little, but then I saw the brown and black puka shell necklace she was wearing.

Riggs's dumb necklace.

What did *that* mean?

I reached out and tugged on it. "What's this?"

Jaylee flinched away. "A necklace," she said, still not looking at me. "Riggsy gave it to me."

"Classy, Jay," Lizzie said. "What, did you wait two minutes after you and Eli broke up before moving on?"

"We're just friends," she said, glaring at Lizzie. "Besides, Eli and I were never going to work out. We all knew it."

Ouch. No one said anything, as if they all agreed with that statement.

Then Jaylee grinned at me, her old self again, and nudged my arm. "It was fun, though, yeah, Eli?"

No, it was not fun, letting this girl mess with my head. It had been a stressful roller coaster of pleasure and pain, and the way she made it all sound like a game made me feel like there was something wrong with me because I hadn't enjoyed every moment.

"Sure," I finally said, walking on.

Footsteps pattered behind me. I imagined Jaylee chasing after me to make sure I wasn't upset, but I was surprised to see Hannah appear on my right.

"She's kind of brutal, isn't she?" Hannah said.

"She certainly has a way of making a guy feel like a moron," I said.

An engine roared nearby, coming closer. Hannah and I both looked toward the sound just as semi-automatic gunfire rang out, echoed with people's screams. Just ahead, an Army Jeep barreled around the corner, straightened, and accelerated toward us. People on the sidewalks scattered, screaming as two men, standing in the back of the Jeep and packing M&P rifles, fired into the crowd. A second Jeep rounded the corner behind the first.

Hannah and I grabbed each other's arms and yelled, "Run!"

# 18

**ELI**

We took off, back toward the pizza place and our friends, who were still standing in a circle on the sidewalk. It took the others a few seconds to catch on, then they, too, turned and ran, Zach in the lead. He darted into Mountaintop Sports. Cristobal, Antônia, Krista, and Jaylee kept running, but Lizzie, Hannah, and I followed Zach into the store where we all ducked behind various circular clothing racks. From where I crouched, I could just see out the wall of windows that faced the road. The first Jeep rolled past, gunmen spraying both sides of the street with bullets. Glass shattered. I ducked down and squeezed my eyes shut, praying someone would stop these madmen and that no one would die.

I counted the roar of four different engines pass by. Only

after a long stretch of silence did I risk a peek.

Jagged shards of glass rimmed the store's window frames. Outside, an army van had rolled to a stop. The back doors sprang open, and a dozen men poured out, each carrying what looked like Smith & Wesson M&P sport rifles. Most of them scattered, but two entered our store. The first walked right behind the counter. His rifle was a Colt, not a Smith & Wesson like his buddy carried. What a stupid thing to notice. It made me miss my gun.

"You!" the Colt guy yelled, looking down near the floor. "Come out of there."

A middle-aged man with thick black hair stood, hands raised above his head, and walked out to the front of the store.

Colt followed. "Load all this in the van." He waved his gun at the racks of clothing.

The clerk grabbed an armful of North Face jackets off a rack and carried them out the door. The Smith & Wesson gunman followed him to the back of the van, where two other armed men stood guard.

Who were these guys?

Nearby, muffled gunfire and screams rang out. I felt naked and vulnerable without a weapon. The clerk came back for a second armload of coats. Colt shouldered his gun and started filling a backpack with candy bars from the front counter.

I tried to make eye contact with Zach but didn't see where he'd hidden himself. Hannah was the only person I could see, and her eyes were fixed on Colt. The clerk came back for trip number three. He'd cleared the first rack and headed toward a rounder of T-shirts.

"Hey!" Colt gestured to a rack with Patagonia coats. "This one."

The clerk grabbed an armful of coats and carried them out, leaving a gap in the rack that exposed Lizzie, crouched and wide-eyed in the center.

I reached through the shirts on my rack and waved at my sister, but she didn't see me. She stood, still hunched and staring at Colt's back. The guy had resumed filling his backpack with junk food. Lizzie lifted one leg over the metal bar on the bottom circle of the rack and lowered her foot to the floor, shifted her weight and lifted her other leg.

I held my breath. Hurry, Lizzie!

She had just set both feet outside the rack when the store clerk returned. He stopped suddenly, staring at my sister. She put a finger to her lips and took one step away from the rack.

Colt noticed the clerk's gaze and turned his head. "Stop!" he yelled. "Don't move!"

Lizzie froze.

Colt approached and circled my sister, gun trained on her. He was youngish—maybe late twenties. He looked her over, appeared to like what he saw, and motioned her toward the door. "Get some coats and take them to the van."

I popped to my feet at the same time as Zach, who was on Colt's right, so when he turned his weapon on Zach, he put his back to me—hadn't seen me at all.

"She's not going anywhere," Zach said.

"You going to stop me, big guy?" Colt asked.

"You going to make me stop you?" Zach shot back.

I needed a weapon. I scanned the wall within my reach and grabbed a red and black Burton board off a snowboard display. I crept toward Colt, raising the board to strike. Zach and Lizzie stayed cool and didn't look at me, but the clerk's head turned and gave me away.

Colt spun around just as I slammed the board against his face. He fell backwards into a rack of snow pants. Zach was on him in seconds, ripped away his gun, and handed it to me.

I ejected the magazine. "Is there a backdoor in this place?" I asked the clerk.

He led the way behind the counter. We passed through a small storage area and out a door that emptied onto a dirt road alley that separated the store from the pizza place. The air smelled like oregano, yeast, and gunpowder.

The clerk stopped and looked both ways. I did too. Gunfire and screaming came from both directions. Too bad we couldn't wait it out right here, but Colt would likely follow any minute. I dropped the gun in a dumpster.

"Where to?" Zach asked.

I didn't know. With only two choices, I went right, away from the street. This led us around the back of an apartment complex. We circled the building and came out on another street where two more army vans were parked. Gunmen were loading people inside. I saw Cristobal help Antônia climb in. My mind spun, trying to think of a way to help them.

Lizzie gasped. "Eli!"

"I see them," I said.

"Who are these guys, and why are they kidnapping people?" Hannah asked.

The question that was on everyone's mind.

"Stop right there!" someone yelled behind us.

Colt and his partner were coming this way, the second guy gripping his Smith & Wesson by the barrel.

"Run," I yelled. "Go, go!"

Zach and I pushed the girls ahead. The clerk was still with us, and he went next. Zach and I brought up the rear as we all ran out onto the street. "Cut across to the bar!" I yelled from the back of the line.

Lizzie, who was in the lead, sprinted in front of the first army Jeep, Hannah and the clerk on her heels. She stopped suddenly and lifted her hands above her head.

Zach and I slowed to a stop just as two new gunmen stepped out from the other side of the Jeep. The closest one was packing a lever-action Winchester.

"Around back, folks," he said. "I've already called shotgun."

"Funny guy," I said, sizing him up. He wasn't much older than me, but I wasn't eager to try and wrestle a shotgun from anyone—especially not in a crowd.

Lizzie, Hannah, and the clerk backed up, and we all grouped together in front of the Jeep. Winchester pressed forward, and behind us, Colt and Smith & Wesson arrived.

We were surrounded.

A chorus of sirens screamed over the distant gunfire as police cruisers sped upon the scene. The gunmen turned their weapons on the enforcers and started shooting.

The enforcers shot back.

The clerk collapsed right in front of me.

"Run!" I yelled, pushing Lizzie back toward the bar. She sprinted away with Zach, but Hannah dropped to her knees beside the clerk and was looking him over. The guy's eyes were open. He was gone.

"I don't see the wound!" she yelled.

I glanced at the clerk, caught a glisten in his dark hair, and grabbed her arm. "Above his left ear. Let's go."

She must have seen it too because she stood and sprinted with me toward the bar. Ahead, Zach and Lizzie reached the door, found it locked, then ran around the side into an alley between the bar and the ice cream shop. Hannah and I followed, but the alley ended in a brick wall.

"Let's hunker down. Wait it out," I said, sinking against the exterior wall of the bar and pulling my knees to my chest. The others lined up along the wall on my right, sitting like I had.

Adrenaline pulsed in my head. That clerk! That could have been me. Lizzie. It could have been any one of us. Had I gotten him killed? Should I have run the other way out of the store?

I could just barely see the street. Even with the wall acting as a partial barrier, the gunfire was deafening as the two sides waged war. Sitting there, my mind calmed a little. Should I go back out and see if we could help anyone? Get Cristobal and Antônia out of that truck? Walking into gunfire would be suicide, right? Might as well let the enforcers to do their job.

I didn't much care for that plan, but what else could I do?

The gunfight ended. Engines roared. Tires squealed. Sirens blared. They were leaving. Still, none of us moved for quite some time. My heart was still thudding when my sister gasped.

"Is that your blood?" she asked.

I glanced down, wondering if I'd taken some blood spatter from the store clerk.

"I'll be fine," Zach said.

I lifted my head and saw Lizzie on her knees before Zach, who was looking quite pale. The right shoulder and sleeve of his white T-shirt was drenched red, and a stream of blood had wound its way down his arm where it was dripping off his elbow.

•　　•　　•

We weren't allowed to see Zach until he was out of surgery, so while I was waiting in the hospital, I went looking for Reinhold. Hannah said he was in room 4B. Even though she pointed me in the right direction, it still took me a while to find it. When I finally did, I was disappointed to see an enforcer sitting on a chair outside the door. I walked up and down that stretch of hall a few times, trying to think of a way to distract the enforcer, but I came up with nothing.

"You lost, boy?" the enforcer said the third time I passed by.

"Looking for the lobby," I said.

"Go back the way you came. Take a left at the end of the hall, walk all the way to the end, then go left again."

"Thanks, man," I said, taking that as my cue to depart.

I didn't make it back to the lobby. I met Hannah and Lizzie on the way.

"We can see him," Lizzie said.

Hannah took us to a room where Zach was propped up in a hospital bed, his arm in a sling.

"Oh, Zach, I'm so glad you're okay," Lizzie said.

"You're glad?" Zach said. "Doc Russell said I'm going to need at least two weeks off. I get a vacation."

"Not from the morning parties," I said.

"Did you find out what happened to your friends?" Hannah asked.

"Cristobal and Antônia are fine," I said. Hannah had loaned me her cell phone, which had Cristobal's number in it. I'd called him and got the whole story. "He said the truck got stopped by enforcers. They were taken down to Rehab for questioning."

"That was insane," Zach said. "Who were those people?"

"Cristobal said they follow a local warlord. I guess they've attacked a few times before. They were the main reason Admin was putting up the perimeter fence, to stop them from entering."

"Fence didn't do much to keep them out," Zach said.

"Which will only make them want to build a better fence," I said.

We eventually left Zach at the hospital and drove home to fill in Dad and Logan on our afternoon. Cristobal and Antônia were already there.

Lizzie hugged them both. "Sweetie, I'm so glad you're okay!"

"I was so scared," Antônia said. "How is Zach?"

"He's good," Lizzie said. "Has to stay in the hospital for a few days."

"When we left, they still didn't have a good report on how many had been hurt," Cristobal said.

"Twenty-eight brought into the hospital," Hannah said. "Fourteen of those had gunshot wounds. Three fatalities."

"Three people killed in this supposedly peaceful city," I said.

"We need to start carrying our guns," Logan said.

"You don't have a gun," I said. The idea of Logan packing heat terrified me almost as much as those warlords.

"Better to just lie low until things calm down," Dad said.

"Or until we figure out how to leave this place," I said.

"Did anyone actually get taken?" Dad asked.

"I didn't hear," Cristobal said.

"One patient said eight people," Hannah said. "Linsey heard three, and Dr. Russell said he'd heard five. The enforcer who'd been shot said none. So there you go. Clear as mud."

Stupid enforcers. "We need to know what's going on."

"I could check the CB frequencies from the shop," Dad said.

"Warlords might be on CB," Logan said, "but I bet the enforcers communicate digitally."

"Wish I could be a fly on Tracy's wall," I said.

"You could," Antônia said. "Cris could put a microphone on the office, and I could record whatever it hears."

Cristobal made a sound of uncertainty. "I don't know about that."

"I could hack into Tracy's computer," Logan said.

"Don't tell lies," Antônia said. "You could not."

"Could too."

"There is a reason you did not get to stay on with the programming and I did," Antônia said. "Two, actually."

"What were they?" I asked, grinning at Logan.

"No," he said. "Don't listen to her."

"He way over exaggerate his programming skills, but they would have kept him if only he didn't talk so much."

"I didn't talk *that* much," Logan said.

"Logan, the IT department takes many prides about secrecy," Antônia said. "They could tell after five minutes of you talking that you were not good for the job. You could still help me, though. If I could send you a link to the microphone, then you can listen here. It would be better for you to record instead of me. That way there would be no—How do you say?—*evidence* on my work laptop."

Again Cristobal groaned. "I don't think so, Tônia. I don't like it."

"*Está bien. No te preocupes*," Antônia said. "No one will catch me."

"It's not *you* I'm worried about," Cristobal said.

Antônia sighed and told me, "We will figure it out."

I liked the idea of spying on Tracy. "That would be amazing," I said. "If you could get that going, we could take turns monitoring Logan's recordings. Hopefully, we'd hear something that gives us a clue about how to get out of this place."

# 19

HANNAH
AUGUST 23

Sunday was the second time I'd been off since I started working at the hospital. I woke to the sound of singing. I listened carefully and realized they were singing church songs. No guitar this time since Zach had left it at Andy's house, and he remained in the hospital, but it still reminded me of the night at Ace Hardware in Flagstaff.

Shyla got up and begged me to walk with her out to the porta-potty. We came downstairs and found Eli, Seth, Lizzie, and Logan sitting in the living room. No one was singing now, but Seth was reading aloud. I stood quietly in the shadows while Shyla pulled on her shoes and listened to words that sounded very old but quickly drew me in.

"'But you, Israel, my servant, Jacob, whom I have chosen,

you descendants of Abraham my friend, I took you from the ends of the earth, from its farthest corners I called you. I said, "You are my servant;" I have chosen you and have not rejected you. So do not fear, for I am with you; do not be dismayed, for I am your God. I will strengthen you and help you; I will uphold you with my righteous right hand.'"

"Ready," said Shyla, whose frizzy red hair was a tangle of knots.

I took her hand, and we slipped outside and visited the porta-potty in our front yard. I was grateful I could walk outside these days without being scared. I'd come a long way.

I spotted a sheet of paper on the ground—several sheets, actually. I picked up the nearest one. It was a flyer, printed on typing paper.

IF YOU AGREE, WHY DON'T YOU ACT?
CALL TO ALL AMERICANS!
WE ARE YOUR CONSCIENCE.

It went on to list ten atrocities the LLC Administration had implemented that were inhumane. I saw withholding water for punitive reasons on the list along with injections of ketamine and denying constitutional amendments like freedom of speech, assembly, and the right to counsel and a jury.

When Shyla and I returned to the house, Eli approached, arms folded and shoulders hunched like he was cold. He shook his hair out of his eyes—it was getting long.

"Sorry if we woke you," he whispered. "We do church on Sundays when we can. You're welcome to join us."

"You should see this," I said. "There's a new flyer out." I handed him the paper.

He smiled, eyes shining as he read the paper. "I've seen it. They're all over town. Wish I could find out who it was. Might be nice to start meeting with the other rebels."

"Don't you think that would be dangerous?" I asked. "Enforcers are probably looking for these people. You could go back to Rehab."

"It wasn't so bad," he said. "Besides, we're probably not going to get out of here without making someone angry. Maybe if we all work together, it will be easier."

Shyla and I followed Eli as he returned to the circle of couches and handed the flyer to Logan. I sat between him and Logan and pulled Shyla onto my lap.

Seth went on to talk about fear and anxiety, how everyone experienced them at some point in their lives. I found myself having a massive resurgence of fear for Eli and the trouble he might get himself into if he went looking for groups of rebels in town. He'd just better be careful. I didn't want him coming into the hospital on a code blue like Andy Reinhold.

• • •

Monday was only the second time I'd been able to attend the morning party. With Zach still in the hospital, we were all able to fit in one van. Cree snuggled me the whole way. He didn't like my schedule at the hospital and often cried if I left the house when he was awake. It was sweet that I meant so much to him, so I tried to give him as much attention as possible when I was not working. Once we parked, I ended up carrying him piggy-back style. Lizzie and Eli were walking up ahead with their dad. Shyla and Davis followed, side-by-side, and Logan was keeping me and Cree company at the back of the line.

"I told Dr. Bayles that janitors played a vital role in protecting the health of everyone in the hospital," Logan said. "We prevent the spread of germs and infections because we keep everything clean and disinfected."

"That's true," I said.

"That's what Dr. Bayles said. He also thanked me for my service."

I smiled, thinking of Dr. Bayles trying to keep his cool while Logan prattled on. I could relate.

"Did you know janitorial workers have one of the highest rates of occupational asthma?"

"Logan?" Eli yelled from the front of their procession.

"Come here."

"Be right back," he said.

Up ahead, Lizzie stepped into the road and waited until I reached her. She fell in step beside me. "Hi," she said, grinning.

"What?" I asked.

"Eli wanted to rescue you. Right now he's telling Logan that I had an important question to ask you about menstruation."

"Eli used the word menstruation?" And he was thinking about me?

"I think he said 'girl stuff,' but you get the idea." Lizzie grinned. "He's very crafty."

I chuckled. "He's strategic." And thoughtful. And at the same time, kind—to try and spare me from Logan and spare Logan from knowing he was making me miserable.

I watched Eli, my gaze flitting from him to Logan to Seth—I barely spoke with Seth anymore. Eli had reclaimed his place at the top of my list of people I most wanted to spend time with. I really hoped I wouldn't mess it up.

•   •   •

Loca and Liberté opened the morning party with a new song—a tribute to those who lost their lives or were taken by the warlords. After the song, Loca spoke to the crowd.

"We are grieved by this senseless tragedy, saddened that these shooters forced their way past our blockades and committed violent atrocities against our residents. Our crews are working tirelessly to complete the fence around Safe Water. Until it is complete, we remain vulnerable to attack. We would ask that you be on guard when you are in public. We also ask that all guns be turned in to enforcers."

"What?" Eli said.

"There are two reasons for this. First, our officers need a bigger arsenal of weapons if they are to stand against such acts of violence. Just as we've asked those of you with medical abilities to come forward, we would ask that those of you with weapons donate them so that our enforcers can stand against future attacks."

"Who would be dumb enough to donate their guns to the enforcers?" Eli mumbled to Seth.

"The second reason we ask you to turn over your weapons," Loca continued, "is because Safe Water is meant to be a peaceful city. Guns are a vehicle of death. Only in the hands of trained enforcers can guns benefit our community. So we ask you, people of Safe Water, to give up your weapons and let our enforcers protect you. Any person who turns in a gun voluntarily by the Safe Day deadline of next Sunday at midnight will receive an extra week's worth of rations. Any who are caught withholding weapons after that date will be treated as a lawbreaker."

"Lawbreaker?" Eli said.

"Shh," Seth said.

As Tracy stepped forward and raved about the brave residents who would donate their guns, Eli exchanged several more glares with Seth, but it wasn't until we were driving home in the van that he voiced his opinion on the new gun law.

"We're not turning in the guns," Eli said. He was sitting in the passenger's seat while his dad drove. I was in the second row with Lizzie, Cree buckled between us. Logan, Davis, and Shyla were in the back.

"But Loca said we have to," Shyla said.

"He's wrong," Eli said, turning in his seat until he could see Shyla in the back row. "Loca can't simply declare himself my ruler. I didn't vote for Loca for president. Did you?"

Shyla blinked her big eyes. "I'm too young to vote."

"These people are on a fast track to creating a dictatorship," Seth said.

"A potato ship?" Davis asked from the back row, his tone incredulous.

"Dictatorship," I said. "A dictator is someone who rules with force over a group of people who often didn't get a vote."

"I would vote for Loca and Liberté," Shyla told me. "They're nice, and they make fun music."

Eli groaned. "I know you like them, Shy," he said. "They're talented musicians. But that doesn't mean they're qualified to rule a whole town."

"Taking away people's guns is against the constitution," Logan said.

"The constitution means squat to those people," Eli said. "They're not even Americans. They're French."

"And they've started their own nation," Seth said. "Can't fault them for that, but I don't want to be a part of it."

"Me either," Eli said.

"But where else can we go?" Lizzie asked. "We need safe water."

No one had an answer for that, but I suspected several of us were thinking of Andy Reinhold and what he would have to say when he woke up.

"How about this?" Seth said.

I looked at him, confused, until I saw the drops sprinkling the windshield.

Shyla screamed.

"Stay calm, sweetie," Lizzie said, hugging her close.

"The rain is bad!" Davis said.

"We don't know that," Eli said.

"And it can't touch us while we're in the van," Lizzie said.

"How can we test it?" Seth asked. "Is there a safe way to find out?"

"We have a minilab at the hospital," I said. "Mr. Tracy has a team in there working on things. They're all set up to test the water if we ever get a good rain."

"This isn't it," Seth said. "I don't even need the wipers." He flicked them on, and the few drops of water smeared blurry arcs across the windshield.

"It won't be long, though," Eli said.

By the time we got back to the house, the sky was bright blue. We still all ran into the house. I found myself standing at the windows throughout the day, watching, waiting, but no more rain came.

# 20

ELI
AUGUST 25

Tuesday at work, to my delight, Nigil promoted me to substitute driver.

"It won't be often," he said. "Just when someone's out and we need to shift everyone around."

We went out into the garage bay where there was a large town map on the wall. There he showed me the route I'd take for my training runs.

"You're going to take Gothic out to Winterset," he said. "Go all the way to the end, turn 'round and come back up the other side. When you reach Gold Link Drive, take that until you come to Silver Lane. Take Silver Lane to the dead end, turn 'round and come back to Gold Link Drive. Continue on until you reach the dead end and—"

"Turn around," I said. "I get it."

"You'll hit Copper Lane on the way back. The rest is a straight shot. If you have any trouble, we've got these maps in the glove box."

"You've got copies of that," I said. "Any extras?"

"Sure, I can get you one. Why?"

"I'd like to study it," I said. "Memorize the route."

"Suit yourself, but I really don't think that's necessary." He went into the boss's office and returned with a folded-up map of town. "Go wild, kid."

While I enjoyed driving that huge truck around town that day, rather than working the back with Bong, I was more excited to bring home the town map to show Dad.

I laid it on the kitchen table, and we stood over it. "I was thinking we could check out every exit and mark how many enforcers are posted at each."

"Let's divvy them up," Dad said. "I'll take the south end. You do north. Hopefully Andy will be able to tell us which side of the mountain he went up."

The familiar worry for Reinhold rose up urgently inside me. "I don't like that Hannah's off today," I said. "I think I'll pay Zach a visit and try again to see Reinhold."

"Take Lizzie with you," Dad said. "She's driving me crazy, pining over that boy."

•   •   •

Susan, the head nurse, greeted us with a huge grin. "I wondered when you two would come a-calling. We've never had such a popular patient as our handsome EMT."

"He's *my* handsome EMT," Lizzie said, winking.

"Oh, you don't have to tell me, honey," Susan said. "That boy talks nonstop about you."

Lizzie beamed. "He does?"

"Mmm hmm." Susan waved us down the hall. "Just so you know, he really likes that perfume of yours, so you best make it last."

"It's lotion," Lizzie told me as we headed toward Zach's room. "I got three more tubes of it at Target in Flagstaff."

I had no comment for my sister's toiletries or what Zach thought of them. We entered Zach's room, but before we could even say hello, he spoke.

"Andy's gone."

"Gone how?" I stamped back the flames of dread inside me. "Dead? Or moved to Rehab?"

"Sorry," Zach said. "Just moved to Rehab."

Well, that was a relief.

"For how long?" Lizzie asked.

"Don't know," Zach said, "but I talked to him."

I sat on the edge of Zach's bed. "What did he say?"

"Is Kimama okay?" Lizzie asked.

"As far as he knows, she's fine," Zach said. "He made her hide when the enforcers came to investigate their campfire. They found him. Exchanged gunfire. That's how he got shot and brought in."

"So she's still up there?" I asked.

"By herself? All this time?" Lizzie added.

"He's not sure," Zach said. "He told her if he didn't come back to hike home."

"All the way to Durango?" I asked. "That's insane."

Zach shrugged. "That's what I said, but he told me not to worry about her."

I had no idea how an eleven-year-old girl was going to hoof it 200 miles with no food or supplies. "It'll take her at least two weeks," I said, "maybe more. But this is Kimama we're talking about. She's been camping with her dad since she was born. If anyone can survive on their own out there, she can."

"Definitely," Lizzie said. "I'm still worried for her. What else did he say?"

"He told her to stay home but doubts she will," Zach said. "She still has the walkie talkie, so he said to keep listening in case she tries to contact us. He figures she's either still up the mountain or she went home and will come back with supplies to build an irrigation ditch."

Hope kindled inside me. "He found out something about the creek?"

"He said there are three branches that feed into that creek higher up the mountain. Said we could divert the one on the east side of the mountain and build ourselves a camp between the base of the mountain and the East River. It's only a couple miles from the resort, though, so they'd know we were there."

They'd see the smoke from our campfire, just like they'd seen the smoke from Reinhold's. Again I wished I'd gone with him and Kimama. I could have helped her. "Wonder what it would take for them to leave us alone?" I said.

"A miracle," Zach said.

"Then that's exactly what we pray for," Lizzie said.

•   •   •

On the way out of the hospital, we passed several men hauling boxes inside. Quinn was one of them.

"McShane," he said, stepping aside to let his coworkers pass.

"What's this?" I asked.

"Got myself on a scavenge team," he said. "They liked my wheels, so now I get to drive around looking for supplies."

"And you came back?"

Concern etched his face. "Darby doesn't get to go out with me. They assigned me a partner to ride along. Hey, you might be interested in this." He shifted the box he was holding to one hip and fished a slip of paper from his pocket. Three more fell out, and I stooped to pick them up. They all said the same thing: 5 East Silver Lane, Sunday, 9:00 p.m.

That address was on the route I'd driven that morning in the garbage truck.

Quinn snatched back all but one of the papers. "That there is a gathering of like minds, if you know what I mean. We all share a common purpose."

"Leaving?" I asked.

"Anarchy," he said, grinning.

"Quinn! What are you doing?" a man yelled from down the

hall.

"Gotta run," Quinn said. "Hope I'll be seeing you around."

• • •

Zach was released from the hospital. I felt better having him home, but I was anxious about Quinn and his hint about anarchy. Sunday was too many days away for me to sit and do nothing. On Wednesday, LLC was hosting a special night party. The official reason for the event was "to celebrate the unity of our community."

We all knew better. They needed to pacify the residents of Safe Water after the recent restrictions had upset so many.

"I'm going to go to the night party," I said. We had just finished dinner, and I was helping clear the table.

"Why?" Dad asked.

"I want to check out the security there to get an idea of the numbers of enforcers they've got working for them," I said. "Cristobal said they sometimes have to call in every enforcer just to keep things from getting out of hand."

"Maybe we should try to escape during a night party," Zach said.

I dropped the paper plates into the trash. "That's what I was thinking. I've been compiling a list of enforcers' names. If we can figure out how many there are, and find out how many work the night parties, we'll have a good idea of how many we'd face trying to leave."

"I'm in," Dad said.

"Me too," Logan said.

"Could I come?" Hannah asked.

We all looked at Hannah. Dad gave her a suspicious look. She'd never asked to join in our investigations before, but I trusted her completely.

"Of course you can come," I said, wondering what was behind that reaction from my Dad.

"Someone needs to stay with the kids," Lizzie said. "Zach?"

"You want *me* to babysit?" Zach asked. "By myself?"

Lizzie rolled her eyes. "I was thinking we could both stay."

"You're actually going to watch the kids, though, right?" I asked.

Lizzie shot me a dirty look. "Yes, Papa Eli."

"You sure?" Dad added.

"Dad!" Lizzie threw one of the couch pillows at Dad.

"I don't know," I said. "Maybe we should ask the kids to watch *them*."

"Just go," she said, throwing another pillow at me.

We ran out of the house laughing.

•   •   •

This was only the second night party I'd been to, and I hadn't missed the ear-splitting music. A sea of dancing bodies writhed between the stage and where we stood in back. Blue lights lit up around us from every wristband. I lifted my own and stared at the glow, wondering how they did that. The wristband lights began to pulse in time with the beat, now turning different colors: red, green, blue, yellow, purple, and white. My gaze shifted back to the crowd and caught on one of those shirtless guys wearing the blinking bicycle safety lights across his chest.

"Isn't that a weird way to sell merch?" I had to yell to be heard over the music.

"I'll go buy something." Hannah slipped into the crowd and started dancing, which totally took me off guard. She looked like she belonged in the scene. Like she was the star of some EDM video.

Dad leaned close. "I'm going to circle around. Count that cluster of enforcers by the exit. Come with me, Logan?"

Logan, who was starting after Hannah, jerked his head toward my dad. "Huh?"

"I could use another set of eyes," Dad said. "Want to help?"

"Sure." Logan followed my dad along the back of the crowd. To his credit, he only looked back at Hannah once. Why had Dad taken him? Logan had never been his favorite person.

I turned my attention back to Hannah, who had reached the

guy with the flashing lights. She leaned close and said something. The guy threw back his head, laughing. Then he scanned Hannah's bracelet and handed her something. She slipped whatever it was into her pocket and turned back.

She'd made it about five yards when some guy stepped in front of her. She darted around him, but the guy followed. He was big, round more than tall. A black bandana had been tied over his hair. Mirrored sunglasses and a short beard covered his face. He'd look at home atop a Harley.

Hannah yelled something. "Get lost!" I think. Then she screamed and elbowed the guy in the face. He must have touched her—I could only see their shoulders up in the crowd.

The next thing I knew I was pushing my way through the mob, headed toward them. When I arrived, the Harley guy had Hannah around the waist, clutching her from behind. From the way he was swaying, I guessed he thought they were dancing.

Hannah jabbed her elbow back and struck absolutely nothing. I grabbed the guy's arm—the one tucked around Hannah's waist—and dug my thumbnail between the bones on the inside of his hairy wrist. He dropped Hannah, who zipped behind me, clutched my arm, and pulled.

"Come on!"

Before I could turn, the guy shoved me, two hands to my chest. I flew back into Hannah, both of us falling against the mob like dominoes. The crowd pushed back, though, propelling me toward the Harley guy. I saw his fist a moment before it smashed my eye.

I collapsed, my face on fire. I couldn't move. Just didn't have the energy. Then my world went black.

When I came to, everything was dark and loud. Several sets of hands were lifting me. Carrying me. The thought crossed my mind that the Harley guy was hauling me off to finish the job, and I thrashed, desperate to escape.

"We got you." Dad's voice. "You're okay."

I relaxed some but still struggled until Dad dropped my legs to the ground and I was standing. I felt dizzy, so I let myself be led. I squinted my eyes open but only one obeyed.

"He might have a concussion." Logan.

"Eli, how you feel?" Dad.

"Hannah okay?" Me. I said that. Classy.

"Eli, I'm fine," Hannah said. "Can you look at me? Look into my eyes?"

Eyes. Mine rolled around in my head, but I couldn't find anything to focus on.

"Let's get him out of here," Dad said.

I stumbled between two bodies, legs moving from instinct alone. The more I walked, the more my head cleared. The pulsing music faded, which eased the ache in my skull. I squinted. Focused straight ahead. Logan waving people out of the way. Looking back, eyes wide and worried. Good grief. We passed a line of vehicles. A parking lot? No, this was the street. We were leaving the LLC compound. Dad had his arm around my waist. So did Hannah. My arms had been slung over each of their shoulders.

How pathetic I must look. I seized control of my body and tried to stop, to get away from them. I could walk on my own, for Pete's sake. I wasn't a baby.

But they grabbed me tighter and continued to compel me forward. A pulsing throb in my head convinced me to give up the fight.

The next thing I knew I was sitting in the middle row of the van next to Hannah. Dad was driving, with Logan sitting shotgun yet hanging backwards over the seat to stare at me.

"Why did we leave?" I asked, coming back to myself.

"Hey, Eli." Hannah brushed her hand over my head, which felt really nice. She pushed back my hair to look into my eyes. My left eye, anyway. My right one was closed.

"What happened to you?" she asked.

I reached up and felt my swollen eye. "I got punched in the face."

Hannah smiled. Smiled! "Why'd we go to the night party?"

"To count enforcers. You laughing at me?"

"Only because you're cute." She held up her finger between my eyes, then moved it from side to side. "Follow my finger with your eyes," she said.

My stomach flipped as I tracked her finger from one side to the other. Hannah thought I was cute?

"Any pressure in your head? Neck pain?"

"A little in my head."

"Dizziness? Blurred vision? Nausea?"

She was doctoring me. "Uh, I feel kind of foggy."

"I wished I'd have been there," Logan said. "I would have punched that guy back."

"That would have been awesome, Logan." Hannah winked at me, which made my stomach zing again.

I scrambled for something to say. "How many enforcers working tonight, Dad?"

"Ten," Dad said.

"That's it?" I couldn't believe that was it.

"Yep, and I didn't recognize one of them," Dad said. "Must be new recruits."

"Guess night parties are not a good time to escape," I said.

"Probably not," Dad said.

I dwelled on this for a bit, then recalled my other question—the one that had gotten me punched in the face. "What did that guy sell you?" I asked Hannah. "The guy with the lights."

"Ecstasy out of a TicTac container," she said. "He also offered crystal meth."

"Free drugs?" I said, shocked. "Those guys were at the night party I went to with Jaylee that first week we were here."

"Not free," Hannah said. "He scanned my wristband. Said it would cost me fifty."

"Fifty credits?" Logan said. "Addicts would be starving at those prices."

"Being broke is a common problem for addicts," Hannah said.

"They'll be able to track which people use and which don't," I said.

"That's good information to have," Dad said.

"It sucks," I said, suddenly angry. Not that I needed a last straw, but this was it. "They're selling drugs. That's so irresponsible."

"I'm sure they think they're just being good party hosts," Dad said. "Helping people have a good time."

"Those are two very dangerous drugs," Hannah said.

"People could die," Logan said.

"They don't seem to care about that," I said.

•    •    •

Back at the house, Hannah bemoaned our lack of medical supplies. She found the remains of someone's half-drunk milkshake in the freezer and made me hold it against my eye.

"I should bring home some things from the hospital," she said. "I don't like being so unprepared here."

She insisted on sitting up with me in the living room, talking. In case I had a concussion, she said. I briefly wondered where everyone else had gone. Especially Logan, who usually hovered around Hannah like a mosquito. It was just the two of us, though. We talked about all kinds of things. My home in Phoenix. Her home in San Francisco. Her high school. My high school. Her trip to Guatemala. How long the enforcers might keep Reinhold in Rehab. Where Kimama might be and what she might be doing.

"What would you do if we could get out of here?" she asked.

"Go back to Reinhold's place and get my truck," I said. "Then set up a camp between the base of the mountain and the East River, like Reinhold said. Dig that irrigation ditch to send some of that clean water right to us. Then build some houses."

"You know how to build a house?"

"I know enough. Dad and I built a shed in the back yard. The task would be a lot easier with tools and a generator, which is why I want my stuff from Reinhold's place. With access to the water, we'd have everything we needed. We could scavenge medical supplies. Find some books on natural remedies. I had a great one in my truck before it was stolen. Lizzie and I used to help Mom grow tomatoes and peppers for her salsa garden. We'd need a bigger garden, though. We'd need to plant a lot and store everything in a cellar for winter. We'd have to dig a cellar. Winter will be the hardest. I don't know if enough animals survived that we could hunt."

Hannah asked me a ton more questions, and I talked and talked. I don't know what possessed me, but it was like I'd been holding it all in for so long, I just needed to get it out. All my ideas. All my plans. Life would be better outside this compound. Sure, we might not have access to restaurants or the Grid or concerts or drugs. But we didn't need any of that to survive.

No one did.

• • •

I must have fallen asleep, because when Dad woke me for work the next morning, I was on the couch, a blanket tucked over me. I still couldn't see out of my right eye. After I got over my confusion and remembered the previous night, I was just plain embarrassed. Some guy had knocked me out with one punch. And what had I said to Hannah last night, anyway?

I had talked. A lot.

I went into the bathroom to see what I looked like and wished I hadn't. My right eye was the color of a plum and swollen just as big. Bong was going to love mocking me all day. I reached for the faucet, turned the knob, and only caught myself when no water came out. I ran out to use the portable bathroom, then got dressed for work. I microwaved a breakfast burrito I'd found in the fridge and ate it in the van while Dad drove me to the Department of Water and Sanitation.

"Where did everyone go last night?" I asked.

"Hannah was taking good care of you, so I went to bed. Right after I encouraged Zach and Lizzie to challenge Logan to a game of Trivial Pursuit up in the attic." Dad winked at me.

"You left me *alone* with her on purpose?"

"I'm sorry, did you require a chaperone? Some sort of babysitter?"

I scowled. I couldn't believe my dad was trying to set me up. "That's not what I meant. I was not myself last night. I was babbling. I might have told her my eighth-grade locker combination."

"Good," Dad said. "It's about time you paid attention to a real woman."

My cheeks blazed. "What's *that* supposed to mean?"

"She likes you. And she likes you even more after you rescued her last night."

I snorted. "Tried."

"You don't have to win the battle to win the war, son," Dad said.

I shot Dad a dirty look, but the phrase played over and over in my head. We'd tried a lot of things so far in Safe Water. Lost more than we'd won. But the war wasn't over. In fact, the time had come to plan for the final battle, and this was a battle I intended to win.

# 21

**HANNAH**
**AUGUST 27**

Eli and his dad got into an argument at dinner Thursday night about whether or not they should turn in the guns. Seth wanted to. Eli did not.

Later that night, I found Eli out on the deck, sitting in one of the wooden chairs.

"You still upset?" I asked, taking a seat in the chair beside his.

"I'm more upset that Tracy and the Champions don't know what they're doing. That they think they can control people. That's not leading. This is supposed to be a free country."

"They do seem to have a shocking lack of common sense," I said. "But I've never been a fan of guns. Kind of a proponent against them, actually. My recent experience with Brandon didn't exactly change my mind."

"Yeah, getting shot at was not fun," Eli said.

"Which is why this thing with the guns doesn't bother me as much as some of the other things, like the ketamine."

"I get that," Eli said. "But if we give up our weapons, how will we defend ourselves against the enforcers?"

"Why would you want to go up against them?" I asked.

"I don't," he said. "It would be suicide."

"You just want to sneak out and avoid confrontation?"

"Absolutely. I'm just not sure we'll be able to."

It was good to hear him say that. Sometimes Eli bravery made me nervous.

"This group of rebels on Sunday night," he said. "Quinn hinted they are all about anarchy, not trying to leave. I don't want to fight Admin or help anyone fight them. You can't win a fight like that—not in one lifetime, anyway. People would have to agree on strategies, be organized, be discreet, and they won't. Someone will screw it up."

"How do you know? Maybe you should have a little more faith in humanity."

His eyes narrowed. "Are you really that naïve?"

I narrowed my eyes right back. "Are you really that cynical?"

We stared at each other. Eli cracked a smile first, and we both laughed and said, "Yes" at the same time.

"Why do you think people won't work together if the cause is important enough?" I asked him.

"Oh, they'll act like they're going to work together—like they want the same things. But I know people. People are selfish. Even good-hearted people. And they don't listen to sense. Unless the one leading happens to be attractive. Or really persuasive. People will follow then. Look at Zach. Guess how many girls I liked who liked him better?"

"Really?" I shot him a look. "This is about girls?"

He waved his hand, as if I was missing the point. "That's just one example. What I'm saying is, those girls didn't know either of us, but they liked what they saw when they looked at Zach, and they didn't see me at all. Riggs is another example. The guy is one fry short of a Happy Meal, but people love him and will do whatever he says."

The Happy Meal comment made me smile. "What you're saying is, it depends who's in charge of this rebellion," I said.

"I guess. I still don't want to start a war with enforcers, but I don't want to live here and be disrespected, either. I'm really curious to see what they talk about."

The sliding glass door whooshed aside, and Logan stepped out onto the deck. "Hey, guys. I stopped at the Avalanche to grab some dinner, and guess who I saw making out in a booth in the back?"

Logan looked at me expectantly, so I finally took a guess. "Cristobal and Antônia?" I asked, remembering seeing them together lately.

"Nope," Logan said, his eyes filled with mischief. "Jaylee and Riggs. Apparently they're dating now."

Eli slouched back in the wooden chair. "Of course they are."

Where was Logan's sense? "What's the matter with you?" I asked him.

Logan eyes widened. "What?"

"That was mean." I gestured toward Eli. "He's your friend. Why would you tell him that way?"

"It's fine," Eli said.

I whirled back to him. "You said you don't like when people disrespect you. Logan just did. Why don't you tell him how it makes you feel?"

"Logan, you're a jerk," Eli said, stone-faced. "You make me feel like the loser I am."

Logan lifted his bony shoulders in a shrug. "Sorry, man," he said.

Emotions warred in my chest. Was Eli laughing at me? After I'd tried to defend him? "You're not a loser," I told him, standing. "But you *are* stupid." I pushed past Logan and through the open sliding door, fleeing into the house and wishing with every step that I'd held my tongue and could take back those toxic words.

But I couldn't.

• • •

"It made me angry."

I was sitting in the wing chair across from Dixie, having just told her about my outburst with Eli.

"The conversation triggered you," Dixie said. "A similar thing happened the day that man came into your patient's exam room. His presence triggered feelings from your past, feelings your body remembered about Brandon, and your body reacted in order to protect you."

Some help that was. "How do I fix it?"

"It's not to be fixed, but you do need to learn when your body is overreacting," Dixie said. "When you feel that rush of energy, ask yourself where it's coming from. What in your story does that pain remind you of? Then you can separate things. 'That was then. That hurt from the past was hard for me, but that's not what's happening here. This is now. This is a different situation, and I'm okay.' If you can practice doing that—put the emotions where they belong—the energy often drains right out of you. Eventually you'll learn to manage your triggers in a healthier way and be left with truth."

That sounded lovely. "It was silly," I said, "but it made me so mad. Then I was angrier that I didn't have any control over myself. Logan was the one being mean, but I ended up looking like the bad guy."

"Control is a coping mechanism," Dixie said. "You were more bothered by what Logan said than Eli was, so you stepped into Eli's yard to deal with Logan's remark the way you felt Eli should have responded."

I frowned. "I totally did."

"Don't beat yourself up. Your heart was in the right place, but now you know that wasn't really your job. Eli is a big boy and can take care of himself."

I sighed, tired of how hard every little thing seemed to be. "What about when I'm afraid? When that man came into the hospital, I didn't have time to separate piles. He was attacking my patient. He was attacking me!"

"Always try and stay with your body in the present. Remind yourself of what is currently happening. 'He's not here for me. He's not Brandon. I need to be strong for my patient.' Then afterwards, give yourself patience and grace if things didn't go perfectly. Be kind to yourself."

"That's hard for me. I get mad at myself when I do stupid things."

"What stupid thing did you do?"

I snorted a laugh. "I picked Brandon."

Dixie pursed her lips. "If I brought in that young patient of yours who'd been abused, and she sat right next to you on the sofa, how would you feel toward her?"

"Empathetic," I said.

"Would you blame her for getting hurt? Would you call her stupid?"

"No. Of course not."

"Interesting. Why does she get grace, and you don't? What makes you so special that you bear so much more responsibility for what happened to you than your patient does for what happened to her?"

I was speechless. I'd never considered I was being cruel to myself.

"Catch those lies when they're feeding you extra helpings of shame and guilt and fear," Dixie said. "You're not stupid and you don't do stupid things. Those are error messages from your story. Call them out, and correct them with truth."

"Okay," I said. "I'll try."

● ● ●

I was a little surprised when Eli picked me up after my shift that day.

"Was there no one else to come get me?" I asked as I buckled my seatbelt.

"Did you want someone else?" Eli asked. "I'm sorry. Logan was still asleep, but I can wake him for you next time if that's what you'd prefer."

"Ha ha," I said. "I didn't want anyone else. I just thought you might be mad at me."

"For what? Yelling at Logan? I thought that was kind of funny."

"Funny! I called you stupid."

Eli shrugged and pulled out of the hospital lot onto Snowmass Road. "Logan sometimes gets under people's skin," he said. "I have a bad habit of trying to diffuse people's anger toward him."

"Like you did on Monday when you told him Lizzie wanted to ask me about girl stuff?"

He chuckled. "Exactly. But you were right. He doesn't think about anyone's feelings before he speaks. It's just not how he's wired. The problem is, I've been his friend since first grade. I'm used to it."

"You had just told me you were sick of people walking all over you."

"I had. You're totally right."

Gosh. All that worry about what I'd said over nothing. "Well, I'm sorry for butting in," I said, thinking of my conversation with Dixie. "It wasn't really my business. My father used to say mean things to my mother, and she never defended herself. I think Logan's insensitivity sometimes reminds me of that."

Had I really said all that out loud?

"You are going to break his heart," Eli said. "You know he's hoping to marry you."

My mouth dropped open. "Why would he hope that?"

"To repopulate the earth, of course. And why wouldn't he choose you? You're a catch."

My cheeks tingled. "I am?"

"Sure."

"Why?"

"Oh, now you're going to put *me* on the spot?"

I grinned. "You brought it up."

"I guess that's fair." He glanced at me, looked me over.

"Okay, well, you're brilliant. You're practically a doctor, which is super intimidating because I always want to say smart things around you, but I'm just not that smart, so . . . You're kind, except maybe to Logan." He chuckled. "You're great with Cree and Shy and Davis, and I don't know, it's just nice to see people care about them. Uh . . . You're really very pretty too." He stopped at the corner, looked both ways, then steered the van out onto the main road.

"You're blushing!" I said.

He laughed. "No, that's called being ruddy and handsome. It's not something I can really do anything about, Hannah, and I'd really appreciate it if you didn't look at me like a piece of meat."

"I'm a vegetarian," I said.

"You are not!" he said, then looked at me again. "Are you really?"

"No," I said.

"Huh. So that's what I get for paying you a compliment? I can see I'm going to have to be more careful with what I say to you."

Silence fell soft and comfortable as Eli drove us out of town.

"Why are you up so early?" I asked him.

He took a deep breath. "Cree woke me to take him to the bathroom. Then he couldn't sleep. I laid down with him, but his feet were like ice. As soon as he conked out, I got up. Played a few games of Boggle."

"With who?"

"Myself. No one else will play with me. Lizzie says it's a mercy because I suck at the game. I don't care, though. I just think it's fun."

"I'll play Boggle."

He glanced at me, then back to the road. "Aren't you tired?"

"I'd like to eat something before I go to bed."

"I can make you some eggs."

"We have eggs?"

"We have eggs. Tracy must have found some chickens because they've got a farm going out past Alpenglow with the

223

most expensive eggs in the history of mankind. Ten credits a dozen, but they taste good."

"Can't wait to try them."

So, Eli made me eggs while I changed out of my scrubs, then I beat him in several games of Boggle before fatigue sent me off to bed. Once I was tucked in, though, I couldn't sleep. I kept replaying Eli's words over and over in my memory. How he'd said I was brilliant and intimidating and kind and really, very pretty too.

I'd never seen myself that way before, and I kind of liked it.

# 22

ELI
AUGUST 29

The next few days passed by in relative quiet. I worked. I picked up Hannah from the hospital whenever I could. She and I played a lot of Boggle, and I had to admit those nights were becoming my favorite part of the day. I honestly don't know why I so thoroughly enjoyed playing a game I was so bad at, nor did it bother me that Hannah was a gifted wordsmith. I liked watching her try to hide her smile every time she beat me.

Whenever we could, Dad and I monitored enforcer shifts and marked them on our town map. We discovered there were always four enforcers on patrol at each gate with the exception of 3:00 a.m. to 6:00 a.m. and the 11:30 a.m. to 1:30 p.m. lunch hours. At those times, there were only two.

We couldn't agree on whether we'd take the northern or

southern gate or how we would get through.

"The south gate will put us on the road back to Durango," I said. "We can head right for Reinhold's place."

"Yeah, but it will also take us through Crested Butte," Dad said. "Isn't that where those warlords are from?"

I wasn't sure. "My biggest concern is that going north traps us. We'd be at the end of the road with no way out," I said.

"We could hike south along the East River," Dad said. "It wouldn't be long before we'd reach County Road 738, which would let us out on the highway south of Crested Butte."

"By that dinky little airport," I said, wondering if Admin had conscripted any pilots for scavenger trips. "The northern gate has less traffic. If we could get past it, it would take enforcers longer to catch us."

"Who goes out of the gates each day?" Dad asked.

"Enforcers and garbage men," I said. "Some big rigs carrying scavenged supplies. None of the trucks go north. Not even the garbage trucks. The closest landfill is in Gunnison."

"Then we need the garbage trucks," Dad said, "and you have access."

"Not really," I said. "I'm only a sub driver. We could actually haul a lot inside a garbage truck." An idea came to mind, bringing a chill over my arms. "Actually, why not haul people? One driver. A load full of people. The guards at the gate would never know how many had passed through."

"Because no one looks in the back of garbage trucks," Dad said. "Can you get a truck?"

"I don't know," I said. "There are no spares. We use every truck every day."

"Then we go at night," Dad said.

"But then it's after hours. The enforcers at the gate wouldn't let a garbage truck leave then. I'll think about it some more and see if I can come up with something. In the meantime, what about the guns?"

Tracy had set up several gun donation locations around town, which Dad and I had ignored so far, though we'd argued about it plenty.

"I still think we should each turn in a handgun," Dad said. "Keep the rifles. That way they'll assume we were cooperating and won't come looking."

I didn't want to cooperate at all. "They already know how I feel about this place," I said. "There's no way they'll believe I'm cooperating. Plus, turning in a gun will only make them suspect I have more. What if we hid the handguns in the house and stashed the rifles out back someplace? That way, if they do come looking, we'll look guilty, which is what they'd expect. They'll find our hidden guns, take them away, and figure they won."

"They'll also punish someone for it," Dad said. "What did they say the penalty was?"

"They didn't," I reminded him. "They only said anyone who turned in guns would get an extra week of credits."

Dad released a deep breath. "I'd like to think about it a little more. I don't want to give them reason to send anyone to Rehab. We'll make a decision by Sunday."

That was fine by me, until the enforcers came by Saturday night. Dad had taken Cree and Davis to bring back dinner when Harvey and Vrahnos banged on the front door. Assuming they'd come to search for guns, I almost lost my cool, but Vrahnos asked for Lizzie. They'd come to conscript her out of daycare and into a new elementary school to work as a kindergarten teacher. She'd start Monday after the morning party.

The whole thing scared me so much that, as soon as they left, I hid the guns myself. I put the first handgun inside a box of garbage bags in the cupboard over the kitchen stove. The second handgun I put in a Ziploc bag and duct taped it inside the toilet tank. I was hoping they'd check that cliché location first. I wrapped Dad's and my rifles and what ammo we'd brought for them in trash bags. Then I climbed one of the blue spruce trees in our back yard and tied the bags to some upper branches. When I told Dad what I'd done, he said to leave everything as I put it. I slept soundly that night, confident I'd done what I could to protect the rifles.

•    •    •

Sunday night, Dad and I drove over to 5 East Silver Lane. It was a little subdivision with five massive houses. The land was fairly barren here. The only trees around had been planted as part of the landscaping. Cars were triple-parked in the driveway and bumper-to-bumper along the road.

"Looks like a good turnout," Dad said.

"I don't like how it feels exposed here," I said. "Our place is much more secluded."

We knocked, and someone opened the door without greeting us. It made me feel like no one was in charge. We entered a modern house with a high ceiling and open living room-kitchen space. The place was packed with people, all listening to a guy sitting on the kitchen counter. He had a narrow face, dark curly hair in need of a cut, and a scruffy beard that was graying at the chin. His eyes were deep-set and intense, and he was wearing an American flag T-shirt.

". . . to our great shame," he said. "Nothing is less worthy for a civilized people than to allow themselves to be governed by those with no morals. We did not vote for Loca and Liberté Champion." The crowd shouted their agreement. "We did not vote for Morgan Tracy." More assents. "So let us not surrender our free will so quickly to their ideals. No. We must resist. We must stand strong. We must fight back."

"How?" someone called out.

"How, indeed?" the man said. "That is why we're here tonight. Let's work together. Make a plan."

"We could take Town Hall," a guy behind me said. "If we planned it out in advance."

"To what end?" asked the guy sitting on the counter.

"Free the prisoners inside, for a start."

Several cheered at this idea.

Quinn appeared out of the crowd. "Hey, you came!"

"This is my dad," I said. "Dad, Quinn."

"Seth McShane," Dad said, shaking Quinn's hand. "Who's the speaker?"

"That's Brett Durzinski," Quinn said. "He organized the

protests at the front gates back at the start of all this."

"So, he's in charge?" I asked.

"More or less," Quinn said. "No one is really in charge."

I met my dad's gaze. We both knew better than that. Someone was always in charge, whether they wanted to admit it or not. And Brett Durzinski didn't look like he was shying away from the spotlight.

"What about the mansion?" Durzinski asked. "It's not enough to take Town Hall if the mansion is still in their control."

"We need to take both," a guy said. I recognized him. It was Rick from Los Angeles who, with his friends, had joined us for our water protest and twenty-four hours in Rehab.

"Champion House is impenetrable," someone said. "They've added every state-of-the-art security feature they could find to that place. It's a fortress."

"Then we need to find a way to take it down from the inside," Durzinski said. "Who do we know who works in the building?"

This was met with silence.

"Come on," Durzinski growled. "Someone here knows someone on the inside. We don't succeed unless we take risks. So, speak up!"

"My son is friends with a guy on the Champions' AV crew," a man said. "They won't betray the Champions, though."

"Ahh," Durzinski said, grinning at the man who had just sold out his son. "Then we must persuade them carefully. Who else? Think, now. Don't hold back!"

"My sister works at Champion House as a maid. Cleans mostly. Sometimes runs errands," a woman said.

As Durzinski seized upon the poor woman with more questions, Dad leaned his head close to mine. "I've seen enough," he said. "You want to stay?"

I shook my head, eager to put some dark road between me and Brett Durzinski.

We said goodbye to Quinn, using the kids as an excuse, then sidled our way back to the door. Neither of us said a word until we were safely in the Silver Bullet, driving away.

"That was reckless," I said. "Enforcers could have walked in at any moment. If they're not more careful, they're all going to end up shot or arrested long before they take Town Hall."

"They sure don't have a healthy understanding of what they're up against," Dad said. "Don't get me wrong, an uprising like that *could* work, in time. But Mr. Durzinski seemed way too eager to risk others for the sake of his plan. A true leader would slow down and think before taking advantage of an already strained father-son relationship."

"So, we stick with the garbage truck plan?" I asked.

"It's better than what Brett Durzinski is planning," Dad said.

"I completely agree," I said, relieved that Dad and I were on the same page.

• • •

At the morning party the next day, Tracy had an announcement he said he was reluctant to make. "We are approaching winter, y'all, and Colorado winters are harsh. Water will still flow under the ice, but the freeze will slow it some. Because of that we've decided to plan ahead across the map. Daily allowance will be dropping to twenty-five credits a day. We'll also be limiting y'all to four showers a week and five gallons of drinking water a week."

The crowd lost it, booing.

Tracy spoke over the noise. "Last night was the Safe Day Deadline to turn in all weapons before midnight. There will be consequences for violators."

He didn't say what those might be, which left me a little apprehensive, but there was nothing to do about it now. So, I tried to enjoy the rest of my day off.

Tuesday morning, I almost didn't want to get out of bed. It was September 1. We'd been here a month already, and it was harder than ever to imagine ever getting out of here. I didn't know how to get promoted to full-time driver at work or steal a truck. I decided to pour a little more effort into Antônia's plan of bugging Tracy's office. At least then we might learn something that would enable us to escape.

The smell of eggs finally pulled me from bed. Lizzie, Hannah, and Shyla were at the kitchen table, enjoying a breakfast of eggs and salsa.

"Where did you get salsa?" I asked.

"Bought a few To Go containers from the Avalanche," Lizzie said. "Today is the first day of school for me and the kids. I thought it would be nice to celebrate a little."

Didn't sound like anything worth celebrating to me. I sat in the empty chair beside Hannah and helped myself to some eggs. "What grade is everybody in?" I asked.

"Kindergarten," Shyla said, glowering. "Again."

"Cree and Shyla will be in my kindergarten class," Lizzie said. "I think it will be safer. And Davis is in fourth grade."

"My teacher is a guy," Davis said, pushing his glasses up his nose.

Well, at least I only had to worry about Davis's teacher. "Where's Dad?"

"He got called in early to fix some enforcer vehicle," Lizzie said. "Logan drove him on his way to the hospital. He said for you to take the van, drop us off at school, then pick him up after you're done today."

"How will you guys get back?" I asked.

"Zach is getting dropped off at the hospital after his shift," Lizzie said. "He'll grab the van keys from Logan and pick us up. One of us can grab Logan later on tonight."

Someone knocked on our door.

"Oh no," Lizzie said.

"What?" I asked. "Are you expecting someone?"

"No," she said, "but it can't be good, can it?"

She was right. I opened the door to Harvey, Vrahnos, Miller, Wick, and two of their friends I'd never met before.

"We have a warrant to search the premises for illegal weaponry," Harvey said.

My pulse shot up, but I'd expected this. "Who is issuing warrants around here?" I asked.

"Admin issues warrants," Vrahnos said.

"Well, I don't have any illegal weaponry," I said.

"We received a complaint that you were seen with guns," Harvey said.

"Really. From who?" I asked, wondering if that were true, and if so, who had sold us out.

"We're not at liberty to say." Harvey patted my cheek as he pushed past me into the house. "Get into a fight, did you? Wait, don't tell me. The other guy looks worse?" He chuckled.

I ignored him and stepped back so Vrahnos and his buddies could also enter. "Can I see a copy of this warrant?" I asked.

"We don't have a copy with us," Vrahnos said.

"I'm pretty sure you're supposed to give me a copy, or I don't have to let you in," I said.

At the kitchen table, I caught sight of Hannah rolling up our map of town. She slid it up her sleeve. Relief flooded me. Smart girl.

"How many people live in this residence?" Harvey asked. He was already in the kitchen, rifling through drawers.

Before I could finish my mental head count, Lizzie said, "Nine."

"How many here at present?" Harvey asked. "Just you four?"

"The boys are still asleep," Lizzie said.

"Get them up," Harvey said. "I want everyone out here where I can see them."

Hannah came with me as we woke Cree and Davis. Hannah led Cree by the hand out to the living room. Davis and I followed. When Davis saw the officers, he darted behind me.

"Davis, sweetie, come have some eggs," Lizzie said, waving him to the seat I'd vacated. Davis obeyed, sitting beside his sister who was staring at the enforcers like a frightened deer.

Vrahnos stayed in the kitchen to keep an eye on us while Harvey and the other three enforcers searched the place. The first gun found was the one I hid in the toilet tank. Harvey himself carried that out and laid it on the kitchen island like evidence.

"No illegal weaponry, did you say?" he asked, looking at me.

"I've never seen that before in my life," I said, hoping I had a good poker face.

"If it's not his, it's the EMT's," Harvey said to Vrahnos. "We'll just have to check them for prints, then see if we have a match."

That I hadn't seen coming. I didn't expect they'd have a crime scene investigation team in their newly formed law enforcement organization.

"Not so cocky now, are you?" Harvey grinned at me. "Where is Mr. Olympian, anyway?" At our collective glares, he added, "That's right. I heard all about what a great swimmer he is. Lot of good that'll do him now."

"Zach is at work," Lizzie said, eyes narrowed.

Harvey grunted. "Well, *Zach* had better watch himself too."

He went back up the stairs. I felt better, knowing there were no more guns in the house but the one in the kitchen, and for a while I thought I might get away with them not finding that one until one of Harvey's minions started emptying cupboards onto the kitchen floor. Shyla began to cry, which made Cree cry too. The boy crawled onto Hannah's lap, and she hummed softly to him.

"Do you mind not making the place a mess?" Lizzie asked, when the lid to a sauce pan rolled over by her feet. "I have to teach school today and don't have time to clean this up."

The enforcer ignored her.

A commotion up the stairs raised the hair on my arms. Harvey returned with Logan's navy blue backpack, and my stomach twisted.

"This yours, Mr. McShane?" Harvey asked.

"No," I said.

Harvey set it on the island and reached inside. "Whose is it?"

I shrugged. "Not sure."

He pulled out a beige canvas Sportlock handgun case. As he made a production of unzipping it slowly, I glanced at Lizzie, but her eyes were fixed on the 9mm Glock Harvey had unsheathed from the case.

All I could think was, *Logan Graham, you idiot.*

But that wasn't all Logan had stashed in his pack. Harvey

also unveiled a Colt Revolver, also zipped in a soft case; several boxes of shells; three tasers; and seven knives, all in sheaths.

"That's quite the arsenal," Vrahnos said to Harvey.

"Boss." This from the enforcer decimating the kitchen. He'd found the gun I'd stashed above the stove.

"This many guns, Mr. McShane . . ." Harvey released a deep sigh, as if the scene tired him. "You're going to be in Rehab a long time."

At those words, Shyla's crying rose in pitch, then Davis started crying too.

"You don't know those are Eli's," Lizzie said.

"Tell me they're Zach Montgomery's," Harvey said, a leer on his face. "I'd love to throw that Boy Scout in Rehab again."

"They're all mine," I said, figuring they'd find my prints if they looked, so I might as well keep the others out of trouble. "The Constitution of the United States gives its citizens the right to bear arms."

"This is not the United States of America, Mr. McShane," Harvey said. "Consider this a private nation. We have different laws here."

"We don't want to live here," I said. "Let us take our stuff and go."

"So you can join the Somerset Shadow?" Harvey said. "You do strike me as the type he'd recruit."

"Who?"

"Guns are for killing, Mr. McShane," Harvey said, "and we're not going to let anyone have that responsibility but us."

"Guns are also for protecting myself and my family from people who would try to harm us," I said. "Enforcers included."

"Obey the law and you have no reason to fear enforcers," Harvey said.

"Loca and Liberté Champion and Mr. Tracy don't get to make laws for me," I said.

"They already did, Mr. McShane," Harvey said. "Now, are you going to come peacefully, or would you like to try the taser?" He picked up one of the tasers from Logan's hoard.

"I'll come," I said.

Harvey smiled and waved the kitchen enforcer over to cuff me. Before he could reach me, Lizzie came and hugged me, which prompted Shyla and Davis to stampede from the table to do the same. Three sets of arms, squeezing at once, felt nice. Hannah got up and carried Cree toward where we stood, all of us in a little cluster.

"Destroy Logan for me," I whispered to Lizzie.

My sister answered with a prayer. "Jesus, go with Eli and keep him safe."

I extended my hands toward the enforcer, hoping he'd cuff me in front, but he twisted my arm behind my back, which shot a spike of pain through my splinted fingers.

"Easy on the fingers!" I said.

This made the kids start crying again. Lizzie shooed them back to the table, but Hannah stayed close. Cree reached for me. Hannah kept trying to turn him away, but he just swiveled back in the opposite direction, arms outstretched, so he could see me.

"Let me tell the kid goodbye," I said to the enforcer.

He shoved me toward Cree and Hannah. Cree grabbed my neck and tried to climb into my arms, but as they were cuffed behind my back, I couldn't take hold of him. Hannah stepped close, supporting his weight.

Cree nuzzled his face into the hollow of my neck, his hair tickling my face. "*Nda*. Don't go away," he said. "Stay home."

"It's okay, buddy," I told him. "You take care of Hannah for me until I get back, okay?" I met Hannah's eyes across Cree's hunched back, and she smiled. I pulled back and tried to see his face, but he grabbed my ears and held me close. "You'll help, right, Cree? Help Hannah take care of everyone?"

"*Goshį̱į̱*, Eli. *Ayóó ánóshí.*" No clue what he'd said, but his tone sounded like an agreement.

"Thank you, Cree. I'll see you soon, okay?"

He turned, laying his head on Hannah's shoulder. Then she leaned in and kissed me softly on the lips.

"Bye, Eli."

Stunned, yet pleasantly surprised, I barely had time to form a coherent thought before the enforcer yanked me toward the door.

"Bye," I told Hannah, then added a pathetic, "Thanks."

The moment the enforcer pulled me outside, all three kids started howling again. The enforcer led me down the stairs and packed me inside his cruiser.

They drove me to Rehab. Again. But Hannah had kissed me, and that was pretty much all I could think about as they processed me, a new procedure that included fingerprinting and a mug shot. They didn't re-splint and bandage my fingers afterwards, either. As I sat in my cell awaiting Connie Lawler's arrival, I fingered the puckered scar on both sides of my hand and inspected my fingers, which were almost able to stretch out straight again.

And I thought about Hannah.

Why had she kissed me? Was she just being nice? Or had she kissed me because she wanted to? Because she liked me?

I suddenly wanted that to be true more than anything—more than even wanting to leave this place. The possibility filled my chest with a kind of fierce pride, which was probably stupid because I was likely reading way too much into that kiss.

I used to think that Jaylee was way out of my league. I was smarter now. I never really knew what I wanted in a girlfriend until Jaylee had shown me what I didn't want. Not only was Hannah everything I'd told her she was—smart and beautiful and completely intimidating—she and I got along. We could have real, two-way conversations about things that mattered.

With Jaylee, I'd been afraid that she'd find me naive and inexperienced compared to everyone she'd dated before, and that I'd be humiliated. With Hannah, I was far more afraid I'd find her to be so perfect I'd never look at anyone else the rest of my life. This was going to kill Logan.

Nothing I could do about it now, staring at the walls of Rehab. This time I would spend ninety-six hours being brainwashed by Connie Lawler that "guns were evil," and I must "trust the enforcers" to protect me. She made me chant these phrases again and again, and they also piped them into my cell through a ceiling speaker and played them at night. There was no point in arguing if I wanted to get out of this place, so I said whatever she asked me to. But me trusting anyone in this place was *never* going to happen.

The second morning, I woke feeling groggy and confused. I had a red mark on my hand and figured something ugly must have bitten me. After that I felt itchy everywhere, which was likely all in my head, but I had a hard time sleeping.

I also spent a huge chunk of each day on porta-potty patrol, wearing a yellow hazmat suit and spraying poo off the walls. Good times.

They released me Saturday afternoon. I walked over to the EMT building and was relieved to find Zach there. He gave me the keys to his van and told me to send Lizzie to pick him up at ten that night.

When I got home, I was surprised to find Hannah on childcare duty.

"You're back," she said.

"I thought you worked Saturdays," was what came out of my mouth.

"We had some shift changes," she said. "Are you okay? Are you hungry?"

"I'm starving. I probably should have stopped and picked up something to eat."

"We have a piece of carrot cake," Hannah said. "Lizzie got it for you to cheer you up when you got back. Said it was your favorite."

"It is."

Hannah removed a plastic clamshell container from the fridge with the biggest piece of carrot cake I'd ever seen. She handed it to me.

"This is huge," I said. "Want some?"

One corner of her mouth tipped up. "Sure."

She pulled two paper plates from the cupboard and grabbed a plastic knife and two forks. We sat at the table, me on one end, Hannah adjacent to me.

"How is your hand?" she asked, motioning to my unbandaged fingers.

I held it up. The middle two fingers still tilted in a bit. It was nothing compared to what it had been before, when I looked like Spiderman trying to shoot a web. "It's better." I was going to show her my spider bite, but I could hardly see it anymore. It didn't seem worth mentioning. "Where are the kids?"

"Upstairs playing Logan's Switch. I was just reading." She motioned to a book laying open on the couch.

"*Dune?*" I said.

"I found it on the bookshelf. It's good."

"It's one of my favorites."

I sliced two pieces off the cake and put them on the plates. As we ate, Hannah filled me in on how everyone had been plotting with Antônia on how to bug Tracy's office.

I was eager to do anything to fight against this place. "What did they decide?"

"Nothing yet. They've been down there a lot, taking turns on reconnaissance. No one has any idea how to get into Champion House without being seen."

"Really." I wondered what the full story was there. I'd have to talk with Cristobal when I had the chance.

We ate in silence for several bites. I felt nervous yet totally comfortable too. Aware, was maybe the word for it. Then for some reason, I said, "You kissed me."

Her gaze flicked to mine, her eyes deep and liquid brown. "Did it bother you?"

"No," I said, scrambling to think of something clever to say next. "I was kind of hoping you'd do it again."

"Right now?" she asked. I couldn't read her expression.

My heart beat faster, and my insides felt hot and electric. "Sure."

She pushed aside her plate and leaned toward me. I did the same and met her halfway. Our kiss wasn't make-out wild like kissing Jaylee. It was soft and careful and tasted sweet, like frosting. I got lost in the moment, wondering why this girl was kissing me, of all people—when the door opened, and Logan walked inside.

"Oh, I see how it is."

# 23

**HANNAH**
**SEPTEMBER 6**

Logan finally trudged out of the front doors of the hospital and crossed the lot. He stopped about two yards in front of the van, staring. I guess he saw who was driving and was trying to decide if he wanted to suffer through the conversation or not. I couldn't blame him. I still wasn't sure myself.

He finally got in the van. "If you're going to tell me how sorry you are about liking Eli, just don't," he said. "I like Eli too, so I'm not surprised."

I frowned and let his words tumble in my brain. "You like Eli? Like him, like him?"

"What! Gosh, no!" Logan rubbed his face and growled. "I'm just saying he's my friend, and he's a great guy, so of course you'd like him. Everyone likes Eli."

"That's funny. He told me everyone likes Zach."

Logan tipped his head, conceding the point. "That's true. Everyone does like Zach."

Another long moment of silence passed.

Logan took a deep breath, paused, like he wasn't sure he really wanted to say whatever it was that he was thinking, then spoke. "Eli and I are the nobodies, see? Zach and Josh are the cool ones. Cristobal rides the line between cool and nobody, but he's an athlete, so that pushes him closer to cool, though none of us three has ever had a girlfriend. Josh and Zach had more than enough for all of us. Then the Jaylee thing happened, and I saw it with my own eyes. It changed everything. Suddenly it felt like if Eli could get a girl like Jaylee, then maybe I could get a girl like you."

I thought of Dixie and decided it might be better for me to just listen and let him get this off his chest.

"I guess I got a little carried away," Logan said. "I said something about you to Linsey last week, and he told me to leave you alone. Said there was a reason Susan had scheduled us at different times. I knew then that I was being delusional. That you didn't even want to be my friend."

"That's not true," I said. "We're friends. I just didn't want to give you the wrong idea."

He scowled at his knees. "Eli knew I liked you. He should have told me."

"Can I tell you my side?" I said.

He shrugged.

"When Eli came into that gas station and saved me from Brandon, he saved my life. And if he hadn't invited me with you guys . . . if I'd stayed on my own in Flagstaff . . . I'd be dead. Or as good as dead, anyway. For that, Eli has always been special to me. And he doesn't know this, but he was so good about just talking to me. He didn't push to get the story about who Brandon was. He just gave me my space. He respected me in a way Brandon never did. He let me be myself. He didn't criticize me. He impressed me. How he kept you all together, despite Jaylee and Krista being so desperately immature in the face of the pandemic. He was so strong and brave yet he doesn't see himself that way, which is endearing. I liked him instantly, but he liked someone else. So I did my best to give him the respect he'd given me. But I did not like Jaylee Jennings for Eli. Not at all."

Logan snorted, and a grin split his face.

"It's no secret that Eli and I have been spending a lot of time together lately. I want you to know that nothing happened until the day he was arrested. The enforcers found all those guns, and Eli said they were his to protect you and Zach, who Officer Harvey was just itching to blame. They put him in handcuffs. And when everyone was saying goodbye, I saw my chance, and I took it. I kissed him. And when he came back, he kind of asked me why, so I kissed him again to make my feelings very clear. That's when you walked in. So, he couldn't have told you because he's been in Rehab the whole time."

"Oh," Logan said.

"I like Eli," I said. "I don't need your blessing, Logan, but I'd like it just the same. Because whether or not you believe it, we are friends."

He looked skeptical. "Why'd you ask to have your schedule changed, then?"

I took a deep breath. "I had just survived Brandon. Your attention at the hospital . . . I know you didn't mean to bother me, but you weren't getting my hints. It was making me uncomfortable."

His eyes bulged. "You thought I was stalking you?"

"I knew you weren't, but it sometimes felt like it, yeah."

"I'm so sorry," he said, looking completely miserable. "I hope you and Eli work out. I really do."

"Thanks," I said. "Someday, you're going to find someone who is as interested in you as you are in her."

"I doubt that," he said.

"Be patient," I said. "The day will come."

•　　•　　•

I wanted to spend every free moment I had with Eli.

Unfortunately, the sheer number of people living in the house didn't make that easy. On Sunday, I replaced the splint on his fingers that the enforcers had removed to fingerprint him, then we had a lovely walk, and we spent most of Monday together—went to the morning party, hung out on the deck, took Cree and Shyla for ice cream, and played Boggle until the wee hours of the morning. Then came Tuesday, and our schedules the rest of the week were opposites. I was on nights from three in the afternoon until three in the morning, while Eli worked Tuesday through Saturday, eight to four.

Eli came to see me after his shift on Tuesday—gave me the keys to the van. He and Seth had driven both vans down here so they could leave one for me. Apparently, no one wanted to pick me up at three a.m. this week. Linsey caught us kissing in the lobby and had been teasing me ever since.

I looked forward to my meeting with Dixie that evening on my dinner break. I was anxious to tell her about Eli. After I finished my rounds, Susan told me Dr. Bayles wanted to see me in his office. I went straight there, a little worried the doctor had also seen Eli and me in the lobby and was going to lecture me about public displays of affection in the workplace.

He'd better not.

I found the door open and knocked on the frame.

"Hannah, come in!" Dr. Bayles stood from behind his desk. "Close the door behind you. I have some news to share that is confidential, and I don't want anyone overhearing."

I hesitated, not sure I trusted this man enough to be trapped alone with him in his office, but finally closed the door and took the seat before his desk. "I hope it's nothing bad," I said.

"I'm afraid it is." He rubbed his chin and sighed. "You've been off for three days, so you'd have no way of knowing, but last Friday we diagnosed two new cases of HydroFlu. Since then, five more cases have come in."

A shiver ran up my arms. "You're sure?"

"Yes, but it's a new strain—a very different strain. The virus has mutated. We don't yet know if it is more or less deadly."

"How are the patients you treated?" I asked.

"Still with us," he said.

"Were you able to identify a common source of contamination?" I asked.

"Not yet, which is why this is extremely confidential. We can't tell anyone, not even our closest friends. If word got out, it would be chaos."

"I understand," I said.

"I believe the virus is no longer waterborne," Dr. Bayles said.

"Why is that?" I asked.

"Because all seven of the patients we've admitted for HydroFlu symptoms also happen to be carrying a bloodborne pathogen—and not the same one."

Another chill ran over me. "You think the new strain is bloodborne?"

"I do, which in a way is good. Bloodborne pathogens are not as easily transmitted as waterborne or even airborne pathogens. I hope that will give us the time we need to get ahead of this. I need you to know what to look for and to keep it confidential, even from patients. We're not telling them we think they have the HydroFlu. Not yet, anyway."

"I understand," I said, though I didn't like the idea of keeping things from my patients.

"I'm also going to need you to accompany me to Champion House at six thirty today. Someone who lives there is infected and wants to keep that private."

"I'm happy to help, sir," I said, wondering who it was, though frustrated that I'd miss my appointment with Dixie.

"Please, Hannah, call me Jason." He went on to describe the symptoms to look for in regard to the new strain of HydroFlu and where we were keeping the infected patients.

I returned to the floor in a daze—scared, to be honest. Just when life had started to resemble some kind of normal . . .

"You talk to Bayles?" Linsey asked me when I returned to the nurse's station.

"Yeah," I said.

"Pretty scary, yo?"

I nodded. "Yeah."

"You be careful out there, you know what I'm saying? You and that boyfriend of yours. You got protection?"

My cheeks burned at the insinuation. "Oh, we're not . . . We haven't . . . He's not even really my boyfriend. Not officially, anyway."

Linsey lifted his hands. "Didn't mean to pry. Just be smart out there, okay? This thing has got STD written all over it, and I don't want anything to happen to you. I'd have to work a lot more hours, and that would upset my wife."

I grinned. "I'll be careful, I promise."

"Good," he said. "Now do me a favor and replace the IV for 7A. She keeps ripping it out so I'll come see her. Tell her I went home, will ya?"

I chuckled and started gathering the supplies. "She won't believe me, but I'll try."

• • •

That night, Dr. Bayles and I followed Jennie up the red-carpeted stairs to the second floor of Champion House. The ornate décor continued to accent dark wood floors and ceilings that were painted emerald green and red. The place would look pretty decorated for Christmas.

"We still on for Thursday at your place?" Jennie asked.

"Absolutely," Dr. Bayles said. "I've been looking forward to it."

As we traversed a long hallway, I pondered the idea of Dr. Bayles dating Jennie when I thought he was with Monica.

Jennie left us in a bedroom in the back of the house, and the fishy odor on the air made my skin crawl with memories of finding the dead kidnappers, the buildings in Flagstaff, and Cree's mom at the Holiday Inn.

We found our patient in bed, already intubated and receiving fluids from an IV stand. He was male, Caucasian, and handsome despite his haggard appearance and the pimply rash coating his face and arms. I didn't recognize him; however, the woman seated on a chair beside his bed and holding his hand was Liberté Champion.

She looked as if her bedside vigil had exhausted her, yet she jumped to her feet and pulled back her chair, motioning us into the space she'd just vacated. "It is about time! I wish you did not make us wait so very long, Jason. It is unkind."

"Hannah, check his IV and fluids," Dr. Bayles said as he approached the patient.

I did as directed, curious how long Dr. Bayles had been coming here.

"How are you feeling today, Mr. Kipp?" Dr. Bayles asked.

The man was beaming at me. "Better since you brought an exotic Asian princess to take care of me," he said.

The term, meant as a compliment, had always pushed my buttons. I normally would have let it pass, but I'd been practicing being brave lately. "Did you know the word 'exotic' means 'rare' or 'unique?'" I asked. "Since there are more Asian people on the planet than Caucasian, I'd say you, sir, are the exotic one."

The man laughed. "Oh, I like you," he said. "Though I'd counter that if Safe Water is the last place on earth with any kind of population, I suspect we're all exotic at this point."

I cracked a smile. "True," I said.

"Barkley Kipp," he said. "What's your name?"

"Hannah Cheng."

Dr. Bayles asked Barkley several questions, the answers of which indicated there had been little change since the previous visit.

"We sent out two more teams," Liberté said. "Everything will be better when we can replace the—how you say?—medicines? I have concerns about the public. Morgan is against my wishes to warn them about this, but I feel we should."

"Mr. Tracy is wise to hesitate," Dr. Bayles said. "It would incite panic."

A chill ran up my arms as I gleaned what they were taking about. "Forgive me, Ms. Champion," I said, "But I thought you were our leader, not Mr. Tracy."

Liberté gaze turned icy. "I am the leader of Safe Water.

Morgan speaks for me."

I raised my eyebrows. "I see."

Barkley chuckled. "I don't think she believes you, babe."

"You believe I am not?" she asked.

"Hannah spoke out of turn," Dr. Bayles said, shooting me a glare. "Apologize."

"*Non*," Liberté said to me. "I want to know your feelings. Tell me honestly."

Was I walking into a trap? Eli wouldn't hesitate to say what he really felt. "Well, I just think if you care about the community you've built here, you should make them a part of this. Include them in the mission. Let them cheer you on. And make yourself an example by getting tested. This new strain is dangerous. The sooner we know who is infected, the better."

Liberté looked to Dr. Bayles. "You disagree?"

His mouth flapped. "Well, it would certainly help to contain it if we tested everyone."

"What would happen to those with a positive result?" Liberté asked.

"We would treat them as best we can," he said. "We have a good pharmacy. It just won't last forever."

Liberté reached for Barkley and took hold of his hand. "What do you think?"

"Do it, Libby," he said. "If anyone can put a positive spin on this, it's you."

Liberté seemed to consider his words, then she kissed Barkley's lips and stroked back his hair. "All right, *mon amour*. Time to spin."

# 24

ELI
SEPTEMBER 9

Wednesday morning, Dad, Logan, and I went to the showers at the crack of dawn to case the LLC mansion. Dad took the front of the house and sent Logan and me around back. It was the first chance I'd had to be alone with Logan since the day I got out of Rehab.

"Hey, I'm sorry about Hannah," I said.

Logan shrugged like it didn't matter. "It's okay. Hannah told me everything." He looked away. "I'll forgive you if you forgive me for what the enforcers found in my backpack."

My eyes widened. "Yeah! Where did all that come from?"

He winced. "Ace in Flagstaff."

"You had it all this time? In a backpack? Where the kids could get to it? Logan!"

"I knew you'd be mad," he said. "But we're even, right?"

I blew a raspberry, then narrowed my eyes, playing it up for all it was worth. "I went to jail for you," I said.

"I'm sorry! If I'd been home, I would have fessed up. I promise."

I slapped his back. "Naw, man, we're cool. But if you get your hands on a gun again, you bring it to me and let me teach you how to take care of it. You can't keep a gun in a backpack under your bed. Especially in a house full of kids."

"They weren't loaded."

I fought to keep my voice calm, but it still sounded strained. "The ammo was in the backpack with the guns! You don't think Davis could figure out how to load it?"

Logan looked miserable, so I figured I'd punished him enough. I nodded to a massive deck on the back of the house. "Think we could get in that way?"

We were careful not to linger too long at Champion House. That night Hannah let me use her cell phone to text Cristobal. I knew he'd been hesitant when Antônia first brought up the idea, but he was the best chance we had to get a recording device into Tracy's office. I suddenly felt like Brett Durzinski, ready to put pressure on whatever contact I had to get my way. I promised myself I would just talk to Cristobal—find out how he felt about everything—but he never responded to the text. Logan emailed Antônia to ask about him, but that also received no reply. I hoped nothing had happened to them.

We spent the next two mornings on reconnaissance, taking turns watching the mansion, specifically the windows that were Tracy's office. What that guy at the rebel meeting had said about Champion House being a fortress wasn't kidding. The property's perimeter was surrounded by an eight-foot-high wrought-iron fence. Sometime after the warlord attack, all the outer doors had been changed to steel. Cameras mounted on the outside of the house monitored the fence. Any movement in unauthorized entry points set off alarms at the gatehouse and somewhere inside—I could hear it but couldn't tell where the interior alarm was located. I'd been hoping we could sneak into Tracy's office through the first-story window, but I witnessed a fan try that very thing and—besides setting off the blaring motion alarm—she was seized by two enforcers in less than thirty seconds.

There was no way to sneak inside that place.

•   •   •

Sunday night, a knock on the door sent a chill up my spine. To my delight, it was Cristobal.

"Hey!" I said. "How you been?"

He darted inside. "Shut the door, quick, man."

I shut the door.

Cristobal paced to where Zach sat at the table and back toward where I stood at the door. "You can't call me or email me or Antônia, okay? They're watching us both, I'm sure of it. I even left my wristband and phone at home. I'm pretty sure they can track me on both."

I didn't doubt that. "Who do you think is watching you?" I asked.

"Enforcers. I messed up. I was translating down at Rehab, telling this woman that her husband was being locked up for the next six months."

"What for?"

Cristobal lifted his hands. "That's just it. He didn't do anything. I think he saw something he wasn't supposed to see. Mr. Tracy and Officer Harvey were both there, and the man—he wouldn't say a word. I think they threatened to hurt his wife because he made me swear to tell her he was guilty."

"Guilty of nothing," I said.

"Right, like she's not going to question that. So, I asked a few questions. I wanted to know what I was supposed to tell her. Mr. Tracy asked if I was deaf. Then Officer Harvey told me I'd better stop asking questions, or I could join the guy in Rehab."

"Stellar legal system we've got in Safe Water," Zach said.

"Weird things have been happening ever since," Cristobal said. "One of those enforcer scooters has been following me around, and I swear someone was in my apartment, going through my stuff. I don't think they trust me, anymore. Now this second wave of HydroFlu. It's all freaking me out."

That comment turned my stomach. "What second wave?"

Cristobal looked confused. "They're dealing with a resurgence of HydroFlu cases at the hospital. Someone who lives in Champion House is infected too. Hannah came out twice last week with Dr. Bayles to treat him."

"She didn't tell me," I said, feeling like I'd just been sucker punched. "Zach? Did you know?"

Zach winced from the kitchen table. "Kind of. My supervisor gave a training on how to spot HydroFlu cases. Said the hospital was worried about a new strain. He didn't think it was true but said to keep it quiet until he knew more." Zach shrugged. "I kept it quiet."

"And so did Hannah," I said.

"Don't take it personally, Eli," Zach said, shaking his head. "Doctor-patient confidentiality doesn't apply to EMTs, but it *does* apply to doctors and nurses."

"This is going live at the next morning party," Cristobal said. "Anyway, I wondered . . . You still trying to get out of this place?"

"Yes," Zach and I said together.

"I want to come. Tônia and me. If you can find a way out, please take us with you."

"You got it," I said. "I don't suppose you have any interest in bugging Tracy's office?"

He winced and rubbed his face. "Tônia wants me to. She thinks we have a better chance of freedom if we have something to use as blackmail. I got to say, the word 'blackmail' freaks me out. All of this freaks me out, man. I just don't know."

This was the first I'd heard about using recordings for blackmail, and the idea excited me. "It would be nice to not feel like they were coming after us," I said. "I mean, we talk of settling on the mountain or down by the East River, but that's, like, two miles away. It's naïve to think they'd just leave us be."

Cristobal sank onto one of the chairs at the kitchen table and sighed. "All right," he said. "If you think it might mean we could actually live free from their reach, I'll do it. I'll try anyway."

"You're the man," Zach said, knocking his fist against Cristobal's.

Cristobal then filled us in on some of the other atrocities he'd witnessed as part of Tracy's team. "They're making plans to set up labor forces, which sound to me like communist labor camps. Eerily similar to what Stalin did."

"But no one owns any farmland," I said.

"And no one will," Cristobal said, "but you'll still have to work it. Someone will have to work it, anyway."

"How can they force people to work more than a regular job and still maintain a party atmosphere?" Zach asked.

"That's the big debate," Cristobal said. "They only want to make people work thirty hours a week, max, but there aren't enough people—especially to plant all the fields they're hoping to plant. Best idea going around at the moment is that everyone will have to serve a term on the fields. They're currently debating shifts. I've heard everything from people working the fields one day a week, to one week a month, to one month a year, to full year shifts that, if you work one, will give you the next four years off."

"I don't envy them the job of figuring that out," I said. What a nightmare.

"Won't we have to do something similar?" Cristobal asked. "I mean, eventually?"

I thought about it. "We can live off scavenged food through the winter," I said, "but if we're going to survive long-term, we'll need to plant crops."

"And you know how to do that?" Cristobal asked.

"My expertise is in salsa gardens, but I know enough to get started." I suddenly realized how ridiculous that sounded. It was like Logan saying he knew how to check oil on a car and therefore could change his own oil as well. "I probably sound crazy," I said. "I totally understand if you'd rather not put your life in my hands."

Cristobal shook his head. "Oh, I'm sure it'll be hard," he said. "The important thing is we'll be away from here. Plus, you just sweetened the deal when you said salsa garden, so I'm down.

Admin, the enforcers . . . they're high on power. I don't want any part of the future of this place."

"I'm with you, man," I said. "It won't be long now."

•    •    •

Around nine-thirty that night, Lizzie and I were sitting in the living room letting Logan cream us at Trivial Pursuit when Zach and Hannah got home with paper sacks from The Divy.

Hannah sat beside me on the couch and pulled out a sandwich wrapped in foil. She was wearing her lilac scrubs today, which were my favorite color on her.

"So, HydroFlu is back," I said, reminding myself I was mad at her. "How come you didn't say?"

She glanced at me. "I was asked to keep it confidential."

"Even to us?" I asked.

"To everyone. That's my job. If I thought any of you were at risk, I would have warned you."

"We're all at risk!" I said.

She wrinkled her nose. "No, you're not. And you're going to have to trust me on that." She took a bite of her sandwich, completely calm.

I fumed inside. I wanted to trust Hannah. I *did* trust her. But it made me angry that she didn't trust me.

"Who's sick at Champion House?" Logan asked.

We all waited while Hannah finished chewing. "Can't tell you that," she finally said.

"Cristobal said Loca and Liberté will be singing on stage Monday morning, so it's not them," Logan said.

"I'm not telling you who I'm treating," Hannah said.

"I know," Logan said, "but if I guess, will you nod or shake your head?"

"No, I won't." Hannah turned back to me, eyes practically glittering. "What I can tell you is that I spoke to Liberté, and I was the one who convinced her to go public about the second wave." She looked so pleased with herself, it was downright adorable.

"And how'd you do that?" I asked.

"Taunted her with a little, 'Are you in charge here, or is Mr. Tracy in charge?' It ticked her off, big time."

Well that was interesting.

"Tracy's in charge," Zach said over a full mouth. He was sitting on the floor in front of Lizzie, who was rubbing his shoulders.

"Yes, but Liberté *wants* to be in charge," Hannah said. "She just doesn't want to do the work."

"So she can be played," I said.

"Like a video game," Hannah said.

"Nice simile!" Logan said, raising his fist to Hannah.

She laughed and knocked her knuckles against his.

I nudged her side. "Now that you've told, will you keep me posted?"

"No, I will not," she said. "At least not when it falls under doctor-patient confidentiality. You're just going to have to trust me. And hope I know what I'm doing." Her tone was a mix of amused and offended.

I scowled. "I trust people just fine."

A chorus of negativity rose up around me.

"What? I do," I said.

"You don't trust anyone easily," Hannah said, "and that's okay. I get it. But I'm asking you to please try and trust me?"

It went against my nature to say it, but I said, "All right."

She leaned against my side, her head falling onto my shoulder. "Thank you."

"You all set up to record, Logan?" I asked. "We want to be ready to go as soon as Cristobal can plant that mike."

"I'm ready," Logan said. "I just need the link from Antônia."

"Perfect," I said. Everything was falling into place.

•   •   •

The next morning, Hannah and Zach were working. Lizzie insisted the rest of us circle up at the back of the Champions' lawn and pray for Cristobal as he attempted to plant the microphone. This we did, but I was too nervous to focus on praying. I kept my eyes on the house's front entrance, wondering if Cristobal was doing it right now, hoping I wouldn't see him come out of the house in cuffs, escorted by enforcers.

The meeting began, and Tracy gave his regular rule reminders: no protesting, no guns, be kind, obey enforcers. Then he called this week's house winners. It wasn't until the winners had all gone forward that Liberté came to the front of the stage, alone.

"My friends," she said, and the crowd cheered. "We are all such good friends, don't you think?" The crowd agreed with more applause and catcalls. "This is why it grieves my heart to tell you that the HydroFlu virus has not left us entirely." Murmurs rolled through the crowd, but Liberté didn't pause to let anyone digest this news. "The virus has changed. This new strain you cannot catch like before. *Non.* This new strain you catch from each other. It has infected a close friend of mine, and because we found out right away, he is getting the medical attention he needs."

Somewhere in the audience, applause broke out.

"*Oui,* it is good." She sighed heavily, then threw a curve ball I hadn't seen coming. "It is imperative that we determine who among us has been infected with this new strain so that we can help our friends recover and prevent further spread. As your leaders, Loca and I were tested just yesterday. Loca is not infected, but I am."

A cheer for Loca cut off mid howl when Liberté's news sank in. She was infected with the new strain? And she had told everyone here? Bold move. And, frankly, brilliant.

Everyone in the crowd started talking at once. The dull roar drowned out whatever else Liberté was saying.

A few seconds later, a siren went off. The front left side of the crowd scattered, revealing an enforcer SUV with its lights flashing. The driver stood behind the open front door, holding a bullhorn to his mouth.

"Let's have some quiet here so Mr. Tracy can give everyone instructions. Quiet please!"

The crowd obeyed.

"Thank you, officer," Tracy said. "I know this is scary, y'all." He set his hand over his heart like he was about to say the Pledge of Allegiance. "I'm scared too. But if we are going to stop this thing before it gets out of control, everyone needs to get tested as soon as possible, m'kay? We've posted a schedule on the Grid based on the first letter of your last name. Names A-E go today, F-K on Tuesday, L-Q on Wednesday, R-V on Thursday, W-Z on Friday. If you're scheduled to task during that time, you can take time off to get tested."

"What if we miss our day?" someone yelled out.

"Anyone can be tested on Saturday or Sunday," Tracy said.

"I beg of you," Liberté said, her voice catching. "If you care for each other. If you care at all for me. Please. We must know who has this strain so that we can save everyone."

The crowd cheered, and Liberté waved and blew kisses as if she'd just been crowned Miss America. Tracy came out beside her, and the two embraced. He gave her a handkerchief from his pocket and she dabbed her eyes.

"Oh, please," I said to Lizzie. "How staged was that? Who carries a fabric handkerchief these days?"

Lizzie wiped away her own tears with the back of her hand. "She's so brave, to tell everyone like she did."

I thought of how Hannah had challenged Liberté to step up as a leader and figured "calculating" was a much better word.

"Friends," Tracy said. "It's been a rough week for our little community, but we are determined to keep as many people safe as possible. If everyone follows the schedule on the Grid, by the next morning party, everyone should be tested. Because this is important, we're making this a mandatory testing. Anyone who has not been tested by next Monday will be arrested. Don't let it come to that, my friends, m'kay? If you have a hardship, call our office or the hospital and make other arrangements. We'll find a way to get this done as quickly as possible."

A prickle ran up my spine. I wasn't about to be tested for this thing—Hannah said I wasn't at risk—but I really didn't want to go to Rehab. Again. I wished Hannah were here. I'd love to hear what she thought about all this.

Tracy ended the meeting, and people started to leave. I stayed put, arms folded, trying to hold in my frustration. The way they had spun this thing . . . as if anyone who would refuse wasn't a "friend" to the community . . . I hated being manipulated.

There was no way I was getting tested.

"Eli, look," Lizzie said.

My sister was pointing toward the fountain in front of the mansion. Cristobal was sitting there with a book in his hand. We made eye contact, and he flashed me a thumbs up.

Relief washed over me, and I pushed through the crowd, making my way toward him. He saw me coming and went back inside. He must have been worried about being seen with a repeat offender. I honestly couldn't blame him.

"Let's get back and start listening," Logan said.

I headed for the exit. "I couldn't agree more."

# 25

**HANNAH**
**SEPTEMBER 14**

HydroFlu testing had turned the hospital into a circus.

A group of about a dozen protestors had set up camp outside the hospital with signs that said mandatory testing was against their rights.

To make matters worse, someone had dropped flyers all over town. The flyer not only questioned Admin's right to mandatory testing, it claimed Admin was wrong to keep people trapped in Safe Water.

Over half of the people I saw brought a flyer into the hospital with them and asked me if, as a doctor, I agreed with its claims.

What could I say? Mandatory testing had been my idea, but no one should be forced to have their blood drawn. I did my best to stress the importance of being tested, but some people left without one. I was certain Eli was seeing his share of flyers as he cleaned up trash around town, and I was grateful his job would keep him so busy he wouldn't learn about the protest. He likely would have joined in.

Dr. Bayles had not only asked everyone on staff to work overtime, he had also given the EMTs a crash course in phlebotomy so they could offer support. He then paired the EMTs up with hospital staff, which often caused more problems than it did good. I was partnered with Amber, who struggled to find veins. I made sure to do all the children and troublesome patients myself, which helped.

Dr. Bayles also called in the enforcers to keep order. The first thing they did was arrest the people who'd been protesting outside, and I was again grateful that Eli wasn't out there.

Then the enforcers brought the protestors into the hospital, demanding we test them for HydroFlu immediately.

Linsey told the enforcers it was antiethical for us to administer care for a non-life-threatening matter without a patient's consent. Then Officer Harvey drew his gun, which only made Linsey dig in his heels more. They were toe-to-toe when Dr. Bayles came in and told us all that HydroFlu *was* a life-threatening situation and instructed us to test the arrested persons. None of us felt right about it, but we did what we were told.

The whole thing was awful and did the opposite of instilling calm in Safe Water. Our patients were hysterical with fear, and while 90 percent of those we tested were uninfected, there were still forty-seven patients on Monday who tested positive.

I was grateful the three doctors took it upon themselves to impart the bad news.

I worried constantly about Eli getting arrested again. I considered faking a test for him. It would be so easy, and he'd probably never find out. I didn't need to consult Dixie to know that such an action would be codependent on my part. It would also betray Eli's trust and be just as much of a violation as we'd all committed today performing blood tests on the protestors who hadn't given consent.

I had to let him choose what he wanted to do, even if that put him in danger of being arrested again.

We tested over four hundred people Monday on top of our regular duties. It felt like we treated more regular patients than normal too. Being in the hospital had inspired people to ask about ailments they'd previously deemed too low of concern to bother with.

I took an x-ray for a man who'd broken his arm, then found Dr. Bayles in the nurse's station to give him my report. "The patient with the broken arm is ready for you in Exam Room 3, Doctor Bayles."

"Diagnosing now, are you?" he said.

"Looks broken to me. You'll have to tell me if I was right or not."

"You're always right," he said.

I grimaced, thinking about how he and I disagreed that HydroFlu testing was a life-threatening situation. I decided not to pick a fight after all I'd already been through this day. So, I smiled and turned to leave.

"Hannah."

I turned back. "Yes, sir?"

"I've repeatedly asked you to call me Jason."

This again. "I'm sorry," I said. "I just wasn't trained that way. You're my superior, and I feel it's important to keep a professional, respectful boundary. Calling each other by our first names changes the atmosphere."

"I suppose you believe dating would change the atmosphere too," he asked.

Warmth flushed over me. I likely turned three shades of red. "It certainly would."

"So, you won't accompany me to dinner when all this is over?"

So awkward! "I thought you and Jennie . . ."

He frowned and shook his head. "Oh, no, she and I are just friends."

I wanted to ask if he was *just friends* with Monica and Asiya too but decided against it. "Well, I'm flattered, but I have a boyfriend." The admission made me smile.

"Oh." Dr. Bayles seemed to think this over. "It's that kid, isn't it? The skinny one who came to visit the EMT?"

I bit back a sarcastic remark and simply said, "Yes, that's him."

"Hannah . . ." He smirked, like he knew a secret and was trying to decide whether or not to divulge the information. "All right," he said, apparently deciding against it. "I won't pretend I'm not disappointed to learn this, but that's what I get for dragging my feet. I should have asked you out the first time I saw you. My loss."

Kind words, but they made me so uncomfortable! Did he really expect me to feel sorry for him for not being more inappropriate in the workplace?

"Thank you for understanding," I finally said, though I had a feeling the man wasn't going to give up that easily.

●　　　●　　　●

I was grateful to have an appointment with Dixie during my dinner break. I told her about the wild morning we'd had at the hospital with the flyers, the protestors, and the enforcers.

It was so nice to be able to talk about it with someone trained to be objective.

"Besides the craziness at the hospital, anything new happen in your life this week?" she asked.

"My boss asked me out," I said. "Though I guess that's more craziness at the hospital."

"Ah, yes. Dr. Bayles . . ." Dixie pursed her lips and left that hanging.

An awkward silence fell between us. I was glad I wasn't the only one who saw Dr. Bayles's behavior as inappropriate.

"But I also have a boyfriend now," I said, smiling big.

"You do? Good! I'm happy for you."

I wasn't sure I believed her. "You think I'm ready?"

"Aren't you?"

I shrugged. "I just wondered if I needed more time to, you know, get healthy."

"Hannah, we are all of us a work-in-progress, and life rarely happens when we're ready for it. You like this person, and he likes you. See where it goes. No guilt. No shame. So, tell me about him."

I told her how I met Eli, what I liked about his intelligence and kindness and strength. "He's an amazing person and he doesn't even know it," I said.

"You're drawn to that," Dixie said.

"From the moment I met him, yes. He fascinates me." Lizzie had told me those traits came from Eli's relationship with God. Eli didn't talk much about his faith, but it obviously made him different.

I told her how Eli had tried to save Brandon and failed. I left out the part about stabbing his hand. I wasn't ready to tell my counselor I was a murderer. Three appointments didn't seem long enough for such a confession. I did tell her that Eli was against being tested for HydroFlu.

"He's also Seth's son," I said.

"The 'Let's get married in ten years' guy?"

I nodded, and the next thing I knew, I was fighting back tears. "I'm sorry," I said. "It's been a stressful day."

"Stop right there," Dixie said. "I can tell by the look on your face that this is more than stress. What's coming up? Your body is trying to tell you something. Don't push it aside. Listen to it."

Annoyed, I gave in, and tears dripped down my cheeks. Dixie handed me the tissue box, and I pulled one out, dabbed my face. "It just sometimes feels risky, being with Eli. This is why it made sense to arrange myself a marriage in ten years—it was unemotional, safe. I know Eli would never physically harm me, but there are other ways of getting hurt. And what if he doesn't forgive me about his dad?"

Dixie tipped her head and gave me the most endearing smile. "You can't control this. It's risky."

I nodded. And I had a bad track record for romance.

"Don't you think it might be risky for him too?"

I thought about it, how Jaylee had messed with him and had always flirted with Riggs and random strangers. "I guess."

"Love is not about power, Hannah. It's the opposite. It's making yourself vulnerable to another person, opening your heart to him and trusting him with it."

Which was what I didn't like about it. "I'm not good at that," I said.

"I know. Next time you're with Eli, tell him all this. About your fears, about what happened with his dad. Get it all out. This is an assignment."

I didn't like that idea. "I've been waiting for the perfect time to tell him."

Dixie shook her head. "There will never be a perfect time. You don't think he'll understand?"

A pang shot through my heart. "I think he'll be hurt. I don't want to hurt him."

"Would it hurt him more to keep the truth from him?"

"If he ever found out, yes." So, I had to tell him.

"Take the risk and see what happens," Dixie said. "I'm excited for you."

Sure. Easy for her to say, but "excited" was one word I'd never use to describe the task that lay before me.

# 26

ELI

That first day, nothing much came through the bug Cristobal had planted—Tracy wasn't even there most the time. Early on he got a phone call from a doctor at the hospital asking for enforcers to help keep order during HydroFlu testing, and when Tracy called Captain Koval to talk about that, he also asked about weapons offenders. We couldn't hear the person on the other side of the call, but it sounded like there had been a couple of arrests. I wondered if Brett Durzinski and his rebels were still planning to take Town Hall.

I picked up Hannah from work that night with a sack of sandwiches and an old quilt I found in the attic. "Want to go for a picnic?" I asked.

"Sure," she said, giving me the fakest smile I'd ever seen.

"What's wrong?"

"I just had a bad day. I'll tell you about it later. Right now, I just want to be away from the hospital for a little while. Spend time with you."

I liked the sound of that. "You got it."

I drove us down a deserted road and led her on a half-mile hike up a hill not far from the house. I stopped under a stately pine tree and spread out the blanket. We sat and enjoyed the view and meatball sandwiches.

"How did you find this place?" she asked, breathlessly.

"When I was out running. Following a dog, actually."

She looked at me. "A brown lab?"

"You've seen it?"

"Once, yeah."

"It looks exactly like the dog that was with the couple who stole my truck. Right before we met you."

"You think they're here?" she asked.

"Don't know. He didn't seem like the type to come to a place like this."

"Well, don't hate me," she said, "but I'm glad he stole your truck."

Ouch. "Why would you say that?"

"If he hadn't, you never would have come looking for a new vehicle and found me."

That earned her a kiss, which led to several more kisses, and I got lost in the pleasure of being with someone who liked me as much as I liked her.

At some point, I began to vent my frustration about mandatory testing.

"Did you know Liberté was infected?" I asked.

"I didn't," she said. "If she is, I've not been invited to treat her, which would be strange since I'm going there anyway for a different patient."

"You think she made it up so people would sympathize with her?"

"Or so people would get tested. By telling everyone she was infected, she removed any stigma from the disease."

"I wouldn't be surprised if people want to test positive so they can be like her," I said. "It's insane."

"You'd be surprised how many don't want to be tested, but Eli, I hope you'll come. I can do it for you at home, if you're afraid of the other nurses or doctors."

"I'm not afraid," I snapped. "It's the principle. I'm not showing any symptoms. Why should I be tested?"

"To keep out of Rehab?" she said.

I chuckled. "Ahh, Rehab isn't so bad."

"But they said they'd keep you more days next time. I worry for you."

"Don't. I can take care of myself." Ooh, that earned me a dirty look. "Why a blood test? Can't you just smell the HydroFlu on people?"

"The fishy odor doesn't come until later," Hannah said. "If we're going to help people, we have to catch it much earlier than that."

I supposed that was fair.

"Look," Hannah said, "I know it bothered you that I didn't tell you about the HydroFlu. I'm sorry I couldn't."

"It's your job," I said. "I get it."

She threaded her fingers with mine, which was very distracting. She was wearing her hot pink scrubs today, and the color somehow made her hair look blacker and softer than usual. I really wanted to touch it and see for myself.

"Thank you for understanding," she said. "The thing is, I'm starting to know you better, and one thing I've noticed is that you don't like surprises."

"I like some surprises," I said, squeezing her hand. "I liked when you kissed me."

She gave me a "be serious" look. "I just don't want there to be any secrets between us," she said, "but I suddenly realize you don't understand that I was the one who convinced Liberté to require mandatory testing."

My chest tightened. "What?"

"See? I thought I told you the other night."

"You said you convinced her to go public about the new

strain."

"I'm sorry," she said. "People are dying. We have to contain this, and the only way to do that quickly and effectively is through mandatory testing."

"But you said I wasn't at risk."

She took a deep breath. "The new strain is bloodborne. So unless you've been sleeping around or shooting up with shared needles . . ."

"Oh," I said, my mind racing with this new information.

"I wasn't supposed to tell anyone that," Hannah said, her eyebrows pinching together.

I now understood why Hannah had pushed for mandatory testing. The way people partied in this town, STDs were likely high. It would be imperative to determine who was infected right away.

"I still don't want to be tested," I said. "Especially now. Blood is drawn with needles."

"Every needle is brand new. There will be no contamination from testing. In fact, I can test you myself."

I shook my head. "I don't think so. I trust you, but it's the principle of the thing."

"I can fake your test, then," she said. "I just need to take your wristband to the hospital next time you're off."

I considered it. In a way that would be sticking it to Tracy, but he would still think I complied. "You're too good to me, you know that, right?"

"Well, I'm sorry I put you in a position where you feel like you need to take a stand."

I shrugged off her concern. "Don't worry about it. It's my choice."

"That's just it." Hannah pulled a folded piece of paper from her pocket and handed it to me. "It's not going to be anyone's choice."

She went on to tell me about her day, how patients had brought the flyers in to the hospital, asking if what they said was true, how the protestors outside had been arrested, how Officer Harvey had ordered Linsey at gunpoint to comply, and how Dr.

Bayles had told them they had to test everyone.

That sent me into a tailspin of ranting that rivaled Brett Durzinski in its passion. Until Hannah started to cry, which finally shut me up.

I hugged her. "I'm sorry for yelling," I said. "They just make me so angry."

"It's hard," she said. "I believe mandatory testing is the best way to stop the spread of the new strain, but I also believe people have the right to refuse testing. It didn't feel right to test without their consent."

"I get that," I said. "I can see how hard this must be for you—for all of you. I wish I could have seen Linsey stand up to Harvey."

A breathy laugh escaped her as she wiped the tears from her cheeks. "He was pretty awesome."

We lay down on the blanket, my arm around her shoulders, and watched the sky, which looked a little gray today. Again I wondered if it might rain. Hannah rolled on her side and brushed the hair off my forehead.

"Your hair is getting long," she said.

"I was thinking of growing it out, like Cree."

"I don't think you can pull that off," she said, laughing.

"Logan picked up a hint of something big on the CB today," I said. "A meeting in Tracy's office Friday morning with Loca and Liberté and Captain Koval."

"That should be interesting," she said.

"I hope so," I said. "We could use a break."

We lay there in silence for a while, and I found it interesting how nice this was, just doing nothing.

"Eli?" Hannah fidgeted with a loose thread on my shirt. "There's another thing I need to tell you, but it's hard. It's dumb, really, but I need to work up to it." The look on her face was so troubled, goosebumps ran up my arms.

"Work up to it?"

Tears glossed her eyes. "Maybe not today, though. It's been a hard day. Would you be patient?"

"Sure." I mean, what else could I say?

"And when I do tell you, do you promise not to jump to conclusions?"

I suddenly felt uncomfortable. Her secret probably wasn't nearly as bad as she thought it was, but my mind was already leaping from one idea to the next to try and figure out what she might think was bad enough that she couldn't just tell me now. Drugs, maybe? She had a juvenile record? She had somehow contracted the new HydroFlu strain?

A stronger possibility clicked in my mind. She could have slept with Brandon. Probably had. That seemed most likely. "You're not a virgin?" I asked.

She slugged me. "No, I'm not. I certainly hope that doesn't matter to you."

I clamped my molars together at this confession and shook my head. It didn't matter, I told myself, and I knew it was true even if the confession did annoy me. Jaylee certainly hadn't been a virgin.

Growing up as a Christian, I knew God wanted people to save sex for marriage, but Hannah's past could stay in the past.

"That's not it?" I asked.

"No, it's not. And I asked you to be patient. Trying to guess isn't being patient."

I deflated. "Sorry."

Something cold touched my cheek. I slapped it away, thinking it might be a mosquito, then I saw a drop of liquid land on Hannah's cheek.

I gasped at the gray sky, a chill dancing over my arms. "It's raining."

We leaped to our feet, grabbed the blanket, and ran to a nearby blue spruce, ducking under the boughs. It wasn't a very thick tree, though. My heart was hammering in my chest just looking at the rain streaking across the mountain. Cold drops sprinkled through the tree and landed on my neck and arms.

"Eli," Hannah said, the fear in her voice urgent.

"We'll wait it out," I said. We sat down, and I draped the old quilt over our heads to protect us from the droplets sneaking through the branches overhead.

I tried to distract us with conversation, but every word felt forced. Forty-five minutes passed before the rain stopped.

"Okay, let's go," I said, grabbing Hannah's hand.

We ran, our footsteps unsteady in the wet grass that soon had both our pantlegs soaked. We were halfway down the hill when the rain picked up again.

Hannah screamed and slid to a stop, pulling at the quilt. "What if it's poisoned?"

I yanked the blanket back over our heads, and we continued down the hill much more slowly. The rain came thick and heavy, and the drops were quickly soaking our quilted umbrella.

I started to pray out loud, like I was Lizzie or something. It was all I could think to do. I asked God to make the water safe, but if this was the end of our story, I knew that would be okay too. I told God I trusted him, live or die, that I was his. Hannah probably thought I was nuts. She was crying, and I started to think my prayer was scaring her more than helping.

I began to pray for Hannah, instead, and asked God to keep her safe so she could help people. I was babbling now, barely knew what I was saying.

Hannah slipped and fell. I pulled her back up, but we were both soaked and crying, even under the quilt. The van was still nowhere in sight.

"I'm sorry," I said. "We should have stayed under the tree."

"Maybe it's safe," she said. "The rain?"

I nodded. "Yeah." If it was, it would change everything.

Hannah lowered her arms, pulling the quilt off her.

"What are you doing?" I asked.

"It's not really helping us anymore," she said.

I put down my arms too. The rain pelted my head and skin. Soon it had matted my hair and T-shirt. Hannah looked like she'd just gone for a swim in her scrubs. It was terrifying to stand there in the open, knowing the rain could be poisoning us.

Our hands were gripped so tightly our knuckles were white. I lifted them between us. "Looks like we might be a little scared right now."

She shivered. "Just a little."

We stood there, staring at each other. Then Hannah kissed me. I kissed her back, overcome with fear and hope and crazy wild attraction for this gorgeous girl. Deep secret or not, nothing Hannah Cheng could say could change the way I felt about her.

The movies always made kissing in the rain look so romantic. In reality, it was just . . . wet. When Hannah and I finally made it to the Odyssey, drove home, and lived to see the next morning, I never felt happier in my life.

We'd lived through the rain. Everyone had. Which was one less thing Safe Water could hold over us.

# 27

**ELI**
**SEPTEMBER 18**

Friday morning marked eight weeks since Hannah had stabbed my hand with a knife and caused Brandon to fall. That morning, before I left for work, she took off my splint.

"Just to see," she said. "If it hurts you even a little as you work, I'll put it back on tonight."

"I'll be fine," I said, eager to not feel inhibited anymore.

"I notice you didn't come in this week," she said as she unwrapped the gauze. "No McShane did. Not even Lizzie."

Mandatory testing again. "Dad and Lizzie are with me on this," I said.

She pressed her lips together tightly as if trying to keep herself from saying anything more. Her eyes were focused on unwrapping my hand.

"So many people asked about the rain," she said. "It was nice to be able to tell them not to worry about that, at least."

"It stirred up the rebels again," I said. "They were over at the gate protesting." Safe rain meant people could survive outside this place. People could go home and harvest rainwater. "I wonder if Tracy will say anything about it on Monday."

"My boss asked me out," Hannah said.

That got my attention. "The old guy? Or the guy who wears the neckties?"

"Neckties."

I grunted and watched her pull the last of the gauze from my fingers. They looked pale and puckered from being wrapped up for so long. "I don't like him."

She laughed, and her eyes met mine. "I told him I had a boyfriend."

I liked the sound of that. "Boyfriend, huh?"

"Is that okay?"

I kissed her, mumbled, "Very okay," against her lips before kissing her again.

"Are you sure you don't want us to wait for you tonight?" I asked her.

Cristobal and Antônia were coming over after dinner to listen to the recording Logan would be making of the meeting happening in Tracy's office today. Only Hannah would miss out since she had to work until ten.

"You guys go ahead," she said. "I can listen to it when I get home."

I flexed my fingers open and closed, open and closed. They were stiff but seemed to finally be stretching to their full capacity.

"Eli?" Davis said, his voice sounding hesitant as he walked down the last few steps into the kitchen. "Is there any more water in the bucket?"

"Why?" I asked, instantly annoyed.

"The toilet is full again," he said.

"Because of you?" I asked.

He shrugged. "I forgot."

"Just because it rained does not mean we get to use the

indoor toilet," I said. "No more."

"Sorry," he said.

After Hannah and I got home the day it rained, I'd put out some buckets I found in the garage and collected enough water to flush down the accidents Cree had left in the toilet our first few days here. The kids had been so impressed, the toilet kept magically getting used again.

"I guess I have to go flush a toilet," I told Hannah.

A grin spread across her face as she got up from the table and tossed out the old gauze. "Lucky you."

After I dealt with the toilet, Dad and I left for work. On the drive over, I thought about what Hannah had said about me being her boyfriend.

"Dad? Is it weird that Hannah and I are, you know, together, but we're on different sides of the whole mandatory testing thing?"

"People in relationships don't ever agree on everything," Dad said.

"I just feel like maybe she's mad at me."

"She's worried for you. That's a very different thing. She doesn't want anything bad to happen to you."

Hearing Dad put it like that made me feel a lot better.

• • •

That night after dinner, we all crowded around Logan's laptop in the living room to listen to the recording. Logan had cued it up to the place he said the meeting started.

"Here it is," he said, pressing play.

"How is Barkley?" Tracy's voice.

"Worse." This from Liberté. "He's so thin and weak. My heart breaks just looking at him."

"Who is Barkley?" Zach asked.

"One of Liberté's male dancers," Lizzie said. "He must be the friend she said was infected."

"Shh!" I said.

"Any word from the research team?" Loca asked.

"They sent a message through the Grid." Koval's deep voice seemed to growl over the recording. "Made it to New Jersey. They're trying to make sense of things at the pharmaceutical company, but it's going to take time."

"We should have sent Dr. Bayles with them," Loca said.

"That would have been ideal," Tracy said.

"Barkley cannot do without Dr. Bayles right now," Liberté said.

"You're absolutely right," Tracy said. "Besides, we couldn't risk our most experienced doctor for a trip that far away. There's no way to know the team will make it back."

"They have to!" Liberté said.

"They'll make it," Koval said.

"Sure, sure," Tracy said. "It's a simple trip. Mendoza is a good pilot too."

"Reggie will help them find what we need," Loca added.

"He's got fifteen years in pharmaceuticals, working out of Dallas," Koval said. "He knows his stuff."

"We're going to need to learn how to produce everything ourselves," Tracy said.

"Eventually, yes, but not today," Koval said.

"Have they seen any other people out there?" Loca asked.

"A few," Koval said, "but no other communities like us. No signs of any other safe water sources."

A moment of silence followed as everyone in the meeting and in our house took this in. Were we really alone in the world? Was this little creek producing the only safe water on the planet?

Loca broke the silence. "I don't like so many people around my house," he said. "We have no privacy."

"Even after the increased security?" Koval asked.

"I still see them out my window," Loca said. "We bought this land because we liked the ski resort and the small population. I don't feel safe with so many people around all the time."

I met my dad's gaze. "Then maybe he shouldn't have invited everyone up here," I said.

"We'll find a way to get rid of them," Tracy said. "They shouldn't be bothering you."

Antônia gasped. "That's so mean!"

"But this is where you wanted the showers built," Koval said, pointing out the obvious.

"There weren't so many people in my yard then!" Loca said.

"People won't need the showers forever," Liberté said.

"That's right," Tracy said. "Once the dam is up and running, we can redirect the city water supply. Then people can shower in their own homes and won't need to come here."

"We want them to need us," Liberté said. "We just don't want them on our property all the time."

"We'll post some showering hours, m'kay?" Tracy said. "People can only shower from nine to five or something like that."

"Perfect," Loca said.

"We don't want to upset anyone, though," Liberté said. "Are people still protesting?"

"No one has challenged with force for a few days," Koval said. "The rain protestors are still grumbling. We disband any gathering minutes after it forms, but we can't figure out who's printing those flyers. Thanks to them, everyone here knows ten ways they could harvest water and survive outside this place."

"Let them leave if they want," Liberté said. "They will not find a better place to live than here with us."

Hope bloomed inside me. Yes, let us leave. Would they?

"We cannot let them leave," Loca said.

"Why not? We're only talking a handful of people, right?" Liberté asked.

"Perhaps at first," Koval said. "If word gets out there are options, others might leave. You'd lose your work force."

"We've been over this," Loca said. "She knows what's at stake."

Liberté huffed. "Don't talk about me like you're my handler."

"You want to clean this place?" Loca asked. "You want to raise cows and pigs, grow vegetables? Do you know how? Because I don't."

"How many have asked to leave?" Liberté asked. "How

many are we talking about?"

"More importantly, how many have refused task assignments?" Koval asked.

"Too many," Tracy said. "You think we need to threaten Rehab?"

"Not yet," Koval said. "We just took their guns. Too much too soon, and you'll have riots."

I snorted. They'd have more than riots on their hands if Brett Durzinski had anything to say about it.

"We must perform a humanitarian action," Liberté said. "Make video of us working same as everyone else, then people will see that even we have to take jobs if Safe Water is going to survive."

"Excellent idea, Liberté, I love it," Tracy said.

"But we already have two jobs!" Loca said. "We're musicians, and we're the rulers of this place."

"King Loca and Queen Liberté," Tracy said. "You're trailblazers. It's a beautiful thing."

Lizzie rolled her eyes.

"Mr. Tracy is like that all the time," Cristobal mumbled. "It's so obnoxious."

"There is no point in being musicians if no one is listening," Loca said. "No point being a king and queen if we have no people to rule."

"Well said, Loca," Tracy said. "You're so wise."

"What a suck-up," I said to Cristobal, who nodded in agreement.

"But still I don't want to work," Loca said.

"We need to be seen out there, setting an example," Liberté said.

"Not for a whole day," Tracy said. "Just long enough to get some footage we can use on the Grid."

"You always wanted a movie, *mon chérie*," Liberté said. "Be an actor. Play well your role. The people will love it."

"It would be easier if I am acting," Loca said. "But I must do something fun, like operate one of those electric ice cream cone machines."

"Done," Tracy said. "You'd be great at that, by the way, and your fans would love it. We'd sell out of ice cream in an afternoon. The Grid ads are pulling in great feedback on the two of you, by the way."

"But not everyone is on the Grid," Liberté said. "How do we get everyone to participate?"

"I've been thinking about that," Tracy said. "I'm not sure everyone has access to the Grid. We need to gift everyone a computer or a cell phone or both."

"We've been over this," Koval said. "There aren't enough for everyone."

"So send another scavenge team," Tracy said.

Koval growled.

"This one stays close to home," Tracy said. "We send them to Denver with one mission: computers and cell phones for all."

"Why not announce this at the morning party?" Liberté said. "We can make it a lottery, like with the houses. Let the public participate."

"To give the phones away? Or to go on the trip?" Tracy asked. "Because we can't just let anyone go on these trips," Tracy said.

"Why?" Liberté asked.

"Gifting everyone computers won't stop people from wanting to leave," Koval said. "Those who want to leave won't care."

"He's got that right," I said.

"How can we convince them to stay?" Liberté asked. "Safe Water isn't meant to be a prison."

"Could have fooled me," Zach said.

"If we had something they needed," Koval said.

"They need the water," Tracy said.

"Yes, but they could look elsewhere for water," Koval said. "Scavenge bottled water or harvest rainwater and snow."

"I have an idea . . ." Loca said. "Maybe it is a little reckless."

"I love it already," Tracy said.

"Speak up, *mon chérie*," Liberté said. "We cannot read your mind."

"Well, what if we make it so everyone becomes . . . how do you say . . . *une drogue addictive? Stupéfiant?*" he said.

"You want to get everyone hooked on something?" Tracy asked.

"Barkley will not give up his *beu*," Liberté said. "He is running low and needs it for the pain."

"We can grow more pot," Tracy said.

"Not everyone smokes," Koval said.

"Have the chefs put it in the food, like with brownies," Tracy said.

This comment got a good laugh from those at the meeting and a round of groans from us at the house.

"Why can we not do this?" Loca said. "Not *beu*. Not something so obvious. Something addictive, but not something that will turn everyone *toxico*. Something subtle. We need them physically able to work."

"Nicotine," Tracy said. "It's the most addictive substance known to man."

"*Non*, it is not," Loca said.

"*Oui*, he is right," Liberté said. "I read this in *le magazine Cosmo*. It is even more addictive than cocaine."

Loca snorted. "I suppose this is why you cannot manage to stop smoking *les cigarettes*."

"*Oui*, it is exactly why, *mon frère*. I do not like who I am when I try to quit them. I get very irritable."

"*Elle devient un monster*," Loca mumbled.

"*Tais toi!*" Liberté cried.

"I disagree," Tracy said. "You're always such a joy to be around, Liberté."

The conversation went on as the four of them discussed other ideas to trap us here. They came up with nothing better than their grand addiction scheme, though, and Koval promised to contact the New Jersey team and ask them to look for liquid nicotine. The meeting fizzled, and they started talking about which songs to perform at next week's party and how Liberté was having new costumes made.

When the meeting ended, Logan stopped the recording.

"Tracy is such a weasel," Zach said. "He had to one-up everything everyone said."

"He sure sounds like a different person when the Champions are in the room," Dad said.

"Loca is so cruel," Antônia said. "Jaylee will never believe it."

"Liberté wanted to let us go," I said. "Too bad we can't just ask her."

"That would be awesome," Logan said.

"She is the softer of the two," Cristobal said. "If anyone would let us go, it would be her."

"Yeah, Loca was pretty ruthless," Logan said.

"I can't believe they sat around plotting ways to addict the entire population," Lizzie said.

"It's pretty despicable," I said, wondering what Hannah would think of that.

"It sure does make it harder to leave everyone else behind," Dad said, "none the wiser to what's coming."

I blew out a long and frustrated breath. "But we have to leave, Dad."

"Oh, absolutely," Dad said.

Everyone agreed, and Cristobal and Antônia took off.

I wondered how Hannah would respond to the recording. I didn't know what to think about Us with a capital U. She loved her work at the hospital, and I was afraid to know how she felt about our plans to leave. Then there was her big secret. It hadn't exactly been fair for her to ask me not to think about it. That was like saying, "Whatever you do, don't think about ice cream." Of course, when you tried *not* to think about ice cream, ice cream was pretty much the only thing you *could* think about.

Well, my imagination had gone completely out of control on this Hannah thing. I'd imagined her having done everything from selling prescription drugs in college to starring in a porn film. The absurdity of that last idea caused me to start thinking of possibilities that better fit her personality. Rather than selling prescription drugs, maybe she'd tried to smuggle meds across the border into Guatemala to help the people there. Maybe she had an international record for smuggling.

"Stop," I said out loud, desperate to reel in my thoughts.

"What's that?" Dad asked.

"I'm going to find something for dessert," I said, hoping that getting out of the house might help keep my imagination in check.

"I'll come with," Zach said.

He and I drove to the bakery and found the place packed.

"What's going on?" I asked the clerk as we waited for our dozen brownies.

"Someone died from the HydroFlu over at the hospital," he said. "People are using their credits to stock up on any food that will keep."

Zach grabbed a handful of candy bars beside the register and tossed them on the counter. At my raised eyebrows, he said, "What? I'm stocking up."

As I drove the van out of town, the foot traffic was thick on the sidewalks, people everywhere carrying bags.

"This is bad," I said. "We've got to get out of this place before it implodes."

"How?" Zach asked.

"Steal a bulldozer. Drive right over the chain-link and barbed wire."

Zach laughed. "If we're stealing vehicles, let's just steal a police car and pretend to be enforcers."

"Sure. No problem. I say we put Logan on the case. He *can* hotwire, you know."

It felt good to laugh, but the situation was grim.

We took the brownies home and found everyone playing Sorry at the kitchen table. We passed out the brownies and sat down to watch the game.

Then Lizzie dropped a bomb. "I'm going into the hospital tomorrow morning to get tested," she said.

Silence fell around the living room.

"Why?" I asked.

She took a deep breath. "Most of my students got tested this week," she said. "I don't think it's right for me, as an educator, to be arrested for noncompliance."

"You're the perfect person to be arrested," I said.

"*Eli.*" Dad shot me a look.

"What?" I said. "She needs to set an example for her students."

"Exactly," Lizzie said. "And since we don't have a plan of escape, I think it's best to model compliance for now."

"Are you crazy?" I asked.

Lizzie speared me with her intense gaze. "Romans 13. Obey the government God placed in power. Those who refuse to obey the law of the land are refusing to obey God."

"Oh, come on," I said.

"If we knew we could leave," she said, "I could see protesting. But we might be stuck here for a long time, and I'd rather maintain a positive relationship with my students—where I can make a real difference in their lives—than ruin that relationship now to make a point. Plus, compliance will keep the enforcers from watching us."

"They're already watching us," I said.

Lizzie shrugged. "Testing doesn't hurt me. Zach and Hannah and Logan all got tested, and they're fine."

"They had to because of their jobs," I said.

She turned away from me, looked at Dad. "Zach's going to take me in tomorrow morning," she said.

"I understand," Dad said. "The kids and I would like to come with you."

"What!" I stood up and almost knocked over my chair. "I thought you were with me on this, Dad."

"I am, in principle," Dad said. "But Cree, Shy, and Davis are kids. I put myself down as their guardian when we checked in here. They're now Cree McShane, Shyla McShane, and Davis McShane. I don't feel right making a choice that might get them put in Rehab or parted from us."

"They wouldn't put kids in Rehab," I said.

"You sure about that, son? Because I'm not."

No. I wasn't sure about anything. I hadn't realized my dad had put himself down as their guardian, either. It made me feel like I had dropped the ball. I had been acting like a man when I decided to take the kids with me, but the moment I'd found my own daddy, I'd let him do the adulting, and I went back to being a child.

"If the kids get parted from us, we might never get them back," Dad said.

"Fine," I said. "I get it. But I'm not getting tested. I've been to Rehab. I can handle it." See? I even sounded like a whiny child. Go me.

"I understand, Eli," Dad said. "If it wasn't for the kiddos, I'd be right there with you."

That, at least, made me feel a skosh better. But when Saturday morning came, and I watched Dad drive the van away with Zach, Lizzie, and the kids inside, I felt completely alone.

# 28

ELI
SEPTEMBER 19

Saturday night, Hannah found me sitting on the deck, staring at the mountain. She'd showered, recently. Her hair was down, and she was wearing jeans and a green Mt. Crested Butte T-shirt.

"I just listened to the recording," she said. "It was pretty awful. How is your hand?"

"Fingers feel a little stiff, but they're working."

"That's a relief. I was afraid I'd scarred you for life."

"I think you have," I said, fingering the welt on the back of my hand. "I don't think this will ever be gone."

"That's true." She was quiet for a long moment. "I saw your sister and your dad at the hospital today."

I grunted.

"You have all day tomorrow," she said. "There's still time

for you to make it."

"I'm not going because I haven't done anything that would give me an STD," I said, my voice raised. "I should have the right to abstain from testing."

"You're mad at the rest of us for getting tested."

"Yes, I'm mad. I thought we were in this thing together." I hated how bratty I sounded. Apparently I'd taken my role as emotional adolescent to heart.

"We *are* in this together," Hannah said. "But you've already been to Rehab twice. Don't you think it would be easier to leave if you weren't 'A Number One' criminal around here?"

I started laughing. Couldn't help it. "Me? 'A Number One' criminal?"

"You know what I mean."

I sighed. "Yeah, I hear you, and I've thought about that. I just can't do it."

We stared at the mountain in silence for a bit. A mosquito buzzed near me, and I slapped at it in a panic. "Can mosquitoes transport bloodborne viruses?"

"No," Hannah said. "Let me ask you this. You want us to leave this place. Where will we go? I'm not saying Safe Water is ideal. It's not. But they do have a clean water source. And they have the resources to get food, medical supplies, law enforcement. Can you do all that for us?"

Anger rushed through me at what felt like an attack—it took me off guard. "Didn't I do all that already on the ride here?"

"I'm not trying to negate what you did," she said. "You're incredibly smart and brave. I'm simply asking you to consider how you will provide for your own community. Because if you and your dad lead our little group out of this place, you guys need a plan that's better than 'We'll figure it out.' Cree and Shyla and Davis deserve better than that. We all do."

I rolled her words around in my head. "I'm not so sure I agree. Yes, we need to know we can get safe water, but the rest? Loca and Liberté and Tracy . . . They don't have much of a *plan*, and what plan they do have is not in any of our best interest. It's all about what *they* want, holding on to *their* way of life. They need fans. A crowd to sing to. A people to *rule* and do their grunt work. And they'll risk who they must to hold on to that. So, yeah, I think my 'We'll figure it out' plan is a whole lot better than staying here to be minions to a couple of narcissistic rock stars."

Silence reigned for a few minutes, and I slapped away three more mosquitoes.

"You could be right," Hannah said.

That surprised me. "I don't want to be right," I said. "I'd much rather live in this house than have to build my own. And I certainly don't want to be in charge of an entire community. It sucked coming up here. I hated having people depend on me. It was scary."

"I like that you're honest to a fault, Eli. You don't care how it makes you look."

That wasn't true. I probably cared too much. "So you still like me?" I asked.

She took hold of my hand and wove her fingers in with mine. "Yeah, I still do. Want to walk?"

"Sure."

We descended the stairs to the street and followed the sidewalk, hand-in-hand. "You can't build a future giving people everything they want," I said. "History has proved over and over what happens with that type of economic system."

"I really do think that Liberté wants to be a good leader," Hannah said. "I've talked to her a few more times, and she's a nice person. She just wants everything to be fair and equal."

"For everyone but her and her brother," I said.

"Yeah, that's true."

"I'm sure they'll make an effort to keep things fair and equal, but at some point, it will crash. People will realize it's not really fair at all. They'll figure out they have no say. That they can have no ideas of their own apart from what the Champions and Tracy decree is acceptable. They must conform. Become slaves. Maybe well-dressed, well-fed slaves who get invited to every party and concert, but they're still slaves."

"Slaves to their EDM gods?" Hannah said.

"And that's not the worst part. Loca and Liberté . . . they act like they care about everyone—like they love their fans—but you heard what they said. They need people to do the work so they don't have to. The new strain of HydroFlu came, and did they cancel their night parties? No. They say party on. That tells me everything I need to know about them. They don't care about anyone but themselves." And I wasn't going to let them destroy our lives.

We walked in silence for a moment, swinging our hands between us, and I thought again about how we might escape from this place.

"It was a conversation I had with your dad," Hannah said.

I frowned, trying to make sense of her sudden comment. "What was?"

"The thing I need to tell you about."

My stomach dropped. I stopped walking and turned to face her, let go of her hand. "So it's recent?"

She nodded, tears flooding her eyes. "It's not what you think, so don't go there."

"Think? What am I thinking?" I couldn't think at all. My dad? What?

The sound of a siren cut through the night. An ambulance turned onto the end of our road, lights flashing off the houses along the street as it approached us, passed by, then pulled into our driveway.

We ran back to the house and saw that Zach was behind the wheel. I glanced up the stairs, my heart hammering in my chest. Had something happened to my dad? Was he sick? Is that what Hannah knew? She couldn't say because of doctor-patient confidentiality?

"Hannah!" Zach said, standing on the running board as he shouted over the hood of the ambulance. "Emergency at Champion House. You've been summoned."

"Oh no." She stepped toward the ambulance, then turned back to me. "Eli, I'll be back. Please don't worry."

"But what about my dad?" I asked.

"I'll tell you when I get back, I promise." She rose onto her toes and kissed me firmly on the lips.

I didn't kiss her back in time, and when I reached for her, she'd already stepped away. Everything felt strange and out of synch. Broken somehow. "Bye," I said, after she'd closed herself inside the cab.

I went inside and found my dad standing at the dining room window, looking out into the dark night.

"Who was in the ambulance?" he asked.

"There was an emergency at Champion House. Zach came for Hannah."

Dad raised his eyebrows. "Mystery patient took a turn for the worse, perhaps?"

"Maybe." If something had happened with my dad, Hannah wasn't the only one who knew about it. "So . . . Hannah," I said, sitting down at the table. "You two don't get along very well."

Dad sat across from me and started studying our map of town. "We get along fine."

"No," I said, thinking it over, remembering things. "You avoid each other."

"Let it go, son."

Wow, okay. Had I stumbled onto something? "I just want to know why you don't approve. I mean, you said you wanted this to happen."

"I think Hannah is great. Ever since I met her, I'd hoped the two of you might hit it off. That thing with you and Jaylee had me worried for a bit."

I decided to take a risk. "She told me, okay?"

Dad's head jumped up so fast I knew I'd struck oil. "Did she?"

"She said she didn't want any secrets between us." Which was true.

All of a sudden, Dad wouldn't look at me. "And you're mad at her for that? Or for what she said? Or both?"

Holy crow. So close, I couldn't stop now. I sought out the perfect response, one that would get me the most information without revealing I didn't have a clue what I was talking about. "What do *you* think, Dad?"

He sighed and rubbed the back of his neck. "Look, I can see

you've already jumped to the wrong conclusion here, but it wasn't like that. She was just talking hypotheticals. Shooting the breeze. I'm still not sure she was even being serious, and there was certainly no attraction."

The word attraction made me a little bit queasy. "Just tell me your side of it," I said, no longer sure I wanted to know.

"All right. We were eating dinner with the kids, just the five of us. Shyla asked us if we were going to be their parents now, then Davis said we should get married. Kind of awkward, right? I explained that Hannah and I had just met. End of conversation."

I narrowed my eyes. "Really?"

"With the kids, yes," Dad said. "Later we were laughing about it, and Hannah started talking about how she thought marriages of convenience were going to come back since this community is so small. She suggested we consider Davis's idea."

What in Hades? "She *proposed* to you?" My voice rose at least one full octave.

Dad scowled. "You said she told you."

"I fibbed. No wonder she was having a hard time admitting that. Hi, new boyfriend. I just want you to know that my ex is your dad."

"No," Dad said. "It wasn't like that. It was one hypothetical conversation. One of those 'If we're not married in ten years' kind of things."

I stood and walked to the door.

"Where are you going?" Dad asked.

"For a run." I left and—juvenile as I knew it was—I slammed the door behind me.

I sprinted until I couldn't breathe. I was halfway back to town when I spotted the brown Labrador. I thought about whistling to call him over, but what would that prove? Instead, I followed at a distance, watched him wander and sniff and mark territory as he explored. The sweat on my arms dried, and I started shivering. I didn't give up, though. I needed this distraction. I didn't want to think about Hannah and my dad and what it meant about her and me.

Three times I almost turned back, yet my feet continued to

follow until a distant whistling perked up the dog's ears and head. He took off at a lazy jog, eventually trotting down a narrow, dirt drive. I followed him to a cabin. He bounded up four porch steps to greet an old woman waiting there.

Parked in front of the cabin was a red Toyota Tacoma access cab.

Dad's truck.

I slowed to a walk, dumbstruck. The woman's eyes met mine, and I stopped, not interested in a reunion with Beardo.

The woman crouched and greeted the dog with a scratch behind its ears. "Didn't expect I'd see you again," she said.

"Same," I said. "Nice truck."

She grimaced. "He's not here, so don't worry 'bout that. Come in, if you want. You can have your gun back."

My throat tightened as I trudged mindlessly toward the cabin and up the porch steps. The woman led me inside an open space. There was a short kitchen counter in the back corner, a fireplace centered on the opposite wall. The dog parked itself on a braided rug before it. Stairs in the back led to a loft. An old plaid couch sat in the middle of the room, cutting the space in half.

The woman walked to the kitchen and used a can opener to open something. "The gun is in the trunk behind the sofa." She nodded to the couch.

I circled it and dropped to my knees beside a large cedar chest. I pushed it open, and my eyes widened. "There must be thirty guns in here."

"Thirty-seven," she said.

"What are you going to do with them all?" I asked.

She set a bowl on the floor and whistled. The dog came running and attacked the food. I noticed the old woman was wearing my mom's hiking boots. The ache in my chest grew.

"Don't know yet," she said. "We'd like to fight for our rights in this place, but we also think that sounds like a good way to die."

"My family has the same problem," I said, shoving down the emotions threatening to choke me. My gaze fell onto a familiar stock, and I reached into the trunk and withdrew my .243, which felt small after holding the .338 Winchester. I fell onto my backside on the chilled wooden floor, read the inscription engraved on the end of the stock, my full name and birthdate—*Elias McShane—March 22*—and cradled it, tears flooding my eyes. I wanted to say "Thank you" but I could barely breathe.

"It was wrong of us to take it," the old woman said, "to take your truck too, though I'm sorry to say I can't give that back. My daughter wouldn't have any way to get to work."

I looked at her. "You have a daughter?"

"That she does," a younger voice said.

I looked up, startled, and saw a woman standing in the doorway, a load of firewood in her arms. She was short and wiry, wearing jeans and worn cowboy boots. Long blonde hair was pulled back into a fancy braid. She looked to be in her thirties, I guessed.

"This is the young man I told you about," the old woman said. "That's his truck out front. I'm giving him back his gun."

"Elias McShane," the daughter said. "The brave young hero who rescued his sister from a sociopath. I've heard all about you."

I narrowed my eyes. "Who are you?"

She crossed the braided rug and dropped the wood onto a mat beside the hearth. "Rebecca Webster," she said. "My friends call me Becky."

"I was just leaving, Rebecca," I said, just to make it clear that we were *not* friends. I stood and spotted Dad's toolbox under the stairs, stared at it. Beside it were several flats of bottled water and two five-gallon Sparklets bottles.

"Take it," the old woman said. "Take anything you see that's yours."

I couldn't carry this stuff all the way back to my house any more than I could carry just the rifle. "Can one of you give me a ride?" I asked. "I can't be seen with this"—I lifted my gun—"out there."

"Be glad to," Rebecca said.

I walked toward the door, eager to leave. That's when I got my first look at a desk in the front corner of the house that held a computer and printer. Beside it and all around the desk on the floor were stacks of flyers and boxes of typing paper.

"You make the flyers," I said.

Rebecca nodded. "You going to turn me in?"

"No."

She stepped outside and held open the front door for me. I walked through. Footsteps followed me as I descended the porch steps and approached Dad's truck, my mind too full for coherent thought. I opened the passenger's door and climbed in. The familiar smell made my chest ache all over again.

"You took out the gun rack," I said when Rebecca got in.

"Didn't want to call attention to myself as a gun owner."

Gun owner. Gun thief. It was a fine line she was straddling. "Smart move."

Rebecca started the truck and backed out of the driveway. The old woman and the brown lab stood on the porch, watching us go.

"What's your mom's name?" I asked.

"Deborah."

"Your dad?"

"Lenny Keele was mom's second husband. I never liked him. When this thing hit, I drove home, saw what he'd been doing, and got Mom out of there."

"You took a lot of his stuff—his spoils."

"Served him right," she said.

I couldn't argue with that, so I stuck to giving directions, which meant I didn't talk much. In the privacy of my head, I railed at God about everything. Why was everything so mixed up? Why couldn't I catch a break? Or had I? I gazed at the rifle in my hands and wondered what God was up to in all this.

Rebecca soon pulled into our driveway. I climbed out, hadn't even shut my door when I heard my name.

"Eli!"

I looked up. Dad was standing at the railing up on the deck.

"Is that my truck?" he asked, his tone incredulous.

"Shocking turn of events, huh?" I said. "It's that kind of day." I glanced across the inside of the cab at Rebecca. "Want to meet my dad?"

Her eyes flickered up through the windshield to where Dad stood. She tipped her head to the side, as if considering it. "Why not?" she said.

I led the woman up the stairs to the deck. "Dad, this is Rebecca. Her stepdad stole our truck and all our supplies, but her mom gave me back my gun. Rebecca, my dad, Seth McShane."

"Nice boots," Dad said. "You ride?"

"Used to. You?"

"When I was a kid back in Montana."

"Beautiful country up there," she said.

"They got you working someplace?"

"Construction," she said. "Foreman, actually. Didn't go over well at first."

"I can imagine."

"I have an architecture degree. Used to build commercial real estate in Albuquerque. You?"

"Mechanic. Phoenix."

Their easy dialogue annoyed me. I went inside and shut the door, went to my room and checked my gun for shells. It was empty. I climbed into bed with my rifle and lay there thinking about Beardo and Deborah and Rebecca and my mom's boots and the flyers and the brown lab and God and Hannah—mostly Hannah—until I fell asleep.

# 29

**HANNAH**
**SEPTEMBER 20**

By the time Zach, Travis, and I arrived at Champion House, Barkley Kipp had died. We found Dr. Bayles and Liberté Champion sitting together on a loveseat adjacent to the bed. The fishy odor was almost unbearable. The room was chilled as several fans had been set up and were oscillating toward an open window. I understood that it must be making a difference, but from the way I kept fighting the urge to gag, it sure didn't seem like it.

Liberté's face was wet with tears and creased in sorrow and fatigue. She jumped up and embraced me. *"Je ne peux pas le croire. Je suis sous le choc."*

I hugged her trembling body, clueless as to what she had just said. "I'm so sorry," was all I could think to say.

"Take Mr. Kipp's body to the hospital morgue," Dr. Bayles told Zach. "It was his wish to donate himself for testing, that we might find a cure for this new strain."

Zach and Travis set to work. Jason stood and motioned for me to take his seat. "Hannah, please keep Ms. Champion company while I speak with her brother."

Liberté released me and fell onto the loveseat. "My heart," she said. "It is broken."

I sank down beside her, remembering how it felt to lose my brother—all the thoughtless, empty words people said to try and comfort and fix me. Better to say nothing. I took hold of her hand and squeezed.

We sat there, watching Zach and Travis load Barkley's body onto their gurney. They were just about to wheel him out of the room when Liberté yelled, "Stop!" She flew to the gurney, took Barkley's face in both hands and kissed his forehead, his lips. "*Adieu, mon amour. Je me souviendrai toujours . . .*" One last kiss and she stepped back to allow the paramedics to take him away.

She broke down and wept, then, and I felt helpless in her presence. Just as I decided to reach for her, she screamed and knocked a vase of flowers off the bedside table.

"Libby." Loca strode into the room, Dr. Bayles on his heels. He reached for his sister. "*Viens là, chérie.*" She embraced him and sobbed.

I felt out of place and wondered why I had been summoned. Dr. Bayles sat beside me and laid his hand on my knee. "Thank you for coming," he said.

I scooted forward and clasped my hands, resting my elbows on my knees and—in the process—causing his hand to fall away. "I'm sorry I was too late to be any help," I said.

"Liberté asked for you," he said.

As I pondered the oddity of such a thing, Dr. Bayles rose and approached the siblings.

"Would you like to do this another time, Ms. Champion? Perhaps tomorrow?"

"*Non,*" Liberté said, wiping her eyes with the back of her hand. "I must know now."

"May I see your meds?" Dr. Bayles asked.

"*Oui.*" She walked to a dresser in the corner of the room and returned with a pill box, which she handed to the doctor. He opened it and inspected its contents. "My doctor said there was no risk of infecting my partner once I had become undetectable," she said.

"How long had you maintained an undetectable viral load?" Dr. Bayles asked.

"Eight months, I believe," she said. "And we have had no problems."

"Did you miss some pills? Even one?" Dr. Bayles asked. "When treatment is stopped, your viral load rebounds to a very high level."

"Of course I missed some pills!" she cried. "I know this is my fault. I know that I killed him."

"That's impossible," Dr. Bayles said. "Even if Mr. Kipp did contract HIV from you, it would not have killed him in a matter of weeks. HIV *may* cause AIDS after you've been infected for several years, but not everyone who has HIV will get AIDS. I'm sure you know this."

"Then what happened?" Loca asked, rubbing his sister's shoulders.

"I have only a theory," Dr. Bayles said. "I think you contracted HydroFlu—the first strain—before you arrived here. I think your antiretroviral treatment saved you—kept your immune system strong enough to fight off the virus, but it mutated with the HIV and became something else. This mutation is what Mr. Kipp contracted from you."

"Then I did kill him," she said.

"He is a casualty of the pandemic," Dr. Bayles said. "Since he was not taking the antiretroviral treatment as you were, his immune system didn't have the added protection yours had."

"This you think is what has happened to the others?" she asked.

"To some, perhaps, though I suspect each story will be different. We found the new strain only in those also carrying a bloodborne pathogen. Not only from STDs . . . We even have one case that is a relapse of malaria that was never properly treated. The point is, you are infected with the second strain, and you have shown us that it can be contained with an antiretroviral treatment. Barkley's death gave us the clue we needed, if not to stop this new strain, to at least control it."

"Then he is a hero," Liberté said.

"He is," Dr. Bayles said. "With your permission, I'll start the infected on antiretroviral treatments."

"Why do you need my permission?" she asked.

"Because with the number of infected, there won't be enough to last everyone more than a few months," he said.

"The trip to New Jersey was just a precaution to make sure Libby had enough," Loca said. "You said the pharmacy was well stocked."

"It was," Dr. Bayles said. "But that was when the number of people needing retroviral therapy was seven. After mandatory testing, we have 178 people who need retroviral therapy."

The heaviness of such a statement fell over the room. Loca broke the silence.

"We'll wait until the team is back," he said. "Until we know more."

Liberté looked at her brother. "*Non*, we must not wait. It took Barkley so quickly."

"If Reggie does not return, you will not have what you need to live," Loca said.

A resolve came over Liberté, and her posture straightened, her chin lifted high. "I will not let my people die," she said. "I am their queen. Their mother. I will care for them as I should have cared for Barkley. If Reggie does not find enough, we will send him elsewhere. We will survive." She nodded curtly to Dr. Bayles. "Help everyone, Dr. Bayles. Is that clear?"

"I'll get started right away," he said.

*"Mon dieu, que tu es bête."* Loca huffed and walked out of the room.

"You're very brave," I told her, awed that someone I had perceived to be so shallow would risk her own future for others.

Liberté smiled sadly, tears filling her eyes. "They are lucky to have us both," she said, looking toward the open door. "Loca is a good man. He worries for me, but I am not afraid."

An awkward silence passed, and I wished I could find a polite way to leave.

"Hannah," Liberté said. "You have a cell phone?"

"Yes," I said.

"May I see it?"

I pulled it from my pocket and handed it over.

"I am giving you my number," she said, "so I can reach you when I need someone to tell me the truth. You can contact me as well. Anytime you need, my friend."

"Thank you," I said, not at all sure I wanted that privilege.

Shortly after that, Liberté had a driver take me home. When I got out of the car, the fresh air was such a relief, I stood in the driveway, just breathing and trying to cleanse my lungs of the fishy odor.

I saw Eli sitting up on the deck. Guilt seized me so completely that I sighed, not at all eager to fight with him tonight. I'd promised him answers, though, so I climbed the stairs and sat in the chair beside his.

"Everything okay?" he asked.

Zach would tell Eli about Barkley's death soon enough, so I saw no reason to hide it. "Barkley Kipp died."

"We need to get out of this place," Eli said.

His irrational fear annoyed me. "You're in no danger at present," I said.

"That's not the point. You heard the meeting. You heard what they want to do to us."

"Wanting to do something is not the same as doing it," I said. "You can't go to jail for wanting to kill someone. You actually have to do it." I hoped Liberté would continue to stand up to her brother and Mr. Tracy. I wasn't willing to count on it, though.

"You proposed to my dad," Eli said.

That stopped me cold. "He told you."

"Eventually."

"*Eli.*" I gritted my teeth, annoyed he'd been unable to wait a few more hours. "I wanted to tell you myself," I said. "It was important to me to tell you."

"Then you should have."

"That's not fair. I was trying to when Zach drove up."

"So, you just want somebody, is that it? You couldn't have Zach or my dad, Logan freaks you out, and Dr. Necktie smells like Old Spice, so I'm the consolation prize?"

"Stop being so self-absorbed," I snapped. "That conversation with your dad had nothing to do with you and everything to do with me and my fears."

Eli said nothing, but the hurt on his face was clear. This had shattered his already low opinion of himself.

"Don't you ever just get to talking with someone and say stupid things?" I asked. "Well, I didn't believe in love anymore. The idea of risking my heart to anyone scared me. I was having nightmares all the time. I figured the best this shattered world had to offer me was a mutual agreement between two consenting, sane adults. When the kids asked if we could be their parents, I just figured, why not? Would that really be so bad?"

Eli looked away.

"I'm not proud of it. It was a mistake. You're the only person I want to be with."

His brow crumpled, and he shook his head. "I don't think you do."

"How can you say that? Haven't I shown you the truth? We're good together."

"It just feels like . . . Like I'm your last resort."

My heart broke at those words. I understood why he believed them, yet I had no way to show him any differently. Despair and panic gripped me, followed by a triggered rush of anger.

I didn't pause to separate the piles. I just let my mind race. How could Eli expect the worst of me? How could he go behind my back and twist the truth from Seth? Why hadn't he been patient enough to wait for me to come back and tell him myself? "Sometimes you're such a child," I snapped.

His wounded expression hardened into something fierce. "I

guess that's why you prefer older men." He stood and walked into the house.

•    •    •

The next day at the hospital, I agonized over my fight with Eli as I helped Dr. Bayles get the HydroFlu second-strain patients set up on their antiretroviral treatments. The hospital was packed—we were so busy!—but still I wanted to call Zach to bring the ambulance and drive me around the garbage truck routes until I found Eli so I could apologize. At the same time, I never wanted to see Eli's face again. I felt both guilty and humiliated. As if that stupid conversation with Seth hadn't been embarrassing enough, Eli's parting words burned deeply. That he would think me so callous and cruel.

Was I?

"Yo!" Linsey approached, two enforcers behind him escorting a man between them. "We got an empty room?"

"Follow me," I said, leading the men to room 118 at the end of the hall. "Where are you hurt?" I asked the injured man.

"My hand," the man said, stretching out his right hand, palm down.

I pulled on a fresh pair of gloves and inspected a swollen red area near his thumb. Didn't look like he'd been in a fight. Looked more like something had bit him.

"What happened?" I asked.

"Patch him up without the questions," the enforcer said.

My back to the enforcer, I rolled my eyes at my patient. I probed the flabby skin between his thumb and forefinger and felt something hard inside. A chip of bone, perhaps? His hand wasn't bruised, though. If he'd been struck hard enough to break bone, his skin would be more damaged than it was.

"You need an x-ray," I said.

"No," the enforcer said.

"Yes," I said, "or I will call Liberté Champion and tell her that Officer"—I read his name tag—"Wick refused to let me treat my patient. And I can do it too, because she personally gave me her cell phone number just last night." Like I would ever really call her.

"I answer to Captain Koval," Wick said, but he looked uncertain and stepped out of the way.

I soon had the images I needed. It turned out there was a slender cylinder about the size of a grain of rice inside the man's hand. He'd been injected with an RFID chip. That reduced my concern for a greater injury to his hand, and I went ahead and treated his infection the best I could and put him on antibiotics.

The knowledge of the chip, however, raised all kinds of ethical red flags. Later, at the nurse's station, I told Linsey and Susan what I'd discovered.

Linsey whistled low. "Human microchipping without consent. That's pretty sneaky."

"Jason mentioned it about a month ago," Susan confessed. "Mr. Tracy had asked him if it was safe for humans. This is the first I've heard that it actually happened."

"Where did they get the technology?" I asked.

"A veterinarian out of Montrose," Susan said. "From what I understand, they wanted to inject repeat offenders with the same tech used to tag pets."

I instantly thought of Eli.

"So they can track them?" Linsey asked.

"Exactly," Susan said. "Too many people don't wear their wristbands at all times."

"But why?" I asked. "If they commit a crime, Rehab would have a record of prior offenses."

"Maybe they're tracking their behavior," Linsey said.

There was no excuse. "I don't like the way Mr. Tracy and the enforcers do their jobs," I said. "It makes me wish I'd never come here."

"Maybe you should call your best friend Liberté and tell her what's what."

I glowered at Linsey. "I wish I hadn't told you about that," I said.

He laughed. "Seriously, though. You think there is someplace better out there?"

"I could live off the land," I said, not sure I really could without someone like Eli or Seth or even Andy—if he ever got out of Rehab—to show me how.

"I couldn't," Susan said. "It takes a special kind of person to be able to survive out there."

"Yeah, this place ain't perfect," Linsey said, "but I can raise my family here. I can make a difference. Admin needs us. We're valuable to them."

He wasn't wrong. I did like having purpose, and I loved working at the hospital. But Mr. Tracy and Loca and Captain Koval were out of control. I wondered what Linsey would say about Admin's desire to addict the population of Safe Water to nicotine.

I remembered my first hospital internship and how annoyed I'd been by the politics—the favoritism. I'd signed up for Doctors Without Borders that summer, hoping I could make a difference in a place where the only thing that mattered was giving my patients the best possible care. This hospital was small enough that I had been able to accomplish that here, but the more Admin meddled, the worse things would get. With no one to stop them, it was only a matter of time before they demanded the hospital staff do something even more unethical than drawing blood from an unwilling patient. What would I do then?

●　　●　　●

After my dinner break, Susan told me Dr. Bayles wanted to see me in his office.

"We have a problem, Hannah," he said, once I was sitting across from him. "I've just learned that you are under investigation by enforcers. Mr. Tracy is concerned that I'm employing a suspected violator."

The words knocked the wind out of me. "I'm not a violator! Why would he think that?"

"Because you live with several violators. Apparently there have been arrests, some weapons seized, and one didn't even come in for mandatory testing." He looked down at some notes on his desk. "Oh, I guess that was your boyfriend, the suspected ringleader."

"Eli's not a ringleader!" I said, leaning forward to read what else he'd written down.

He turned the paper over. "I assured Mr. Tracy that you're completely trustworthy, but he wants to reassign you. He's also concerned about three minor children living in that environment."

My eyes filled with tears. "Those children are perfectly fine," I snapped.

"Oh, I don't doubt that for a minute, Hannah, since you live there. But you can see how this must look to Mr. Tracy."

What if the enforcers took away the children? I had to warn Eli and the others. "What should I do?" I asked.

He sighed, clearly troubled by my situation. "The hospital can't afford to lose you," he said. "I'm prepared to stick out my neck for you, but I'd need some assurances."

And suddenly I saw right through him. "What kind of assurances?" I asked through gritted teeth.

"I didn't tell Mr. Tracy that you were dating the ringleader, but if enforcers were to learn that bit of information, I'm afraid Mr. Tracy would insist upon you leaving the hospital."

"You want me to break up with Eli?"

"I think that would be wise, yes. You should also move out of that house right away. I can show you the available apartments upstairs after your shift."

"Move here?"

"And if I could tell Mr. Tracy that you and I are dating, all of that together would convince him, I'm sure."

"Dr. Bayles! Are you blackmailing me?"

He winced, as if I'd misunderstood him completely. "I'm just trying to help, Hannah. These are simply ideas I thought I'd run past you."

Sure they were.

# 30

ELI
SEPTEMBER 21

Monday morning, I woke up on the wrong side of the bed. I didn't want to attend the morning party and listen to Tracy spin lies, though I was curious what he'd say about the rain being safe. I wanted to talk to Hannah, but she'd already left for work—asked Logan to drive her in early. That worried me. We'd argued before, but not like this. Was she avoiding me? The idea made me feel like a fish being gutted. I don't know why I thought talking to her would change things. I didn't want to be her last resort.

Tracy must have agreed to Liberté's idea of involving the public in scavenging, because at the morning party, he announced the Denver Technology Research trip. Any citizen in good standing could enter on the Grid, and five lucky souls would be chosen for the adventure. Tracy said we were needed—that it was important we all do our part. If I had planned to stay here, I might have entered. I knew better, though. Tracy would never choose me for anything but an all-expense-paid visit to Rehab.

"This is a load of bull," I said to Zach. "Tracy will handpick the Denver team."

Zach nodded. "Probably so."

"You doubt it?" I asked. "Of course he will. He decides everything."

"Chill, man," Zach said. "How about you don't make a scene today?"

I glared at Zach. What was *his* problem?

Tracy switched to the topic of HydroFlu testing and thanked all who had gone in voluntarily. "The patience and kindness y'all showed our medical staff was so impressive. We are thrilled to have such wonderful citizens living in this community. Give yourself a hand." He began to clap, and the audience joined in.

When the applause died down, Tracy let the joy fade from his face. "Unfortunately, not everyone here shares the same values. We had twenty-eight violators who did not appear for their blood test last week."

Someone booed, which caught on, and a chorus of negativity rang out. Twenty-eight? So, me, Rebecca and Deborah in their cabin, and Brett Durzinski and all his rebel friends.

"I understand how you feel," Tracy said. "I was disappointed, to say the least, and decided it was important for y'all to know who's causing trouble in our little utopia."

My cheeks burned as faces flashed across the big screen, the word "VIOLATOR" under each picture in all caps. "What a clever way to *not* talk about the rain being safe," I said.

Zach tugged my sweatshirt hood over my head. "Don't want that eye suffering a relapse," he said.

I shoved him away but left the hood, thinking he could be on to something. With each face that appeared, the crowd grew more agitated, booing and catcalling some nasty names. Mr. Tracy had just waged war upon me and everyone else who refused to submit to his every whim.

Most the people on the screen were old—Dad's age or

above. Brett Durzinski came up early, and sure enough, I also saw Rebecca and Deborah. I appeared about halfway through. Kimama wasn't far behind. I hoped she was still alive.

After the slideshow, Tracy reminded people to enter for a place on the Denver trip. I wondered if they'd take many enforcers with them. If so, the enforcers might be a little shorthanded when trip time came. Might work to our advantage to plan our escape then.

I pondered this as we left the field and headed for our truck. We had just passed through the gate when I heard my name.

"Eli!"

I looked up and met Krista's gaze. She was sitting on the hood of a red truck with some buff Asian guy I'd never seen before. The guy had gauges in his ears as big as half dollars.

"Hey," I said.

"He's one of the violators!" she yelled, turning to knock on the windshield behind her.

The truck doors opened, and two guys climbed out. Marco and Riggs. The Asian guy with the gauges slid off the hood and approached slowly, like his muscles actually weighed him down.

I doubted that was true. Where had Krista found this guy?

"Why am I not surprised?" Riggs said, walking toward us. "You think you're better than everyone else, don't you, twig?"

Zach pulled me to his other side, putting himself between me and the muscle. "Run to the van," he said.

"I'm not running from Riggs," I said, annoyed.

Marco elbowed Lizzie aside to get to me, and Zach lunged forward. "Hey, why don't you watch where you're going, man?"

Marco shoved Zach, who fell against Lizzie. Zach caught her around the waist and spun her behind him to keep their balance.

"You got a problem?" Zach asked Marco.

"Yeah," he said. "You're hiding a violator."

"We don't want any trouble," Zach said, waving me to go.

"Then your friend here should have gotten tested," Gauges said, pushing me so hard I stumbled on the soft gravel on the shoulder of the road.

My anger boiled over, and as soon as I had my balance, I

shoved the guy back. "I don't need a test to tell me I'm not sick," I said. "I have a brain."

Gauges swung a fist at my head. I ducked, but his next punch bruised my shoulder. Desperation fueled a few punches, and I swung wildly. When my fists managed to land, the impact was weak. My knuckles stung, and I don't think I did any damage.

Shyla darted into the fray and pushed Gauges' leg. "Leave him alone!"

Panic flashed over me at the idea of Shyla getting hurt. "Shy, let go." I pulled her off the guy and handed her to Lizzie.

Behind me, I heard Dad's voice. "Take the kids, Liz."

I spun around and saw Dad standing between me and Gauges, his palms raised. "We don't want any trouble," he said.

But I did, and while Dad was playing high school principal, I shoved Riggs. He snapped his fist at me, grazing my cheek. It felt like it had shredded some skin. I punched him back, thrilled when he staggered. It felt good to hit Riggs, who had annoyed me for so long and epitomized the typical Safe Water sell-out. Logan joined the fight by kicking in the back of Riggs's legs. Knees buckling, Riggs managed to keep his feet and twist around. Logan sprinted away like a frightened cat. Then Riggs came at me.

For a moment, things seemed almost even, despite the fact that Logan had fled and I weighed thirty pounds less than anyone out there. Time passed by in a mess of fists and pain. Dad knocked Gauges flat, but he was already getting up again. Zach and Marco went to the ground, rolling like wrestlers on a mat. I tried to dodge Riggs's fists, but he clipped my chin and kicked me so hard in the stomach, I lost my breath. Someone yelled for the enforcers.

Logan came back, but Riggs elbowed him in the face and sent him sprawling. Riggs got a hold of my arm. I swung away, trying to use my weight and momentum to break his grip, but he yanked me toward him and punched my face. Pain exploded in my nose. I clubbed his chin, then dodged in time to take a blow to the ear rather than another to my face. Before I had a chance to strike back, my nerves lit on fire. I lost control of my body and found myself on the ground, shaking from an enforcer's taser.

• • •

By the time I could move again, I was in an ambulance. Drool trickled from my mouth, but when I wiped it away with my wrist, I saw it was actually blood oozing off a fat lip. My face stung, and when I tried to sit up, a sharp pain spiked in my stomach and made me whimper.

"Dude, lie down." Zach appeared over me, not nearly as bloody as I felt.

"Am I dying?" I asked.

"No," he said, "but you're in some serious trouble. What's with you today? You've been looking for a fight all morning."

"Me? What about Krista?"

"We could have walked away, man," Zach said. "Why didn't you run when I said to?"

"So Riggs could laugh at me? Oh, look at the scared little boy running away?"

"Who cares what he thinks?"

"I do, okay? I'm tired of being a weak kid."

"Something happen with you and Hannah?"

I frowned. "Why? She say something?"

"She doesn't have to. You're like a billboard with the scowling and the attitude and the yelling."

I was about to tell him where to shove his observations, but I gagged on a glob of my own bloody spit and had to let him help me not choke to death. Once I was breathing again, I told him about Hannah and my dad.

"Ouch," Zach said. "I see why you're mad, but honestly, it kind of makes sense."

"Are you kidding me right now?" If Zach took my dad's side, I was going to punch him.

He shrugged. "I mean, you were in charge of our group until we reached Reinhold's place. As soon as Jaylee kissed you, you regressed to middle-school kid with girlfriend."

I snorted. "What, like you?"

"Exactly like that, only more sickening."

"Nobody is more sickening than you and my sister," I said.

"Disagree," Zach said. "But that's beside the point. When you picked up Hannah from that gas station, you were our fearless leader. And she would not leave your side from the time you found her until she stabbed you. Then you paired off with Jaylee and let your dad take over. Once we got here, the rest of us kept ditching Hannah and your dad with the kids to go off and pretend life was normal. What was Hannah supposed to do?"

"Not try and hook up with my dad?"

"Why not? We're living through a freaking pandemic, Eli. Life is about survival now. Don't punish Hannah for trying to survive."

I slugged him in the gut. My angle was bad, though, and there was no force behind it. "How would you feel if Lizzie tried to marry *your* dad?"

"Honestly? After I busted my gut laughing, I'd feel grateful my dad was still alive. At least you still have your dad, man. Stop whining."

Zach's verbal blow hit hard. "Sorry," I said.

"Hannah likes you. Always has. Stop doubting it."

"I . . . can't," I said.

"That's because you're you. Trust me on this. I've seen the way she looks at you. You got it good, man! Well, not at the moment. You're being arrested again, after you get patched up, of course. The rest of us got off with warnings because, you know, you're the violator."

"Of course. My cot is probably still warm from the last time I was there."

"Just do what they say and get out of there, okay?" Zach said.

I closed my eyes. "I'll try."

●    ●    ●

By the time Officer Wick led me into the hospital, my wrists were burning from the pinch of the handcuffs. I instantly started looking for Hannah but didn't see her. Monica nodded to Wick like they did this every day, and we strode right past the reception desk. One pro to being arrested: no waiting.

We met the male nurse, Linsey, coming down the hall. He took us to an exam room where Wick removed my cuffs. Linsey told me to put on a hospital gown that sat folded on the exam table, shooed out Officer Wick, and shut the door behind him. I stood there, thankful to have some alone time, wondering if I'd get necktie doctor or the old guy.

Five minutes passed. I opened the door and peeked into the hall. Wick glared at me and pulled the door shut. I tossed the gown onto an empty chair and sat on the exam table, the paper crackly beneath me. Another five minutes passed before the door opened, and Hannah walked in. My pulse started racing. Her eyes met mine, widened. Other than that, she looked at her chart as if she didn't know me.

"Mister, um . . . McShane. Let me inform you that this exam room is for violators. Do not try anything. The enforcer is right outside the door. He can hear everything we say."

"Wonderful."

"First things first," she said. "One blood test, coming right up."

I sighed. "Whatever." Guess I lost *that* battle . . .

The next few minutes passed in silence as Hannah tied a tourniquet to my arm and took a vial of my blood. I'd never felt so defeated, losing my fight against Safe Water, losing Hannah.

"Can we talk?" I asked.

"I suggest we keep this strictly professional, Mr. McShane. What happened to you?"

"There was only one last Snickers bar at the mercantile. I reached for it at the same time as this other guy. Big guy. I wasn't about to let him have it."

"You got in a fight over a candy bar."

"It was a Snickers," I said. "Could be the last one on earth."

She smirked, which made me feel good, that I'd cracked through whatever act she was performing here.

"Your face hurt?" she asked.

"Not really," I lied.

"Any pain elsewhere?"

I wanted to say no, but the ache in my gut spoke up. "My stomach is a little sore."

"Show me where."

I straightened, winced, and ran my hand over the sore spot.

"Could be a bruised rib." She motioned to the gown on the chair. "I need you to remove your shirt, so I can listen to your heart and examine your ribs."

I didn't really want to take off my shirt in front of Hannah. We'd already established I was an immature teenage kid, and I'd just gotten my butt kicked. Did she need to see how skinny I was to rub it in? "Isn't that the doctor's job?" I asked.

"I'm your doctor today," she said.

"Oh. Congratulations."

She smiled to herself. "We're kind of busy, and Dr. Bayles thought I could handle it."

I didn't have any other logical reason to refuse, so I started to pull my shirt over my head. Pain shot through my side. I froze with my shirt tangled around my head and made the most pathetic whimpering sound.

I felt Hannah's hands on my back. She pulled the shirt the rest of the way off. I snagged it from her and held it balled up in my lap. "Thanks."

She pressed the cold stethoscope against my back and chest in several places, telling me to breathe in and hold it, breathe out. Then she asked me to lie down. I did, and the paper crumpled under me. I felt vulnerable and exposed with my legs hanging off the end of the table at my knees. Hannah put her fingers against my stomach and pushed in several places. Her touch felt good— better than I wanted it to—until she hit the sore spot.

"Whose side are you on, anyway?" I asked.

A grin. "I think you have a bruised rib. We'll get you an x-ray to make sure it isn't broken."

"I don't want an x-ray."

"Don't be stupid, E— Mr. McShane. The technology is available. Use it."

I said no more while she continued her examination. The

whole thing totally impressed me. I felt like a thug compared to all the things she knew. It didn't help that my dad had fought way better than I had. It suddenly seemed ridiculous that Hannah would pick me over him. What could I offer someone like her? A patient to practice on. That was about it. I wanted to say something about our fight, but I didn't know what.

She left with my blood sample. Linsey came and took me for x-rays. He not only x-rayed my chest, but my hand too, which I thought was weird. He didn't seem to like what he saw.

As he took me back to the exam room for criminals, I saw Dr. Necktie standing super close to Hannah. Practically had her pinned to the wall. He was holding her hand. We passed them, and I heard him say, "It's a date."

Hannah met my gaze for the briefest moment, swallowed in this super guilty way, then said, "Okay." Then—then!—Dr. Necktie kissed her hand.

I faced forward, my chest tight with shock, which made it difficult to breathe with the bruised/broken rib. Linsey steered me back into the exam room. I almost asked him about Hannah and Dr. Necktie, but what did it matter? The guy was a flipping surgeon. How was I supposed to compete with that?

Hannah finally returned to tell me that two of my ribs were bruised. Probably when Riggs had kicked me in the gut.

"So, you and Dr. Necktie?" I said, wincing as I tried to breathe normally.

She handed me a tiny paper sack. "I've given you some painkillers."

I let out a short breath. "I thought you didn't like him. I thought you told him I was your boyfriend."

"Paracetamol can be taken with or without food."

"Come on, Hannah. Talk to me. We had a fight! People do that sometimes. Then they, you know, make up." My pathetic panting was really starting to annoy me.

"Take two tablets up to four times in twenty-four hours. Always wait four hours between doses." She wouldn't even look at me.

"You can't go out with that guy. He smells like Old Spice!"

She pulled open the door and told Officer Wick, "I'm all done here," as if we didn't know each other at all.

"Love you too, Hannah," I yelled as Wick dragged me out.

"Be sure to read the After Visit Summary in the bag," I heard her say from behind me. "Mr. McShane?"

Wick had me by the arm, but I was able to turn my head enough to see her and managed to squeeze out the word, "What?"

"There are instructions written on there," she said, and I noticed that her eyes were red.

Instructions?

But Wick took away my little bag. He hooked my cuffs in front and led me toward the exit. I trudged along beside him, confused and hurt over everything I'd just seen and experienced. Some people were coming down the hall, so Wick moved us to the right to wait as Linsey led a female patient past. She was dressed in a paper gown and pink socks. Our eyes met.

It was Jaylee.

Wick pushed me onward. I looked over my shoulder and saw Linsey lead Jaylee into an exam room. What was she doing here? She didn't look sick. I hadn't seen her face on the list of violators this morning, so she likely wasn't here for a blood test.

Later. I'd ask Hannah tonight.

I shifted my arms so that my cuffs didn't touch my stomach and remembered I wasn't a free man.

Fine. I'd ask Hannah when I got home. If I could get her to speak to me.

Stupid Safe Water Mountain Refuge, anyway. As soon as I got back to the house, I was planning some kind of escape. I was more than done with this place.

●　　●　　●

Over at Rehab, they put me in a plain, cinderblock room with a beat-up laminate table in the center and two chairs. Thankfully, Wick dropped my prescription bag on the table before he left. My handcuffs made it tricky, but I managed to grab the sack and dump its contents: a bubble pack of painkillers and a sheet of paper that said "After Care Summary." I scanned it, didn't see anything interesting. I turned it over and spotted Hannah's narrow and neat handwriting in the bottom corner.

Tracking microchip in your hand.

My face tingled from the shock of those words. Panicked, I knew I needed to destroy the evidence. I ripped off the corner of the page and put the paper in my mouth. I chewed on it until I had a nice wad, which I spat at the wall where it stuck with a satisfying thwack.

I was admiring my work when the door opened behind me. I figured Connie Lawler had come to lecture me, but this was a day of surprises. Tracy himself loped into the room, shut the door, and sat across from me.

"Mr. McShane," he said.

"I want a lawyer," I said.

"Lawyers died with the rest of the world," Tracy said. "We don't need them here."

"You can't just change the law," I said. "I have the right to legal counsel."

"Are we really going to do this again?" Tracy asked. "The United States of America has died, m'kay? It's history, like Czechoslovakia, Prussia, and the USSR. You are now in the jurisdiction of the Safe Water Mountain Refuge. Here, I decide what's law."

"I thought Loca and Liberté were in charge," I said.

"They're figureheads, like the royal family of England. I'm the prime minister. The president. The Commander in Ch—"

"The dictator?"

His lip curled, but he managed to force a smile. "If that helps you."

"I know the drill," I said. "Put me in my cell until Connie is ready to try and brainwash me."

"It's not going to be so easy this time, Mr. McShane."

Great. Just great. "I didn't do anything wrong."

313

"You missed your blood test and started a fight at the morning party."

"You're the one who flashed my face on the big screen. That's like putting a 'Kick Me' sign on my back."

"If the citizens of this town are upset at you, perhaps you should try a little harder to support the community. This is your third infraction, Mr. McShane. This time you will remain here for seven days."

"A week without water? I could die."

"You will get one, eight-ounce glass of water per day. You will get one meal."

"I need more food than that to digest my painkillers." I nodded at what was left of the crumpled After Care Summary on the table.

"No painkillers for you, Mr. McShane. The goal is to make you miserable enough that you'll fall in line."

"Look," I said, "you don't want me here. I don't want to be here. Why continue to annoy each other? Open the gate and let me out. Then I won't be your problem anymore."

"You'd like that, wouldn't you?" Tracy said. "Despite how much you annoy me, I can't let you leave. One person gets to leave, then everyone wants to leave."

"Gee, I wonder why? Maybe it's because you're a psychopathic dictator."

His eyes flashed, but he held his fake smile steady. "Next time you're arrested, Mr. McShane, you will be sentenced to six months. I promise it won't be pleasant."

That sobered me. I didn't doubt he was serious. If I was going to get out of town, I couldn't get locked up for that long.

Tracy stood. "From the look on your face, I see we understand each other. Have a good day, Mr. McShane."

He left me there alone. I wondered about the tracker in my hand, wondered if Reinhold was in here for a six-month stint, wondered if I'd lost Hannah to Dr. Necktie. A week was a long time. I somehow doubted she'd still be waiting when I got out.

# 31

HANNAH
SEPTEMBER 23

I'd agreed to Dr. Bayles's offer. I'd taken an apartment above the hospital and said yes when he asked me to dinner right in front of Eli—the jerk. But I hadn't actually moved. At the moment, I was living two lives. I'd warned Zach and Lizzie and Seth and Logan—told them what had happened and that we needed to leave soon. We couldn't go anywhere without Eli, though, and none of us knew when he was coming back.

Wednesday, one of my days off, I was sitting in the living room reading *Dune* when the walkie talkie radio crackled. "This is Grizzly Cub to base. Anyone there?"

Kimama!

I jumped up, but before I could take one step, Logan sprinted across the room and yanked the walkie talkie to his mouth. "Yes! Hello, Grizzly Cub. This is Graham Cracker at Home Base. What happened to you? Over."

He pressed record on his computer, then stared at me as we waited for the static to clear. Besides the children, he and I were the only ones home. I wished Eli were here. He would hate to miss this.

"That's a story for another day," Kimama said. "Just want to say the original plan is good. I repeat. The original plan is good. You still in Alcatraz?"

For eleven, Kimama's intelligence surprised me.

"Affirmative," Logan said. "Ready to find a new Home Base. Any recommendations?"

"The best property is always on the water or in the hills."

"She means by the river or on the mountain," Logan told me.

I nodded and imagined Eli saying, "Thank you, Sherlock," which made me smile.

"You stopping by for a visit, Grizzly Cub?" Logan asked.

"No can do," Kimama said. "I've made my home on the cliffs of paradise. Know where that is?"

Logan turned around, gaze fixed on the map Eli and Seth had left on the kitchen table. He motioned to it and hissed, "Grab the map!"

I complied, studying it as I carried it to the desk. I set it down and continued to search for something that matched Kimama's description.

"You copy that, Graham Cracker?" Kimama asked. "Can you find my address?"

"Hold that thought, Grizzly Cub," Logan said, then to me, "Any ideas? Cliffs of paradise. What's that mean?"

I recalled where Eli had wanted to build and pointed to the area between the base of the mountain and the East River. Then I ran my finger up the mountain's slope. "She has to mean up the mountain where the third arm of the creek splits off," I said.

"Here." Logan pointed to a small typed name: Paradise Cliffs. He pressed the call button. "We found you, Grizzly Cub."

"Good to know. You serve your time yet?"

"Affirmative," Logan said. "Our sentence is over and done. We'll stop by first chance we get. Over."

"Sounds like a plan, Graham Cracker. Any sign of Grizzly Bear?"

Logan winced. "We think he's in the real Alcatraz, if you know what I mean."

"Try to bring him when you visit," Kimama said. "Over and out."

Logan set the receiver back in the cradle and offered me a high five. "She's okay!"

I slapped his hand. "I'm so glad."

"Wonder how she's been living out there all by herself."

"It's pretty impressive," I said.

"It won't be long now," Logan said. "We're almost out of here."

He looked so excited, but for me, hope felt far away. I wanted to believe that Eli and I would mend things. He had said he wanted to talk. But if I couldn't be with Eli, I didn't think I wanted to escape with them. It would just be too strange. But staying here, knowing the kind of man Dr. Bayles was—not just a womanizer but someone who would blackmail to get what he wanted—the hospital was no longer a safe place for me. I regretted taking an apartment upstairs. I regretted agreeing to date him. I didn't want to do this, but I saw no other way to buy time until Eli came back. I just hoped they didn't keep him too long.

•   •   •

"I'm ready," I said to Lizzie.

She looked me up and down. "You still look pretty."

I rubbed my neckline, self-conscious about the spaghetti straps. Lizzie had gone shopping with me and helped me pick out the ugliest dress we could find for my forced date with Dr. Bayles. It was black with huge red and orange flowers—hands-down hideous—but I'd have preferred something with sleeves.

"I'm nervous," I said.

Lizzie handed me the keys. "It'll be okay, sweetie. Just eat your dinner, then come home."

"But he thinks I live next door to him now."

"Then say you're going to go visit Antônia afterwards."

"Okay." That was a good idea.

Lizzie pursed her lips, but a smile broke through. "You're not going to give up on my brother, right? He can be a complete idiot sometimes, but I just think—"

I held up my hands. "This wasn't his fault. It was mine."

"I still think you two are great together."

We could have been. "It's really up to him." And he'd said he wanted to talk.

"Try to have a little fun?" Lizzie said, wincing. "Maybe the food will be yummy?"

Fun? Oh, my date. Right. "Maybe," I said.

Yet as I drove myself to the restaurant, the dread almost choked me. From what I had learned during my time spent with Dixie, it was clear my body didn't want to go on this date. I only hoped this dinner would tide Dr. Bayles over long enough for Eli to return so we could get away.

That seemed an impossible dream.

Racines was a French bistro located on the northern end of the downtown area in a tiny log cabin. It was the only restaurant in Safe Water I'd yet to try, because it served five-course meals at $100 a person. I'd never felt inclined to spend all my weekly credits on one meal, but Dr. Bayles had made it clear that he would be paying. He must somehow receive more credits than the rest of the population.

I felt only apprehension as I parked the van on the street out front. I went inside. It was so dark I had to let my eyes adjust before taking another step.

"Hannah!"

Movement drew my attention. Dr. Bayles sat at a table in the corner, arm raised in my direction. The place was tiny—no bigger than most living rooms. I counted nine tables, draped in white linen tablecloths, all filled with people. I supposed it was charming, but I already felt crowded. I took a deep breath and approached. Dr. Bayles jumped up and greeted me with a peck on the lips that shocked me with its boldness.

"You look amazing," he said, pulling out my chair and helping me remove my jacket, which he draped on the back of my chair.

As I sat, his Old Spice smell gusted over me and my anxiety skyrocketed. Separate the piles, I reminded myself. Dr. Bayles was a completely different, far more civilized, predator than Brandon.

The sarcastic thought made me smile over the tears burning my eyes.

"Wait until you meet Don," Dr. Bayles said. "He's amazing."

"Don?"

"The sommelier. The entire staff here is excellent."

How could he be so calm when coercing a woman on a date? "You come here often?"

"At least once a week. The chef is great, and the wine is excellent."

I didn't mind wine, but for too long I had associated any kind of alcohol with Brandon's rages. It annoyed me how much he came to mind when I spent time with Dr. Bayles. I didn't think of Brandon nearly as much with Eli.

Don arrived with our waitress, Annette, and they recited our choices for the amuse-bouche. The escolar ceviche would be served with a German Riesling wine, the beef tartare with a French red. I didn't like either dish, but I chose the ceviche, as did Dr. Bayles.

"And, Don, bring a bottle of that Napa Valley Shiraz," Dr. Bayles said.

"Of course, sir," said Don, striding away.

Dr. Bayles leaned across the table. "Any good sommelier will tell you not to match spicy food with a Shiraz, Zinfandel, Cabernet . . . The heat of food is amplified by the presence of alcohol, but"—he leaned closer—"for someone like me, who enjoys the burn and heat of spice on my tongue, I love that."

Which at the moment only made me despise him. He could have told me he watched *Sesame Street* growing up, and that would have annoyed me too. Did he honestly think blackmailing me into a date would trick me into liking him? Or did he just not care about my feelings at all? Either way, he was as insanely self-absorbed as Brandon.

At that moment, Don returned. He set down a fresh wine glass and poured the dark Shiraz. "How about you, miss?" he asked me. "What do you prefer?"

"I'm not much of a drinker," I said, then added, "I like the Riesling," just to be polite.

"A fine choice," Don said.

Dr. Bayles drank the Shiraz with his ceviche, and once he'd finished the course, he drank the Riesling too. Turned out he loved wine and talked about it all night. His favorites were heavier, muscular, fuller-bodied wines with strong, peppery aromatics. It was not lost on me that these wines also held the most alcohol.

"What do you like to do for fun?" Dr. Bayles asked me, finally changing the subject.

"Besides go on dates with men who blackmail me?"

He frowned. "That was unkind. I'm only trying to help you, Hannah."

I stifled a sigh of frustration. Fighting with him would not make the evening any easier. "Fine. I read books. Go hiking. Play board games. Do you like Boggle?"

"Never heard of it. I played blackjack in Vegas. That's as close as I've come to a board game since Candyland when I was seven years old."

"Oh, Candyland is fun," I said.

Dr. Bayles laughed. When I said no more, he answered his own question. "I ski," he said. "Can't wait until it snows. They say this is one of the best slopes in the country."

"The former country," I said, darkly.

"I like exercising. I'll text you next time I work out, and you can join me in the gym."

The private gym above the hospital, just a few doors away from my new apartment.

When I didn't react to the invitation, he continued, "I listen to jazz and classical music. Mostly I work. Helping people is my life."

Gag.

Don and Annette stopped by so often it almost felt as if they were on the date too, for which I was grateful. Each course had two options. I enjoyed the scallops and the crab tower—the strawberry grouper was delicious. The best part was the chocolate ganache cake topped with raspberries. The dessert course was the longest time the wait staff left us in peace, so I asked a question that had been bothering me for some time.

"How far is too far before you speak up about the unethical practices of the enforcers?"

Dr. Bayles looked up from his cake. "What unethical practices?"

"Starving detainees of food and water? Demanding EMTs sedate patients? RFID microchipping?"

He grimaced. "That's Mr. Tracy's domain."

"It's your domain too," I said. "The hospital should put its patients first."

"Honestly, I've said plenty. Mr. Tracy doesn't much care for the mantra of 'First do no harm.' He cares about the success of his plan. People who get in the way get removed."

That statement intrigued me. "Has he threatened to remove you?"

Dr. Bayles laughed. "Oh, all the time. But since I'm the most qualified medical professional here, he's stuck with me. That knowledge gives me the courage to stand up to him when it really matters."

The question was, what really mattered to Dr. Bayles? Certainly not respecting women. Certainly not Eli.

"Have you ever thought about going someplace else?" I asked, gesturing toward the door. "Living out there."

"Outside Safe Water?" His tone was incredulous. "Whatever for? There's nothing out there. Believe me. I know."

"There are people out there, though," I said. "They need medical services too."

"Undoubtedly so," Dr. Bayles said. "They should move here, where the doctors are."

321

If Eli and the others left without me, who would help them when someone got sick or wounded? Zach, I supposed, and he wouldn't do poorly.

"You're thinking about him, aren't you?" Dr. Bayles asked.

"Who?"

"Who, indeed? You're here with me now, Hannah. That's what matters." He reached across the table and brushed his thumb across the tops of my knuckles. "You're better off without him."

I completely disagreed but kept that thought to myself as I withdrew my hand to take a sip of water.

"You still haven't seen my place," Dr. Bayles said. "How about we head over there now? Have a little more wine? Talk?"

*So* not happening. "You're very kind, but I actually have plans."

His expression darkened. "With who?"

"Some of my girlfriends who live in the Snowcrest." He looked so angry, I added a little something extra to my lie in hopes of appeasing him. "They wanted to hear about our date."

"Just dinner is not much of a date. Don't you want to have a little more to tell them?" He leered at me—the man actually leered.

"You should know something about me, Dr. Bayles," I said. "I'm kind of an old-fashioned girl. If you want this to work, you're going to have to be patient."

"Jason, Hannah. Call me Jason."

I shrugged, grimacing like I had no control over what I called him. "Like I said. Patience, please?"

Don returned. "How is everything?"

Dr. Bayles growled softly and stood. "Everything was excellent, as always. I'd like to sign the bill now."

"Of course."

Dr. Bayles followed Don to a table beside the door. I stood and put on my jacket, nervous about how we would finally part ways. I thought about running outside, jumping in the van, and driving off while he was still paying. I was still smirking over the thought when he opened the door for me, and I stepped outside.

"What's got you smiling?" he asked.

"Nothing," I said. "Thank you for a lovely dinner."

"I don't want the night to end, Hannah."

"Then we'll have to do this again sometime," I said, fighting to sound like I meant it.

"You could stop by my place after visiting your friends." He stepped close and slid his hands around my waist, grinning. "I'll wait up."

I stepped back out of his reach. "That wouldn't be appropriate." I turned, unlocked the door to the van, and opened it.

A step behind me triggered the memory of Brandon's hands on my throat. It felt so real I started to tremble. I reminded myself Brandon was not here. That was then. I was safe. Sort of.

"May I at least give you a goodnight kiss?" Dr. Bayles asked. "I can be patient, Hannah, but I want to be able to assure Mr. Tracy that this is going somewhere."

The jab sent fire through my veins. I didn't want to kiss Dr. Bayles, but I also didn't want to anger him. Feeling like I had no choice, I faced him.

Dr. Bayles leaned forward. At the last second, I panicked and turned my head. His kiss landed on the corner of my mouth.

He chuckled, pulled me against him, and pressed his open mouth against mine. Trapped between him and the van, fear engulfed me, made me hot all over and my heart rate rise. I turned to stone, clamped my lips tightly, and held my breath so as not to smell the alcohol and Old Spice clouding him. He seemed to get the hint because he ended his kiss and stepped away, watching me with a funny little smirk that told me he'd understood perfectly that he'd been shot down.

"See you tomorrow," I said, fumbling for the door handle, my hands trembling.

"Thank you for tonight, Hannah. Let's do it again very soon."

"Okay." I climbed into the driver's seat and shut the door before he had a chance to say or do anything else. He was still there, staring intently at me and holding up his hand in a motionless wave. I faked a grin and waved, started the van. He didn't move, so I checked the mirrors and pulled out into the road.

My heart was still hammering.

On the off chance he might follow me, I drove over to the Snowcrest. Only when I had shifted into park in the lot did my emotions take over. I started to cry, and before I knew it, I was sobbing. All along my body had been telling me no. I hadn't wanted to go out with Dr. Bayles or kiss him. I'd made myself do it, and now my body was responding to my poor decision.

"I'm sorry," I told myself. "I'll never do that again."

# 32

## ELI

My cell in Rehab was in a new part of the Town Hall building—a long hall with cells on both sides. Everything had been freshly whitewashed and smelled of latex paint. No propaganda posters in this wing. Impressive how quickly they'd built this. Were there really that many criminals in Safe Water? Or were they all *violators* like me?

After the guard left, the first thing I did was try and find the microchip. My hands were so cut up from the fight, I barely knew where to look. Eventually, I zeroed in on the old bug bite between my right thumb and first finger. A little massaging, and I could feel a tiny stick inside the flabby skin.

How had they done this? Drugged me the last time I was here? That seemed like a much greater violation than anything I'd ever done. I fumed about Tracy and this messed up town, then moved on to Hannah and Dr. Necktie for a while. But something had been off there. Her red eyes. And she'd slipped me the message. She cared enough to warn me. What did that mean?

•     •     •

The days crawled by. My daily meal was a bowl of broth and a hard dinner roll. That was it. My body was going to eat what little muscle I'd gained working at the Department of Water and Sanitation, so I tried to exercise, but my sore ribs wouldn't put up with much. I desperately anticipated my tiny meal and even looked forward to porta-potty detail and my sessions with Connie Lawler, obnoxious as they were. It was something to do.

When I slept, I dreamed about food and eating and shopping for food. I slept so much that by night I lay awake, mind racing with thoughts of food and Hannah and Dr. Necktie, and missing my mom. I also prayed for God's mercy and help and sometimes flat-out yelled at him. It all brought some pretty rough breathing on my sore ribs.

One night I was lying on my cot, remembering how I'd challenged Hannah's use of the word *zax* in a game of Boggle, when a guard led someone past my cell.

"What did the kid do? He looks too young to be here."

I sat up. That had been Reinhold's voice. I waited for the enforcer to leave, which seemed to take forever. When the exit door finally clicked shut, I walked to the bars, gripped them, and peered down the corridor.

"Andy Reinhold?" I meant to keep my voice soft, but I was surprised when the sound that came out was more like a whisper. I was so thirsty my throat hurt.

"I thought that was you, kid. What you doing in here?"

"Me?" I pressed against the bars, trying to see out—to see him. I couldn't. We were on the same side of the hall. "What about you?"

"They didn't like my gun," Reinhold said.

I grinned. "Didn't like mine either, though they didn't get it

326

yet."

"That a kid. Any word from Kimama?"

"No." I wished I could have told him differently.

"How many times you been in here, McShane?"

"Third visit," I said. "Tracy said next time he'd keep me six months."

A snort. "He will, so keep your skinny butt out of here."

"It's not that easy," I said, though this last time could have been avoided. I should have listened to Hannah and taken the stupid test.

"Want to know what I do all day?" Reinhold asked. "I work like a dog. They've got about thirty of us doing penal labor."

A chill ran over me. Of course they did. "What kind of work?" I asked.

"Prepping fields, mostly. Lots of fields. Some construction. We're putting up two massive barns. Apparently someone is expecting a lot of livestock."

"From where?"

"No clue."

"No Connie?"

"Oh, yes. We listen to the shrink at every meal."

"They feed you meals? I'm surprised."

"Even Tracy knows a man can't work hard if he's starving."

I guess that didn't apply to porta-potty duty. "You in for six months?" I asked.

"A year. I'm lucky I didn't kill anyone. Tracy would have had me for life."

My mind raced, wondering how I could possibly break him out of here. "He's got people in here for life?"

"Three of us," someone else said.

"That's Nick," Reinhold said. "Him and some buddies shot up the town a while back. They're a little deranged."

"We were trying to free people," Nick snapped.

"By shooting them?" Reinhold said.

I thought back to the name of the group Harvey had accused me of being a part of when he'd found Logan's guns. "Somerset Shadow?" I asked.

"Yeah, that's right," Nick said. "Who wants to know?"

"Eli McShane," I said. "Why'd you guys come in here shooting and kidnapping people?"

"We wanted to free people. We were shooting enforcers."

"No you weren't," I said. "I was downtown when your brigade rolled in. One of you shot my friend."

"Who got shot?" Reinhold asked.

"Zach. He's okay."

"We were trying to help people get out. Took them to our village over in Somerset. We didn't mean to kill anyone."

"Too many of their guys were high," Reinhold said.

"It's true," Nick said, sadly. "Hard to get everyone on the same page. Mostly we just wanted to scare the enforcers. They're getting stronger. Soon, no one will be able to stop them."

I didn't doubt that was true. "Still sounds like kidnapping," I said. "At the very least, it's a jerk way to recruit people to live in your town." Though I wished they'd taken me.

"Never underestimate the capacity of young people to do stupid things for what they perceive to be perfectly good reasons," Reinhold said. "Nick and his gang are young and they're angry. But they need to learn that real heroes use their brains before they use their weapons."

"Bite it, old man," Nick said.

"Listen, McShane," Reinhold said. "When you leave, promise you won't try and bust me out of here."

Was he kidding me? "You want to stay?"

"Swear it to me, boy. Especially if you find Kimama. She'll want to come for me, but you have to tell her I said no."

"Why?"

"I don't want any of y'all stuck in here. Besides Nick and his pals, they lock up innocent people in this place every day."

Nick not-so-politely told Reinhold where to shove his opinions.

"Don't you worry about me," Reinhold said. "Once I break out of here, I'll come find you. Promise me, Eli. That you won't come after me."

Though I didn't want to, I said, "I promise."

• • •

At 3:30 in the afternoon the following Monday, I was released. A guard led me to the lobby and told me to use the computer sitting on the counter to contact a ride. I sent everyone I knew a message on the Grid, and still it was another two hours before Dad stopped the Odyssey out front to pick me up.

"You bring anything to eat or drink?" I asked. "I'm so thirsty."

"This is all I brought." Dad tossed me a package of crackers. "Slowly or you'll get sick."

"Probably get sick, anyway," I said, tearing into them.

I told him about Reinhold and the work camps and Nick and the Somerset Shadow. I told him about the tracker in my hand and Tracy's warning that next time I'd be in for six months.

"We've got to get out of here," Dad said, "but we've got to get it right."

"Or I'll be plowing fields with Reinhold," I said.

We rode in silence for a while, and I nibbled a cracker. It was nice, being with my dad.

"What happened with you and Hannah?" he asked.

Well it *was* nice. Just thinking about Hannah made me ache. "I guess we broke up. Why? She say something?"

Dad eyed me. "You're still mad about what she said to me over a month ago?"

The question made me all squirmy inside. "I don't know."

"You don't know. Well, here's what I know. I know she took her own apartment above the hospital. I also know she went out on a date with some doctor. Borrowed the van from Lizzie."

I slumped low in the seat. "Our van? You let her take our van to go on a date with another guy?"

"I don't *let* Hannah do anything. She's a grown woman. And she asked Lizzie—not me—about borrowing the van. Instead of getting mad at me for nothing, how about you tell me what happened with you two?"

"I told her I didn't like being the consolation prize."

"Ah, son." Dad clenched his jaw. "Don't you get it? *I* was the consolation prize. She liked you from the beginning. Ask Logan. He told me all about how Hannah picked him up from work one day and confessed how much she liked you, but you were obsessed with Jaylee."

I perked up. "She liked me before Jaylee?"

"Apparently. Look, Eli, you can't afford to be petty in this new world. There is no room for getting offended over every little thing."

"It wasn't a little thing!"

Dad held up a hand. "Let me finish. The problem is, there aren't plenty of fish in the sea anymore. Do you know what I'm saying? What happened upset you. Fine. But this is about your ego, and you can't afford to let your ego win this one. Humility is going to have to become a bigger part of your life if you want to be happy. Don't screw this up."

Dad's words hit hard. "You think I can fix this? Win her back?"

"Not if you do nothing but mope."

"Okay. What should I do?"

"I've always found, 'I'm sorry. I was wrong,' to be very effective."

"What about a present? Flowers or something?"

Dad shook his head. "Guilty men use gifts to distract from what they did wrong. Just say your piece. The truth hurt your feelings, and you responded badly. You're sorry."

"I *am* sorry."

"So, tell her."

But when we got home—and after everyone mobbed me with hugs—Logan told me the truth about Hannah's new apartment and her "date" with Dr. Necktie.

"He coerced her into going out with him? Because of me?" I spun on my dad, who was sneaking out onto the deck. "Why didn't you tell me?"

"You needed a little scare. And what I said *was* technically true."

"*Dad!*"

"Calm down," Lizzie said. "Hannah gets off at eight. I said I'd pick her up, but you go instead—after you shower and brush your teeth, of course, because you stink."

"Thank you?" I said. "But no. I'll talk to her when you bring her back. I don't want to risk Dr. Necktie seeing us together. Not if it might get her in trouble."

"I second that plan," Zach said, thumping my back. "Enough Rehab, already."

"Fine," Lizzie said, "but clean up while you wait. Please."

"In a bit," I said, sinking onto the recliner in the living room. Cree crawled up onto my lap. "You were gone a long time."

"A reaallly long time," Shyla added.

"I got a needle," Cree said, showing me the remains of a Band-Aid outline on the inside of his forearm.

"We all did," Shyla said. "Mine didn't hurt, but Davis cried."

"I did not!!" Davis said.

"Sounds like you were all very brave," I said, feeling foolish that I hadn't just gone with them.

"Was it scary in jail?" Davis asked. "Did you try to escape through the toilet?"

"No," I said, smirking. "Only cartoons can do that. And it wasn't really scary. It was mostly boring."

I told everyone about Reinhold and the tracker in my hand, then Logan told me about Kimama's call on the walkie talkie.

"I can't believe she's up on that mountain," I said. "That girl is amazing."

"She's got great radio etiquette too," Logan said.

"Oh-kay," I said, slightly confused by Logan's compliment. "I just wished she'd called a couple days earlier so I could have told Reinhold she was okay."

Dad rolled out the city map on the coffee table. "It's bad timing," he said. "Would have been nice to let Andy know."

"Maybe we can get him a message?" Lizzie said.

"I don't see how," I said. "I wonder if there is any way to get him out of there."

"We're going to respect his wishes on that," Dad said. "If I was in his place, I'd have wanted you to leave me behind too."

331

A very unpleasant thought. "All right," I said. "It's not going to be easy out there. We're going to be roughing it for a really long time. Maybe forever."

"What about water?" Davis asked.

"We're going to use the same water we're using here," I said. "Only we're going to get to it higher up the mountain."

"Kimama confirmed what Reinhold told Zach," Logan said. "But rather than setting up camp where you want to, she's up on the mountain."

"They'll be able to see us a lot easier up there," I said.

"And we'll be able to see them," Dad said.

"We'd have to have someone on watch 24/7," I said.

"We'll probably need that anyway," Dad said. "Neither location is far enough that they won't see smoke from our campfires. Logan, make a copy of that meeting. I'll leave it with Becky as insurance."

"Who's Becky?" Lizzie asked.

"The woman who has my truck," Dad said. "She owes us."

"What good would that do?" Logan asked.

"Don't know," Dad said. "But it wouldn't hurt to have it in our back pocket, just in case."

"Maybe we should go back to Reinhold's place," Zach said, his eye twitching. "Hole up there for the winter, then come back in the spring when Tracy will have forgotten us."

"I'm for that," I said. "I'd honestly like to get out of his range for a while."

"But we'll need the water eventually," Dad said. "Bottled water could last us years, but at some point we'll have to start harvesting. Better to stake out a place up that mountain or down by the river before someone else does."

"The Somerset Shadow," I said. "Wherever we end up, it needs to be off road. I don't want to make it easy for anyone to reach us."

"We still need an exit plan," Zach said.

"Yeah, how we going to get out of here?" Logan asked.

"It's got to be with the garbage truck," I said. "I just can't figure out how to steal one during the day without everyone knowing. They're always in use."

"I've been considering that," Dad said. "What happens if one breaks down?"

I thought about it. "I don't know. It's never happened."

"How about this?" Dad said. "Just before you leave for the day, pop the distributor cap from one of the trucks. In the morning, when it won't start, they'll call me in to take a look. I'll make up some complicated problem."

"We'd have to rework the routes to cover for the missing truck," I said.

"Leaving it for me to fix," Dad said. "Then I'll steal it."

I was excited now. "The guards at the gate won't have a clue that a truck is down that day. Why would they?" It could work.

"We're going to be in the back of a garbage truck?" Lizzie asked, her nose wrinkled.

"Yep!" I said. "It's going to be awesome."

"Who's going to drive?" Zach asked.

"Dad," I said at the same time as my dad said, "Eli."

"You know the trucks," Dad said. "And you're employed by the Department of Water Sanitation. It should be you."

I nodded, nervous about the idea, but also kind of fired up. "I'll need to remove the chip in my hand," I said.

"I can try," Zach said.

"Hannah will do it," Lizzie said.

"You can't know that," I said.

"Stop being so negative," Lizzie said. "You guys are going to be fine."

My sister's optimism was great, but it wasn't contagious. "We'll see," I said.

"What will you tell the guard at the gate?" Logan asked.

"They won't ask anything," I said. "Bong said they just wave the trucks by. We just have to pick the right time."

"We need everyone's work schedules," Dad said. "Then we'll see what day and time makes the most sense."

After that, Dad led us in prayer. He asked God to guide us and give us wisdom. Then everyone split up to gather supplies.

Lizzie warmed me some soup. "Hannah brought it home.

Said you should have liquids the first couple days after a fast."

Hannah got me soup. My eyes stung, which completely shocked me. I was just tired, which made sense after my week in Rehab. The hot soup, and the warmth of Cree snuggled beside me, was making me drowsy. I finished the soup, then went up to my room and took a nap. By the time I returned downstairs, looking for more food, the whole day had gone by. Lizzie, Logan, Davis, and Shyla were packing in the kitchen.

"Ice cream," Lizzie said. "And chocolate. Oh, chocolate chips!"

"I'm going to miss video games," Logan said.

"Swimming," Zach said. "I miss it every day."

"What are we talking about?" I asked.

"The things we'll miss when we leave this place," Logan said. "I'm going to miss pizza."

Everyone groaned their agreement.

"We can still have some of that," I said. "It depends what we find and what we learn how to make. I'm willing to bet there are still some back-up generators running out there. We might find some frozen stuff. And we can play video games. We just need to siphon gas for the generators we picked up at Ace. Then we'll have electricity."

"How long will it take to scavenge the games I want, though?" Logan asked. "I should have brought my games from home. I didn't even think to pack my PlayStation."

"We have all these games," Davis said, tottering toward us with a stack of board games that was listing sharply to one side. Zach tried to catch them, but they slid off Davis's arms and crashed in a heap on the floor. Thankfully, they didn't open up and spill, though I bet they were all a mess inside.

"What about you, Eli?" Lizzie asked, dropping to her knees to help clean up the games. "What will you miss?"

"Hannah," I said, picking up the Boggle game box and staring at it. "I'm going to miss Hannah."

Lizzie shook her head at me. "It's going to work out," she said. "Trust me."

But I wasn't so sure.

# 33

**HANNAH**
**SEPTEMBER 28**

When my shift ended, and I saw Lizzie behind the wheel of the van, I was so disappointed my chest ached. What if they kept Eli in Rehab indefinitely? My eyes stung at the idea of never seeing him again. Today was Monday, which marked a full week of him being in Rehab. Surely they wouldn't keep him longer than that.

Lizzie seemed extra hyper, prattling on about how adorable her kindergarten students were. I tuned her out, staring at the dark trees as we sped along the familiar path to Eli's house. I had barely climbed out and closed the van door when the sweetest sound met my ears.

"Hannah!"

Eli descended the steps toward me, thin and pale. Hair wet,

he must have showered recently. Wrinkles circled unsmiling eyes. He looked fierce.

I did *not* want to fight with this boy anymore.

"You're back," I said, stamping down the hope inside me just in case I was about to be disappointed.

He reached me, took my hands in his like he was trying to warm them, and said, "I'm sorry." His voice sounded different, husky. He swallowed, which made his Adam's apple shift. "What happened hurt my feelings, but I shouldn't have made it about me. I should have listened and believed the best about you and my dad. I wish I'd never said those mean things. I want to fix us more than anything. Please say it's not too late."

The emotions tumbling through me at that moment left me reeling.

"Dad and Lizzie and Zach and Cree and everyone . . . we're leaving," Eli said. "I understand you might not want to come with us, and if you want to stay . . . Hannah, I'll stay with you. I want to be where you are."

Was he serious? "You would be so unhappy here."

He fake-frowned, shook his head. "I don't mind the garbage job. Not really. I hate the MPs. I hate Tracy. I hate Koval. I hate Loca. Liberté, I can take or leave her. She's snobby, but I like that she's willing to do the right thing. Sometimes." He pressed my hands to his chest. "But I'll learn to be an obedient Safe Water citizen, for you."

He was so full of it. He would never be a good Safe Water citizen.

He lifted his eyebrows, like he knew I wasn't buying it, and he had to convince me. "I'm not as smart or suave as Dr. Necktie, and I don't know how to put in an IV or take out an appendix. But I can do other things. Keep house and cook you eggs. Lose at Boggle."

"What about your dad?" I asked. "Your sister? Your friends? Won't you miss them?"

"Sure I would," he said. "But they have each other. And I just feel like . . . What if Hannah Cheng is the girl for me? What if I leave, and I miss out of discovering if it was true? I can't pretend that doesn't matter." He swallowed again. "I could get some neckties."

I grimaced. "It wouldn't feel right, Eli, you wearing neckties. Besides, I don't like them."

His frown faded into a hopeful smile. "What do you like, then?" he asked, his voice still hoarse. He was clearly dehydrated. I needed to get some fluids into him.

But first, I was going to answer his question. I grabbed the front of his T-shirt and pulled him toward me. I didn't want to leave any doubt in his mind about my feelings.

"I like Boggle." I rose up on my tiptoes and lifted my face toward his.

As always, Eli met me halfway.

• • •

Once we had made up, we went inside the house. I hooked up Eli to the fluids I'd swiped from the hospital, knowing he'd be dehydrated and malnourished after so many days in Rehab.

We talked long into the night about so many things. I told him about Mr. Tracy's investigation and how Dr. Bayles had used it to blackmail me. He said Lizzie had already told him about it, but he insisted on hearing every detail from me.

I confessed that I'd let Dr. Bayles kiss me goodnight. I told him how awful it was, and how I'd asked Susan to schedule us at opposite times at the hospital as much as she could.

"It's actually helped," I said. "I haven't seen him very much at all the past few days."

"Good," Eli said, his gaze distant and steely. "That guy deserves six months in Rehab after what he did to you."

"He's such a jerk," I said.

"So, you missed me, then?" he asked.

"I waited for you every day at the end of my shift, hoping I'd see you behind the wheel. I was worried they'd keep you locked up forever. Or that you'd come back with hypophosphatemia, so I stocked the fridge with soup and IV fluids."

Eli's brows wrinkled. "Hypo-what?" he asked.

"It's an electrolyte disorder that can happen when refeeding a malnourished person."

"You're amazing," he said, his gaze flitting over my face.

"I'm going to leave with you," I told him.

His eyes returned to mine, filled with hope and wonder. "But you love working at the hospital," he said.

"I did, and I learned a lot. But I can't work for Dr. Bayles anymore. Besides, I've always been drawn to areas of need. I figure a burgeoning little settlement like yours will need a good doctor much more than Safe Water."

Then we were kissing again.

•   •   •

Work the next day was a distraction, and the first time I found myself counting the hours until my shift ended. Now that Eli and I had made peace, I wanted to be with him all the time. I couldn't stop thinking about him throughout the day. I swiped the supplies I needed to perform a little surgery on his hand to remove the microchip, then watched the clock tick ever-so-slowly.

When I got home, I rubbed some EMLA cream on the top of Eli's hand between his thumb and forefinger. "We'll check after dinner to see how it feels," I said.

"How long does it take?" he asked.

"You'll feel it going numb in ten or fifteen minutes," I said, "but it will be at least an hour before it will provide any pain relief. Even better if we wait a couple hours."

Cristobal and Antônia came over, and we all sat in the living room, discussing everyone's schedules. Between the eight of us who worked full time, we couldn't find one day that we were all off to stage our escape.

"We have to go on one of Hannah's days off," Eli said. "She'll be missed at work more than the rest of us."

"And you, Eli," Cristobal said. "If you don't show at work, enforcers will be notified. Standard procedure for those with a record of two or more arrests."

Eli grimaced. "Good to know," he said.

"Speaking of record," Zach said to me. "You're going to remove that microchip, right?"

"Tonight," I said.

"Good," Zach said. "I really didn't want to have to do it."

"Don't destroy it," Cristobal said. "That would alert them that you know about it."

We checked work schedules again, and this time Lizzie drew up a weekly calendar so we could have a visual. It took some careful planning, but we finally determined that next Saturday, October 3, would be our best chance to escape. Only Zach and Logan would have to call out sick. Eli would still be scheduled to work, which was why we were going to leave before his shift started at five that morning.

While this wasn't ideal, Eli said there were only certain days of the week and times each day that garbage trucks passed through the gates. Sundays and Mondays were out since the Department of Water and Sanitation was closed. Early mornings were better than the afternoon since only two enforcers would be on duty before 6:00 a.m. Plus, Eli would be missed at work in the afternoons. That's why we ultimately decided to sneak out before his shift started.

It was our best chance.

"I can't believe it's almost October," Zach said.

"How long have we been here?" Lizzie asked.

"Since August 1," I said.

"Two months? That's it?" Logan said. "It seems longer."

It really did.

"We should tell the others we're leaving," Eli said. "Josh and Riggs and Jaylee and Krista."

I stared at him, completely shocked.

"*Eli!*" Lizzie said.

"Are you kidding me?" Logan said.

"After Krista turned you in, and you fought with Riggs?" I said.

"That was so cold," Zach said. "You can't trust either of them."

"I'm afraid I agree, son," Seth said. "They might report us."

"Krista won't want to leave, anyway," Lizzie added.

"None of them will," Logan added.

"I know. I know," Eli said. "It just feels wrong not to tell them. How about I say we're thinking of leaving and see how it goes? If any of them act interested, I'll bring it back here for a vote. But if they don't care, well, then we'll know, and then I won't have to live the rest of my life wondering if we left them behind."

No one objected to that, but Zach insisted on talking to Riggs and Josh.

"We don't need another game of Death Match right now," he said. "Let me handle those two."

"Fine," Eli said. "I'll talk to the girls after I get off work tomorrow."

"Let's do your hand," I said before Eli could make any more trouble for himself.

He and I relocated to the kitchen table where I spread out an exam drape sheet. I used an alcohol swab to wash my hands, then pulled on a pair of gloves and prepared to remove the microchip.

"How many stitches am I going to need?" he asked as I opened a fresh scalpel blade and attached it to the handle.

"Hopefully none," I said.

An audience gathered around the table, and I had to shoo them back since they were blocking my light. I took Eli's hand in my left hand and held it so that the skin between his thumb and forefinger was taut.

"Ready?" I asked.

Eli winced adorably. "Yes?"

I made the incision. His hand tensed in my grip, then quickly relaxed again.

"It doesn't hurt," he said.

"That's the idea," I said.

The cut was about a half centimeter long. Blood escaped in a growing bead atop the incision. I set down my scalpel, took his hand in both of mine, and used my fingers to feel out the microchip and pinch it toward the cut. "It's like a very thick sliver," I said, just as one end of the foreign object appeared at the mouth of the cut. Blood smeared a little as I pinched the microchip out the opening.

Our little audience released a collective breath, then gave a variety of reactions, some grossed out, some impressed. I wiped the chip on the exam drape and pressed a cotton swab over the cut. "Hold that."

Eli obeyed. I opened my surgical glue applicator, prepped it, then cleaned the wound and applied the liquid adhesive over the cut. I waited a minute, checked that the adhesive was dry, then said, "All done."

"Whoa!" This from Logan.

I removed my gloves and cleaned the table. I carried the trash over to the can under the kitchen sink.

"You're a rock star, Hannah," Zach told me. "That was awesome."

"I really thought it would need stitches," Eli said.

"You would have if I'd done it," Zach said.

"Lizzie," Eli said. "Think you could sew this thing into my work gloves? That way if anyone is watching me, it will look like I'm doing what I'm supposed to be doing. Until we leave and the gloves stay here."

Lizzie walked up to the kitchen table and inspected the microchip. "I think so. I'll just cut a little hole and stuff it inside the lining. Pretty much the opposite of what Hannah just did."

"That should work." I came back and sat beside Eli, took his left hand in mine. "How are your fingers?" I asked, massaging his hand.

"Ah!" He tensed. "Fingers are fine. Hand is still a little tender."

I shifted my ministrations to the outside of his hand and his fingers. "I'm sorry," I said.

"You apologized a long time ago," Eli said. "No worries."

"I wish I could promise I'll never hurt you again, but I'm starting to realize that's not possible." I brought his hand to my face and kissed the scar I'd put on the back of his hand.

The tiniest smile appeared on his lips. "Mom used to say 10 percent of conflict is difference of opinion, and 90 percent is the wrong tone of voice."

"That she did," Seth called from the living room. "She also said, 'Don't make conflict a win-lose battle, because it's an opportunity to love people better.' One of my favorites."

"She sounds like a wise woman," I said.

Eli grinned, his eyes glistening. "She was."

# 34

**ELI**
**SEPTEMBER 30**

After work on Wednesday, I drove over to the Snowcrest Condominiums. No one answered at Unit 34. Considering it was nearly dinnertime, I shouldn't have been surprised. I walked over to the restaurant and grabbed myself a meatball sandwich and a milkshake to go, then sat in the Odyssey, savoring the food, though I was full after four bites.

What was my milkshake made of, anyway? The brown lab and those cows up by the compound had survived the pandemic. One cow, or even a goat, and we could have milk. But were there any others out there? Grains would be much harder to produce. Scavenged flour and sugar would last a while if we could keep it in airtight containers, but once we ran out, we'd need to learn to grow our own or do without.

Do without sugar. Zach might die.

I was so caught up in my reverie, I almost didn't notice Krista enter the apartment with a takeout box. I pondered my next move and decided to talk to her first. She'd know where Jaylee was.

I'd barely reached their door when it opened, and Krista stepped out.

"Gosh!" She clapped her hand over her heart and scowled at me. "You scared me to death, Eli! Knock next time."

"I was about to."

She checked me over, smirking. "Your face healed fast."

"No thanks to you."

"You got what you deserved. For the guns too. I knew you wouldn't have donated them."

"*You* told the enforcers we had guns?" Good thing I hadn't mentioned we wanted to leave. She probably partied with Harvey.

"Duh. What do you want, anyway?"

"To talk to Jaylee."

"Jaylee is resting."

"She's here?"

"That's what I said."

Then why hadn't she answered the door? Had she looked through the peephole, saw it was me, and ignored me? Or had she been sleeping? "It will only take a minute," I said.

"Whatever. Just be nice, okay. She doesn't need your lectures." She walked past me, exiting the apartment. I caught the door and turned around, but she was already halfway across the parking lot.

I found Jaylee on the couch, tucked under a pile of blankets. Her hair was tangled and frizzy, her eyes puffy and red. Krista's takeout box sat on the coffee table, unopened.

"Hey," I said, wondering if she'd had a fight with Riggs.

"She told you, didn't she? She's such a blabbermouth."

"Told me what?"

She looked me over, like she was trying to decide if I knew whatever it was she was worried about. "Nothing. Why are you here?"

"Well . . ." How could I say this in the vaguest of ways? "We were talking about how great it might be to leave Safe Water. Go someplace else."

Jaylee folded her arms, like the topic was making her uncomfortable. "You can't leave. It's not allowed."

"Oh, we know that. We're just thinking about it," I said. "Look, I know it seems good here now, but the people in charge, they don't have our best interests at heart. They're in it for themselves. And it's going to get worse. If we can figure out a way . . . want to come with us?"

She fidgeted with the edge of her blanket. "It's not that I don't want to come, Eli. I mean, I wouldn't have before. But now I would. But since it doesn't really matter, I'm staying here."

"Huh?"

"I'm infected, Eli. With the second strain."

I lost my breath for a moment and sank onto the end of the couch. "How?"

"Riggs thinks he caught it from one of Liberté's dancers."

And Jaylee caught it from Riggs. Wow. I guess she'd finally got her man. "Oh, Jaylee." I didn't know what else to say. I just sat there, arms pimpling with a chill that wouldn't leave.

She burst into tears.

"Hey." I swallowed my own sadness and scooted closer. "Hey, I'm sorry."

She threw herself against me, hugging me tightly. I just held her while she cried. It was desperately sad.

"Is there anything you can do?" I asked.

She shrugged. "The doctor says there's a good chance at stopping it, or at least slowing it down, since I didn't have any health problems before. He put me on some medicine to help. Said it was good I found out early, so I could start treatments right away. He thinks I might beat it. Or at least last longer than some."

Longer than Barkley Kipp and the others who'd died from the second strain. I fought back the emotions that threatened to take over. Jaylee's eyes met mine, and she started bawling again.

I stayed with her for an hour or so. I cried with her, prayed

345

with her. The weird thing was, she let me.

"You probably think I wasn't listening all those years in youth group," she said, "that I just came for Josh and Riggs." She gave me a sheepish smile. "Okay, I did come for them. But I listened too. I know I made some bad choices, but I asked God to forgive me. And you know what? Me and God, we're like this now." She held up two fingers, twisted. "So, that's one positive about my situation. I'm going to meet Jesus before any of you perfect people get a chance to."

I snorted. "We're not perfect, Jay. We're all just doing the best we can."

"I'm glad you're getting out of this place," she said. "Something's not right here. The moment I found out I was infected, people stopped talking to me. I don't have any friends anymore. What does that mean?"

"They're just afraid," I said. "And maybe they weren't very good friends to begin with."

"Krista is. She takes care of me."

"I'm glad. Please don't tell her we're trying to leave."

"I won't. I promise. She's kind of a nark."

"Tell me about it." I couldn't believe that girl had turned us in for our guns. "Are you sure you don't want to come with us?"

She shook her head. "Krista needs me more than I need her. I'm hoping my situation will make her think a little more carefully than I did. I don't want her to end up like me."

"I'm glad she has you," I said.

"Me too." She smiled, and I swear, I had never seen her more beautiful. It was a different kind of pretty, though. Vulnerable. Honest. At peace. "You'll keep praying for Krista and me? Tell Lizzie to pray too."

"Like I could stop Lizzie from praying," I said. "You pray for us too. If we get caught, Tracy is going to put me in Rehab for six months."

She squeezed my hand. "I'll pray, Eli. This time I mean it."

●　　　●　　　●

As I finished my shift Thursday and checked the oil on the garbage trucks, I removed the distributor cap from one of the vehicles, took it home, and gave it to my dad. Sure enough, when I went in Friday morning, Nigil had reworked all the routes so we could cover for the truck that was out of commission. I worked a hard day with two hours overtime. When I got home, Dad told me he'd been called out to look at the truck.

"I told the guy the truck should probably be taken out of circulation for a couple days next week, unless he'd approve me working overtime this weekend."

"What did he say?" I asked.

"Said he didn't have any extra trucks and gave me the code for the garage door so I could let myself in this weekend and do the repair."

"Excellent," I said.

We were set.

Friday night we packed everything we wanted to take with us in the vans. We'd move the stuff into the back of the garbage truck once I brought it to the shop. We'd have to leave the vans behind, which was unfortunate. The Odyssey was the last tangible thing I had of my mom, though I knew Lizzie still had Mom's Bible and some photo albums.

Zach had been as unsuccessful at inviting Josh and Riggs to join us as I'd been with Krista and Jaylee. It was unsurprising, really, but I felt better knowing we'd given them the option.

Logan had made two copies of the audio file from the meeting in Tracy's office, one for us and one that Dad drove over and gave to Deborah and Rebecca. I still thought that was crazy, but I had other things to worry about. I went out back and retrieved the rifles I'd hidden in the trees, thinking over what we'd do first once we got out of here. While I liked the idea of building a camp nearby with access to the clean water, it made better sense to winter at Reinhold's place. Colorado winters were harsh, and with it already being October, I doubted we could build a decent shelter fast enough to prepare for the coming cold.

At 3:00 a.m. Saturday morning, Dad woke me, and we headed out, the kids half asleep in the van. Dad dropped me off at the Department of Water and Sanitation, then headed to the auto shop to meet Zach. I returned the distributor cap, put on my work coveralls, then climbed up into the beast.

I'd always enjoyed driving the garbage trucks. The dual drive cab was a cross between a video game and a spaceship. It had two steering wheels, one on the left side for driving on the highway and one on the right for driving on route. You could stand while driving on the right too, so you could look out back and work the joystick for the automated arm. Pretty fun.

I drove the beast across town, anxious about being seen at this hour. But I saw no one and hoped that meant all the enforcers were asleep at this hour.

Dad had already raised the biggest of the five bay doors at the auto shop when I arrived. He and Zach had parked the vans on the far left, and I was able to roll right in. I parked, activated the hydraulics to raise the rear loader, then climbed out. The shop was filled with the nostalgic smells of my childhood. I'd grown up in an auto shop with my dad, surrounded by dirty motor oil, chassis grease, brake dust, solvent, petroleum, and new tires.

Everyone was standing in a row, holding their belongings and staring at the truck.

"Let's do this!" I clapped my hands, a little hyper from excitement and lack of a good night's sleep.

"That engine is loud," Zach said.

"Good," I said. "It will hopefully muffle any noises you guys make back there."

"I can't believe I'm going to ride in the back of a garbage truck," Hannah said. "It's so unsanitary."

"A little dirt is good for you," I said.

Hannah wrinkled her nose adorably. "A garbage truck has more than a little dirt."

"It's shocking how much it stinks," Cristobal said.

I hardly noticed the smell anymore. "Try not to think about it," I said.

Since we only had the one walkie talkie, Zach gave me his cell phone so I'd be able to communicate with everyone in the back through Hannah's phone. Zach and Logan put down a tarp in the hopper, then we made quick work of moving everyone's belongings inside, which included a box filled with all the board games from the house. I put the .338 Winchester up front, since we had more ammo for it, and Dad put our old rifles in the back.

I called Hannah, then slipped Zach's phone into the front pocket of my coveralls. "If you need anything, talk loud," I said. "I can't hear much in that cab."

"We won't need anything," Dad said. "It's going to be fine."

"I hope so."

Dad gathered us at the end of the garbage truck. We all linked hands, and he prayed that God would set us free and keep us safe.

Hannah kissed me for luck, then everyone climbed inside the hopper.

"It smells gross!" Davis said.

Shyla was already crying. "I don't like it in here."

"Shh," Lizzie said, pulling Shyla onto her lap. "Remember how we talked about being brave? Get your flashlight. Cree? Do you have yours?"

"*Aoo*." Cree held up his flashlight.

"Eli, don't crush us flat, okay?" Antônia said, looking up above her.

"I won't."

Still, it was harder than I thought it would be to close the rear loader with everyone I loved inside. Once it was closed, I checked in with the phone.

"Everything okay in there?"

A chorus of yeses came out of the phone in my pocket.

So, I climbed back into the driver's seat and started the truck. The engine rumbled around me as I backed out of the garage. I saw the open bay doors and briefly wondered if I should get out and shut them. I decided it was too late to worry about that now. We were off.

I headed out of town. Two right-hand turns and I was cruising along Gothic. It was 5:05 a.m. now. We were right on schedule. Hopefully Nigil and Bong would give me a half hour or so before reporting me to the boss as a no-show.

A few turns, and I was slowing to a stop at the gate. I'd never seen it from the road like this. There were two gates about thirty yards apart, each made of nothing but a drop arm. In between was a huge space for making U-turns that was probably used more often than the actual road. I didn't see the enforcer SUV that was usually parked here. I thought about how easily this truck could crash right through both drop arms, but I doubted I could get up to faster than sixty, maybe sixty-five. Even if they had to call the enforcers, they'd still catch up to us in no time.

I put the truck in park. "Keep everyone quiet," I said. "I'm at the gate."

A guard approached my window, tablet in hand. Why was he coming over? Bong said they waved the trucks right through. I held my breath and prayed.

*Please let us through, God. Please.*

The guard motioned for me to roll down my window. I complied.

"Name?" he asked.

I didn't want to give my name. "Nigil Evans," I said.

The guard extended his tablet toward me. "Scan your wristband, please."

Gah! Why hadn't I seen that coming? "Can't," I said. "Accidentally dropped it in the hopper when I was taking off my gloves yesterday. Got to wait until Monday to get it replaced."

The guy looked at me like he was trying to understand Loca and Liberté's French lyrics. "Hold on." He walked back into his little booth.

This was bad. Why hadn't I thought to investigate the procedure at the gate? What did Bong know? Of course they'd check wristbands. It was Admin's way of tracking everyone who didn't yet have a microchip in their hand. Duh.

"We might have a problem," I said, cursing my stupidity. "The guard wanted to scan my wristband—He's coming back."

I watched the man approach, hoping yet terrified the axe was about to fall.

"Please complete a U-turn, then park in that space and wait." He pointed to a pullout on the other side of his booth.

"Someone will be coming to issue you a new wristband."

"I can't do my job for one day without a wristband?" I asked. "My boss isn't going to be happy about the delay."

"Sorry, sir. I need you to complete a U-turn and—"

"Yeah, yeah." I stepped on the gas and cranked the wheel. I was so glad the enforcer SUV wasn't here, but I wasn't about to sit here waiting for them to return, either. My best plan was to get the truck back to the garage so we could scatter. Enforcers would surely come investigate, but I was out of options. I accelerated past the pullout and headed back into town.

"How we doing?" Dad asked.

"We're going back. This isn't going to happen today."

"Copy that," Dad said, and I could hear the groans of those around him.

I kept my eyes glued to the rearview mirrors, but no one was following. When I saw the shop and the open garage door, I thanked God that I hadn't bothered to shut it. I activated the hydraulics to raise the rear loader as I coasted to a stop inside.

I hopped out and was halfway across the shop when the rear loader stopped raising. I hit the button to lower the garage door. As it started coming down, I had second thoughts. Maybe we should have jumped into the vans and driven off in a hurry. But as I turned toward the truck and saw how slowly everyone was moving as they pulled on backpacks and grabbed their gear, I was glad the door would hide us from the street.

Dad handed Cree out to me. I set him on his feet, then reached for Shyla. Lizzie was already passing her my way.

No one spoke as they climbed out of the hopper. The garage door stopped, leaving the only sound the truck's engine ticking as it cooled down. This made me think of the seconds on a clock tick, tick, ticking as some enforcer came back from his coffee break, talked to the guard at the gate, called my boss to ask about Nigil, and heard I wasn't at work today.

This was bad.

"I need to go to work," I said. "Now."

Dad nodded. "Let's get everything back in the vans."

I grabbed my pack out of the hopper and took the guns

from Logan. I carried it all to the Odyssey, opened up the back, and dropped my stuff inside. I was ejecting rounds from Dad's Remington when Hannah slipped up beside me.

"You okay?"

I shook my head. "I blew it. I didn't think they'd ask to scan my wristband. And I gave them Nigil's name. It won't take long for them to trace this to me. Even if I do make it to work before enforcers come asking questions, it's still going to be trouble. I don't have my gloves with the tracker. Left them at the house."

Hannah hugged me, and it wasn't until her arms squeezed that I realized I was shaking. *Help us, God. What do we do?*

"Circle up," Dad said.

I caught Davis eyeing Dad's Remington and shut the back of the van. Hannah took my hand, and we joined the others in the narrow space between the garbage truck and the vans. The lights were out, but there was plenty of morning light coming in the high windows above the five bay doors. Dad was now holding Cree—had set his rifle on the roof of the truck. The boy had snuggled up onto Dad's shoulder, probably still terrified from being shut in the back of a garbage truck.

"How about we say I was driving?" Dad said. "I haven't been to Rehab yet, so they'll go easier on me than you. Plus, I can play up the mechanic angle, say I wanted to test the truck on a long stretch of road and didn't even think that it wasn't allowed."

Despair threatened to overwhelm me. "I don't think they'll buy that," I said.

"It's still better than you getting picked up," Dad said.

"I guess."

Hannah squeezed my hand, so I squeezed back.

"Zach, drive Eli to the house, then to work," Dad said. "Lizzie and the kids can go with. The rest of you, head out the back door. Split up. Shop in a few stores until Zach comes back for you. The Odyssey needs to stay here for me."

"How will we leave Safe Water now?" Cristobal asked.

"We can try this again," Dad said, "depending on what happens with my story. If they believe me, we wait a couple months and steal another garbage truck."

"We could try the fence," Logan said.

"It's electrified," Zach said. "We can't get past it."

"No, I think we could," Dad said. "We've got everything we need in this shop."

"Which is . . . ?" Antônia asked.

"Cable cutters and some electrical gloves," Dad said.

"Cut through the fence?" I asked.

"Might as well try," Dad said. "We'd be on foot, but . . ." He shrugged.

Seemed as good of an idea as any at this point. I was feeling better now that we had a—

"Open it." The voice was not one of ours.

All heads turned toward the main door positioned at the end of all the bay doors. The voice had been muted—outside. Keys jangled, and my knees turned to jelly.

Dad handed Cree to Hannah and whispered, "Back door. Go!"

The group scattered.

"I don't want to split up," I said.

"I have a reason to be here, you don't," Dad said, grabbing the Winchester off the truck. He stashed it inside a row of tires. "I can stall them long enough for you to get over to one of the restaurants. Get going!" Dad grabbed a pair of coveralls from a hook on the wall and pulled them half on, then popped the hood on the garbage truck.

Hannah and I ran to the back. Logan was holding the door, letting in the pleasant scent of fresh bread. The shop lights flickered on—horrible white halogens that blinded me and lit up the bay like a hundred spotlights.

"Come on! Come on!" Logan said, waving us out.

An alley ran between the backside of the shop and a bakery. Lizzie, Zach, and the kids had followed Cristobal and Antônia to the left, toward the auto shop's parking lot. I glanced right, which led to the main road. I didn't like the look of either direction. If enforcers were out front, they'd likely surround the place. I panned back, trying to decide what was best.

"Eli?" Hannah said. "What's wrong?"

My gaze caught on a door in back of the bakery, propped open with a rock. I grabbed Hannah's arm and pointed. "There. Take Cree inside and go out the front. Don't run. Act natural."

"What about you?"

"I'll get the others and follow you. We'll meet you at the pizza place."

With her free hand, Hannah grabbed the back of my head and kissed me. "Be safe," she said, then crossed the alley.

*Protect her, God. Protect us all.*

The others were now gathered at the corner of the building behind Zach, who was looking around the side. "We need to bring them back," I said to Logan, walking toward them.

"Zach!" Logan yelled. "Back this wa—Ah!"

I shoved Logan against the wall of the shop and clamped my hand over his mouth. "Let's not tell the world we're here, okay?"

"Sorry," he whispered.

Two shots rang out. Sounded like a handgun. A girl screamed. Lizzie? Antônia? I saw both run across the alley with the group into the parking lot.

Movement to my right. A woman peeking out the bakery door. She scowled at us, kicked the rock aside, and pulled the door shut. It had no exterior doorknob.

"There went our exit," I said to Logan, then sprinted toward the others, pulling my rifle off my shoulder as I went. Logan's sneakers slapped the pavement behind me.

I reached the corner and peeked down the side of the shop, which was a driveway to the parking lot that met the alley where I stood. I didn't see anyone, but the red and blue lights of enforcer cars flashed in the windows of businesses across the street.

"What should we do?" Logan asked.

I eyed the parking lot. It was small, about fifty meters square, and completely fenced in. No more than twenty vehicles: mostly cars, a couple of pickups and vans, and what looked like a repurposed UPS truck in the back. Could we wait it out here? Should we go back the other way?

A siren blipped behind me. A patrol car was approaching from the other end of the alley. I sprinted into the parking lot and crouched as I darted down the first row of cars. Logan was right behind me.

"Get inside one of these cars. Or under one," I said, in case they were locked. "Stay put until someone comes for you."

I kept going, zig-zagging my way to the UPS truck. I needed a better view. I slung my rifle strap over my shoulder and tried to climb up the back. Easier said than done with my sore ribs. I had to first climb into the old turquoise fishing boat sitting on a trailer beside the UPS truck and launch myself off the narrow side, but I finally managed to get on top of the brown beast.

I slid prostrate to the front and positioned my rifle facing out, careful not to move as the steel roof popped under my weight. This was an ideal spot for sniping, though I really didn't want to shoot anyone. I realized in a hurry that we were trapped. There were two ways out, and both were now blocked with enforcer cars. Two cars likely equaled at least four enforcers.

*We need help, Lord. Please help us!*

I studied the lot, looking for movement, for any other exit. I spotted Cristobal and Antônia lying in the back of a pickup truck. Not exactly hidden. Logan was curled into a ball on the ground behind a Nissan Rogue. Or maybe he thought he was under it. The sob of a child brought my gaze to an old Astro van. Lizzie was standing on the far side, Shyla tucked under one arm, Davis under the other. Zach crept down the side and tried the passenger door. Locked.

Movement drew my gaze back toward the shop. The top of an enforcer's hat glided along the other side of a Chevy Tahoe.

"Stop!" someone yelled.

Gunfire rang out. One, two, three pops of a handgun, then a fourth rifle shot in reply. I wildly searched the lot to see who was shooting, figured my dad had come outside. The enforcer by the Tahoe had stopped moving. Didn't seem to be a shooter.

"Put down your weapon and come out!" a man yelled from somewhere near the street. "Hands above your head where I can see them."

Had someone seen me? Or was Dad out here? This was insane. I didn't think it was possible to escape at this point, but the alternative was to spend six months in Rehab—likely longer now that I was part of a standoff with enforcers.

Zach had moved up beside a glossy Mazda CX-9 that was parked in front of the Astro. The rear passenger door opened, and he motioned for Lizzie and the kids to come. Lizzie sent Davis first, and Zach helped the boy inside.

The enforcer's hat was moving again. It stopped at the nose of the Tahoe, and his face came into view. Officer Harvey. He slipped around the front of the SUV and headed toward Zach and the kids. My heart throbbed in my chest. I aimed my rifle at Harvey and ran my thumb over the safety to make sure it was on. Didn't want to shoot unless I had to. Didn't want to even then.

"This can end peacefully," yelled the voice from before. "Don't do anything you'll regret." The guy sounded closer now.

A guttural cry pulled me back to Zach, who collapsed. Harvey had found him, and from the way the enforcer was holding his gun, he'd used it to knock Zach over the head. I didn't see the others, so Zach must have gotten everyone in the Mazda, though the door was still open.

"Get out!" This from Harvey, who was standing over Zach's motionless form.

Lizzie slipped out of the Mazda, and Harvey grabbed her. "I knew it was you people," he said, then raised his voice. "I got your woman!" he yelled, holding his gun to Lizzie's head. "Come on out, and let's end this once and for all."

I felt helpless. What could I do? Someone ran between two rows of cars at the far end of the lot. Dad, rifle in hand. If he could get to Lizzie, maybe there was still a chance we could get out of here. *Please, God!*

Before Dad even got close, Zach tackled Harvey, knocking them both against the Mazda. Lizzie dove aside as they struggled. Zach got in a good punch, but Harvey knocked Zach across the face with his gun. Zach fell to his knees, clutching his eye.

"I've had enough of you, boy scout." Harvey aimed his gun at the top of Zach's head. "Time to die."

"No!" Lizzie screamed.

I fired at the same time as Harvey. Zach fell, and the enforcer flew a good three feet before landing on his back. I figured he was wearing a vest and waited to make sure he was down. My ears were ringing from the shot. My whole body tingled. Zach was clutching the side of his head, but he was moving. *Let him be okay, God.*

To my left, Logan got up and started walking. What was he doing? He stopped at the pickup and motioned Cristobal and Antônia to follow him. They shook their heads, no.

Officer Miller stepped into view at the end of the row, handgun pointed at Logan. "Stop!" he yelled. "Hands above your head where I can see them."

Logan pushed his hands into the air, then turned and ran. Miller shot at him, missed, and the back window of a blue Kia spider-webbed.

A rifle shot cracked, and Miller went down, gripping his thigh. I could no longer see Logan. I glanced back to Zach, saw Lizzie pressing a wadded up sweatshirt against his face. Behind them—Harvey was gone!

Dread filled me as I scanned the lot to find him. I was about to climb down when the UPS truck shifted and the metal roof popped.

I rolled. Down by my feet, Harvey was just pulling his second leg onto the roof. Our eyes met. We both froze for a breath, then launched into action. I kicked the leg he was standing on. He fell on his side, reaching for his belt, but seemed to find it empty. I stomped his face and whipped my rifle toward him, but before I could aim, Harvey was on me, swearing and cursing and promising to kill me. Teeth bared, eyes filled with rage, he grabbed the barrel of my rifle and ripped it away, let it fall off the side of the truck.

"You shot Zach!" I yelled, swinging at his face.

He caught my fist and twisted it, brought it down in a move to cuff me that went nowhere since I was on my back and he didn't seem to have any handcuffs. I bucked, trying to get out from under him, but it was no contest. I was a ten-year-old boy to this MMA fighter. Still, I thrashed and punched him as best I could. His free hand closed on my throat and squeezed. I couldn't breathe. My pulse throbbed in my ears. The sound around me went funny. *Please, God. Please!*

I thrust my free hand at his face and dug my thumb into his eye socket, grinding it deep. Harvey roared and clutched his face while his other hand reached for me. He was disoriented, though, and I wriggled free. I pulled my knees to my chest and kicked him as hard as I could. He fell to his back and quickly rolled to his side. I kicked him again but missed. He was out of range now, pushing to his feet, wobbling, but widening his stance.

Shots rang out below us as I stumbled past Harvey toward the front of the truck, thinking I could slide down the windshield and front hood to the ground. Harvey grabbed the back neck of my coveralls, pulling me off balance. I grabbed him to keep from falling, but it was too late. We spun and tipped over the truck's side.

We landed in the boat, hard. My right arm was pinned underneath Harvey, who wasn't moving. I scrambled back and gaped at the unnatural way his body lay over the boat's convertible windshield, his open, glassy eyes widened in shock, one red and swollen.

Vomit climbed into my mouth, but I choked it back, which burned my throat. I scrambled over the boat's side and dropped onto the asphalt. After I found my rifle, I crept toward the Mazda, where I'd last seen Zach and Lizzie. My heart was beating so fast, I could hardly breathe—emotions threatening to choke me as much as Harvey had. I was just nearing the back of the Astro when something pressed against my back.

"Drop the gun."

Officer Vrahnos. I recognized his voice. I crouched and lay my rifle on the ground. The next thing I knew, Vrahnos was pressing my face against the cool pavement, digging his knee into my back and cuffing me. After all I'd been through with Harvey, it seemed unfair to get arrested.

At least Hannah and Cree had gotten away. I prayed that God would keep them safe. But me? Looked like I would be plowing fields with Reinhold and Nick on the chain gang.

# 35

**HANNAH**
**OCTOBER 3**

Cree and I waited at The Secret Pizzeria. Neither of us had our wristbands since we'd left them at the house, so I couldn't order us anything. I told the server we were meeting someone, which didn't bother him at all.

When the gunfire started, I knew Eli's dream of leaving this place had died. There was no escaping a standoff. Not in this place.

I wasn't sure what to do. Walk toward the auto shop to see what I could see? Walk back to the house and wait there? Walk to the hospital and see if anyone had been brought in?

I didn't know.

I finally decided to walk toward the auto shop. I took Cree's hand, and we set out. I had barely turned down the block when flashing enforcer lights told me everything I needed to know.

Eli arrested again. Now what?

"Let's go to Seth," Cree said, looking at the shop.

"Seth is working," I said, heading back to the pizza place.

There was still no sign of any of the others when I arrived, so I didn't bother going in. Cree and I sat on a bench overlooking the mountain. I started to cry, imagining of all of the bad things that could have happened. I didn't like my wild thoughts, so I grabbed Cree's hand, and we set off again, this time walking to the hospital.

"Hannah!" Monica leapt from her seat behind the reception counter and ran toward us. "He's okay. He's going to make it."

"Who?"

"You don't know? Your friend Zach was shot."

I shivered. "Shot how?"

"I don't know, but two enforcers were shot as well."

"Killed?"

"Officer Harvey died at the scene."

"Oh!" My mind raced as I thought about the implications. It had to have been Eli or Seth. They were the only two with weapons. But who would have shot Zach?

"Danny Miller took one in the leg," Monica said. "He's going to be okay. Jason is working on him now."

"And Zach?"

"He's lucky from what I hear. Bullet grazed his face. But, Hannah, he's under arrest. He was part of this."

"Zach would never shoot anyone," I said.

Monica shrugged. "All I know is he's under arrest, and that gorgeous face of his will never be the same."

Poor Zach. "They arrest anyone else?"

"Bunch of people, I think. Heard Officer Miller say something about it to Susan. Want me to page her?"

"No, but I'd like to run back and check on Zach. Would you mind watching Cree for five minutes?"

"Does he like computer Solitaire?"

"I have no idea," I said, then told Cree I'd be right back.

Monica got up and let Cree sit in her office chair. She gave him a spin as I slipped down the hallway. I pulled on a lab coat and stethoscope, then headed for the exam room where we always took prisoners.

I recognized Officer Wick at the door. He nodded and asked no questions as I let myself into the room. He'd been decent ever since I threatened to report him to Liberté.

At first, I thought Zach was asleep, but his eyes flashed open as I neared the bed. The left side of his head was covered in thick white gauze.

"Hannah," he breathed.

I put my finger to my lips. "Quietly," I said. "He's likely listening. What happened to the others?"

"They arrested everyone," Zach said.

"Who killed Officer Harvey?"

His eyes glistened. "I-I don't know. He shot me. But someone shot him. Lizzie said the shooter saved me. But Harvey ended up in the boat. I don't know how he got in the boat because somebody shot him on the ground and saved me."

"Shh," I said, patting his arm. "Try to get some sleep. I'll come back later."

He closed his eyes—the antibiotics must be kicking in.

Cree and I left the hospital without anyone else on staff seeing us. We walked back to the shopping area, then up onto the pedestrian bridge that led to the Snowcrest condos. I stopped on top to think and grieve. Zach's story hadn't been the clearest, but I believed Officer Harvey had tried to kill him. I also believed that someone had saved him.

The truth of what really happened didn't matter, though. Mr. Tracy would write his own version that locked Eli away for a long time.

My eyes caught sight of a new billboard at the foot of the mountain. Liberté's face smiled at me from the surface. I recalled her words when she'd given me her number.

*"So I can reach you when I need someone to tell me the truth. You can call me as well. Anytime you need, my friend."*

I fished the phone from my backpack and pulled up Liberté's contact information, wondering if asking for help with this might be pushing my luck. If she knew I was involved with a group that had tried to escape and was responsible for the death of an enforcer, it might get me arrested as well.

I decided to risk it. For Eli.

She sent a car to pick me up in the parking lot of the Snowcrest. Ten minutes later, Cree and I walked into Champion House, where we were escorted to Liberté's apartment.

"Hannah, you look terrible," she said. "Who is this child?"

"This is Cree," I said.

"He is yours?" she asked.

"Kind of, yeah."

"Tell me, what has happened to upset you?"

Apprehension warned me that this could go very badly. I had no reason to believe that Liberté, when she heard what had happened, wouldn't just arrest me too, but she was the most trustworthy of anyone in Admin. I had to try.

I started talking, thinking I'd only tell her about the atrocities I'd seen through my position at the hospital, how Tracy had spearheaded several unethical practices like putting microchips in prisoners, using water and starvation as punishment, and forcing paramedics to administer ketamine to anyone who resisted arrest. I explained why these things violated my calling to first do no harm and to treat all people with respect.

Once I got going, however, I couldn't stop. I told her everything, how we'd been wanting to leave and couldn't, how I wavered and almost decided to stay. About Mr. Tracy's investigation and how Dr. Bayles had used it to blackmail me into dating him. Why I ultimately made my choice to try and leave. I told her about our morning and how Eli had sent me and Cree into the bakery. "That's the only reason I'm here now and not arrested," I said.

"Why didn't you come to me earlier about all of these concerns?" Liberté asked.

I'd only had the phone a little over a week. It seemed a little presumptuous to start calling the woman and lodging my list of complaints. "I don't know. I guess I figured you would take Mr. Tracy's side."

She pressed her lips into a tight line. "I know much of what Morgan has done, but not everything. I did not know about any microscopic chips or harming prisoners."

"He said you are nothing more than a figurehead," I said, passing on the words Mr. Tracy had told Eli. "That he is the ruler of Safe Water. He called himself the prime minister, and when pressed, the dictator."

She raised her hands in frustration. "This makes me feel tired, Hannah. You may not realize the difficulty of my position. People want to be close to me, but they also deceive me. Fame gives people a taste of power, and many cannot resist it. Morgan is one of those people, but he is also wise in many ways that I am not wise. So I have need of him. I have been lazy, though. You are right about that. I will not be so distant from my responsibilities any longer."

"I'm glad of that," I said. "Your people need you."

"Yet you still wish to leave?"

"I'm sorry," I said. "I love Eli."

"Ahh, I see now. Your heart is divided. Love against duty. Of course you must choose love. I insist upon it, *mon amie*. So you want I should open the gates and let you and your friends go outside to live?"

Hope blossomed in my chest. "Could you?" I asked.

"Of course I can do anything that I want," she said. "I suppose your Eli is arrested?"

"Yes," I said, wondering again who had killed Officer Harvey.

She sighed. "Very well. Let us take a ride to the Rehabilitation Center and see what we can learn. It is time I have a grand tour of that place, anyway. They built it so much larger. I would like to see what exactly is going on inside."

I hugged her. "Thank you."

"I only wish for you to be happy, Hannah," she said. "But I will not promise I can help your Eli until I know the truth."

"No matter what happens, I will never forget your kindness," I said.

•  •  •

We arrived at Rehab, where Liberté demanded to see Captain Koval immediately. An enforcer scrambled to his feet and led us to a spacious office. Captain Koval wasn't alone. On the other side of his desk sat Morgan Tracy. Both men turned toward the door when we walked inside, Cree still holding my hand. When they saw Liberté, they leapt to their feet.

"Morgan," Liberté said. "How curious to find you in this place. I have been hearing things, *messieurs*, and I need for you to tell me the truth. Have you been drugging prisoners when they are arrested? Are you inserting tracking devices into their bodies without their knowledge? Are you starving the men and women incarcerated here?"

The men looked at each other. Mr. Tracy stammered something about it all being Captain Koval's idea.

"Don't you even try to blame me for everything," the captain said.

"I see," Liberté said. "You both have taken your authority too far. We must remedy that in the coming days, or my brother and I will have to replace you both. From now on I will know every decision you make, no matter how little. Is that understood?"

Both men looked completely humbled.

"I asked a question to you," she said.

"Yes, ma'am," Captain Koval said. "You're the boss."

"I serve at your pleasure," Mr. Tracy said.

"I hope so," Liberté said. "We have betrayed our people, and some have fought back. This is Hannah Cheng. She was a doctor at our hospital. Today she has turned in her resignation to me, and I have accepted it."

"Hold on just a minute here," Mr. Tracy said. "We need every capable doctor right now, especially with the new strain and all the—"

"Perhaps you were not listening," Liberté said. "I told you I have accepted her resignation. I am not a woman to go back on my word."

"Of course not," Mr. Tracy said. "You are wise and honorable."

"*Oui*, I am," Liberté said, "which is why I have also granted Hannah's request that we let her and her friends leave Safe Water forever."

"No one leaves," Captain Koval said.

"Except Hannah and her friends," Liberté said.

"They attacked two enforcers," Mr. Tracy said. "One died. The other is in critical condition at the hospital right now. We're still trying to figure out who did what."

Liberté glanced at me, then back to the men. "Did enforcers shoot the guns first?"

"Absolutely not," Captain Koval said. "There was an exchange of gunfire, yes, but the violators shot first."

Liberté approached the desk and folded her arms. "Is that what the prisoners will tell me when I ask them?"

"I doubt they'll tell you anything," the captain said. "They're not talking."

"None of them will speak their side?" Liberté asked.

"The kids told us some," Captain Koval said, "but they're kids. They didn't know anything anyway."

"We were thinking of bringing in some pharmaceuticals to act as a truth serum," Mr. Tracy said. "Sodium something?"

"Sodium thiopental," Captain Koval said. "It's not fully reliable, but it makes people more inclined to talk."

"That's a barbiturate," I said. "It's not only extremely addictive, it's been known to be lethal."

"I want to talk with the prisoners," Liberté said.

"All of them?" Captain Koval asked.

"One by one. Show me to your interview room. You do have such rooms?"

"Yes, ma'am," Captain Koval said.

"How many prisoners are there?" Liberté asked. "Do you have a list of their names?"

"We brought in nine," Captain Koval said. "Arrested seven adults: five males, two females. Dropped two children with social services. A boy and a girl."

"No," I said. "The children belong with me."

"Bring back the children immediately," Liberté said. "Hannah will wait for them in the lounge. I will speak with the women first, then the men, oldest to youngest. Take me there now." She turned her attention to Mr. Tracy. "Ms. Cheng is my personal guest. Treat her so."

"Of course," Mr. Tracy said.

"I will get to the bottom of this, Hannah," Liberté told me, then she left with Captain Koval.

"Allow me to escort you to the waiting room, Ms. Cheng," Mr. Tracy said.

Cree and I had no choice but to follow him.

# 36

## ELI

I lay in my cell, torturing myself over all that had happened. It was my fault I couldn't get through the gate. I should have known they'd check wristbands. And I'd killed a man. It was an accident, though. We only fell because he grabbed me. Still.

"Mr. McShane?"

I looked up. A guard was unlocking my door. "Come with me."

I climbed off the cot and followed the guard. He led me back to the interrogation room. I'd been here once already. I'd told them nothing. If they thought that would change, they were wrong.

At the auto shop, right after Officer Vrahnos had cuffed me, Dad had told us all to say nothing. I had no idea how the others had fared, but I'd kept my mouth shut—except for asking Koval for a lawyer. So far he hadn't sunk to torture, but I wouldn't put it past him. Maybe that's what they were going to do now. They'd lost one of their own today, and I didn't blame them for being angry. I was angry too. Why would Harvey try and execute Zach? He wasn't even armed.

The interrogation room was empty. It had a shiny window that I couldn't see through. I figured someone was on the other side, watching. Probably Tracy.

It wasn't Captain Koval who came to speak with me. It was Liberté Champion, which shocked me so much I almost didn't hear her first question.

"You are Eli McShane?" she asked, sitting with her back to the window.

Man, the gobs of makeup on her face was like circus paint. "Yeah. I'm Eli."

She lowered her voice. "Hannah called me. That is why I'm here."

"Hannah," I said, confused.

"Did she tell you we were friends?"

Was she kidding me? "Uh, she said she'd met you, but that was it."

"She was kind to me when I was in grief. I care for my friends." She set a slip of paper on the table and slid it before me. Her position blocked her actions from anyone who might be watching through the interrogation window.

I read it. *Tell me your side, but do not confess to any altercations with enforcers.*

She raised an eyebrow at me, like she was waiting for a response. I didn't dare speak out loud, so I nodded, hope blossoming inside me. Had Hannah somehow saved us? Would Liberté let us go?

She questioned me as thoroughly as Koval had, but this time I told my story honestly, except for the part about climbing onto the UPS truck and shooting Harvey.

My hands were shaking. I wanted to believe that we might walk out of here, but Harvey had died. They would want someone to pay for his death.

When Liberté finished, the guard took me back to my cell. I sat there for at least an hour before the guard returned with my dad—put Dad in my cell—then left.

"What's going on?" I asked.

Dad paced in front of where I was sitting on the cot. "We've got a deal on the table, but it will require your cooperation."

"Do I want to cooperate?" I asked.

Dad swallowed, crossed his arms. "Probably not," he said. "But I want you to."

I didn't like the sound of that. "Just tell me," I said.

"I confessed to shooting the two enforcers and pushing Officer Harvey off the truck," Dad said.

"What?" My mind spun at the strangeness of his words. "But you didn't! I shot—"

"I did," he said, cutting me off. "I was just trying to help my kids and stay alive."

I suddenly knew exactly what was happening. "Liberté set me up."

"*We* set you up," Dad said.

"No," I said, shaking slightly. "Don't do this."

"Liberté is letting our group leave Safe Water," Dad said, "but someone has to pay for that enforcer's life."

"He was about to kill Zach!" I said. "And he tried to kill me. I just . . . Dad, no."

"It's done," Dad said. "My confession is recorded on video. Decision made."

I stood and faced him. "No!"

He grabbed my shoulders, looked me in the eyes. "Listen to me. You have your whole life ahead of you. I want you to live it. Promise you won't interfere with this. It's the only way."

"Dad . . ." I broke down.

He put his arm around me. "I made a deal with Liberté. They're not to bother you, or the recording I gave Becky goes on the Grid. They're not to interfere with your lives, whether you build one village or twenty. As long as you stay outside their fences, they'll stay outside yours. And apparently Hannah has

Liberté's phone number if she needs anything."

I made no sense of that as my mind spun with ways to help Dad. "I'll go back to the house," I said. "Stash your rifle in the tree. That way when you get out, you'll have a weapon."

"My rifle is in the van where you left it," Dad said. "It's likely been impounded. Besides, I'm probably not getting out."

"You might," I said, my voice cracking, but I remembered Reinhold telling me of the men in Rehab for life.

Dad pursed his lips like he was thinking about it. "If you can, take the gun to Becky. Tell her what happened—about the deal I made. Come up with some way to contact her if you need her to upload the recording to the Grid. Tell her where I am, and that if I get out, I'll come for my gun. Maybe by then, if I do ever get out of here, Andy and I will have a plan to leave."

My chest hurt. It felt like I'd bruised my ribs all over again. "You have to get out, Dad," I said.

A bang at the end of the hall preceded the return of the guard.

"I love you, kid," Dad said. "Now, get out of here."

But I didn't move. I just stood there. Eventually, the guard cleared his throat. Tears had flooded my eyes. "I can't just leave you," I said.

Dad hugged me, and I squeezed him back as hard as I could. "You're going on a trip. Just like when you went camping with Andy. We'll see each other again."

"How do you know?"

"I don't, but that's what we're going with, okay?"

I nodded.

"You take care of Lizzie and those kids. You take care of Hannah."

I nodded again, completely unable to respond coherently. I just hugged him and refused to let go. I finally said, "I can't do it without you."

"Yes, you can. I know you can."

"But I don't want to."

"Well, that's a different story," Dad said, slapping my back. "I'll be praying for you. Always."

"Me too," I managed to croak.

Dad had to push away to get me to let go. "Take good care of yourself, okay? And get a haircut."

A smile broke through my sorrow. "You too."

Dad and I hugged again, and somehow, at some point, I finally walked away.

● ● ●

The enforcer led me out to the lobby that was now filled with people. Besides our group, I saw Tracy, Koval, Liberté, as well as several more enforcers, all glaring at me.

Hannah tackled me in a hug. "I'm so glad you're okay," she said.

*Okay* didn't seem the right word, but Hannah's arms around me felt good. Over her shoulder, Liberté Champion watched us with interest. Her presence here confused me so much. I wanted Hannah to tell me exactly how she'd befriended this woman, but that would have to wait.

Hannah released me, and I did a head count. Everyone was here. Except my dad. I bit the inside of my cheek and fought to look like the confident leader everyone needed me to be. I could lose it about Dad later. Right now I had to get us out of here, together.

When I spoke, I addressed Liberté. "We're leaving," I said.

She tipped her head in a single nod. "*Oui.*"

"We want to be able to set up a village," I said, "either by the river or on the mountain or both. And we don't want any trouble from anyone in this place."

"You will have no trouble from us," Liberté said.

"I'm having second thoughts," Tracy said. "If we allow one group such a privilege—"

"I decide," Liberté said to Tracy. "That's what you've always told me. I am deciding now."

"Yes, of course," he said, shrinking back from Liberté's sudden burst of authority.

"We will let them leave," she said to him. "And we will not

pursue them. Is that clear?"

"Absolutely," Tracy said.

"We will not interfere with them," she added, "or spy on them or track them or anything at all. We will pretend they are not there. Is that clear?"

"Yes," Tracy said.

Seeing Tracy put in his place made me smile. "We'll need our vehicles out of the impound," I said. "And all of our things."

Liberté nodded. "Mr. Tracy will see to it immediately."

I looked to Lizzie, whose eyes were so puffy I almost didn't ask. "You said goodbye?"

She nodded and whispered, "We all did."

"You must pack your vehicles and leave this city before nightfall," Liberté said, and I suddenly felt like she was running out of patience. "Pool your credits to purchase food or clothing, fill up your vehicles with petrol, whatever you want. Then go."

"Thank you," I said.

She turned her attention to Hannah. "I'm sorry I disappointed you, *mon amie*. If ever you need anything, you have the phone to call me. I wish you joy and peace in your life."

"I wish you the same," Hannah said. "Thank you."

Liberté embraced Hannah, then left.

And so did we.

# EPILOGUE

**ELI**
**APRIL 6**

The following spring, I was sitting on a flat rock on a bluff that overlooked the valley. The city of Safe Water had grown some, though it still looked dinky. The fence was now stone in parts. The dam was almost complete. I'd hiked down there yesterday with Davis to check it out.

"Been looking for you."

I glanced over my shoulder as Zach approached and sat beside me on the rock. "You okay?"

I fought back a sigh. "I feel like Jonah."

"From the Bible? You do stink like fish."

I laughed. Hannah had conducted several experiments on the fish that came down out of the mountain. After she'd declared them safe to eat, we'd built a smokehouse down by the river. I'd spent the last few days filling it with fish.

"I mean later," I said. "At the end, when he's sitting on the hill, looking down on the city he thought God was going to destroy. But God granted them mercy, and Jonah was ticked off. I used to feel so awkward reading that part. Like, Jonah was a jerk, you know? But I get it now."

"It's not the same," Zach said.

"I didn't say it was the same," I snapped. "I just said I was thinking about it."

Zach wisely remained silent, and I felt badly for biting his head off. We'd spent the winter at Reinhold's place, though we'd driven back and forth dozens of times. Last fall, we'd managed to dig and pour a foundation for a cabin before it snowed, which enabled us to continue working on it through the winter. It now had skeleton walls. We also tried to start the irrigation ditch, to funnel water to us from the mountain. That had been a disaster, so we'd given up on that project until spring, which was why I was up here on the land Kimama said was hers, trying to survey the area and choose the best route for the ditch.

"You're not thinking about going back in there, are you?" Zach asked.

"I think about it every day."

"If it means that much to you—and if we planned carefully—"

I looked at him. "No, Zach. That's not going to happen. It *can't* happen. And I need you to remind me when I start talking like it can, because I'm sure there'll be a day when I think I'm clever enough to pull it off."

Zach thrust his hands into his pockets, looking relieved.

"I want to save him, but to do so—to even try—it goes against my promise to him, against what Liberté asked of us, and it would put everyone at risk. Right now . . . it's quiet. They let us go. So, I have to let him go."

"It sucks," Zach said.

"Yeah. It really does."

A stretch of silence passed. I glanced at my friend, who was studying the town of Safe Water as I'd been before. This offered me a rare peek at the wide scar that slashed across his cheek to the missing bottom half of his left ear and the shriveled remains of what was left of the top. The scar, horrible as it was, reminded me daily that my sin had not been without good reason.

"You know what Lizzie says about your dad being stuck there?" Zach asked.

"Oh, who knows? Probably, 'God has a plan.'"

"Pretty much." Zach laughed, his expression practically glowing with affection for my sister. "She thinks your dad is going to do more good helping people down there than he'd do with us. Reinhold too."

I didn't doubt it one bit. "I know it's selfish," I said, "but I really don't care about anyone down there."

"You will someday, man," Zach said.

Yeah, I probably would.

"So, listen," Zach said. "I still want to marry Lizzie."

A subject he'd only brought up every week for the past six months. "That's her problem," I said.

"I was hoping you'd marry us."

"Lizzie's our pastor."

"Yeah, but she can't marry herself to anyone. That leaves you or Logan."

"Or Hannah or Cristobal or Antônia or Kimama."

"Come on, man. I'm asking you."

I scowled, my mind racing for something clever to say. I'd known this was coming, but I just wasn't ready to deal with it yet. Too bad for me, I guess.

"I talked to your dad about it once," Zach said. "He seemed to think it was a good idea."

"He *did*?"

Zach's voice went soft. "You think it's a bad idea?"

"That's not what I meant. I just . . . How? It's not like there are any churches or anything."

"I'm asking for your blessing, Eli. And I'm trying to ask if you will marry us."

I cringed inside. The moment one of us got married, we were all going to get married. Well, not *all* of us, but Cristobal and Antônia, and me and Hannah, anyway. That would leave Logan waiting for six years for Kimama to grow up, which frankly, weirded me out. Kimama had already claimed Logan, too. They talked about it with a complete lack of emotion, like they were discussing what supplies we should look for on our next scavenging trip. I was sick of hearing Logan tell me how great his and Kimama's house was going to be—he'd even picked a spot.

Zach and Lizzie would be the first wedding for our little group. How could I use it to set a precedent? "What do you have to offer her?" I asked.

"My heart."

I snorted. "You're talking to me, not her," I said. "Your heart isn't going to put food on the table. You don't even have a table. You know what? Build her a house."

"What? How am I supposed to build a flipping house?"

I slapped his shoulder and nodded down the mountain toward our half-built cabin. "That's for you to figure out, my lovesick friend."

"Come on, Eli."

I chuckled, liking this idea very much.

"Ah, you're joking."

"I am not. This is a good idea. It shows your commitment— not just to Lizzie, but to everyone. Someday we might all have kids thinking they need to marry each other. This would be a way to ensure they're mature enough to take care of themselves."

Zach seemed to mull this over. "I get that. I do. But—"

"You want a family, you need a place to live. You saw how we built the first one."

"Barely," Zach said. "You and Cristobal did most of it."

"Just do what we did. About twenty yards from the first one."

"Who gets to live in the first house?" he asked.

"It'll be for the girls and the kids," I said.

"What about us?"

"The goal is to finish at least two cabins before next winter. One for girls, one for boys."

Zach sighed. "So no one will be able to help me with mine?"

I shrugged.

"Dude."

I broke, and a smile stretched across my face. "Fine. If you ask me nicely, I'll help you."

"Will you help me build a house, o wise village elder?" Zach said, his voice jilted and voice monotone.

"We'll need some new shovels," I said.

"Then you'll marry us?" Zach asked.

"I'll figure out something," I said.

We walked down the mountain and over to the makings of our new village, which consisted of the half-built cabin, the smokehouse, and a garden the size of a tennis court that Hannah, Lizzie, and Antônia were trying to cover with net.

"You have to cover the whole thing?" I asked as we stopped to watch.

"Who knows?" Hannah said.

"Build us a greenhouse, and we won't need to," Lizzie said.

"Build us a greenhouse . . ." I turned to Zach and mumbled, "You know that once you marry her, she gets to boss you around instead of me?"

Zach looked like he was thinking it over. "How do you build a greenhouse?"

I shook my head. "And you want to be my brother-in-law."

Zach grinned. "More than anything."

I thought about Zach and Lizzie the rest of the day. An idea came to me over dinner. We were sitting in our camp chairs around the fire, eating grilled rainbow trout with white rice—one staple that was lasting us a long time—and drinking bottles of Gatorade we'd found searching houses in Gunnison.

When I finished eating, I stood up and cleared my throat. "Can I have everyone's attention, please?"

With only eleven people present, I pretty much had instant silence.

"Zachary Montgomery has a request to make of our community," I said, trying to sound as official as possible.

"I do?" Zach deadpanned.

"Don't you? If so, stand up and make your request."

He looked like he didn't trust me, but he stood. So I went ahead and sat down.

"I have asked Lizzie—" he began.

"Who?" I asked.

He narrowed his eyes at me. "I have asked Elizabeth McShane to marry me," Zach said.

Shyla squealed and danced in place.

Zach went on. "And she said—"

I cut him off. "Elizabeth McShane, please stand."

Lizzie was blushing. She stood up, hands on her hips, and looked right at me. "Yes, *Papa* Eli?"

She thought this was a game, but I wasn't playing around. "Zachary Montgomery has asked to marry you. Please tell us how you will answer."

"I said yes, of course," she said.

Shyla squealed again, Cristobal wolf-whistled, and our little group cheered. Before I let anyone speak, I asked another question.

"Does anyone in this community have a reason why these two should not marry?"

No one said anything.

"Can anyone speak *for* them, then? How about some witnesses to their commitment? Anyone? How can we be sure they're a good match?"

Lizzie narrowed her eyes at me. "I think I can decide that for myself, thanks."

"I'll speak for them," Logan said. "I've never seen any guy so devoted to his girlfriend."

"Thanks, man," Zach said.

"Do we have a second?" I asked.

"*Eli!*" Lizzie said. "This is not up for a vote."

But Hannah said, "I'll second. They're great together. A team. And good friends too."

I met her gaze and could tell from the way those dark eyes of hers seemed to be smiling at me that she approved of this little ceremony. "Perfect," I said. "We have an offer. An acceptance. A witness. And a second witness. I hereby declare Zachary Montgomery and Elizabeth McShane engaged to be married. We are all invited to the celebration, which will happen after they build a house they can live in. And after both parties have reached eighteen years of age."

"*Eli!*" Lizzie said.

"That's non-negotiable," I said.

"You'll be eighteen way before we have a house built," Zach said to Lizzie. "In fact, everyone is invited to the house building too."

I raised my bottle of Gatorade. "To Zach and Lizzie. May you know nothing but happiness from this day on."

Everyone agreed and drank their Gatorade. My best friend and my sister looked blissfully happy now that my little initiation was over, but I felt restless. We weren't kids anymore, and I was going to have to get used to that idea.

●　　●　　●

"This seat taken?"

I looked up at Hannah. I was sitting on a stump—the only one around. "What seat?"

She sank onto my lap and put her arms around my neck. "This one."

I laughed. "I guess not."

"What's wrong?"

Over the last seven months, Hannah and I had become so close that I no longer felt embarrassed to tell her exactly what I was thinking. "I just feel a lot of pressure," I said. "I don't want to let anyone down."

"You're not responsible for all of us," she said.

"Sure doesn't feel that way," I said. "I'm not sure Zach can build his own house."

Hannah's face lit up with a wide grin. "Poor Lizzie. At least help him with the roof."

I smiled, imagining Zach patching up his roof with a myriad of umbrellas. Lizzie would probably build more of the house than

Zach, though not for lack of Zach's effort. He was a hard worker, but construction was not one of his gifts. "Can I ask you a question?"

"You're not going to propose, are you?"

I frowned and looked into her eyes. She was so close, her eyes blurred into one. I pulled back my head so I could see her better. "You don't want me to?"

"Someday. I just think Zach and Lizzie should have their time."

I thought about it. "So, we celebrate Zach and Lizzie until their house is done. Then they get married?"

"Yeah. That gives everyone plenty of time to see how it works out."

"They're our 'get married' guinea pigs, you mean?"

"Exactly. Let them make all the mistakes so we won't have to."

I chuckled. "You are extremely clever, Hannah Cheng."

"Which is why I picked the smartest guy in town to kiss." She lowered her mouth to mine and I kissed her right back, amused that she'd called our two buildings and a campfire a town. Kissing Hannah always intoxicated my senses and made me feel wild and reckless and strong, yet at the same time, falling without an end.

When we finally broke apart, she set her chin on the top of my head. I started playing with the ends of her hair as I stared out into the dark night. "Did we do the right thing?" I asked. "Coming out here?"

"I don't know. Ask me in ten years."

"You think we're going to last ten years?"

"I know we are."

Her words were a net that corralled my spiraling fears and kept them from growing irrational. While I still felt uncertain about the future, I was so grateful that Hannah had come with us. I tried to imagine what the last seven months would have been like without her—what I would be like without her. I didn't like that Eli very much. She helped me stay focused yet reminded me to be patient and calm. When we'd first left Safe Water, I'd been anxious to make everything perfect, but Hannah pointed out that there was no hurry. We had all the time in the world to build our futures. Easy does it, trial and error. Better, she said, to also enjoy each day for the gift it was.

She was a gift, God's gift to me—to all of us. I would forever be grateful that our paths crossed in Flagstaff, and she'd gotten into my truck. With her by my side, I would be brave, no matter what challenges or fears came along—and there would be plenty. But we would deal with them—we would survive—together.

## THE END

# Acknowledgements

I want to thank Stephanie Morrill for being my first editor on *Hunger*. Stephanie's feedback made this book so much better, and I'm grateful for her keen eye for characters, plot, and storyworld.

Thanks also to my husband, Brad, who listened to me read the whole book aloud and offered great feedback. It's due to Brad that this book has such a good ending. As I was reading him the early draft, he kept saying, "Um, no," because he wanted Eli to be more active, which was exactly what Eli needed to be.

Thanks to Kaitlyn Williamson, Margaret Williamson, and Kim Titus, for listening to me talk, talk, talk (and sometimes text) about my challenges with *Hunger*. It was incredibly helpful to have so many empathetic ears, and I'm blessed to know each of you. Thank you!

A huge thank you to my proofreaders! You all were SO AMAZING! I'm in awe over how many typos I made while writing this book, and I'm thankful for your keen eyes that helped me find them and polish this manuscript to perfection. You readers might think, "Wow! That's a lot of proofreaders." But while my proofreaders found many of the same errors, they also all found things that were completely unique. It was magical to search through each list and be surprised time and again. A special thank you to Bethany Baldwin, Carol Brandon, Jessica Dowell, Julie Fugate, David Hawkins, Jane Maree, Meagan Myhren-Bennett, Crystal Nielsen, Nathan Peterson, Jennie Webb. The ten of you rock!

To the writers at GoTeenWriters.com who read *Thirst* when I first blogged it back in 2016 as part of the #WeWriteBooks series, thank you so much! Your comments and excitement and feedback helped me realize I needed two books instead of one. Hunger would never have been written if not for you. I consider the *Thirst* Duology a product of the GoTeenWriters.com blog and a collaboration of young, talented authors.

To my readers, as always, thank you for reading the books I write. I hope you enjoyed the end of this story and that it inspires you to re-read *The Safe Lands* trilogy (or read it for the first time). I'm grateful to God that I have the amazing privilege of creating characters and stories for people to read. What an adventure! Thanks for joining me on the ride.

~Jill Williamson

# ABOUT THE AUTHOR

Jill Williamson has written over twenty books for teens and adults, including her debut novel, By Darkness Hid, which won several awards and was named a Best Science Fiction, Fantasy, and Horror novel of 2009 by VOYA magazine. She has also written a handful of books on the craft of writing fiction and teaches writing in person and online at storyworldfirst.com and goteenwriters.com, the latter of which has been named one of Writer's Digest's "101 Best Websites for Writers."

To be notified of new releases and to get a free short story, visit jillwilliamson.com/sanctum and subscribe to her email newsletter. You can also find Jill on the following social media platforms:

 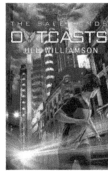 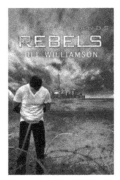

# AWARD-WINNING FANTASY FROM JILL WILLIAMSON

"Wonderfully written with a superb plot, this book is a sure-fire hit with almost any reader. An adventure tale with a touch of romance and enough intrigue to keep the pages turning practically by themselves."
—*VOYA* magazine

"This thoroughly entertaining and smart tale will appeal to fans of Donita K. Paul and J.R.R. Tolkien. Highly recommended for . . . fantasy collections."
—*Library Journal*

"Williamson crafts a complex and vividly portrayed epic fantasy reminiscent of George R.R. Martin's *A Song of Ice and Fire* series but less edgy."
—*Library Journal*

"[*King's Folly*] is an intense drama of biblical proportions... Wilek, Mielle, and Trevn in particular are intriguing, and the ending leaves readers wondering what adventures await this group of young people searching for truth."
—*RT Book Reviews*

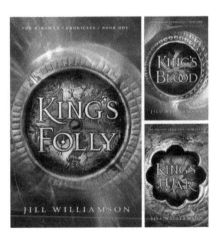

TO LEARN MORE VISIT
WWW.JILLWILLIAMSON.COM

# WRITING RESOURCES

READY TO WRITE THAT BOOK?
NOT SURE HOW TO BEGIN?
YOU NEED THIS BOOK!

Learning to write a novel from
beginning to end is a challenge.
But with this book as your guide,
you'll see that when you're in
possession of the right tools,
you're capable of finishing what
you start. You'll be empowered
and encouraged—as if you had
a writing coach (or three!)
sitting alongside you.

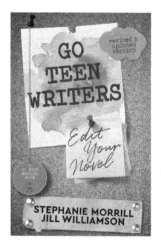

REVISED & UPDATED EDITION!

You know your first draft has
problems, but what's the best
way to fix them? How do you
know where to start editing?
Or for many writers the bigger
question becomes, "How
do I know when I'm done?"

Teaching yourself how to edit a
first draft can feel overwhelming,
but using this guide, you'll feel
as encouraged, empowered, and
capable as if you had a writing
coach sitting alongside you.

TO LEARN MORE VISIT
WWW.JILLWILLIAMSON.COM

# MORE WRITING RESOURCES FROM JILL WILLIAMSON

Jill Williamson

PUNCTUATION

101

A fiction writer's guide to getting it right

You don't need to be an expert in grammar and punctuation to write great novels, but you do need to learn the basics.

This handy reference book includes all the need-to-know punctuation rules for fiction writers, and it's presented in a clear, user-friendly format with many examples for the visual learner—including some from popular novels.

*Punctuation 101* will save you time and energy, which you can spend writing your novel.

BUILDING A STORYWORLD? WONDERING WHERE TO START? THIS BOOK CAN HELP YOU.

Whether you're starting from scratch or looking to add depth to a world you've already created, *Storyworld First* will get you thinking.

Includes tips on the following worldbuilding subjects: astronomy, magic, government, map-making, history, religion, technology, languages, culture, and how it all works together.

Jill Williamson

STORYWORLD FIRST

Creating a unique fantasy world for your novel

TO LEARN MORE VISIT
WWW.JILLWILLIAMSON.COM

Come hang out with us!

# GO TEEN WRITERS

honesty, encouragement,
and community for writers

www.GoTeenWriters.com

Lightning Source UK Ltd.
Milton Keynes UK
UKHW010047170223
417092UK00013B/734/J